Praise for

THESE SHATTERED SPIRES

'*These Shattered Spires* is a grotesque extravaganza of a book, with a labyrinthine quest and complex, morally grey characters you can't help but root for. I've never had so much fun'
Bea Fitzgerald, author of *Girl, Goddess, Queen*

'Utterly fabulous and darkly imaginative. Complicated, flawed characters shine in a world of grit and bloodshed, all brought to life through effortlessly evocative prose. I devoured every page'
Elise Kova, *New York Times* bestselling author of *Arcana Academy*

'Part fantastical court intrigue, part murder mystery, part lush queer romance, and part dysfunctional found family. At times the writing is humorous, at others it bites like a scorpion's sting'
Katy Nyquist, author of *A Holy Maiden's Guide to Getting Kidnapped*

'Absolutely perfect for fans of *Gideon the Ninth*, *These Shattered Spires* pulses with the weird and wonderful macabre. Salter weaves a ragtag crew of loveable misfits with uniquely grim worldbuilding that is impossible to forget'
Catelyn Wilson, author of *All the Devils*

'Gruesome, gothic, gay and glorious. I ate this up from cover to cover. Addictively weird, heartfelt and a bloody good time!'
Kat Dunn, author of *Bitterthorn*

'*These Shattered Spires* is the weirdest book I've read this year, which is the highest praise I can give. It is delightfully grotesque, exquisitely macabre and viscerally strange'
Alwyn Hamilton, author of *Rebel of the Sands*

THESE SHATTERED SPIRES

Books by Cassidy Ellis Salter

These Shattered Spires

THESE SHATTERED SPIRES

CASSIDY ELLIS SALTER

BLOOMSBURY
LONDON OXFORD NEW YORK NEW DELHI SYDNEY

BLOOMSBURY YA
Bloomsbury Publishing Plc
50 Bedford Square, London WC1B 3DP, UK
Bloomsbury Publishing Ireland Limited
29 Earlsfort Terrace, Dublin 2, D02 AY28, Ireland

First published in Great Britain in 2026 by Bloomsbury Publishing Plc
This paperback edition published in Great Britain in 2026 by
Bloomsbury Publishing Plc

A catalogue record for this book is available from the British Library

ISBN: PB: 978-1-5266-8298-7; HB: 978-1-5266-8297-0;
Waterstones: 978-1-0372-0851-5;
Export PB: 978-1-5266-8299-4; eBook: 978-1-5266-8296-3

2 4 6 8 10 9 7 5 3 1

Typeset by Six Red Marbles India
Printed and bound in Great Britain by Clays Ltd, Elcograf S.p.A.

FSC www.fsc.org MIX Paper | Supporting responsible forestry FSC® C018072

To find out more about our authors and books visit www.bloomsbury.com
and sign up for our newsletters
For product safety related questions contact productsafety@bloomsbury.com

Fourspires Castle
The Ulcer
The Academy

THE DESECRAE
The University

You should turn around now.

If you insist on coming inside the Desecrae, be wary of:

- Bones, blood, teeth and general bodily goop
- Swearing (you would swear too if you lived here)
- Gender dysphoria, gender scrutiny, threat of outing and triggering pronoun talk
- Mortality in its many inglorious forms, including murder and mass background death
- Violence, such as: terrible sword-fighting, stabbing, dismemberment of monsters and neck-breaking
- Memories of atrocious parenting and abuse at a so-called 'school'
- Control and physical pain
- Fire (accidental. Sort of.)

Got it? Good.

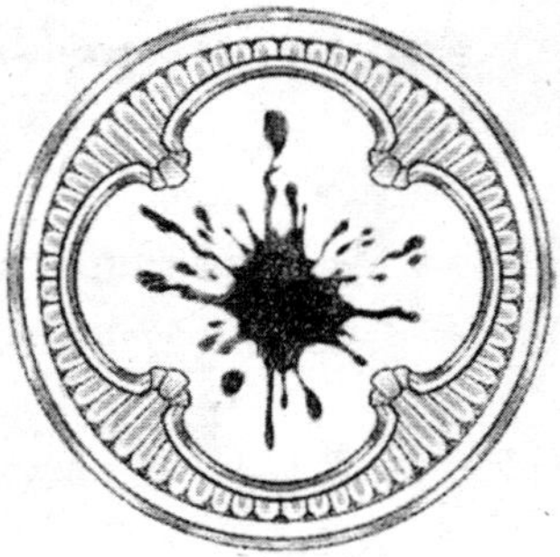

A short introduction to the four towers for new familiars

As a familiar, you will serve your arcanist by providing them with power for their spells, regardless of the pain it causes you.

If you receive the honour of serving one of the four head arcanists, the power you create will be used for the Suppression. The Suppression, a spell performed by each head arcanist every morning, prevents the daily apocalypse.

This task will be your greatest work.

It will also eventually kill you.

Blackspire

Without which the dead would rise
from the gravemounds

Arcanic Discipline

Bone

Head Arcanist

Jonathan

Current Familiar

Tarenteeno, graduate of ~~the Academy~~ *You mean the Torture Pit*

Mascot

Skull

Blackspire is built from dark stone inlaid with polished human bone, believed to be those of deceased arcanists. Bone arcanists, who derive their power from skeletal remains (channelled, of course, through their familiars) are viewed as 'morbid' and 'arrogant'. This opinion is rarely expressed openly due to the fear of having one's kneecaps dissolved.

Taro

Redspire

Without which we would drown in the effluence of the dead

Arcanic Discipline

Blood

Head Arcanist

Morgan

Current Familiar

~~Toben Petre Aziz Rhys Unknown Castriel Hemlock~~

Unknown, graduate of ~~the Academy~~ the Torture Pit

Mascot

Drop of blood

Redspire is constructed from a crimson stone which, due to its distinctive gloss, appears to bleed at twilight. Prominent blood arcanists are agreed to be salacious in manner with a prodigious appetite for criminality. Their familiars can produce arcania from any kind of blood, but arcanists often find it amusing to use human sources.

Elliot

Greenspire

Without which our flesh would be food for the garden

Arcanic Discipline
Botany

Head Arcanist
Kellan

Current Familiar
Nixeen, graduate of ~~the Academy~~ still the Torture Pit

Mascot
Sapling

The crest of Greenspire, which is covered in thick ivy, resembles an elaborate greenhouse with vicious iron spikes. Botanic arcanists are often viewed as docile, but they are skilled poisoners and assassination attempts between colleagues are frequent. Do not eat anything they (or their familiars) give you.

Nixie

Greyspire

Without which our very foundations would fail

Arcanic Discipline

Stone

Head Arcanist

Geraldin

Current Familiar

~~Alis~~ Cassia, graduate of ~~the Academy~~ *TORTURE PIT*

Mascot

Cuboidal stone

Greyspire, through its brutal design of overlapping grey scales and lack of windows, maintains complete impenetrability. Stone arcanists have the reputation of being difficult to read and enjoying the application of obscure and often arbitrary laws, usually to their benefit.

I beg of the universe that everyone loyal to Greyspire is painfully eviscerated. My name is Alix Alix Alix Alix Alix Alix Alix Alix Alix Alix Alix Alix Alix Alix Alix Alix Ali

Alis

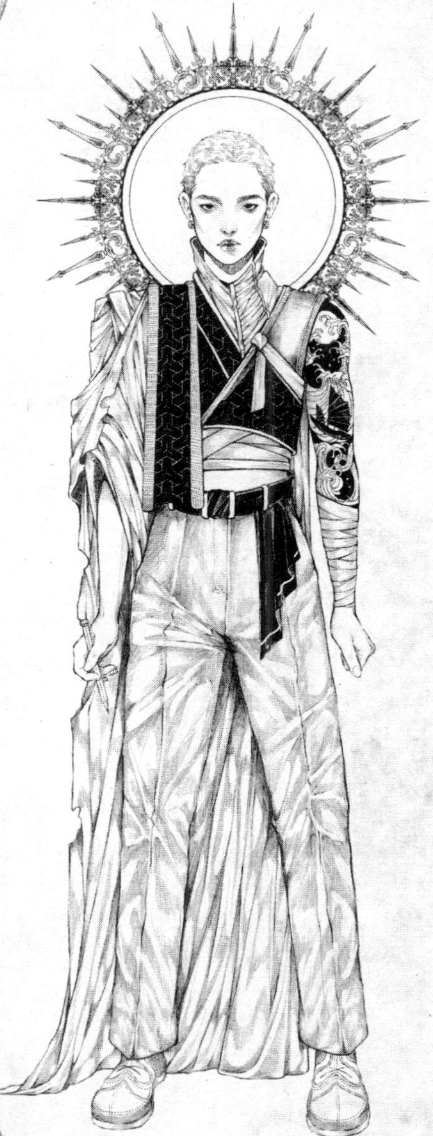

The Fifth Tower

The centre of our universe

You will bow to the Fifth Tower.
Pray its ruler does not fall in your lifetime.

One

Taro was a bone fanatic with a sugar headache and an unhealthy obsession with black eye liner. Her pockets were always filled with vertebrae and boiled sweets, and her eyes were as dark as the crux of night. She also lovingly nursed an attitude problem that rivalled the direness of the rotting castle she lived in. She knew this about herself, and she was at peace with it. Plenty of people thought she was abominably irritating, and quite frankly it was the only thing that got Taro through the day.

She had considered herself mentally unbreakable until this tortuous procession to the dining hall. It was screwing with the timing of her stunningly crafted, hideously dangerous and incredibly clever escape plan.

Taro kicked her heels and worked remnant toffee from her molars with her tongue. It was all the sustenance she had for three hours of queuing through the castle's grossly misshapen guts. She'd spent those hours picking over her escape plan with the determination of a starving crow stripping meat from a bone. For this to work she had to be perfect. So while scheming, she'd quietly queued past the kitchens where the screaming cooks were presumably killing each other with spoons. She'd obediently dragged herself by the malevolent library, where one could suffer the worst boredom of one's life. She'd even walked through doors held open by skeletons, fighting the urge to steal one of their ribs.

Now there was a bottleneck at the entrance to the dining hall. Something tiresomely ceremonial was happening. Taro, whose life literally hinged on executing her escape plan in the next few hours, hoped whatever awaited her in the dining hall involved the sacrifice of whoever had organised this puffed-up yawn-fest.

'Look less miserable, Taro,' Jon snapped. Taro stopped kicking the floor and blew her cheeks out. If she had been allowed to speak she would have told her master, the apparently extraordinary bone arcanist: *Suck it, Jonathan.*

But she wasn't allowed to talk, and she quite liked being alive. So.

The line jolted past a window, and Taro subtly craned her neck to look at the world below. Most of her and Nixie's planning had used out-of-date maps, and nothing outside the castle walls stayed still for long. She needed to know just how doomed they would be when they escaped into the streets.

Fourspires Castle topped the perpetually collapsing city like a loathsome hat, casting it in shadow darker than an armpit. Through the window Taro could see the grey peaks of the University, with the city dripping and sprawling around it. The dome of the Desecrae, the grisly tooth-filled sky, arched over the mountain like a cloche, occasionally raining saliva on the more unfortunate of its ten thousand inhabitants. It was an ugly and vicious world.

To her and Nixie, it was also freedom.

An elderly blood arcanist coughed, snapping Taro out of her reverie. His deep burgundy robes were spattered with darker patches of red. He had probably killed his familiar by using too much power, then come straight to dinner. Jon leaned away from the man with a curled lip, as though *he* was any better in his midnight-black robes, which were speckled with bone dust from the corpses he made Taro wrest power from.

The queue shuffled towards the last part of the ordeal, where tradition had them bow to the food displayed by the trembling chef. Taro regarded the offerings she wasn't allowed to eat: life-size jellies in the shape of the Thaumaturge, ruler of the city; roast turkeys with rubies poked into their eye sockets; a chocolate rendering of Fourspires Castle, complete with the looming Fifth Tower in its centre. It was all covered by a sugar dome, an unconvincing replica of the Desecrae that bubbled over their heads.

Taro imagined licking it. She wouldn't, obviously, because of the Unholy Mother stuck to the ceiling above her. Its feet were pointing backwards. Taro *nope*d back to Jon's side.

'Stop drooling,' Jon said to her, without looking.

I know you have an emergency sandwich in your pocket, Jon. PS I sneezed on it.

The procession jolted. Taro leaned against the last window and, when she was fairly sure Jon wouldn't slap her, rubbed a patch of grime off the glass.

She stared past the reflection of her white face and into the city, which was slowly melting like a Gothic ice lolly. Taro had a deep appreciation for the never-ending cycle of renewal. She admired the way the city oozed down the side of the mountain, and how people hauled the stone back to the top when they ran out of building material. The castle was pretty much the only thing that stayed still, held in place by impressive amounts of stone arcania.

The castle faced a slower cycle of decay, collapsing in on itself over decades, instead of hours like the rest of the world beneath the Desecrae. In fifty years a room at the top of Fourspires would sink to the ground floor. Whole wings would become wormy basements before finally collapsing into mangled, chandelier-spangled bedrock. A few things were successfully propped up: the main walls, the library, the courtyard and the grim Fifth Tower – but little else survived.

Jon pinched her. Taro jumped, then seethed. No evening in the full eighteen years of her life had been this slow. The only thing stopping her from flinging herself out of the window was the promise of escape. That and being flirtatiously ignored by Nixie, which was always the highlight of her pathetically sad week.

'Don't smile *that* much,' Jon hissed.

Taro flattened her face. She could do it. Just six more hours. One more dinner. A final evening sucking up to Jon before she hauled her arse out of here. Taro's guts lurched at the prospect of their knife-thin opportunity to get out, a tiny fracture of *maybe* in a huge wall of *never*. She and Nixie had spent months planning this. They had watched the Unholy Mothers and their rotations around the castle. They'd stolen clothes that screamed *Don't mind me, I'm normal!* instead of *I'm an escaped familiar*. Tonight was their only hope, the serendipitous collision of a ceremonial dinner with the changing of the nuns. The serving Unholy Mothers would be put in a cupboard to recoup their necromantic energy while refreshed ones were put back into service. The human guards would watch over the dining hall until the early hours. At first greylight Taro and Nixie would burrow through the subcutaneous layer of the castle, and by the time their arcanists realised they had vanished, they would be hidden in the city like fleas in a rotting mattress.

The wait was excruciating, but Taro was well trained in the art of quiet suffering. The Academy, that horrendous institution which forced familiars to operate past the limits of normal human pain, had taught her too well.

Suckers.

The last five yards took an agonising ten minutes to walk. The closer Taro came to the nuns' inspection, the more certain she was that something would go wrong. The merest suspicion that Taro was anything but simperingly obedient, and the nuns would crush her skull like an overripe plum. She had been so careful recently, but a tiny part of her was convinced that her habitual treachery stuck to her clothing.

Three Unholy Mothers flanked the dining-room door. Their faces were obscured by hoods, which stopped flies laying eggs in the delicate flesh behind their eye sockets. They were human, sort of, with patches of hair on their scalp and receding lips that didn't cover their too-long teeth. Taro, in a bid to look unsuspicious, forced herself to look into the eyes of the nearest Mother. Its nostrils flared, and she immediately twitched her head away again. These were the creatures who would come after her and Nixie the moment someone realised they were gone.

They all stared at Taro. Sour sweat cooled her temples. One of the nuns crooked their finger at the hall.

'Finally,' Jon said, and yanked Taro through the door.

Decay had brought the room to its knees. The walls were a deep, greasy black. Servants muttered and clicked their tongues. Green-clad botanic disciples grew hideous bouquets of flowers while bone specialists directed skeletons to lay cutlery. Even though nothing in the castle happened without arcania, no pot stirred or sewage flushed, the two disciplines ignored each other completely.

Jon clicked his fingers in Taro's face.

'Now you're not smiling at all,' he said. 'It's embarrassing having the most miserable high familiar in Fourspires. I raised you to the highest echelons of the castle …'

Taro checked out at 'echelons' and admired herself in a silver bowl. Her hair was so lacquered she looked like a beetle. Hot.

'… let you wear those ridiculous shoes, which I did *not* sanction …'

A bright scent filled the air. Taro twitched, immediately on high alert. Most people wouldn't have noticed it, but Taro was so attuned to the distinctive, sticky-sweet friction of botanic arcania – OK, *fine*, because she associated it with Nixie – that she immediately knew when something was wrong with it.

A servant arcanist was growing a spray of sickly flowers, and his familiar, who was doing the *actual* work of wresting power for him, was near the end of her sad young life. Taro could see the burned blackness of her skin, a kind of rot reaching from her fingertips up her arm, where it was creeping towards her heart. She was about to burn out and die very publicly. If that happened, the nuns would fall on her fresh body, and with their bloodlust triggered they would hunt in a frenzy for the whole night. Taro and Nixie wouldn't even get past their tower doors, let alone out of the castle.

Taro wasn't going to let anything mess up their escape.

She thrust her hand into her pocket and pinched her emergency vertebrae between her fingers. White-cold pain snapped through her arm as she drew its osseous power into her body, changing it into bone arcania, which gathered on her skin. Before it could leech too far into the air – before Jon could notice – Taro took a sharp breath and gathered the arcania beneath her tongue. Oh, the throat-scratching taste of *power.* She wanted to gulp it down. Instead she pushed it into shape with her mouth. It was like moving her tongue through a gobful of cold porridge.

A skeletal hand obediently popped out of the floor. It grabbed the botanic familiar's ankle and wrenched her sideways. The girl shrieked and dropped the plant she was wresting from, cutting off her arcanist's power. The skeletal hand around her ankle crumbled into dust before the girl even hit the floor. A nun looked down, and for a sickening moment Taro thought it might slaughter the girl for making a noise, but it only watched her briefly before resettling its gaze on the hall.

Nothing's going to rile the Mothers tonight, bitch!

Even though her insides shrieked with sour pain, and she had probably taken another few months from her own life, Taro wanted to scream her triumph.

Jon stared at her. She flattened her face into an expression of beatific innocence.

'Taro,' Jon said, his voice dangerously low. 'Why is your hand in your pocket?'

Bone clicked against the flagstones. Every head in the room swivelled towards the Unholy Mother coming from the doorway. Its nostrils flared, and Taro knew, with sickening dread, that it had sensed her unauthorised arcania. The botanic familiar scrambled up, but there was nowhere to turn. The nun backed her into the wall. It raised its hands, grabbed the girl's head, and twisted hard.

There was a loud crack like a raw carrot being snapped. Fresh blood spattered against the smooth floor. Everyone averted their eyes as the nun hooked its fingers under the dead familiar's armpits and dragged her body from the room.

Sparkling horror pattered against Taro's skull. The Unholy Mothers shifted, excited by the blood even as someone hurried to mop it up. *You shouldn't even have tried, you ass,* Taro thought. If any of them realised she had self-wrested …

A couple of people laughed awkwardly. Noise washed back into the room. Jon brushed his robes and smoothed his hair again.

'Well,' he said.

The imperative not to scream with guilt was unbearable. If Taro hadn't stuck her neck out to help, the botanic familiar might have lived another full day. Taro, trying to calm down, remembered that she had an aniseed ball in her pocket and distracted herself by sneaking it into her mouth. Jon slapped the back of her head so hard the aniseed ball launched itself across the floor.

'Not before dinner.'

Taro briefly considered an addendum to the escape plan, namely, to slit Jon's throat before leaving the Blackspire tower. But if she was going to get out of here alive, without drawing attention to herself, she had to look meek and nod … like *this*.

'Now walk.'

The botanic disciple's blood glimmered in Taro's peripheral vision. *She was close to death anyway,* Taro reminded herself, but it didn't lessen the pit in her stomach. Her eyelid twitched with barely contained stress as they began their procession to the front of the hall, where the Thaumaturge waited. *It was her or me,* Taro thought. *This is the price of survival.*

'*Slower*,' Jon said, with the attitude of someone who had been given a dense child for a familiar, rather than Taro, an uncommonly talented and deliciously wonderful piece of joy who was – no matter how you looked at it – walking at the right pace, *unlike a certain someone who moves like a skeleton with wet celery for feet.*

They reached the front. Jon bowed to the floor, his skull-embroidered robes fluttering. He loved slapping the icon of his tower on everything, including Taro, just in case anyone forgot who he was. Good job skulls looked awesome on her. Taro grudgingly bowed before the Thaumaturge too.

'My lord,' Jon murmured, which was the cherry on top of the five-tier cake of Taro's humiliation. Taro took a deep breath – *look innocent, not like you just saw a girl's head snapped off* – and made eye contact with the creature to whom this whole procession led. The Lord of Clockwork, Master of Fourspires, Two-Hundred-and-Tenth Stone Arcanist of His Bloodline, Emperor Against Time, His Frozen Highness the Tick-Tock King.

The Thaumaturge.

This monster was so compellingly awful that even Taro flinched when she heard one of his names. They – *they* being Jon when he was scheming to sit on the throne – said that you could shake the Thaumaturge by his shoulders and only his eyeballs would move.

This was the creature everyone in the world lived for. From the hundreds of arcanically gifted to the thousands of normal people who lived beneath the Desecrae, they all bowed at the feet of a man who couldn't sneeze without forward planning.

Geraldin and Morgan were already at the head arcanists' table. Morgan snapped his book shut as Jon and Taro sat, almost taking the nose off the white ferret around his neck.

'How lovely of you to join us,' he drawled at Jon, flicking a lock of hair over his shoulder.

Morgan was an abomination.

A sexy abomination, Taro thought grudgingly. A masterclass in style. A perfect example of how, if you made something tacky enough, you could elevate it to fine art. His deep crimson robes shimmered with glass droplets of blood, the insignia of the Redspire tower, which was built with stone that looked as wet as a fresh wound. His fingernails were the gold of the leopard sitting at his feet, his perfume intoxicating enough to cover the stench of blood, his silver-lined eyes bright against his tawny face and so snarky they made Taro swoon.

'Morgan,' Jon said stiffly. 'I see you have a new familiar. Your third this year.'

Morgan ruffled his familiar's curls. Taro wondered if they were having an affair. Morgan had famously slept with his fourth familiar, Rhys, and even more famously killed him. Morgan saw Taro looking and grinned.

In a better world Taro would have directed a wolf whistle at Morgan, but even coughing out loud was an adrenaline sport. So she chewed her tongue and imagined that she was screaming instead. *I! Hate! This! Place! And I'm leaving you all the fuck behind!*

'What's wrong with your girl?' Geraldin barked.

'She's an idiot,' Jon said without hesitation. Geraldin narrowed her eyes and studied Taro anyway.

Geraldin, the head stone arcanist of Greyspire, was the opposite of Morgan's resplendence. Her tower was made of bristling slate, but rather than lean in to the brutalist look – which could have been hot – she dressed in bland grey robes that made her look like a grave marker. Her tower's icon was a yawningly dull cube of stone, and her joyless aesthetic was matched only by her hobby of memorising cruel and ancient laws. She had found the one sentence in an ancient manuscript that allowed her to burn her former familiar's tongue out with poison, then had thrown her into the swirling Desecrae for a teeny-tiny cock-up with a spell.

Taro held her face so still she felt as if her skin was melting off, until Geraldin finally turned her attention to the door.

'Oh, look,' Geraldin sneered, 'the fourth horseman of the anti-apocalypse.'

Taro fought the urge to vault over the table and fling herself at the girl walking in. She was always rendered inoperable by that gorgeous face, the intensely clever eyes, the serious crease between the girl's brows. Nixie was born for the deep emerald of the Greenspire robes, the embroidered mascot of the sapling crawling up her thigh and blooming on her hip. The flowers, which would have looked stupid in anyone else's hair, cupped the soft shell of her ear in a way that made Taro's heart flop.

The man striding ahead of Nixie was her opposite. Putting the head botanic arcanist in green floral robes was like throwing a tablecloth over a crocodile and hoping nobody would notice. People had tried to murder Kellan and failed, as evidenced by the scars running up his forearms where the Librarian had ripped him with her sharpened nails. He'd probably enjoyed the murder attempt; he carried a pocketbook full of notes on inflicting pain, which he experimented with in his greenhouse-like tower, watching his subjects with flat, pitiless eyes through half-moon glasses.

'Keep an eye on him,' Jon murmured to Taro as Kellan strode towards them. Taro leaned slightly to keep Nixie in view. 'He's been trying to kill me since he fell down the stairs.'

Because he tripped over a skull. Which you put there. To kill him.

'How dare he accuse me of treachery?'

... because you also sent a creature made of zygomatic bones to his room. In the middle of the night. With a sword.

'I hope he poisons himself with his ... *stupid* potions.'

Good one, Jon.

Kellan clicked his fingers. Nixie smoothly drew up beside him, which predictably made Taro's stomach boil over. She dared flick her eyes over Nixie's face: her deep brown skin, the bow curve of her lips, the dips above her collarbones that Taro knew by heart. Only the twitch of her eyelids showed her exhaustion.

Kellan murmured something in Nixie's ear. Nixie's expression barely flickered. Kellan could have told her to slaughter a nun and she wouldn't react. Nixie was perfect.

Taro clung to the edge of the table as they sat down. Nixie gazed past Taro's left shoulder as though she was looking at the Thaumaturge, but her right index finger twitched: *Hello*. The gesture was as intimate as a kiss. Taro felt a lump in her throat as she remembered those fingers walking over her hip bone, the arch smile Nixie gave her when she wanted to be touched. God, it had been so long since they could be themselves.

'Stop fidgeting,' Jon said, and Taro's bliss was annihilated.

'When the familiars rise up,' Morgan opined, 'you'll die first.'

'I hope your leopard bites off your—'

Jon's lips kept moving, but his teeth had become glued together. So had Taro's. The Thaumaturge had bonded the calcium in everyone's molars, which he always did when he wanted silence. It used so much stone arcania the familiars at his feet twitched like beached fish.

He constantly cycled through five of them, ripping out the power he needed and giving each one just enough time to recover from a near coronary incident before circling back. During the day, Unholy Mothers dragged those familiars from place to place. Their hands were always tied to stone cubes for constant wresting while the Thaumaturge's tongue squirmed, making crystals swirl around his feet. Yet this was little compared to the arcania that kept him alive. His whole corpse – uh, body – had been arrested mid-cell death using arcania so potent that the excess power in the air had made everyone in the castle blind for three days. It had taken someone from every discipline and killed all their familiars, as truly batshit spells were prone to do. His heart pumped to a rhythm set by blood arcania. His skeleton was held together with the precision engineering of bone. The minerals in the soft tissue of his muscles and brain were kept functioning by stone. The delicate microflora of his internal organs was an ecosystem balanced by botanic arcania.

The Thaumaturge raised a hand, and his nuns crawled up the walls, clinging to the cornices with their fingers bent backwards. They were twitchy, too watchful; their nostrils were still filled with the dead familiar's blood, and they were looking for an excuse to eat. Some had gore around their mouths. Taro pushed her dread away and tried to concentrate.

'Subjects.' The Thaumaturge's voice was a dead shudder. 'Tonight we toast to my two-hundredth year on the throne.'

Taro swallowed. Four and a half hours until she and Nixie could escape.

'We also give thanks to stone arcania, without which our very foundations would fail. To blood arcania, without which we would drown in the effluence of the dead. To botanic arcania, without which our flesh would be food for the garden. To bone arcania, without which the gravemounds would burst. In the name of the iron crown, eat as worms do of the earth.'

Taro's teeth unstuck as the spell was broken and the Thaumaturge's familiars came to, gasping. A rush of bottled-up words echoed around the hall. The Unholy Mothers licked their gory lips.

Taro, seized by relief, bumped her oil-black shoe against Nixie's toes. Nixie, whose face was still angled modestly to the table, briefly looked up through her eyelashes. She was saying: *I love you so damn much.*

Joy crept through Taro's chest, washing away her fear. *I love you too, you idiot.*

They were getting out. Tonight.

Ceremonial dinners were Taro's time to shine. Jon didn't feed her often, and this would be the last food she saw before they escaped, so she ate with an enthusiasm that would make the insane chef weep. She gnawed peacocks made of cheese, demolished fist-sized dumplings, and drank scalding gravy. If something was a liquid or wobbly, she swallowed it. If it was solid and didn't smell too bad, she quietly put it inside her robes to eat on the run.

After the initial rush to fill her stomach, Taro poked Nixie with her foot again, several times and with increasing force. Nixie pretended not to notice. Five years of schooling, plus four years as familiars in the castle, and Taro still couldn't get a smile from her in public. Nixie didn't even glance at Taro as she rose from her seat and vanished to use the bathroom, accompanied by a pair of nuns who fell from the ceiling like sycamore seeds. The idea of Nixie being alone with them made Taro ill. She couldn't stop her eyes roaming to the dark patch on the wall where the Mother had snapped the girl's neck. Taro could feel the danger like a knife against her throat, and she didn't breathe properly until Nixie came back. Even then she couldn't shake the wrongness of the night, as though the execution was a warning.

There were so many ways their escape could fail. Their route through the subcutaneous layer of the castle, where the rooms were crushed and barely accessible, could have collapsed. They might be eaten alive on their journey through the Ulcer, the city's unhinged park full of monsters. Their survival hinged on them fading into obscurity at the edge of the world, where the Desecrae met the ground, just two of the thousands of people living in collapsing houses in the shadow of the castle. It wasn't fair. All Taro wanted was for her and Nixie to be able to hold each other.

Three hours.

At midnight the roasted birds appeared in pastry cages, their eyes stuck with jewels. Taro considered pocketing one to swap for dirty books. She liked those tragic sapphic romances where someone died at the end. She'd need something to read when she and Nixie were free.

'Charming!' Morgan cried at the sight of the birds, as though the same thing wasn't served at literally every dinner. Taro had to admire his relentless enthusiasm. 'Can I cut you something, Geraldin? No? Jon? Cut you something? Kellan? Cut you?'

The Thaumaturge rose. He didn't need to stick anyone's teeth together this time. Everyone went silent of their own accord.

Something was wrong.

Ice clattered behind Taro's ribs.

The Thaumaturge blinked rapidly. The crystals around his feet shuddered in waves as his grey tongue flicked uncontrollably between his teeth. His familiars twitched and jerked while their unused arcania gathered in the air, making the stone cups on the table crack and bleed wine. Taro froze with soup in her mouth.

'Continue,' the Thaumaturge whispered finally, his voice so thin it could slip under a door. He touched the crown on his brow, which made the nuns shudder.

Two servants rushed up with bags of gravel and scattered it before him. And the Thaumaturge ... *flew* was only an approximate word, because he was carried on a rolling crest of grit, with his legs dragging behind him like wet noodles. This should have been funny, but it wasn't. He looked like a corpse being dragged out of a pond.

And it was not part of Taro's plan.

He couldn't leave this early.

He needed to be here if they were going to escape.

Five nuns unfolded themselves from the back of the dais and dragged his familiars away by their feet. Everyone stared, wondering if the Thaumaturge would roar back to see if anyone had dared continue eating.

He didn't.

Taro swallowed the soup, which now had the consistency of phlegm. Something was wrong. The whole room knew it. The air was thick with unease, and it was setting the head arcanists on edge. Taro tried to communicate this to Nixie with nothing but the power of her eyeballs, but Nixie continued to gaze at the wall, betraying nothing.

Jon, who was incapable of reading the room, dropped his spoon loudly.

'Finally,' he barked. 'Taro, we must prepare for tomorrow's Suppression. The dead won't keep themselves in the ground.'

'Nobody cares about the skeletons,' Geraldin muttered, eyeing the door through which the Thaumaturge had vanished. This practically made Jon's eyes spin in their sockets.

'You have no concept of the strength it takes to control osseous matter,' he rasped, as though he had *any idea* what it was like to wrest instead of just flapping his jaw.

'Geraldin, darling,' Morgan said. His tone was light, but Taro could tell he was rattled as well. 'We know your Suppression keeps the castle from melting, but you would be doing us a *massive* favour if you collapsed a teeny-weeny bit of it on Jon's head.'

Geraldin unfurled an incantation as short as Taro's bitten nails. The floor beneath Morgan's chair snapped like a cracker, toppling his chair, but the head blood arcanist was already on his feet. Before anyone could move Morgan gripped his familiar's wrist. The boy must have been palming uncooked gristle, because Morgan's lips had barely twitched before Geraldin's nose spurted blood. Geraldin lifted Morgan by the throat, squashing his neck with her fingers. The smell of violence made the Unholy Mothers writhe down the walls.

The Thaumaturge's early departure had rattled everyone, and now everything was going to shit. If there was an honest-to-god murder between the head arcanists, Taro and Nixie wouldn't even get out of the room before the nuns went feral.

'Don't be silly, Geraldin,' Morgan rasped as he dangled in the air, still with that interminable grin. 'Kill me and we'll drown in blood tomorrow.'

'Enough,' Jon hissed, and yanked Taro away before either of the arcanists could turn on him. 'We're returning to Blackspire.'

The thought of that loathsome obsidian prison of skulls and bones turned her stomach. If Taro didn't escape tonight—

The air warped and Taro staggered. She grabbed the wall, dizzy from the crackle of power – an appalling soup of bone and stone and botanic and blood arcania – which sucked at the window. As it ebbed, the Thaumaturge screamed.

Taro knew instinctively that the world was about to change for ever, in the same way she knew who she loved – with every bone in her body, with every scrap of skin, violently and fearfully. She twisted around and shoved through the confused diners, who were beginning to stand and shout. The dining room spat her out and she pounded towards the noise, leaping down damp staircases, back past the sweating kitchens and the deathly library, towards the scream in the courtyard. Jon followed asthmatically, not even yelling at her for running without permission. Morgan overtook them, his leopard running low to the ground beside him.

'Faster,' Jon gasped, then ran past Taro anyway, hitching his robes over his knees to catch up with his fashionable arch-nemesis.

Taro stumbled through an ivy-covered archway. The courtyard was ankle-deep in blood – no, not blood, *thank the holy boneheap*, but a sticky, ghoulish light that was falling from the Fifth Tower. A window at the top pulsed red. The nuns guarding the Fifth Tower thrashed and scuttled over each other like spiders, clamouring to reach the top.

Blue-black smoke oozed from the roof, filling Taro's nostrils with the stench of singed hair. The castle vomited its hundreds of servants and dignitaries into the courtyard until they were pressed elbow-to-elbow. Taro thrust her hand into her pocket to protect Nixie before remembering she had no bones left to wrest with.

The courtyard stilled. Arcanists held their tongues against the backs of their teeth. Their familiars gripped the raw materials of their disciplines in their pockets. Nobody dared move. The seconds became an agonising minute as the smoke curled into the Desecrae.

It was nothing. The Thaumaturge was just doing some messed-up experiment. Everything was fine, and Taro and Nixie were still going to escape.

Oh fu—

Taro doubled over with a scream caught in her throat. It was as though someone had plunged a knife into her spine and was rolling it between their hands. *Nixie*, she tried to gasp, but nothing came out. She twisted her hand to her back and felt a huge wet circle. *Nixie—*

'Control yourself.' Jon grabbed the back of her neck. His voice was high and urgent. 'It's finally happening.'

It's happening?

Taro felt a swirling emptiness as the blood rushed to her head. She sagged to her knees. A space cleared around her as she keeled over, and even Jon stepped away, leaving her writhing on the ground. Taro saw Nixie hit the cobbles a few yards away, her black braids splaying away from her head, the flowers crumpling as she jerked. A bloody red patch was spreading across her back. Taro crawled a hand towards her, even though she was hopelessly far away. She would always reach for Nixie, even at the end of the world, even when the light had faded from her eyes.

Taro knew that a clock was being carved into their backs. The same one was being etched on Morgan and Geraldin's familiars. Its face was bloody, its hand singular and knife-sharp. It had five numbers, each one signifying twelve hours, scored so deeply she could feel them in the back of her ribs. Jon grabbed Taro's arm, pulling her upright and digging his fingers into the fleshy part of the elbow. He shook her once, twice. Taro's head lolled with shock.

'Tarenteeno,' he said, grabbing her cheeks and twisting her face towards him. As though she wasn't paying enough attention. As though she didn't have a *goddamned clock carved into her flesh.* 'Do you know what that is?'

Of course she knew.

Just as she knew, deep down, that she was never going to escape.

The Thaumaturge was dead. A piece of ancient arcania, as unchangeable as the Desecrae, was uncurling its fist inside the familiars of the four towers. It was counting the hours until the competition for the new Thaumaturge would begin, and it could not be stopped.

In three days the Slaughter would start. It would be the bloodiest and deadliest event of Taro's wretched life.

Two

Fifty-seven hours until the Slaughter

Nixie woke up and made three disturbing observations.

One: she was bleeding profusely from a burning circle on her back. It hurt. A lot.

She ordered herself to move past it, ignoring the pain through sheer willpower.

Two: cobalt glass peppered the flagstones around her, bloody like her hand. Her emerald robes, embroidered with the curling Greenspire sapling, shone with razor-sharp glitter.

You fell and cut yourself. Careless.

Three: she was in the Greenspire tower, where she was never meant to be alone. On pain of death.

Panic rose in her throat, and she allowed herself a moment to – what would that idiot Taro say? – *freak out*. With monumental effort she flopped over before vomiting.

The sacred chamber where Nixie gave Kellan her power was a huge greenhouse dominated by snarling plants, mushrooms and verdant moss. The only evidence of the horrors that took place here were the deep scratches she had left in the table after Kellan's last arcanical experiment. A terrarium was stuffed with rampant ivy and the exploded shell of a snail, warning what would happen if the botanic Suppression failed for even one morning.

Nixie raised her eyes to the shelves, to the cold rows of night-black and cobalt-blue poison bottles. Her fear bared its teeth, and she hiccupped the rest of dinner into her lap before getting her body under control.

The escape. With Taro. It was meant to be tonight. But for some reason she was here, smeared in her own blood. She could feel the hand at the twelve o'clock position on her back, the sliver of raw flesh that would grow with the countdown.

She would rather lose all her skin than never leave this place.

Calm down and think, she ordered herself. *What happened?*

The Thaumaturge. The scream.

The layers of her memory came apart like the petals of a rotting flower. The Thaumaturge was dead. Murdered, because only treachery would make him lose his grip on mortality. She had been in the dining hall when they heard the scream. She had fled from Kellan and lost herself in the crowd in the courtyard.

She remembered the clock tearing into her flesh, and crawling away as the Unholy Mothers closed in. She remembered pushing through the shouting bodies and running to Greenspire. She had ripped through the forest of cultivated vines and raced up the narrow, twisting steps to this chamber, and while the confusion rose outside, she tore through Kellan's bottles of poison. Looking for—

A memory potion.

She had tipped it down her throat. Then she must have collapsed, taking the bottle with her, gashing her hand.

Motive?

Nixie scoured her memory again. She could account for everything that day until the middle of dinner. Twitching her right index finger at Taro, putting the full force of *I loathe you* behind it. Looking through her eyelashes at Taro to say *Don't ruin the plan, you impulsive witch*, which had made Taro grin stupidly. And after that her memory was a huge gap like a missing tooth. She felt around the edges, replaying the meal and Taro kicking her. Then there was nothing until the Thaumaturge had abruptly left the room.

Nixie put a hand to her aching temple. A scrap of paper fluttered from her sleeve and landed in the congealing blood. It bore her own floral handwriting.

Clean up. Don't look for answers.

Nixie bristled at being told what to do, but she also trusted herself completely. She dumped the vomit- and blood-stained glass into the terrarium, then ran.

The stairs from the holy chamber of botanicals were neck-breakingly steep, choked with toxic weeds and poisonous nettles. Nixie had secretly memorised the path through them long ago, revelling in the fact that Kellan thought she was too stupid to learn what would kill her.

As she twisted down the stairs, Nixie's eyes snagged on the single ivy-choked window. She could see the glowing white stone of the Fifth Tower in the courtyard, its slick sides bathed in hellish torchlight. Its spire touched the Desecrae, almost piercing the thick clusters of teeth and plasma. Nuns crawled its walls. They endlessly swivelled their heads to look at the other four spires, which each straddled a corner of the courtyard. Together they stood sentry over the city: the slick scarlet of Redspire, the bristling slate of Greyspire, and the emerald-and-glass peaks of Nixie's own tower.

And the tower where *she* lived.

It was impossible for Nixie to ignore Blackspire's Gothic arches. It watched her constantly, just as Taro did. Its light-sucking stone matched the bone witch's soul. Nixie ducked, heart thudding in disgust, and hurried to her room.

The centuries hadn't been kind to the forgotten chamber. Even Geraldin, the head stone arcanist, couldn't prevent its eventual slump. Kellan, who had assigned Nixie the room without setting foot inside, had recklessly given Nixie all the things a familiar shouldn't have: books and letter openers, nail clippers and cutlery. If anyone came for Nixie in the night they would leave with a non-consensual lobotomy.

She leaned against the closed door and enjoyed the relief of her own space, the sagging bed, the decaying furniture, the buckled shelves.

And the mirror.

That goddamned immovable, spirit-riddled piece of haunted *trash.*

It was door-sized, its gilded frame as thick as her thigh. The bedsheet she'd flung over it hardly lessened its malevolence. As if it could hear her, a hand slammed into the glass behind the bedsheet. The sheet slipped from the frame, landing in a puddle at the foot of the mirror-bound Ghost.

The Ghost was already screeching.

'—en will you get my things for me? The skull is *right under your feet*, you boring worm. I'm offering you a life-changing opportunity—'

She's just a kid, Nixie reminded herself curtly. *You can't hate her. She's only, what, fourteen?* Give or take a few hundred years.

The Ghost trapped in the mirror was barely out of her training corset, but she had the raised chin of someone who had whipped servants from the crib. The Ghost's perpetually teenaged body was translucent, but traces of colour suggested she had burnished brown skin and dark eyes like Nixie's. Unlike Nixie, her teeth were visible through her lips, including their roots.

'—live in a place where the sky doesn't smell like halitosis, you idiotic wyrdo. Find some friends, go pick up my stuff, and climb the Fifth Tower—'

Nixie threw the sheet back over the mirror.

She hadn't slept well in four years. The Ghost constantly begged and pleaded and snarled and screamed. She poured ideas into Nixie's ear as she lay with a pillow over her head: *Stab the Thaumaturge. Poison his tea. Pull his entrails out.* It was unclear why anyone would have let a mirror that big exist, seeing as the tiniest sliver of mirrored glass tended to warp arcania. She should have smashed it. But something – Nixie was loath to call it superstition – made her hand falter every time. She suspected that if she broke the mirror, all the power it had soaked up would be unleashed on her.

Nixie went to her cracked sink and splashed metallic-smelling water on her face. She needed to think. To look at the shreds of her and Taro's escape plan and find something salvageable. She wriggled out of her vomit-stained robes so only her rough slip remained, the back stained red with blood from the clock carved into her back. She picked the pins out of her hair and scrubbed the make-up paste from under her eyes, revealing purplish shadows in the water's reflection.

In a fairer world the arcania she wrested would leave its marks on Kellan's body instead. Death was a pit by her heels, and she had always known – as all familiars did – that one day Kellan would take too much power and her life would end. Escaping had been her only chance to avoid that fate.

'Shit,' she whispered, which is when the assassin hiding in the shadows jumped out at her.

It was three heads taller than Nixie, a malformed hump with deeply gouged eye sockets, sheathed in a black cloak with stark white bones for arms. Nixie didn't have time to panic or the materials to wrest. She grabbed the dagger-shaped letter opener hidden behind the soap, turned, and thrust it into the assassin's body.

The creature convulsed and the knife was wrenched from Nixie's grip. The assassin's right arm fell to the floor with the letter opener hilt-deep in its bone. It tried to hit her with its other arm, but she grabbed its neck – the bit below its ghoulish face, anyway – and shoved it into the wall.

The creature flailed as she pressed her fingers into its windpipe. It was lighter than she had expected, just a frail construct of bones beneath a cloth covering.

Options?

She could snap it into pieces and throw it out of the window. She could grind it up and wash it down the sink. She could even shove it through the mirror into the netherworld. Whichever one she chose, nobody would look for it. Most likely it was a construct put together by Jon of Blackspire to get a head start over Kellan in the Slaughter.

Nixie was about to drive her knee into the creature's ribs when she realised it was trying to speak. She released the pressure on its neck, just enough that it could gasp its final words.

'Hello, darling.'

Nixie dropped the assassin.

It collapsed at her feet and raised its remaining arm. It pulled the black cloth away from itself, revealing—

'I was going to kill you,' Nixie said icily.

Taro howled with laughter. She was no longer wearing her customary brick-red lipstick and dark eyeliner. She had scrubbed herself clean, revealing her stubby nose and a new green bruise on her pale forehead, presumably from Jon throwing something at her.

'You thought I was a monster!'

Nixie put her foot on the broken arm and yanked the letter opener free, and without missing a beat flicked it at Taro. Taro shrieked as the blade buried itself in the bedpost behind her.

'You're never pleased to see me,' Taro said.

Nixie considered shoving her out of the room, but Taro had already plonked herself on the bed. With a manic grin, she reached out and pulled Nixie down beside her.

'I've missed you,' Taro said, as though this was a normal evening. They should have been running from the castle by now. When Nixie didn't answer, Taro picked a smear of bone paste off her neck and flicked it at Nixie's face.

'Don't do that,' Nixie said.

'Don't make a mess, or don't miss you?'

The idea of Taro missing her was nauseating, but Nixie was good at pretending otherwise.

'You shouldn't have been able to disguise yourself.'

'Because of the mirror? Yeah, the arcania warp gave me a headache.'

Taro snaked an arm around her waist. Nixie could feel the warmth of her fingers through her slip. She didn't pull away, which she told herself was part of the illusion, and absolutely not because she secretly liked being held, or because she ached to be touched. Like she and Taro had touched each other in the Torture Pit.

'Cut it out, Taro.'

'Cut what out?'

'*Taro.*'

Taro's grin faltered. Her shoulders slumped.

'The plan's ruined, isn't it?' she croaked. 'We were going to start a new life, and now we're going to die instead.' She clenched her fingers together for a moment. Then her voice cleared, and she was all lightness again. 'But it's just a snag. We've got a couple of days to get this clock off our backs. Then we can run away.'

Nixie took a deep breath, trying to summon her patience.

'You know we can't run now.'

'The alternative's the Slaughter. Do you remember what they told us in the Pit about the last one?'

Of course Nixie did. The ascension of the ninety-eighth thaumaturge was legendary. He had played the game quickly and brutally. Two minutes after they went into the Fifth Tower, the head blood arcanist and his familiar were defenestrated in a tangle of bones. Thirty seconds later the head botanic arcanist rolled out of the door with a knife in his chest, a long clump of hair between his fingers where he had torn the head blood arcanist's scalp off. Whatever the Fifth Tower held made monsters of them all.

And when the Thaumaturge lifted the crown to his brow the Unholy Mothers, now at his command, devoured every familiar who wasn't a stone disciple. Hundreds of people dead. Every trainee familiar from the Torture Pit forced into early service to fill the gaps. A blood-splattered message to the world: *stone wins.*

Yes, Nixie knew the story as well as Taro, and if she didn't force it down the horror would burst her open.

'We can't avoid the Slaughter,' she said levelly, her voice barely shaking. 'We're marked, Taro. The nuns will be watching us.'

Taro practically spat her teeth out.

'Are you insane? Nixie, we need to *leave*, just like we planned. Find a way to get this thing off our backs. Escape—'

'No,' Nixie said sharply. She hadn't meant to sound so vicious. She did want to escape, didn't she? She struggled to control her voice. 'We can't undo the countdown.'

Refuse to take part in the Slaughter, and on the last stroke of the bloody clock they would die. The spell, a piece of ancient blood arcania that ran deep through Fourspires' belly, had its fist around their hearts. The only way to live was to follow their arcanists into the Fifth Tower to face the nameless horror inside, wrest for them, and hope they were the one to survive.

'Someone in the city can help us,' Taro said, but Nixie knew she didn't believe what she was saying. 'Nix. If we stay here, we're stuck between a coffin and an open grave.'

The floor creaked. It was a tiny sound from outside, lighter than breath, but Nixie hadn't survived Greenspire by being careless.

She dragged Taro to the floor. Taro kicked and squawked until Nixie hissed: 'They're coming.'

She shoved Taro under the bed, ignoring her curses. The bone witch's foot disappeared as the door swung open.

Two Unholy Mothers sailed in, their faces as blank as mushroom soup. Nixie clasped her hands in front of her and fixed her eyes on the sink as her heart thumped. The Mothers stopped in front of her. They didn't move for several moments, and Nixie wondered if they were stuck. In theory they were in a holding pattern, and they would police Fourspires until the crown was on a new head. But the last Slaughter had been so long ago nobody could be sure how it worked.

One of the nuns finally cracked its jaws open. Bits of skin swirled from its jowls as it exhaled a plume of dust.

INQUISITION, the dust formed, hanging in the air for a moment before pattering to the ground.

Nixie kept her face perfectly still. The Unholy Mothers doggedly ignored whatever they weren't looking for, which meant she might get away with the mirror, and Taro hiding under her bed, as long as she didn't draw attention to them. The Mothers' nostrils flared. Nixie prayed the stink of her vomit covered Taro's self-wresting.

The second nun worked its jaws loose, grinding them until they fell open, displaying two rows of brown teeth.

DID YOU KILL THE THAUMATURGE? it asked, each word hanging in the air for a moment before dissipating.

Nixie resisted the urge to run her fingers through her braids which Taro said made her look guilty as hell, and shook her head.

LYING IS POSSIBLE, the second nun observed. It opened its fist, revealing a thumb-sized purple vial. *DRINK IT.*

Please not this.

The liquid in the nun's fingers was Nixie's worst nightmare. The Unholy Mother waited with its hand extended.

Options?

DRINK IT, the nun said.

Only one.

Nixie took the vial and ejected the cork with her thumb. She drank it in one gulp, before she could change her mind.

The first nun began to ransack her room systematically. Its grey toes scraped the floor by her bed, inches from where Taro lay. Nixie kept her eyes fixed on an empty corner of the ceiling, suppressing the urge to look at the bedsheet over the mirror in case she drew their attention to it.

IS YOUR NAME NIXEEN? the nun in front of her asked. Nixie could see all the way down its throat. She nodded stiffly. *YOU HAVE BELONGED TO KELLAN GREENSPIRE FOR FOUR YEARS. YOU ARE EIGHTEEN.*

Nixie hesitated. Her memory had been wiped in the Pit. It was one of the many delights familiars suffered when they drew the short straw in the raffle that created arcanists and their slaves.

APPROXIMATELY EIGHTEEN, the nun clarified.

Nixie attempted not to move, but the moment she resisted the poison it tightened around the base of her throat. She nodded, and the pressure eased.

WERE YOU IN THE DINING HALL THIS EVENING?

This time Nixie fought, but her throat swelled so quickly it burned. Her neck cracked as she nodded. The other nun ripped the sheets from her bed.

DID YOU KNOW HE WOULD DIE?

Nixie shook her head. She didn't wait for the potion to help.

DID YOUR ARCANIST COMMAND YOU TO KILL THE THAUMATURGE?

This time Nixie hesitated. Had he? She prodded the gap in her memory again. It ached like a rotten cavity, but it was impenetrable. She shook her head again, minutely. The nun stared through her skull.

PASS.

It pivoted to the door, taking the smell of dry rot with it. The other nun cocked its head at Nixie and then bent down to look under the bed.

Nixie's limited options, all terrible and fatal, flared like a match to paper. She could disable the nuns with a spell, but she didn't have plants to wrest with. She could fight them with the letter opener, but she was outnumbered. Feigning innocence wasn't an option. Two familiars from opposing disciplines in one room screamed treason. They would end their lives as fodder for the Unholy Mothers—

EMPTY, it said, looking up from the bed. The letter opener, still buried in the bed post, shivered by its face. Nixie adopted an expression of utter neutrality as they left, and she stayed that way until their stench had faded.

Taro had vanished. The whole room was empty.

'Maybe she's dead,' the Ghost said from inside the mirror.

When Nixie's heart ceased its acrobatics, she strode to the mirror and yanked the sheet away, revealing the perfect face of the teenaged milk-cold spirit.

'If she was dead she'd be in the netherworld fighting you,' Nixie said coldly.

'She could try,' the Ghost scoffed. It was worse now she wasn't screaming. It meant she was going to ask for something. 'I'm sorry for shouting,' she added sweetly. 'I just really, *really* want you to help me.'

'No.'

The Ghost pressed her face against the glass, squashing her nose and her eyeballs flat as the mirror resisted her body. She grimaced and twisted her neck until finally, with a wet *pop*, she broke through. The back part of her body stuck to the glass like toffee, and from the elbows down she was a swirl of ectoplasm. Behind her, the mirror showed Nixie's bedroom, darker and twisted out of shape.

The Ghost regarded Nixie with a hungry smile.

'Was it you?' the Ghost asked.

'What?' Nixie snapped, wondering why she suddenly felt so guilty.

'You who committed the murder. I just found a creepy old man calling himself the Thaumaturge wafting through the netherworld. He was angry about his soup.'

The thought of the murdered Thaumaturge roaming the world behind her mirror, in the space between life and death, made Nixie want to vomit again. What if he had heard her speak? She fought the impulse to smash the glass with her boot.

'He isn't … ?'

'Hanging around? No, he vanished like a slick of butter on a starving man's sandwich.' Despite her smile, there was an urgent set to the Ghost's eyes. 'Was that really the current Thaumaturge? Or just another mediocre man having a post-life crisis?'

'He is – *was* the Thaumaturge,' Nixie said, pulling herself together with extreme effort.

The Ghost drifted closer. The effort it took was palpable; her skin warped back to the mirror like tightening elastic. The Ghost beckoned, and Nixie resisted for a full second before inclining her ear to the Ghost's lips.

'You look guilty,' the Ghost whispered.

'I have no reason to kill the Thaumaturge.'

The Ghost smiled.

'Don't you?'

Someone rapped on the window. Nixie jerked away from the Ghost in time to see a hand gesticulating through the curtains. It didn't have any flesh on it.

'No,' Nixie said. She truly wished Taro would stop using bone arcania for everything. 'Not again.'

'Very much *yes* again,' Taro said outside the window.

Nixie marched over. Taro was attached to the exterior wall of the castle by a ribcage that had sprouted from the crumbling stone and wrapped itself around her chest. The skeletal hand was connected to an arm, which was at least three elbows too long.

'That's disgusting,' Nixie said.

'I had to hide somewhere. Give me a hand … get it?'

'You got out there, so you can bring yourself back.'

'I know you've uncovered the mirror. If I try anything too clever my teeth are going to burst through my cheeks.'

'So don't be clever.'

Taro rolled her eyes, pinched a rib between her fingers, and muttered. The ribcage scuttled to the window. Nixie fought her instinct to punch the gruesome vehicle, grabbed Taro under the armpits, and dragged her into the room. The ribcage dissolved and pattered to the ground.

Taro cleared her throat, then neatly coughed up a tiny pile of bones.

'Where were we?' she said as Nixie stared at the lightly scorched skeleton.

'Is that a *mouse*?'

'I found it under your bed.' Taro prodded the skeleton with her toes. 'Already dead,' she added.

'You ate it?'

'I couldn't reach it with my hands.'

Before Nixie could tell Taro that wresting with her teeth was impossible as well as foul, Taro sauntered to the mirror. The Ghost bared her teeth. Taro pretended not to see her, adjusted her hair in the non-existent reflection, and slung her real arm around Nixie's shoulder.

'Oh, hi there,' Taro said, as though just noticing the Ghost. Nixie unslung her arm. 'Any new floaters, or are you the only one stubborn enough to hang on?'

'I'm still the sole occupant of the netherworld, *Tarenteeno*,' the Ghost said, her sweet voice whetted to a point.

'Don't call me that, you ectoplasmic smear.'

'*Wyrdo*.'

'Don't use that word,' Taro snarled. She jabbed her finger into the Ghost's frontal lobe. 'Arcanists wouldn't be anywhere without us doing the hard work for them.'

The Ghost wasn't remorseful. She settled into the glass, floating there like a bather.

'You might want to be nice to me,' she said, 'because it seems like you're in a bit of a pickle, and you need help.'

'We know what we're doing,' Taro said. 'We're running away, and to hell with the Slaughter.'

Nixie crushed her frustration with extreme difficulty.

'The clocks,' she said. Why didn't Taro *listen*? 'If we're not at the Fifth Tower when the countdown ends, we'll drop dead.'

'Yeah, and if we stay for the Slaughter we have to *kill each other*.'

Nixie visualised it: swinging at Taro's face. Choking her with plants. Taro's expression as she realised that Nixie had loathed her all along, and had spent the last four years using her. The imagined pleasure was like picking a scab; she didn't want to, but it felt good.

The Ghost coughed delicately.

'Huge dilemma,' she said. '*However*.' She held the pause until it was deeply uncomfortable. 'There is a third option—'

'No,' Nixie said. 'I swear by the Desecrae, if you start going on about murder again I'm going to push you out of the window.'

'I know you've never wanted to engage in our partnership, Nixeen, but consider this: the plot has been put in motion for you. However it happened, and whoever did it –' the Ghost looked at Nixie meaningfully here – 'the Thaumaturge is dead. The hardest part has been done for you. Tell me I'm wrong.'

Nixie dug her fingers into the hole in her memory, but the blank gap around dinner was impenetrable. She loathed not knowing her own mind.

'I've been listening to you – against my will – for four years,' she said. 'There's nothing beyond this city. There's no *outside* beyond the Desecrae.'

'Idiot child,' the literal child in the mirror said. 'If you'd read anything more than smut smuggled in from the bottom of the city you would know that this mountain is a prison in a universe so vast it would make your brain leak through your ears. What do you think is on the other side of the dome of teeth and bones?'

'Your mum's ass,' Taro said.

'Don't goad her,' Nixie said, and turned back to the Ghost. This was stupid. But maybe she was desperate enough to grasp for the green shoot of any idea. 'There is no other side of the Desecrae. Everything that exists is inside it.'

The Ghost beckoned Nixie closer and lowered her voice. 'I know you've always felt like something's wrong with this world.'

Nixie wanted to laugh in the Ghost's face. She couldn't. The Ghost knew that Nixie was scared.

'The Desecrae is a big fat veil over your eyes,' the Ghost said. Taro possessively shuffled closer. 'The world is huge, and you know it. I've seen you reading those manky old books.'

Nixie shrugged noncommittally. Sure, her room was full of rotting books that someone had never returned to the library. Yes, they told of obscenely fantastical places with weirdly consistent descriptions. But they were fiction.

'When I was alive, I lived in that world,' the Ghost said. 'This city was just the centre of it. It was the capital, and Fourspires was its castle. There was no Desecrae. We didn't fight the elements. There were no rituals to stop the whole shitty mess collapsing every morning.' The Ghost folded her arms, knowing she had Nixie on a hook. 'If you do as I say, Nixeen, you won't have to fight in the Slaughter *or* hide in the city for the minuscule amount of time you have left. In both of those scenarios, you die. In mine, you're free.' She smiled slyly. 'And if you want to spend the rest of that life with the bone witch, so be it.'

Nixie resisted the urge to punch the mirror. *Idiot.* She shouldn't have told the Ghost anything.

Taro beamed at Nixie with such guileless devotion that Nixie wanted to scream.

'Obviously she wants to spend her life with me,' Taro said. Nixie was saved from having to reply – god, there were so many lies she told the repugnant bone witch – by the Ghost.

'Don't you want to know the rest?' the Ghost asked, lounging against the mirror frame.

Nixie wanted to say *no* out of spite. But she was desperate, and desperation made her weak.

'I can't stop you,' she said.

'Here's the deal, my mortal babies,' the Ghost said. 'The whole city, and this castle, has been under a curse for six hundred years.'

'Cool,' Taro said. 'I love hearing the same boring story every time I'm here.'

'Silence, meat-sacks,' the Ghost said. 'This jumped-up arcanist called Hallow Myre loathed Fourspires, and he hated the thaumaturge of the time, Sobweb. He wanted the city off the map. So he laid the curse that makes the apocalypse happen every morning – you know, the thing your four head arcanists have to stop with spells. What do you call it? The *Suppression* – and he put the Desecrae over Fourspires for good measure. He probably thought that would be enough to kill everyone. But he was an idiot, because we've been crawling around like ants under a picnic blanket ever since.' The Ghost paused for dramatic effect. 'Now the stars are aligned, children. I've missed every Slaughter because you numpties broke all the mirrors, but this time I have *you*. So you, Nixeen and Tarenteeno, are the lucky winners of this epoch's greatest raffle. You get to save the world and your own asses at the same time.'

The Ghost flicked her hair over her shoulders and waited.

'You're saying we're trapped in a terrarium,' Nixie said flatly. She prayed that neither the Ghost nor Taro could tell how hard her heart was beating. What if there really was a third option?

'Yep,' the Ghost said.

'What would arcanists do if they didn't have to stop the apocalypse every day?' Taro said, clearly not taking it seriously.

'They could learn how to pull gold out of their private orifices for all I care.'

'Bullshit. If this story was true, everyone would know.'

'Why would I lie?'

'I don't know how you get your rocks off.'

'*I was there.*'

The Ghost hissed the words with such violence that ectoplasmic spittle flecked Nixie's face.

'Calm down, you antique freak,' Taro said to the Ghost, but Nixie could tell she was rattled.

'I'll calm down when I'm ready,' the Ghost rasped. 'If you don't do as I say, you'll both die while your arcanists fight over the crown, and Fourspires will rattle on like a corpse full of maggots until everything collapses.'

Nixie knew that it was insane to listen to the dead girl. But she had bet her entire life on being able to escape the castle tonight. She wanted so badly to believe there was another way out that it almost hurt.

That didn't mean she trusted the Ghost.

'What do you get out of helping us?' she asked.

'Nothing.'

Now it was Nixie's turn to snort.

Everything had its price. The price of arcania was pain and bodily degradation. The price of love was betrayal and lies. Secrets, once spilled, became fodder for blackmail. They stared at each other, botanic disciple and dead girl, until the Ghost tilted her head and regarded Nixie with something loosely resembling respect.

'You got me. The Desecrae covers the netherworld too. I want to get out of this hellhole and enjoy my death.' There was nothing like seeing two whole eyeballs swivel towards you to make you feel exposed. 'You know when I'm telling the truth, Nixeen. We've been friends for so long.'

'Gross,' Taro said. 'Are you hitting on my girlfriend?'

'Ex-girlfriend,' Nixie muttered.

'OK, it's a situationship.'

'Excuse me?' the Ghost said, her smirk reappearing.

'It means "when you used to bang and you still love each other but now you're slaves to the patriarchy and if you talk to each other you'll get fed to a swarm of dead nuns".'

'Oh,' the Ghost said. 'You still love each other?'

Nixie wished the Ghost was corporeal enough to kick in the shins. She stalked to the window so Taro couldn't see the revulsion on her face and gazed at the Desecrae while the Ghost snickered.

The Desecrae was all she knew. What would the sky look like without teeth? It was as unimaginable as having the clock removed from her back.

The goddamned clocks. Even if they got rid of them and evaded capture, Nixie would have to spend the rest of her life in the city with Taro. Because that was all that existed under the Desecrae: Fourspires Castle and its tiny, rotting kingdom.

She had never really wanted to pay that price.

'Nixie?' Taro was by her side again. She desired Nixie's space with the same jealousy that ivy choked the light from windows. 'You don't believe any of this, do you?'

Nixie wanted to live. Everything did; it was why weeds grew in cracks and mushrooms grew in puddles. If the Ghost was right about the curse – if there was a world beyond the Desecrae – then at least they had a chance. And the prize was so much bigger than escape from Fourspires.

True freedom.

'Whatever she wants us to do, I refuse,' Taro said.

But Nixie had already made her mind up. And like a weed growing through a crack, she was indiscriminate about what she destroyed to survive.

She turned to Taro, her expression a beautiful lie, and gently knitted her hands around the back of Taro's head. Taro shuddered softly as Nixie pulled her in, so they were standing hip-to-hip. Their lips were almost touching.

It was so easy to fool Taro. Perhaps because there was always a silver thread of want running through the darkness inside Nixie, a small knot of old love that she hadn't been able to destroy. The most effective lies were based on a kernel of truth. She breathed into Taro's mouth.

'Screw you,' Taro said, and Nixie knew she had almost won.

She drew Taro's mouth to hers, and their bodies responded to each other automatically. Taro's fingers slid into her hair, and Nixie's thumbs to Taro's back, which was damp with blood from the clock. Everything fit together. For a moment Nixie was catapulted back to a time when her heart was whole.

Then a great darkness swelled inside her, the bleakness of betrayal and rage. It was all she could do to squash it down, packing it into the dark space behind her ribs where all her destructive feelings went.

She fucking hated Taro. Her barbed lies were so deeply embedded in Nixie's body that they made her sick. She was kissing a monster with black eyes and an empty heart.

She dropped her hands from Taro's body, feeling grubby, and turned to the Ghost. The deceased teenager had watched the whole thing.

'OK,' Taro said, her face flushed. 'Cool. We'll do what the dead girl says.'

'You heard her,' Nixie said to the Ghost. She clenched her fists to hide the shaking. 'Tell us what we have to do.'

The Ghost grinned at Nixie's discomfort. She knew what Taro had done to her.

'I need you to steal those things you have embroidered on your robes,' she said. 'You call them the mascots of your disciplines.'

'The— Excuse me?' Taro said. 'The skull on my robe? The sapling, and the piddly drop of blood, and the … lump of stone?'

'They're real, you plebeian. They're the keys to stopping the apocalypse and smashing the Desecrae. I need you to find them and bring them to the Fifth Tower when the doors open for the Slaughter. It's the only place we can break the curse.'

'That's it?' Nixie said.

'No. You need help. You need it fast, and you need it from the right people.'

'Fine,' Nixie said. Her lips were still burning. She couldn't tell if it was desire or loathing; the two had always felt very much the same. Either way, it was just one more thing to bury. And she had buried a lot. 'Tell us who we need.'

Three

Fifty-seven hours until the Slaughter

Elliot was a slave to the bloodiest family under the Desecrae. He was cursed, and almost brain-dead with exhaustion. Most of all he was pissed off. He squashed a spider between his fingers and flicked it at a book, watching it bounce into the shadows of Fourspires' library.

It brought little pleasure. Elliot couldn't know joy while Tamsin Redborn wore his sanity around her neck.

Tonight, he smirked, *that will change.*

He watched hungrily as Malachi Redborn, Tamsin's husband, paced around the issuing desk. Elliot imagined impaling him on his own umbrella, which Malachi ostensibly carried because it was impossible to tell when the Desecrae would rain saliva. In reality, he used it to hit Elliot's head when he was irritated. But Tamsin – oh, Elliot would make her death far more painful.

'They'll think we killed the Thaumaturge,' Malachi said.

'Darling,' Tamsin cooed, 'we never left the dining hall. We have our alibi.'

Elliot raised his thumb and forefinger and pretended he was crushing Tamsin's head. She was lithe and tawny like her son, Morgan, with lips and nails painted the colour of blood arcania.

'That won't stop the nuns ransacking our house,' Malachi said, his gaze sweeping right past Elliot. Elliot crowed inwardly: *The fool.* 'We've voiced our desire to have Morgan on the throne. We look suspicious, *darling.*'

Elliot raised his hands to the level of Tamsin's neck, where the necklace was, and squeezed his fists as though he were strangling her. The spark of nasty enjoyment was small but sharp.

He had never been closer to grabbing the object of his obsession. Tamsin, the heinous witch, only wore the necklace during public appearances. She knew it sharpened Elliot's humiliation whilst making it impossible to snatch. But tonight, the Thaumaturge's unexpected death had distracted her. Elliot, who was supposed to be on the other side of the library door, was the last thing on Tamsin's mind. And now he was going to take back what was his.

He smirked through his teeth. It helped him suppress the unbearable pain and desperation that he tried, at all times, to keep hidden.

Elliot finally dragged his eyes away from Tamsin and refocused on his incantation. The open vein on his wrist bubbled as he wrested from his own blood. It was an unthinkable act of self-cannibalisation, but disgustingly clever too. He was sure none of those idiots in the so-called Academy for Familiars, the Pit, had worked out how to wrest and shape arcania at the same time. They certainly weren't brave enough to use their own flesh for it. The wresting burned like hellfire, but the arcania it produced was dark and rich. He breathed the thick, cloying power into his mouth and slipped his tongue around it. Lesser people would have choked, but Elliot was proud of his talent.

He had slowed his heart rate to approximately fourteen beats per minute. He had cooled his body to the verge of shutting down. The Redborn family were preternaturally observant, having survived an onslaught of assassination attempts, but even they couldn't sense a near-dead body in the room.

To every single person in this library, Elliot was completely invisible.

Malachi leaned on his umbrella, casting a long, crisp shadow over Elliot's face. His ignorance was delicious.

'Do you think Morgan killed him?' Tamsin asked Malachi. 'Perhaps he's finally graduated from petty theft.'

'That would make him more ambitious than we thought.'

'I would be proud. Nonetheless—'

'—my ancestors have a history of attempted regicide,' Malachi finished darkly. 'It would look bad if we left.'

He savagely jabbed his umbrella into a pile of books. They smacked into the desk, and Elliot flinched.

Sharp noises were the only thing that could break him. The shock thrust Elliot into memories that should have been erased in the Pit. The book smacking into the desk was the Unholy Mother slamming into the wooden chest his parents had locked him in, and he remembered: *he was ten years old, panicking, his elbows digging into the wooden sides of his almost-coffin, with the Unholy Mothers scrabbling at the lid. He was fumbling for his penknife, the one he'd been given to protect himself, but he couldn't find it—*

Elliot's nails scraped against the bookcase, rucking up splinters. He gasped for air.

'Who's there?' Malachi snapped. Elliot was slumped against a shelf, his elbows hemmed in by books, hands reaching for a blade that was no longer there. He knew where he was. Yet part of his mind still lingered in the memory of life at the bottom of the city, where the Desecrae met the ground and hunger had carved a hole below his ribs.

Tamsin touched her husband's shoulder.

'It's a rodent,' she whispered, and kissed his earlobe. 'Relax, precious.'

Elliot's heart spasmed as he dug his fingers back into his bleeding wrist. He pressed his lips into a rotting book to muffle himself, whispering his monstrous incantation into the leather. The burning sensation of wresting crawled up his arm again, deeper and hotter than before, but at least the pain anchored him to the present. *Pain is part of the power*, he told himself.

Only the tiniest fraction of his soul longed for the memory again, because it reminded him of being needed. Before the nuns took Elliot away, he had been a hero. He had been the centre of someone's universe.

Focus. Work out how to get the necklace from Tamsin's neck.

It had been months since Tamsin cursed him with the inability to sleep. If Elliot didn't find an opening soon, he might snap and drag Tamsin into the shadows, consequences be damned.

Saul, the Redborns' arcanist and Elliot's master, coughed.

Elliot had almost forgotten he was there. Malachi's nephew had his own invisibility trick: lurking and not making a noise until it was least appropriate. His hands, formerly clasped behind his back, came together at the front.

'I have an idea,' Saul said, stepping out from a dark corner of the library.

'Yes?' Tamsin's voice was cold.

'If we go back to the mansion,' Saul continued, 'the Unholy Mothers may think we have something to hide.' Elliot noted the glittering-eyed use of *we*. Saul went to great lengths to insinuate himself into the Redborns' inner circle. 'What if we stay here? I could find a set of rooms. We'll frame it as assisting with the nuns' enquiries. Then they won't come to the house and see anything they may wish to … confiscate.'

Malachi's lip twitched at the impertinence, but Elliot knew Saul had a point. Morgan wasn't the only Redborn who stole things for fun, and there were plenty of things in the mansion that should have been in the possession of the crown.

'Do it,' Malachi said, thrusting the umbrella at Saul.

Saul bowed deeply before scuttling towards the door.

The door Elliot was supposed to be waiting behind.

Elliot felt a spasm of panic and almost dropped the incantation again. The Redborns would find him in the room with them, self-wresting and practising arcania, and Elliot would have no choice but to fight.

Someone coughed, and everyone looked up.

A girl was standing on a tilted, book-laden mezzanine above their heads. A cigarette dangled from her slim fingers, its smoke forming a delicate question mark in the air. It was impossible to tell how long she had been listening.

Elliot didn't recognise her until she raised her eyebrows. The golden skin of her forehead was naked, her scalp covered in a dark, super-cropped fuzz, her eyes no longer hidden by the thick black fringe she used to live behind. They had been trained together in the Pit – the Academy – for the same five years, never speaking, barely even looking at each other.

It was Alis. The old stone disciple, excommunicated from her role as familiar to the head arcanist of Greyspire, Geraldin. Elliot's position with one of the richest families in the city – a family that had birthed one of the four head arcanists – was coveted, but Alis's had been a phenomenal achievement. She had beaten all the other stone disciples to the castle. The last he heard, Alis's tongue had been burned out. Everyone thought she was dead.

Elliot held the next spell back with the tip of his tongue, bewildered.

Alis mooched down the rickety stairs and leaned against the issuing desk. When she had the family's full attention, she removed a pencil stub from behind her ear and wrote on the wood.

The library is closed.

Malachi's lip curled so far Elliot could see his gums.

'You must be the Librarian's assistant,' Tamsin said silkily. 'It's fortunate that you're working so late. You can find a room for us.'

Alis stubbed her cigarette out.

'Well?' Malachi said.

Alis thought for a moment before using her pencil again.

I work for the Librarian.

Malachi hissed between his teeth. Tamsin touched his arm, stilling him before he could grab Alis's neck.

'This isn't a day for us to mete punishment,' she said softly, but she was looking at Alis as she spoke. 'Saul. Find a room and call for our belongings.'

Alis pointed to the door and bowed sarcastically before sitting and flipping open a book. Elliot remembered that she had always been like this: casual, sarcastic, deadpan.

Her intervention had given him enough time to plan his next move. He would knock Saul unconscious, and while Tasmin and Malachi were distracted, rip the necklace from Tamsin's neck. His desperation was so hot and hungry he no longer cared about the consequences, as long as he could feel the necklace between his fingers.

Now.

Elliot thrust his fingers into the congealing blood on his wrist and wrested from it. His tongue shaped a new incantation that pulled at Saul's blood, draining half a pint from his head. Saul stumbled and grabbed at Tamsin on his way down, digging his fingers into her cloak. It ripped from her shoulders.

Elliot was already moving when he saw Tamsin's bare neck. He pulled himself back mid-lunge, a scream of rage sticking in his throat. Neither Tamsin nor Malachi heard. They were too busy kicking Saul away, disgusted by his groans. Elliot felt sicker than he did even in the depths of night, when he writhed in sleepless agony. The necklace that Tamsin had put on that evening, and which had taunted him all night, was *gone.* Elliot's sleep was still locked inside it. And Elliot knew who had taken it.

Tamsin had worn the necklace to the Thaumaturge's dinner. Elliot had spent the whole evening staring at it. Then the scream – the murder – and the chaos of hundreds of people pressed together in the courtyard, shouting as the clocks were arcanically carved on the high familiars' backs. Only one person was brave enough, or stupid enough, to use that distraction to take a necklace from Tamsin's throat.

Morgan fucking Redborn.

Not because he knew what it was, but because everything was a game. Larceny just happened to be his favourite.

'Get up, you lumpen idiot,' Tamsin hissed, dragging Saul up by his shirt.

As they struggled with each other, Elliot slipped past the issuing desk and through the library door. He turned and caught a last glimpse of Alis, who was casually doodling in the margins of the book she held. Her sleeve rode up as she twitched the pencil, revealing a flash of something black and intricate drawn all over her skin. It vanished before he could get a good look.

Elliot stalked into the hallway, wiping his bloody hand on his robes as he stopped wresting. Moments later Saul was thrown through the door behind him. Elliot tried to look bored as Saul, his face puce, grabbed Elliot by the collar.

'We're staying in the castle,' he said. 'Come!'

Elliot followed, his rage incandescent. He had been so close to getting what he wanted. The necklace that could break his curse would be in his hands if not for the Redborns' malicious offspring.

Morgan had left him no choice.

Elliot would have to break into the Redspire tower. He would steal his life back, and he would do it before the Slaughter. Morgan was powerful enough to win the throne, and once he became the Thaumaturge, sequestered in the Fifth Tower and flanked by nuns, Elliot wouldn't have another chance to get close. But tonight …

Saul glanced back. His face darkened.

'You dare scowl, wyrdo?'

Elliot didn't even think. His patience was already paper thin, and it ripped under his exhaustion. He bit his tongue as hard as he could and stuck his fingers against his teeth. With a silent hiss he drew a long smear of blood beneath Saul's feet. The arcanist slipped and plunged headfirst into the wall.

Saul hit the stone with a visceral *crack* and fell sideways, his nose gushing. Elliot bit down harder, arcania gathering between his fingers. The spell on his lips was bright and shockingly violent, irresistible in its simplicity.

Finish him.

Elliot could do a hundred things to Saul. He hadn't almost killed himself secretly studying arcania for nothing. He could cause him pain. He could draw Saul's death out. But Saul whimpered, and some unfathomable force made Elliot unclench his teeth. The blood on the floor whispered away to nothing.

Weakling. Coward. Child.

Saul clutched his nose as he rose to his feet. When Elliot didn't help, he shook his scarlet-smeared hand so violently that his blood flecked Elliot's face.

'Walk faster,' Saul rasped, and stalked away.

Elliot didn't move. He waited until Saul's blood, violently red against his warm olive skin, was cool. The part of him that still enjoyed things, which flickered only briefly from the cold ashes of his broken mind, rejoiced in Saul's humiliation.

Elliot's parents had raised him to be a hero, but he was born to be a villain.

Elliot lay in wait on the rotting boards beside Saul's bed.

The room they were staying in was lavishly decrepit and had clearly once belonged to a cartographer. The walls were plastered with curling papers: diagrams of the city and the Desecrae above. His eyes roamed over the positions of important landmarks and their predicted trajectories towards the bottom of the city. One picture showed a cross section of the mountain, with Fourspires on top and hundreds of rooms crushed beneath it. Elliot stared as the shadows slowly travelled over his face. It was long past midnight, and the Redborns were asleep.

His one weakness was that he never stopped attempting to join them.

He had tried everything. Potions. Incantations. Counting the stars bursting behind his eyes. Goading Saul into striking him so hard he fell over. Starving himself so he would pass out. More potions. So many he should be comatose. He had prowled the Redborns' black mansion and had staring contests with the caged wolves. He practised arcania, using blood from the vast stores beneath the floors or, when he was in a particularly foul mood, taking it straight from his veins.

He still couldn't sleep.

Elliot should be dead, but somehow his miserable body clung to life, surviving on those few restless hours that he lay in the dark with his eyes squeezed shut, knowing that he wasn't asleep but pretending for his own sanity. Elliot would have murdered to cure himself of his unending wakefulness, but Tamsin Redborn had made sure there was no release without the necklace.

The deadly truth was that his eternal insomnia was breaking him. His mind was stretched so thin that the wall the Pit had built around his childhood memories was falling, and each time a crack appeared another piece of his sanity died. Since the age of ten he had been trained to wrest, even when he was in so much pain a normal person would have collapsed. He had been locked in dark rooms, stuck with pins, strangled, half drowned and chained to a furnace. But nobody had taught him how to withstand the suffering behind his eyes. Now his memories had come back, nothing could make him forget that life had once been beautiful, and that Elliot had been important.

Elliot counted six hundred more of Saul's undisturbed breaths, then eased himself from the room. Fourspires was a maze of crooked halls and nameless horrors. Moulds and mushrooms glistened stickily in the candlelight as the walls, barely held together by Geraldin's stone arcania in the Suppression, bulged inwards. Instead of turning himself into a corpse again and catching the nostrils of the roaming Unholy Mothers, Elliot pressed into the shadows. Every time a nun passed he hid among slime-obscured effigies of the first Thaumaturge, Sobweb.

The air cooled as Elliot slipped towards Morgan's tower. Blood arcania had its own rich scent: the sweet undertone of rotting flesh, the metallic tang of iron. It was so thick here it was chewable. It tasted of power.

With the stink of blood between his teeth, just a few minutes from Redspire and his prize, Elliot heard footsteps.

This was no auditory hallucination borne of sleep deprivation. Someone was coming. He slipped into an empty niche, burning with impatience. A snail oozed past his foot as he waited. After a minute the noise resolved itself into a mutter, then a voice.

It was that repellent bone disciple.

Taro.

He recognised her even without the ghastly make-up, the lack of which made her look young, even though she had been a full school year above him. She still had the same Gothic clothes, angry black eyes, and severe haircut that had made everyone stare at her in the Torture Pit. The professors would have fed her to the Unholy Mothers if not for her scores, which were perfect in every practical exam she took, including the ones she wasn't supposed to.

Elliot frowned. Jon must have sent Taro to slit Morgan's throat to get ahead in the Slaughter. It would be just like a bone arcanist to cheat; its adherents were literally grave robbers. If Taro got rid of Morgan, Redspire would be swarming with nuns, and Elliot wouldn't be able to steal anything.

He sorted through the killing blows in his repertoire, but some instinct, the one that had spared Saul, made him hesitate. *Weak*, he hissed at himself. Taro paced the hall, her black cloak swirling around her ankles, gnawing dead skin from around her fingernails.

'Find betrayers,' she spluttered to herself. 'Sure thing, dead girl. Let me get my evil address book out.' Her heels clicked against the floor. 'Won't even tell us what's in the tower. She's insane. Unless she isn't. Shit.'

Elliot, furious at his inability to murder her, crushed the snail under his foot instead. Taro's head swivelled to Elliot's hiding place.

'What the hell do you want?' she snapped, as though they had last seen each other yesterday.

He *would* kill her. Soon. As Elliot stepped out of the shadows he turned his cheek and showed Taro the old scar under his jaw.

'You still haven't apologised,' he said.

'For what?'

'Lobbing a rock at me when I walked in on you and Nixie four years ago.'

'It was a private chat, you pervert.'

'Some chat.'

Elliot didn't have time to ask what Taro was doing away from her tower, or why she was talking when they both knew it was a capital offence, before she smacked him in the face.

Using arcania.

He didn't even see her pluck the bone from her pocket. Her words were twisted and rib-shaped, every syllable screaming textbook bone arcania. But there was something else in there, too; an utterance that was cold and hard, and another that trickled like blood. Before Elliot could account for the weird inflections in her voice, or untangle her rough, panicked way of casting, the spell caught him in the jawbone.

His face was punched backwards. Something broke in his mouth. Elliot gasped and spat a piece of tooth into his hand.

Impossible. He was the only person who could wrest and incant at the same time. Everyone else in the Torture Pit had been too stupid to consider it. Hadn't they? Or were they all part of some secret club he'd never been invited to?

Elliot, his mother said behind his eyes, cupping her hands around his. *You're the only one who's clever enough.* Her love burned a hole in his aching chest, even now. Remembering that love, and knowing he would never feel it again, was another curse. *Show them what you can do.*

Elliot spat blood into his hand and threw a spell that split Taro's lip. It was worth the pain that bloomed behind his eyes. Taro gargled furiously and locked his wrists together without touching him. She didn't even flinch as she controlled his bones. The spell yanked his hands above his head and pushed him up against the wall.

'I could bend your elbows backwards,' Taro said. She released him so sharply he fell.

'And I could explode the blood vessels in your eyes,' Elliot said. He would have done it, too, if he weren't shaking with exhaustion. Definitely.

He expected Taro to run away, but she just cocked her head.

'You use your own arcania,' she said. 'Knew you weren't any better than the rest of us.'

'I *invented* self-wresting.'

'Cute,' she said, and before he could ask what the hell she meant, she added: 'You were bought by the Redborns, right? You're their arcanist's familiar.'

'I would have been Morgan's familiar if there had been an opening.'

Taro snorted.

'It's not a dick-swinging match,' she said. 'Why are you creeping around, Elliot?' She stepped closer, her smile twitching. 'Did the Redborns stick a knife in the Thaumaturge? Have they sent you to murder someone else?'

'Why are *you* here, Tarenteeno?'

Taro pursed her lips, suddenly sheepish. He sized her up. Even though she could wrest, he could probably take her down. Yes; he was absolutely capable of crushing her. It just wasn't worth his time. Elliot wiped his foot on the floor, removing the crushed snail, and continued walking.

She caught up with him.

'I'll tell you why I'm here,' she said. 'But you'll be shocked.'

'I don't want to know.'

Taro dropped into step beside him, apparently unimpeded by her ridiculous pointed shoes.

'What would you say if I told you I was going to take the throne and punch a hole through the Desecrae because a snotty teenage ghost told me to?'

Elliot snorted. The Redborns' animals became hysterical when the monthly culling and blood collecting began. He suspected the same thing was happening to Taro. Everyone knew that Jon was the weakest head arcanist, which meant Taro was going to die in the Slaughter. She had been pushed over the edge.

'Insane, isn't it?' Taro said, unperturbed by his silence. 'But there *is* a ghost in a mirror, and she says we can get out of the Desecrae if we listen to her. Nixie and I won't have to fight in the Slaughter, and we won't be familiars any more.'

Against his better judgement, Elliot glanced at her.

'You're not trying to be funny,' he said.

'No. And look, I trust this ghost as far as I can chuck a bone, but she's offering proof. We're going to find a skull that was lost a bunch of years ago. We need a stone arcanist and a –' she quirked her lip and waggled her fingers in obvious disdain – 'a *blood* arcanist to help us.'

Of course she needed him. Didn't everyone, sooner or later?

'You want me to help you go digging around the castle?' Elliot asked.

'Oh good, you understand.'

'And you want to find a special skull.'

'It's adorable that you learn by repeating.'

Just explode one eyeball, he thought. *That would shut her up.* But his own eyes were throbbing, and he needed to save his arcania for whatever was waiting in Morgan's tower.

'Fourspires has twenty miles of hallway,' he said. 'There are literally thousands of skulls.'

'I know. I live here.'

'That skull probably doesn't even exist.'

'Killjoy.'

'Even thinking about stealing from the castle is treason.'

'Like you care.'

True. Elliot was all for treason when it suited him.

They rounded another corner. The stone here was red, making it look like Redspire was seeping into the castle's skin. Taro stopped dead, as though the rivalry between the spires physically repelled her.

'Nice to see you, Tarenteeno,' Elliot said. His pulse quickened at the thought of entering the tower. As an afterthought he said: 'If you draw blood from me again, I will kill you.'

'Did you hear anything I said?' Taro snapped. 'We need you.'

Elliot flinched at the word *need*. He hated himself, but he couldn't help it. As a child he had never been allowed to walk away from it, and the word still had its thumb on his throat. His eyes fluttered closed, and this time he didn't fight the memories.

His mother used to drag him through the door. Parents watched, fearful of Elliot, as he tried to cool fevers. Gifts appeared at their home in the morning. His mother only smiled when he saved someone—

Enough. He crushed the memory and slipped his hands into his pockets. He was carrying a scrap of bloody meat from Saul's stash and, should that fail him, a razor blade to cut his fingers.

'Elliot?' Taro said. 'You know Morgan will probably win the Slaughter. He'll chop our heads off just because we aren't blood arcanists, even if we make it out of the tower—'

'He won't kill me. I'm a blood disciple. I don't care what happens to you.'

This silenced her. When he rounded the corner he turned back, expecting her to ask again, only to realise she hadn't followed him.

Good, he told himself. *She's a distraction.* A shameful sliver of him wanted to run back and give Taro another chance to beg. But the thought of giving her anything, when he despised Taro more than any bone disciple under the Desecrae, made him shudder.

Redspire was the colour of injury and violence, its stone polished to wetness. A ruby window curved over the door, showing a pulsing red light inside the tower, an illusion made by candlelight. Elliot trailed his hand over the wood, his breath catching.

He had been so close to taking the necklace back. He had dreamed about this moment ever since Tamsin had cursed him months ago, locking Elliot's sleep inside the hateful pendant and hiding it deep inside the labyrinthine mansion. The necklace was a chain of agony linking him to the Redborns; they owned it and therefore his freedom, and he couldn't rebel in case they destroyed it.

And now it was just behind the black door.

'Peridot!'

Elliot snatched his hand back. He jammed himself into the embrace of a leering statue as the head blood arcanist swept around the corner. Elliot's heart turned somersaults. His mouth tasted like mud and metal.

This was the closest Elliot had ever been to Morgan Redborn, he of the glittering robes and deep perfume and handsome face. Elliot found himself lingering on that face for longer than strictly necessary. He had heard about Morgan's paramours. How strange it must be to hold that cruel face in your hands and know that you would never touch anything more powerful.

The leopard, Peridot, trotted by Morgan's side. Morgan's familiar trailed a few yards behind, dead rabbits slung over his narrow shoulders. Morgan got through four familiars a year. Each was as beautiful as the last, which only added credence to the rumours.

Morgan unlocked the door. As he turned the handle his sleeve slipped and Elliot saw a thin black vial, half empty, tucked neatly against his wrist. The kind of vial that might be easily accessed with a twist of the fingers, its substance administered with a flick of the hand. The kind of thing you would use to murder someone.

The door swung open. Elliot saw a shred of the tower's forbidden interior, shining like the inside of a grapefruit. The walls shivered with jewels and vials and the history books Morgan was obsessed with. Flame-coloured beetles clattered silently over a bowl of purple apples and plums.

'Go on,' Morgan said impatiently to his familiar, waving at the door. The boy sloped into the tower. Morgan pulled a grotesque face at his back.

This was Elliot's chance. It was dark; he could dart in after Morgan, before the door swung shut. If he could hide somewhere and wait for the blood arcanist to fall asleep …

Morgan paused in the doorway and looked at the shadowed statue, right through Elliot's forehead. Elliot stopped breathing.

'I smell you,' Morgan said, flashing his snow-white teeth.

Elliot jerked a hand to his broken tooth. He'd forgotten Morgan's ability to smell blood among blood. It was sharper than Malachi's hearing, and stronger than Tamsin's sensitivity to anything with a pulse.

'Did my parents send you to spy on me?' Morgan asked lightly. Even though Elliot knew Morgan was only looking at shadows, he felt the blood arcanist's gaze stripping him down to his veins. 'You can tell me. I might even make it worth your while.'

He left the idea hanging in the air, fragile and thrilling. Elliot imagined it: holding Morgan's face. Kissing his mouth. Snapping his neck. Everyone knew that Morgan was a great arcanist, but given the chance to attend the University, Elliot would have been better. He might even have been the master of Redspire. Killing Morgan would show everyone, from the monstrous teachers in the Pit to the sneering Redborns, that they had grossly underestimated him; that all the times they had looked down on him, they should have feared him.

Then Morgan laughed, and Elliot's fantasy evaporated. He was exhausted by the curse, and by wresting. Conversely, Morgan took arcania from his familiars until they were corpses, and felt nothing. Elliot would be lucky to get within touching distance of his neck.

Peridot slunk forward and sniffed at the shadows around Elliot's feet. The leopard had teeth like needles.

'Who is it, Peridot?' Morgan said. 'Is it your dinner? Is it a walking wyrdo steak? Shall I put their skin down as my carpet?' Elliot flinched as Peridot flicked his ears and swung his head. He suddenly ached for his old penknife, the only physical weapon he'd ever known. His fingers tightened automatically, remembering what it felt like to hold the blade in the dark while he was being hunted.

'Go on, Peridot,' Morgan said. 'Kill it.'

Peridot looked at him. In three seconds, Elliot would be in ribbons. He was too broken by the evening to deliver a fatal arcanic blow. He looked for a weapon, but he could only see the lavish interior of Morgan's tower and the pale smirk of its master.

Peridot twitched. Instinct took over. Elliot thrust his hand into his pocket and formed a shape with his lips. He had never uttered this spell out loud, but he knew its pattern by rote. His spine buckled as he wrested from the hidden scrap of meat, drawing power into his fingertips.

Like the Redborns' home, everything inside Morgan's tower was covered in a fine spray of blood. And blood could be manipulated. The bowl of fruit toppled over. Purple orbs rolled over the floor, flinging beetles over the leopard-skin rug. Peridot lunged at it, claws clattering on the stone.

Morgan was not as easily fooled as his pet. He moved his eyes languidly through the shadows. The spell had taken everything out of Elliot. His ribs were cramped with nausea, and he knew he was too weak to do anything more.

'Uncanny,' Morgan said. He spoke lazily, as though he wanted Elliot to know his death would be slow. 'I only smell one person. But you're doing the work of two.'

Elliot closed his eyes. Knives slid into his temples. He was moments away from bringing his guts up with pain. Morgan could wrench him from the shadows right now, and Elliot would break in his hands.

But instead of drawing a blade or calling his familiar, Morgan squashed one of the escaped fruits under his toe, spattering the flagstones with gore.

'I look forward to becoming better acquainted,' he said. He walked into the tower and flashed Elliot a wicked grin.

This couldn't be it. It couldn't be this easy.

He closed the door, leaving Elliot in the dark.

Elliot slumped to his knees. He retched, but nothing came up. The castle walls quivered. He pressed the heels of his hands into his eyes, wishing he could dig the pain out, breathing through gritted teeth until the castle stopped spinning.

He knew he should feel relieved at being alive. Instead he felt deep black fury. Morgan had the necklace, and Elliot had fewer than three days to steal it back.

He would find it even if it killed him.

Four

Forty-eight hours until the Slaughter

Alis lounged in her kingdom of books, chin tilted back, feet kicked up on a stack of dictionaries. She drummed the fingers of one hand against a manuscript and dispassionately smoked with the other.

May the Desecrae spit its teeth at Malachi's head, she thought. It was less than he deserved. Last night he had swept a pile of books from the desk with his umbrella, and only she was allowed to do that. *I beg of the universe to make him perpetually hungry*, she decided savagely. *And for everything he eats to starve him.*

Alis stubbed her cigarette out on the spine of an encyclopaedia, leaned forward in her chair, and looked over the balcony. Trainee arcanists from the University scuttled through the library's belly, followed by their hapless new familiars, most of them barely in their teens. She had been like them once. Trailing after Geraldin, having the arcania sucked out of her as though she was a bottomless crucible. Poor sad saps.

But then the castle had gobbled Alis up and taken her into its bones, and now she was the library's king and queen. Every day she slithered through its veins, delivering books and filing them away again. It was no longer her job to wrest for

Geraldin, who performed the part of the daily Suppression that stopped the castle melting. Since her expulsion from Greyspire, her life had been … almost OK.

'Alis,' a voice sang. It was as old and soft as vellum, lovingly buffed and hideous in its cadence. 'I have a question for you.'

Alis was the king and queen, but the realm had an enemy. She shouldered the books she was meant to be filing and swaggered away from the voice.

Centuries of collapse had turned the hallowed hall of books into a sponge. It was riddled with passageways that looped back on themselves to create suffocating chambers of words. A wrong turn could lead to starvation, and removing a load-bearing dictionary might bring the ceiling down. That was how the last assistant had died: under an avalanche of books in Wyrd Botany, her body stripped to the bone by the feral library cats.

Alis was smarter. She respected the library's traps, and she fed the cats. She passed through Monstrous Anatomy, looked up, and nodded to the gnarled wooden beam that held the sagging walls of the library apart. Legend said it had come from a tree in the Ulcer, the decaying, starveling-filled garden below the castle. She enjoyed the reminder that even Geraldin couldn't keep the library fully upright with arcania. Instead the stone arcanist patched things up, her jaw clenched, every time a load-bearing wall collapsed under the weight of paper.

Alis snorted with derision. It was worse now Geraldin had her new familiar, Cassia, who was barely capable of keeping the bedrock steady. Cassia was a pathetic, milksop version of Alis, who had been – *let's face it* – incredible at her job.

Alis ducked into Dead Languages. Suitably sequestered, she dropped the books and sat on them. She nimbly retrieved another cigarette from the spine of a bone-setting manual, lit it, and resumed her observation.

The library was tense this morning. Not like the time a student cursed the filing system by spraying the directory with blood; no, it was far worse. Nervous energy flowed through its rotting boards and curled the pages of its books. Last night had been dark as hell. First the Thaumaturge's murder, which was so catastrophic Alis couldn't quite hold it in her head, and the countdown to the Slaughter. Then the Redborns turning up in the library, which was closer to home and therefore concerned her even more. And that humourless familiar she remembered from the Torture Pit – Elliot, the sour boy with dark curls, who used to carve monstrous little figures with his penknife. It was laughable that the Redborns hadn't noticed him hiding because the entire library had been holding its breath against him, this intruder like a speck of grit in its eye.

'Alis, sweetie.'

Bastarding hell.

The Librarian had a special way of forming Alis's name, curling it up behind her tongue and letting it flutter out like a mouthful of eyelashes.

'You're so quiet, my mousey girl.'

Alis scowled. No doubt the Librarian knew her secret. Maybe Cassia had found a way to tell everyone. Either way, the Librarian said the word *girl* as though it had spikes.

'Alis …'

Ash fluttered from the end of Alis's unfinished cigarette. The shelves were as dry as kindling. One wrong move and the whole place would go up in flames.

Alis's hand hovered over the books, cigarette glowing. It would be so easy to let go. Two seconds until absolute carnage. She loved the library, yet part of her wanted to hurt it for imprisoning her. She should never have been kicked out of Greyspire. She was the best thing to have ever happened to Geraldin, who was insultingly quick to believe Alis had messed up. Alis was the strongest stone disciple to come out of the Pit in decades, and they were *wasting* her.

'Alis!'

Alis sighed and stubbed the cigarette out as the old woman wafted around the corner.

The Librarian's skin was soap-sallow, her face stretched taut by the pins that forced her grey hair into a hard bun. She was heralded by perfume from the unguents she applied several times a day. She was deeply handsome from the elbows up, but the ends of her hands were pure violence, her nails thick and dagger-sharp. She used them as paper spikes during administrative tasks.

'Alis, petal,' the Librarian said. Her eyes were clouded, but that didn't impede her hunting skills.

Alis grabbed a book for protection and backed away. The Librarian matched her step for step, along a row of manuscripts and around a corner. They performed the same dance every day, sometimes fast, sometimes moving in slow circles. Alis stopped against a window overlooking the courtyard, clutching the book to her chest.

The Librarian plucked it from Alis's hands. She trilled her fingers over the cover, noting the gilt edges and the age of the leather.

'You're in the wrong section,' she said. She had possessed this skill her entire life. The attack on her eyesight, much to her enemies' disappointment, had barely affected her. She dropped the book and clicked her tongue. 'I *said*, I have a question for you.'

The Librarian asked this question every morning, sometimes after hours of lead-up, sometimes by surprise. She had once yanked books from the other side of a shelf Alis was tidying and stuck her head through the hole. Alis had nightmares about that one.

'Alis, how old do you think I am?'

So old the skeletons are holding a gravemound open for you, Alis thought, but she never wrote an answer and the Librarian had never enlightened her. It was possible the Librarian didn't know herself.

Alis shrugged. The Librarian smiled in a manner that would have been coquettish had her face possessed an average range of movement. She inclined her head to the window.

'It's going to be a bloodbath,' the Librarian said of the nuns swirling outside. 'I knew the Thaumaturge would die soon. He was as brittle as pork crackling. I offered him my unguents.'

Alis knew she wanted a response. Even if she had been able to give one, she wouldn't have touched her pencil.

'It's so elegant,' the Librarian sighed, as if overcome by the beauty of such violence. 'For something as big as the Slaughter to be triggered, you need a giant wresting that nobody could survive. When the Thaumaturge took his last breath, all the arcania in him spurted out like someone grinding their foot into a sponge. A thaumaturge dies, the spell is triggered, and the countdown to the Slaughter begins. The nuns see it through. Another thaumaturge comes. Familiars of the losing disciplines must die. The new thaumaturge rules, and when he or she dies, it begins again.' She sighed wistfully. 'I wonder if he suffered.'

Alis hooked her fingers into the corners of her mouth and pulled a grimace that the Librarian couldn't see. The Librarian chuckled. Alis wondered what the Librarian thought she was doing: cowering from her? Awaiting instructions? If she'd lacked the iota of self-preservation she still had, Alis would have stabbed the woman with her pencil.

'I would want a botanic arcanist on the throne next,' the Librarian mused, 'if only Greenspire wasn't held by Kellan.' Her lip curled like burning paper. 'It should have been me in Greenspire.' She tapped the space between her eyes. 'Do you know what I did after he blinded me?'

The whole castle knew. She had used her nails to split Kellan like an overstuffed sausage.

'Who do *you* want to see in the Fifth Tower?' the Librarian asked, leaning closer. 'Another stone arcanist?' She stroked the back of her index finger over Alis's cheek, her nail drawing a crescent under Alis's eye. 'Or do you hate them now? You can talk to me.'

Alis raised her middle finger at the Librarian, who stared right through it.

'I forgot,' the Librarian said. 'You can't talk.'

Alis added the other hand and thought: *I hope the library cats murder you in your sleep.*

'What does it feel like to have a dead tongue, my poor sweet? Does it roll around when you eat?'

Alis waggled both fingers, imagining they were in the Librarian's eye sockets. *I pray that an encyclopaedia of different shit stains falls on your enchantingly symmetrical head.*

'Do you miss being a familiar? Are you angry with yourself for ruining your life?'

Alis mimed shoving her fingers into the Librarian's nostrils. *I beg of the universe that the dead rise and drag you screaming through a very small hole.*

Maybe she brought her hands too close. Maybe the Librarian could smell her curses. Either way, the Librarian suddenly grasped Alis's throat, her thumb on her gullet, her fingers wrapped around the back of Alis's neck. She ran her thumb up and down Alis's skin, pressing hard enough to bruise her windpipe.

'No Adam's apple,' she whispered. 'I always said you were a girl.'

She released Alis and swept away.

I beseech the cosmos to make your hair fall out and your skin sag to the floor so you trip over it, you anciently foul hag!

Alis kicked a shelf. *Girl.* It was hilarious and sad and shameful all at once. Alis called herself 'she' because that was how it had always been, and it had left a dent in her skin, like when she fell asleep on a book. But the word, and her name, felt like poorly fitting garments that she wore out of habit rather than desire. In the dead of night, when she had nothing else to occupy her and everything had an awful clarity, Alis knew who she was. She was just a person, a brain in a body, and instantly – temporarily – she felt complete. *I am, I am, I am.*

But look where sharing it had got her.

She – they, she, they – Alis – rested her head against the cool window until the Librarian was safely ensconced behind the issuing desk. Alis waited for the throbbing in her temples to pass. Then she smiled.

One day the Librarian would die, and Alis would officially rule the library. She would burn everything in the Librarian's office except her gilded chair, which she would use as a footstool. She would smash the windows and let the rain form a sea on the floor. She would build islands out of books and bonfires from encyclopaedias. When Alis hurt the library, it would only be like cutting her own fingers, painful but uncriminal, because it all belonged to her.

Providing she wasn't slaughtered by the new thaumaturge.

She nervously ran her fingers over her stubbled hair. That wasn't going to happen. She hadn't been a familiar in years, so she would be spared.

Surely.

She slipped through a gap in the shelves and entered a new, leering passage of books. A cat slunk alongside her, eyeing her pockets in case she had any food, before oozing down the side of a bookcase. This was the heart of Alis's kingdom. It was where she slept and silently screamed into her hands. It was where she kept all the things she had stolen from the Librarian's office: the scissors she cut her hair with, the ink and needles she used to draw on her arms. Most importantly, it was so deep in the library that nobody else came here unless they were hopelessly lost or they wanted to die.

Which made the next intrusion particularly shocking.

Alis stiffened as robes whispered over the floorboards on the other side of the shelf. She knew exactly who walked with that determined cadence.

Nixie.

Alis had last seen her four years ago, when nuns had dragged Nixie away from the Torture Pit to the castle and a new life as a familiar. Alis's heart hammered as she peered through a gap in the shelf. The smudges under the botanic disciple's eyes were the colour of bruises.

Nixie turned left at a junction of mushroom-covered scrolls. She was as welcome as a tooth in soup, yet Alis was compelled to shadow her from the other side of the shelf. She couldn't help it; the part of her that despised Nixie also longed for her smile. It had once felt like home. They were getting deep into the stacks now, to the places where even the Librarian couldn't keep the mould at bay. It was where cats and pigeons came to die when they were sick from ingesting too much ink. Nixie wrinkled her nose at the smell, a gesture she had picked up from Taro.

Odious bone witch.

Alis yanked her hood up and stalked ahead of her old friend, who was about to turn into a dead end. She flirted with the idea of causing a small avalanche to block her in, but nothing would be as good as stepping out, cutting off her escape, and waiting for her to turn around – like *this*.

Nixie jumped, but to Alis's disappointment she didn't scream. Alis opened her arms and held her palms out, letting Nixie observe her shaved head and tattooed arms. When Nixie had taken her in, Alis drew a pencil stub from behind her ear.

It's been a while, she wrote.

'Not on the book,' Nixie said, wincing, which was as characteristic an opening statement as Alis could have asked for. It was a joke, how typically botanical she was: fluttering and delicate, full of emotion instead of violence. Alis pressed the pencil into the edge of the victimised textbook. It was ancient, gilt-edged and goddamned exquisite.

Four years, to be excruciatingly accurate, she added. Her hand was already cramping. Nixie waited awkwardly until she finished, pretending not to flinch with every stroke.

'I know,' she said. 'I wanted to see you.'

I tried to find you once, Alis wrote. *You never tried to find me.*

'It was too dangerous.'

I bet you see Taro though.

Nixie turned red, and Alis felt a bolt of triumph. She was right. But it hurt knowing the bone disciple was worth the risk, and not Alis.

'I know we drifted apart in the Pit,' Nixie said. 'I wish that hadn't happened.'

Alis pressed the tip of her pencil into the paper so hard she made a hole in it. Biting responses jostled for attention in her head, but she couldn't get a single one out.

You say it like it was a mutual decision, she wrote finally, loathing the inability of the paper to convey her anger.

Nixie ignored her, which made Alis want to scream with frustration, and gestured at the book.

'I heard about your tongue,' she said softly. 'It is true?'

Alis burned with rage. *True?* Nixie didn't know half the truth. She had been there at the beginning of Alis's downfall, and had been oblivious. The event that had exiled Alis from Greenspire had started with their friendship in the Pit, even if the consequences had come much later.

She swallowed and waved the pencil: *what do you think?* Nixie glanced away awkwardly, and Alis, against her will, found that her capacity for sympathy wasn't totally depleted. Nixie had always been excruciatingly awkward. It made it hard for Alis to stay angry with her.

It's not unpleasant to see you, Alis wrote, loathing herself.

'You too,' Nixie said. Formal as hell; so that was how they were doing it. 'Do you know what happened last night?'

Even a corpse would know what happened.

'You could just nod.'

Alis yanked a wad of pre-written notes out of her pocket and flicked to the one she showed students in the restricted section of the library.

Why are you here?

Nixie chewed her lip, and a humiliating hope swelled in Alis's throat. That perhaps Nixie missed her. Or even that she wanted to apologise, a fantasy so embarrassing that thinking about it made Alis want to fling herself off a balcony.

'We need your help.'

And there it was. Nixie had come crawling back because she wanted something. Alis dug her nails into the pencil, trying to breathe through her choking disappointment. She could only manage one word.

We?

'Me and Taro. Please don't roll your eyes,' Nixie added, suddenly acidic. 'She hasn't done anything to you.'

Alis's pencil flew.

Before you left the Pit you told me what she did to you. Is she aware that you know?

Nixie stiffened.

Didn't think so, Alis scribbled.

'You were always an ass,' Nixie said, talking over Alis, who was still writing. 'Some things never change.'

Alis thrust the note under her nose.

You should be furious with her.

Nixie looked away, and Alis knew that she had hit a nerve. But even though she had rehearsed this moment for years, it didn't taste as sweet as she'd imagined.

So what do you want? Alis conceded. *A book to help Kellan win the Slaughter?*

'No.' Nixie seemed bewildered by Alis's question. 'Aren't you worried? If Geraldin doesn't win – which she won't, because Morgan exists – they'll kill you too.'

I'm not a familiar.

'Not now. But an arcanist will want you when all the other familiars are slaughtered. You're better than an unfinished kid from the Academy. Morgan wouldn't like them using a loophole like that.'

Alis shrugged stiffly. Most people had forgotten about her, and the ones who remembered probably thought she was dead. The new thaumaturge wouldn't trouble themselves with her.

Probably.

She tapped the pre-written note again.

Why are you here?

Nixie took a deep breath. She had always been serious, but now she was unfathomably grave.

'I need you to listen to me for a minute. Will you do that?'

Alis rolled her eyes, but she already knew she would do anything Nixie asked. She ached to be important to the plant witch again.

You're pathetic, she told herself.

'I'll take that as a "yes",' Nixie said. She glanced down the stacks and lowered her voice to barely more than a breath. 'We want to overturn the Slaughter.'

Alis waited, but Nixie's mouth was unflinchingly serious.

'I know you can't use your own power any more, because of …' Nixie gestured awkwardly at Alis's mouth. 'But you can wrest, and that might be enough. We need an arcanist from each discipline, and you're the only stone disciple I trust.'

Alis moved her pencil slowly.

You're joking.

'No. We're meeting in the tunnels under the castle tonight. There's an entrance by Greenspire, inside a niche. I'll explain. I promise.'

You want me to follow you into the catacombs?

Nixie nodded. Alis snorted.

'If you don't think the new thaumaturge will kill you, do it for revenge instead. Geraldin took your tongue and Cassia stole your place. They expelled you even though you were the most phenomenal stone disciple Greyspire had ever seen. The only reason you're not dead is because the Librarian snatched you out of the nuns' mouths. I know you want to see them burn.'

I should thank them, Alis scrawled, so violently she was pretty sure Nixie couldn't even read her handwriting. *I escaped being a familiar.*

'I wouldn't ask if I wasn't desperate.'

So I'm a last resort?

What she meant was: *I don't want you to die. I hate how you broke me and I hate that I miss you.*

The universe interceded. The shelves rustled. A book smacked into the floor by Nixie's feet. Alis felt a stab of glee, and she clung to it so she wouldn't have to think about Nixie begging her, or the way it made her willpower crumble.

'Are we alone?' Nixie whispered urgently.

Another book eased itself from the shelf and hit the floor with a resounding *smack*.

'Alis, are we being watched?'

The library has a mind of its own, Alis scribbled, her hand throbbing with overuse. *Better get out.*

Nixie lunged at her.

Alis choked back a scream as Nixie embraced her. She hadn't been touched kindly in years. She was choking, overwhelmed by Nixie's physical warmth and familiar sap-stained smell. She gasped for air.

'For the love of light,' Nixie said, releasing her. 'It was just a hug.'

Alis fumbled for her pencil, but Nixie had fled. The lump in her throat choked her. She simultaneously wanted to howl for Nixie to come back and throw her through the rotting floorboards.

The books twitched again. Alis saw a flash of fingernails at the back of the shelf and heard the light *scritch*, *scratch* of disconnected fingertips pattering over wood. She gratefully kicked the defaced book under the shelves, shoved her hands in her pockets, and stalked to her lookout point.

The wonky, long-abandoned balcony was only accessible by a worm-eaten ladder. Alis clambered up and swept her fingers along the top of a dust-smothered shelf until she found her third cigarette and a book of matches she had hidden months ago. She lit the cigarette and inhaled deeply, trying to ignore her skipping heartbeat. She wasn't going to help Nixie with … whatever this was. Nixie had never acknowledged her abandonment or apologised to Alis. She couldn't just come back and pretend that Alis owed her anything.

Oh, she absolutely could, a nasty voice said. *And you would bend over backwards to please her.*

Something moved behind her, as light and cunning as a rat.

Alis knew Mr Fingers had been eavesdropping on them. He was nosy and fast and he liked the smell of trouble. She heard a gleeful pattering as he scuttled over the books and came to rest on an encyclopaedia.

Mr Fingers was either one entity or five, depending on your outlook. He was five fingers without a palm, a collection of digits ranging from thumb to pinkie. They either dragged themselves along like caterpillars or, if speed was essential, jumped like fleas. They usually travelled as a pack with the thumb leading the way, and holding a pencil was a group activity, but Fingers was more than capable of having several misadventures at once. Each digit consequently had its own scars. The ring finger was singed, the thumb was missing half a nail, and the knuckle of the middle finger had a dent.

It was funny, Alis thought, that he was unanimously agreed to be *Mr* Fingers. She suspected it was due to his general aura of maliciousness, which people naively assumed was male. Those people had never met Geraldin or the Librarian.

She tapped the spine of the encyclopaedia, which Mr Fingers recognised as 'hello'. He slyly wriggled his middle finger in response. Alis already had a pre-written note just for him.

Don't be a dick.

Fingers rolled his thumb over the note to read it, then all his digits fell and jerked in a way that Alis had come to understand as breathless laughter. She flicked the spine of the encyclopaedia as hard as she could.

The haunted set of fingers had been around for as long as Alis had been in the library. On her third day there she had slumped between the stacks, hiding from the odious Librarian, when a pinkie tapped her on the shoulder. She almost flattened it with an almanac before the other fingers jumped out, stole the pencil behind her ear, and started writing.

Mr Fingers still wouldn't tell her where he had come from, but she guessed he was an arcanical experiment gone wrong, something that had escaped its cage. Nobody was going to own up to creating something as weird as Fingers. So he lived gleefully in the library by himself, and for some reason he had chosen Alis as his friend.

Question, she wrote. Fingers felt her scrawled handwriting and picked up the pencil.

It is about Nixeen from Greenspire, he replied. He did this by pinching the shaft between three fingers while the other two kicked the point around.

Does she really think she can stop the Slaughter?

Fingers hesitated, and for a moment Alis sensed he was going to run away. He twirled the pencil before changing his mind.

Nixeen can be trusted.

Alis shook her head.

That's not what I asked.

It is what you want to know, Alix.

Alis's stomach churned. She felt too exposed, as though someone had taken her bedroom door off its hinges.

It's Alis, she wrote.

Alas, he scribbled. I forget myself.

She screwed the parchment up and shoved it deep inside her pocket. Fingers tapped the end of the pencil against the shelf to get her attention, then scrawled on the wood.

Shall we play a game?

Alis shook her head quickly, but Mr Fingers had already produced the die from between his knuckles.

She knew it well. It was brown and shiny and rounded at the corners from years of being rolled across the floor. It was hard to believe that something so tiny could be such a massive pain in the backside.

Fingers flicked the die. It bounced against her left shoe and spun away. Alis tried to grab it, but Fingers got there first.

It was a six.

The rules of his game were simple and calamitous. Each number had a different outcome. One, and Fingers would vanish for three days. Two, and he would steal her left sock. Three to five were variations on hide-and-seek, and if Alis didn't play, Fingers jumped out at her at night, landing on her head like a rat. Six meant—

Fingers vanished the die under his thumb and scuttled across the floor, avoiding Alis's desperate grasp. He jumped on to a pile of books stacked on the balcony railing and turned to face her.

He wriggled his fingers slyly in farewell.

Then he kicked the books from the railing. They smacked on to the ground, spurting dust. Alis craned over the edge of the balcony, but Fingers was gone.

'Alis!' the Librarian screamed.

She glided into view, clutching a dripping quill. She found the splayed books and hissed, clutching her heart. Alis almost laughed explosively.

The Librarian dropped to her knees and stroked the books.

'She'll be gone soon,' the Librarian murmured, loud enough for Alis to hear. 'I won't protect her. When the nuns knock on the door I'll cut her into little pieces and slide her through the letter box. Then we'll really see what she's made of, won't we?'

They won't kill me. Someone has to look after the books when the old bag is gone.

Why was Alis thinking about Nixie's plea, then?

Alis instinctively touched the scrap of paper in her pocket. *Nixeen can be trusted.* The idea of going under the castle's skin, where the dead were piled up and the rooms were collapsing under the ever-increasing weight of the towers, was insane. But technically speaking, it wouldn't be dangerous to find out what Nixie was doing. Alis didn't have to agree to anything. Besides, Fingers thought it was safe. While he could be selective with the truth, he never lied.

It wasn't because Alis was worried about being culled by the new thaumaturge. And it certainly had nothing to do with the aching feeling behind her ribs, as though after Nixie had hugged her she'd left with a portion of Alis's heart. It wasn't because Alis missed her, or because she was infatuated, or because she couldn't say no to the girl who used to be her best friend.

Absolutely not that.

Alis pressed the sharp point of her pencil between her thumb and forefinger. By the time it snapped she had made her decision.

Fuck it. She was going underground.

Five

Forty-eight hours until the Slaughter

Taro sifted yellow knucklebones through her fingers, stifling a yawn while Jon tried – for the *fifth time* – to animate a hench-ass skeleton with axes for arms. It wasn't going well. The knives sticking out of the skeleton's eye sockets were throwing it off balance. It fell and stabbed the table every time Jon brought it to life. Daggers McDaggerface was more likely to lop Jon's balls off than help him win the Slaughter.

Jon screwed his finger into Taro's chest.

'You need to get this right,' he said, as though she was in any way responsible for his incompetence. 'When the clock on your back runs down, everyone's going to watch us and our … *colleagues* …' He couldn't even bring himself to say the other head arcanists' names '… race into the Fifth Tower for the Slaughter. If we don't get to the top first, or defeat whatever's inside, someone else will become the Thaumaturge. And *you*, Taro, will be executed, along with every other familiar who's from the wrong discipline.'

Taro looked at him blankly. He turned back to his work with a scowl.

'Well, it's not my fault this is going badly,' he muttered.

'There must be a mirror somewhere in the castle. It's warping everything.'

Taro tried to keep her face straight. Nixie's mirror was too far away to affect Jon, who was just being extra shit at his job. His obsession with creating a skeletal soldier was also keeping her from the grisly treasure hunt the Ghost had sent them on. Taro didn't trust the Ghost, but she grudgingly admitted that the slimmest chance of escaping the Slaughter was worth taking. Nobody knew what was in the Fifth Tower, or what the Slaughter exactly entailed, but it would probably involve her and her beloved having to bludgeon each other to death.

Her stomach heaved. *Forty-eight hours to find a blood arcanist who isn't that shitbag Elliot.* Time was getting shorter with each breath.

'Femur.'

Hurry up and go for your morning nap, you total waste of bones. I have treason to commit.

But Jon refused to rest. His face was three shades paler than usual, the whites of his eyes yellow, his lips worm-thin. He had fumbled his way through their quarter of the Suppression without a second of pre-show monologue, which was how Taro knew he was absolutely shitting himself. He had shut the windows for fear of assassination, which meant the walls were feverishly damp from both their breaths condensing on the stone.

Yum.

'Ribs,' Jon said.

Why hadn't she been bought by an arcanist-doctor? Or a bone manipulator who did cute things like getting skeletons to do the gardening? Why was she in Blackspire, a place so hardcore that one of its previous head arcanists had his bones made into a chandelier upon his death? Why was she stuck with this donkey whose one strength was his ability to wield arcania like a hammer and hit things *really hard* with it?

'Ribs,' Jon repeated. 'From the cupboard, now.'

Screw it.

Taro pressed a knucklebone between her thumb and forefinger, feeling the deep hum of power that only the arcanically gifted knew, and wrested until it bloomed over her skin. The pain was immediate and exquisite.

She breathed it in – inhaling bone arcania felt like sucking a mouthful of ants – and readied her tongue. As Jon swore at the tortured skeleton, Taro used the racket to cover her invented incantation, an arcanical mash-up of spells that she had stolen from one of Jon's grimoires. Incantations weren't taught in the Pit, least of all ones that made bones vanish, but Taro had the uncanny knack of making spells work by instinct.

The knucklebone between her fingers crumbled and the bones in the cupboard poured away like milk.

'Ribs!' Jon screeched, and when she didn't answer he finally looked up.

When Taro had his full attention she gestured grandly to the open cupboard behind her, which was now as boneless as a sock. Jon's eyelids twitched. He was so far gone he didn't even register her Level Ten Sarcasm.

'Get more,' he said.

Taro bowed: *My master, my ruler.*

Arsehole.

The graveyard was a rare open space inside the castle gates, a patch of marshy ground penned in by four high walls. The bodies in the graveyard were grossly ancient, having been buried before the undertakers ran out of room and started shoving the castle's dead in abandoned rooms instead. Taro heaved the swollen castle door open and stepped out into Fourspires' cemetery.

Each discipline had been sequestered to different corners of the graveyard, where they huddled together like conspiracists. Just visible beneath the yellow lichen were the symbols of each dead person's discipline: the skull, the sapling, the blood or the stone, just in case anyone wasn't sure which club they had belonged to.

Except they weren't just symbols. They were pictures of four powerful arcanical objects that had been lost. *Curse keys.* Apparently.

Taro mooched around the graveyard, taking a minute to pay her respects to the unfortunate souls who were rotting in the ground. She'd left Jon's rooms because she needed to look for a blood disciple, and nobody would question her clattering around the castle if she was holding bits of skeleton. So she dug around until she found a few femurs and a jawbone.

'Cheers,' she said to the dead people, and let herself enjoy a moment of the graveyard's deathly silence before she went back to plundering.

As she plucked another bone shard from the grass, a cold hand gently entwined its fingers with hers.

Taro's scream – of course she screamed, anyone would – was drowned out by the sound of headstones toppling. Taro wrenched her hand away, sending chunks of the dead one splattering all over the graveyard. She stumbled backwards and immediately tripped over a spine that was undulating like a snake. She slammed into the ground and felt the ragged edges of the gory clock carved into her back split and bleed.

What! In! The! Fiery! Mouth! Of! Hell! Is! This?

She looked around in horror as the ground heaved like a vomiting body. Small hillocks bulged and popped open, revealing jellied limbs. Taro rolled to her feet, grabbed the writhing spine, and used it to smack an errant arm out of the way.

She *knew* Jon had screwed the Suppression up, the pasty-faced *knob.* He had been rushing to finish so he could concentrate on preparing for the Slaughter, and had consequently skipped at least two lines. All four head arcanists had to do their part perfectly every morning. It was literally their only job: to stop plants rising from the ground and strangling them, the castle from bleeding and drowning them, the walls from collapsing on their heads, and *this* – a catastrophic osseous uprising.

This was apocalyptically bad, *literally* apocalyptic. Because if the dead had broken the surface this far up, there would be hundreds more wriggling in the subcutaneous layer beneath the castle. Taro had never gone far beneath the habitable surface, but she knew what was down there. Not just abandoned ballrooms and crushed kitchens: gravemounds, tangled balls of bone, and all the desiccated corpses that hadn't been chucked into the Desecrae.

Taro stamped on a set of ribs that were walking towards her like a spider. No matter how many times you pulled the ravenous dead apart, they got up and kept going. A skull chattered towards her, mashing its teeth so violently it propelled itself faster than most people could run. Taro smashed its cranium with the spine, shattering it into a dozen quivering pieces. The lower jaw of the skull hit the far wall, releasing teeth like necrotic spores.

As much as Taro would have loved to whip out some serious moves, take down a few skeletons, and shatter some kneecaps, she was outnumbered. On a good day – definitely! Pretty much any other day! Honestly! – she would have kicked the arse of every dead body here. Instead she bolted for the door to the castle.

She crammed herself through the door just as an entire skeleton, complete with gristly nose cartilage, tried to bite the back of her neck. She couldn't slam the door because the skeleton was in the way, snapping its teeth an inch away from her. So she did the first thing that came into her head, which was to turn around and punch it.

Taro gurgled as fire bloomed through her knuckles. The skeleton, wedged between the door and the doorframe, grabbed her throbbing fingers. She couldn't utter a spell because wresting and incanting at the same time required a modicum of calm. Doing it wrong could precipitate something explosively gross like sucking all the moisture from her body.

She yanked against the skeleton, which had almost succeeded in mashing her fingers through the half-closed door. Maybe Taro should have written a will. Not that she had anything to give away. A letter, maybe. *Nixie, babe, I have to tell you something. Four years ago I did something Really Bad—*

Footsteps!

Taro twisted her neck and almost perished from humiliation. Elliot was walking towards her, carrying vials of blood in a long rack. When he saw the skeleton mashing its lips through the castle door he stopped and regarded her darkly, as though he had caught her kicking a puppy. Although knowing Elliot, that was something he might enjoy.

'Oi!' she yelled. 'Give me a hand.'

Fourspires had a sick sense of humour. It had sent her the one person who probably liked watching human bodies being dismembered. Blood disciples were famously into gore, and Elliot had always struck her as the kind of person who secretly killed butterflies for fun. This was the one time she wanted an Unholy Mother to swoop down and give in to bloodlust, but the crusty nuns were nowhere to be seen.

'Is that your way of asking for help?' he drawled. It was impressive how, despite being objectively hot – whole armies would die for his cheekbones – Elliot managed to make himself so odious at the same time.

'So *sorry* to be *disturbing* you,' Taro panted, still pulling back with all her weight to stop the reanimated skeleton crashing through the door. 'It's just that the dead are trying to drag me into the ground and I'm a bit outnumbered, yeah?'

Her shoulder was burning. She was pretty sure the skeleton had torn a few ligaments. Its fingers scrabbled at her wrist, looking for a weak spot where it could punch through to her veins.

Elliot gazed at her for a few moments.

Shitting Unholy Mothers, he wants me to beg.

'Elliot,' Taro said, the words burning on her tongue, 'please help me.'

Something changed behind Elliot's eyes, just for a second: a flicker of pain, or longing. Taro hadn't expected to see anything like a soul in the malignant bloodsucker, and it almost touched her. Then she remembered how much Nixie loved his hair, and she went right back to hating him.

'Fine,' Elliot said softly, and before Taro could protest he grabbed the wrist of the skeleton in both hands and snapped it in half.

Taro fell backwards with the rotting fingers still wrapped around her own. Elliot slammed and bolted the door, flinging several more of the undead backwards.

Taro decided to thank him.

'You look like shit,' she said.

Shit for someone gorgeous, anyway. He had truly incredible shadows under his eyes, the colour of plums, as though he hadn't slept in months.

Elliot inspected the graveyard through a knothole in the door.

'What happened?' Elliot asked, somehow managing to sound incredibly bored.

'None of your business, you vampiric leech.'

'Really? Because I think I just saved you.'

'I could have dealt with it on my own.'

Elliot deigned to look at her.

'Fine,' Taro said. 'My arcanist's an idiot and he didn't do the Suppression properly.'

If Elliot was impressed that Taro, a mere year ahead of him at school, was the high familiar of Jon of Blackspire, head bone arcanist of Fourspires Castle and sole protector against the undead, he didn't comment.

'Why were you creeping around the castle last night?' he said.

'Why were *you* creeping around last night?'

'I asked first, and you owe me. Twice over, because you almost broke my jaw.'

He folded his arms and lounged against the wall, long and lean, with eyes that were striking in a deeply unfair way. Taro reviewed her options. She'd already been gone too long. She had approximately three minutes before Jon's axe-armed skeleton got up of its own accord and Jon started screaming for her.

'Listen, vampire,' she said, 'last night I offered you the chance of a lifetime, and that offer still stands.'

'You mean that ridiculous story about ghosts?'

'One ghost. Do you want me to hit you again?'

Elliot raised an eyebrow.

Oh hell.

'I'm sorry for punching you in the face,' Taro said through gritted teeth. 'And I'm *ever* so grateful that you swooped in and saved me. You're my hero. Now accept my offer.'

Elliot smiled like Taro had debased herself. Which she basically had.

'Tarenteeno,' he said, 'you really need me, don't you?'

And that's when Taro realised, with bewilderment and not a small amount of horror, that Elliot was an absolute sycophant who would do anything for affection.

'Bye, Elliot,' she said.

His expression flickered with disappointment before he went back to his shit-eating smile. He picked up the rack of vials and waltzed off to wherever he had been going without a backward glance. *Where is that, anyway?* He didn't live in the castle, unless he had somehow landed himself a new position, the ladder-climbing slimeball.

'Nobody liked you in school!' Taro hissed at his back. She had done so much talking today it was a miracle none of the nuns had heard. 'I hope Morgan's leopard eats your special appendage, and I hope it's *grim*!'

She stalked in the opposite direction with her cloak swirling around her ankles in a way she hoped was suitably impressive. If the dead weren't clamouring for flesh right now she would—

Elliot yanked her into the shadows. Before she even had time to wonder how he had moved so fast, Taro slapped him.

'It's incredible you've stayed alive this long,' he snarled. Taro glared at him. 'What if someone heard us talking?'

'How did you do that? Creep,' she added.

'You're not the only one with a roster of spells. You have thirty seconds to persuade me to do … whatever you're asking for.'

'You're desperate for me to beg, aren't you?'

'I'll leave, then.'

'Wait!' Taro grabbed his collar. 'Listen. Do you want to spend the rest of your life with the Redborns?'

'They're the least of my worries. Ten seconds.'

'Don't you want to stop being a familiar? Get out of that grim mansion they keep you in? If you help me I can make it happen.'

'What would I do with freedom?'

'Whatever stupid stuff you want.'

'Sounds illegal.'

'So's talking to me.'

Elliot fingered his curls out of his eyes and shrugged. For the love of osseous matter, it was *so tempting* to break another tooth.

'I want to get into Morgan's tower,' he said. 'He has something that belongs to me. That's the price for my help.'

'What the hell does he have that you want?'

'It's not important.'

'How about we make a deal,' she said. 'I'll help you get into his tower, and you come to the catacombs tonight to help me and Nixie.'

The door to the graveyard groaned. It was buckling under the weight of animated bodies. Taro only had a couple of minutes before Jon would have to recast the Suppression, or everyone in Fourspires would be ripped apart by an apocalyptic army.

Elliot waited until she really started to sweat, almost as if he enjoyed it.

'OK,' he said. 'It's a deal.' He folded his arms and leaned back against the wall, cocky and pleased with himself. 'But admit that you need me.'

'Excuse me?'

'Say you need me.'

Taro was dangerously close to giving Elliot what he wanted, and he knew it. On the one hand, she would gain a powerful blood disciple who could both wrest and incant. On the other, she would be satisfying his desire to bathe in the glow of his self-importance.

The smirk on his lips made the decision for her.

'No,' Taro said.

She strode away, leaving him alone in the corridor. When she was sure Elliot was no longer within earshot she picked up her robes and ran.

Jon was pacing at the base of the tower with an axe in his hand. Above him, at the top of the stairs, something incredibly heavy and very determined – something like a skeleton-monster with twenty-six fingers and a handful of knives sticking out of its eyes – was throwing itself against the other side of the chamber door.

'Where have you been?' Jon snarled.

Taro grabbed the disembodied hand from her pocket and plunked it at his feet. He yelped and kicked it away.

'What is that?'

Taro pointed at the writhing hand, then slowly, deliberately, at his mouth.

Jon turned as white as a cracker.

Yep. You screwed it up, Jonno. If the Slaughter wasn't two days away the nuns would have you swinging from the ramparts by your definitely below average-sized ding-dong. The last time the Suppression totally failed was fifty-three years ago, when the head blood and bone arcanists got into a fight and murdered each other. Five hundred people died. Half of them drowned in the blood pouring from the castle walls, and the rest were dismantled by skeletons. The nuns were eating corpses for days. You have literally birthed one quarter of the apocalypse.

'Start wresting!' he yelled.

Taro didn't have time to brace herself before he thrust the writhing hand into her arms.

The arcania had barely bloomed over her before Jon tore the power away, winding it around his tongue as though he was slurping the skin from her arms. Every time he inhaled he wrenched away more of Taro's arcania. He screamed the incantation in Taro's face between breaths, furiously, as though she was responsible for him messing up. Taro had never felt so small or powerless.

You absolute fucker, Taro thought before slumping to the floor.

The incantation rattled over her. The pain of wresting spread up her arm and bloomed through her chest. Someone was sewing red threads of agony through her body and pulling them out through her eyes. It wasn't just power leaching out of her any more, but something that felt like her actual life. She choked and thought of Nixie, just like she always did when her mind was grasping for an anchor. If she died now, Nixie had no chance of survival. If she died now, she would never be able to atone for what she had done to Nixie four years ago, which the botanic disciple still knew nothing about, and which lurked in Taro's chest like a toxic fungus.

Taro closed her eyes and let the pain take her. She couldn't hear the rest of the incantation over the blood rushing through her ears. The seconds stretched out.

After an endless five minutes, Jon spat the last of his incantation, and the skeleton behind the chamber door fell silent. Taro's fingers went slack around the hand, which twitched like a fly suffocating on a windowsill before crumbling. Her nails were bleeding.

'Stand up and work,' Jon said, stepping over her body.

Taro grasped the rough wall and pulled herself up, her fingertips leaving red marks on the stone. She still didn't feel anything. Certainly not the cold, hard fury she knew was coming. She was an empty sack. She was nothing.

Funny, then, that some part of her brain still knew what she had to do. It made her follow Jon to the chamber and step over the twice-dead pile of bones. She went to the cupboard and pretended to rummage for something. She grasped a curl of paper and wrote with her bloodied index finger, drowning in self-loathing.

Elliot. It's a deal.

We need you.

Six

Thirty-three hours until the Slaughter

The subcutaneous layer beneath Greenspire, Nixie thought, was as damp as its fleshy name. The weight of the slumping castle had pushed the rooms so far underground they had turned into catacombs. Ancient windows were blocked with wet sludge. Rubbery fungus oozed from the dank walls, which bowed from the pressure of being endlessly crushed.

Down here, the Ghost had said, was where they would find the forgotten chapel: deep beneath Greenspire, where the worms fed.

Nixie carefully inspected the stonework above her and Taro's heads. Dried vines snaked across the ceiling from the last time the botanic Suppression had failed. Sixty years ago, the story went, ivy had burst from the heart of the mountain, ripping the surface apart, reaching through people's noses and eye sockets and pushing their ribs apart from the inside. People sneered at Nixie's discipline, supposing that they couldn't be killed by flowers.

People were stupid.

'I'm not sure about this, Nix.'

Nixie turned and slipped her hands around Taro's waist, drawing her close, rib-to-rib. She knotted her fingers together at the small of Taro's back, which made the bone witch melt into her. The move was coldly calculated, and Nixie had to swallow her disgust to do it. But a sliver of her found comfort in holding Taro, too. The silver thread that was caught around her heart stretched back in time, where it was tied to their relationship in the Pit, before Taro had betrayed her. To a time when Taro was a breathtaking splatter of stars that lit Nixie up in the dark.

'I know you're brave enough, Tarenteeno of Blackspire,' Nixie said. She raised Taro's hand to her mouth and kissed it. A thin tendril of old love uncurled from the dirt, tiny and weak. It wasn't enough to change anything. 'We'll be fine.'

'We're not fine,' Taro whispered. 'We won't be fine until we get out of here and it's just you and me.'

Nixie dropped her hand and moved on.

They reached the bottom of the sloping hallway, where the Ghost said the chapel would be. Nixie prayed that Alis would find it without drawing the Unholy Mothers' attention, and fervently wished she had given better instructions. Necrotic fungi cast the door in a greenish light. Nixie reached into her pocket and withdrew the thick shard of glass the Ghost had made her break from the mirror. It had taken every ounce of nerve for Nixie to crack the glass, even with the Ghost's wry observation that nothing worse than *her* could come out of it. Nixie wasn't so sure. There was a reason most mirrors had been destroyed. It wasn't just because they warped arcania; they also gave birth to malefici, malformed creatures of flesh and endless hunger that hid in Fourspires' dark corners, or in the Ulcer outside the castle, or even in the thick soup of teeth at the bottom of the Desecrae.

She unwrapped the cloth she had bound tightly over the mirror's surface.

'We're here,' she said to the glass, but the Ghost remained conspicuously absent. They had been given their task, and the Ghost was now refusing to speak until it was complete. It was neat, which Nixie appreciated. It also felt like a kick in the teeth.

Taro whipped a bag of sweets from her pocket and started crunching loudly as they waited for Alis and the mysterious blood arcanist that Taro had apparently recruited. She still hadn't told Nixie who that was.

'Taro, why are your fingers bleeding?'

'Don't ask.' *Crunch.*

'Did Jon do it?'

'You sound like the-mum-I-never-had-slash-can't-remember.' Taro swallowed and poked an ear-shaped piece of fungus on the wall. It wheezed asthmatically. 'You've never told me what you and the Ghost chat about when I'm not there.'

'Nothing important.' *Liar.*

'I don't trust her. She's too dead.'

'Just help me look for this skull. If it's as powerful as the Ghost says, we'll be able to use it for something. Even if we don't find the other curse keys.'

Taro crunched another sweet, slowly and deliberately, before speaking.

'The curse keys being mysterious objects that – stop me if I'm wrong – we could wrest so much power from they'll undo the curse this randomly evil guy called Hallow Myre put on Fourspires. Which will bring down the Desecrae – the *literal sky* – and halt the apocalypse that we're always trying to suppress?'

'It sounds ridiculous when you say it like that.'

'And someone from each discipline – assuming the other two turn up, by the way – has to take their curse key into the Fifth Tower as soon as the Slaughter starts, while hoping our arcanists don't get in the way. Then the Ghost … who you may or may not be in love with … I'm *joking* … will use a special incantation to break the curse while we're all wresting for her.'

'You're being sarcastic.'

'I want you to hear how stupid it sounds. Like, how do we even get into the Fifth Tower?'

'The Slaughter. It's the only time the door opens. We'll fight our arcanists.'

'Cool. Yeah. Easy.' Taro went silent.

'I know you're waiting to say something else.'

'Don't you think it's dodgy that the Ghost won't just give us the incantation?' Taro burst out.

'You can't even remember what you ate for dinner yesterday,' Nixie said. *Neither can I*, she thought bitterly. That goddamned memory potion. 'You're not going to remember a spell that big.'

'Maybe,' Taro said. She elbowed Nixie gently, becoming more serious. 'I know you wouldn't do anything you weren't totally sure about. I do trust you.'

'You trust me,' Nixie said blandly. She couldn't quite hide her scorn. 'Just like I can trust you?'

'Exactly.'

Sometimes Nixie wanted to push Taro against a wall and kiss her like the world was ending. More often, that desire was drowned by the urge to throw her down a hole. She bit her tongue and turned to the chapel door. She couldn't afford messy feelings when survival was at stake.

'They're late,' Nixie said.

'I told you Alis wouldn't turn up. She stares at me like she wants to dig my brains out with a spatula. Also, she literally can't talk, which makes her useless.'

Nixie wondered how it felt, knowing you could produce enough power to destroy worlds, but not being able to use your tongue to bend it to your will. Alis could charge the air with arcania until the smallest utterance fractured the castle and still be helpless.

'Don't,' Nixie said softly. 'It's cruel.' The memory of Alis's expression in the library, that frosty hatred when Nixie asked about her tongue, made thorns crawl up her throat. Sometimes Nixie wondered if she was the cruel one. She changed the subject. 'Why won't you tell me who the blood disciple is?'

'It's a surprise.'

Nixie inspected the door. It was fused shut by a sheet of gluey mycological life and she could see ridges of bone running beneath the wood. It had been sealed by an unholy combination of bone and plant arcania. Whoever had closed the door wanted it to stay that way.

'There's something very … bony behind there,' Taro said, sniffing the air. 'Possibly an active spell. You said this skull was lost, right?'

'You heard the Ghost.'

'You'd have to be especially dim to lose something like that.' But she didn't take the thought any further.

Footsteps squelched behind them. Nixie slid her letter-opener knife from her robes and held it at heart level. She had no formal training, but she had spent hours parrying the air in her bedroom. Her perpetual anxiety meant she was already ready for the worst.

'Who is it?' she said sharply.

A low, sardonic huff of air said: *This had better be good.*

Nixie lowered the knife as Alis mooched out of the shadows. She was hidden inside a moth-eaten grey cloak, a relic from the Greyspire tower, the embroidered stone cube still visible on her chest. Nixie slid the knife back into her robes. She hadn't known if Alis would come. Wasn't sure, deep down, if she even deserved Alis's help.

Stop it. Alis probably doesn't even think about you.

Alis produced a burning cigarette from between her fingers and held it to a cluster of squelching fungi. She watched with mild curiosity as they screamed and shrivelled away.

'You're smaller than I remember,' Taro said.

Alis flicked cigarette ash in Taro's direction. Then she produced a scrap of paper from her pocket and handed it to Nixie.

I get to fight Geraldin in the Slaughter, then?

It was strange for Nixie to feel the brunt of Alis's flat, sarcastic bent, which she used to reserve for strangers. Nixie shrugged, keeping her face untouched by the unease roiling in her stomach.

'If that's what it takes to reach the top of the tower,' she said. 'How long have you been here?'

Alis began writing again. Nixie found herself holding her breath in frustration as the words travelled across the page. *It's not her fault that writing's slower than talking*, Nixie reminded herself, biting her tongue.

Long enough to hear about the Ghost and the curse. You're both deluded.

'You came, though.'

Morbid curiosity. Alis's fingers drummed against the paper scrap, smudging the words. *And maybe I've read some things in old books. But I'll reserve judgement until we're through that door*.

Nixie nodded curtly and touched the chapel door. A faint buzz told her that fungal spores ran all the way through it. She could feel the mycological life pulsing in time with her own heartbeat.

'We'll break it down,' she said. 'Taro?'

'Ready, babe.'

Nixie closed her fingers around the white roots she had packed into her robe. Her arm spasmed in white-hot pain as she wrested, but when she drew the power into her mouth, it was simultaneously sticky and sweet. She exploded the spores of mould in the wood. The door shattered. Shards of wood cut Nixie's face and flecked her closed eyelids with blood.

'Interesting,' a male voice said.

Nixie had her knife out so fast Taro didn't have time to finish swearing.

'—cker,' Taro said. Nixie held the knife at the intruder's throat, her flesh still burning. His face was invisible under his hood, but something about his languid air made her skin prickle in a way that had nothing to do with fear.

Taro gently pushed her arm down.

'I would love to see you rearrange fuckboy's face, but then we'd need a replacement.'

Nixie lowered the knife, and the intruder relaxed.

'Good evening, Nixie,' Elliot said.

Nixie felt her cheeks turn traitorously red.

You aren't attracted to him. His personality is a zero out of ten. It's just his hair.

She'd always had a thing for it. It was dark and curly, and in the Pit she hadn't been able to stop watching it swish over his eyes while he carved tiny figurines, his graceful neck bent, his green eyes intent on the knife. She was, Alis once said, a sucker for a tortured artist.

Alis and Elliot sized each other up. Neither looked impressed by what they saw.

'I told you I'd get someone,' Taro murmured. 'You don't seem happy.'

'He works for the Redborns,' Nixie whispered, hoping indignation would cover her mortification. 'Are you insane?'

'Probably,' Taro said. 'Also, we owe him a favour now. Remind me to tell you about it later.'

'Can we get on with it?' Elliot said loudly.

They all looked at Nixie. Their expectation made her flounder, but she was damned if she would let them know. Which was why, instead of answering, she raised her knife and marched right through the shattered door, into the centuries-old chapel, as if she knew exactly what she was doing.

The chapel had the deathly proportions of an open grave. Thousands of human skulls were stacked up the walls with a squirm of luminescent mushroom in each eye socket. Nixie surveyed the onyx-black floor, the yellow-boned pews, and the tall windows with sludge pressed against them. Wormy roots were crushed against the glass. The chapel groaned under the weight of the encroaching earth. She heard Taro enter behind her and release a great, exultant sigh.

The grisly centrepiece was an archway running between the pews, formed from two rows of monstrously tall ribs. A full skeleton was strung over the front of the arch. Its flesh had dried and peeled back in grey curls that had begun to slough. Written on the floor in dried blood, with the last letter trailing up one of the ribs, to the skeleton's index finger, were the words: *He who steps first shall suffer.*

'Sexist,' Taro muttered.

Nixie had already shifted her attention to the altar at the front of the chapel. More specifically, the skull.

Even though Nixie couldn't sense bone arcania, she knew the skull was significant. The velvet cushion it rested on was as scarlet as a splotch of blood. The skull had a zigzag crack from its dome to its jawbone, and it stared at them with a grin.

'Interesting,' Elliot said softly. 'It looks just like the Blackspire mascot.'

It was exactly what the Ghost had promised them. The first of four curse keys.

Nixie was a hair's breadth from stepping over the bloody writing on the floor when Taro caught her elbow.

'Are you mad?' she said. 'It's swirling with grade A bone arcania. If you walk through that archway your head will explode like a pumpkin.'

She pointed at the human-shaped shadow burned into the floor. It was surrounded by a halo of teeth, and there was a green stain near its former midriff. Nixie couldn't believe she'd been so stupid. The indignity of having Elliot watch her was throwing her off.

Even Alis had stopped smoking. The cigarette hung limply from her fingers as she surveyed the carnage.

'Nice trap,' Taro said. 'I bet if you cross the line your gut flora and bones explode. Looks like your blood evaporates too. And those knobbly lumps were probably the minerals in his body. They've clumped together and torn him up. Four disciplines at once! *Disgusting.*' Then quietly, in Nixie's ear: 'Looks like the Ghost missed some important info. You freaking out?'

'No.'

It was true, if only because Nixie usually packed freak-outs away before she could feel anything. Alis shoved a note into her hand.

What now?

Nixie calculated the distance to the altar. The idea of wresting again made her bones weep, but she was the one who had brought them all here.

'I'll handle it,' she said curtly.

By *handle* she meant that she would animate a slick of moss, turn it into a creature with tendrils, slide it up the altar, and carry the skull to safety. It was complex arcania, but she was good. Her control was so precise that she had manipulated every exam in the Pit, engineering her results so finely that she could choose which arcanist would buy her after graduation.

Kellan had never been on that list.

She once again reached for the pale roots in her pocket, bracing herself for that first snap of pain, which she would take on the inhale, like *this*—

The mushroomy light splintered and the chapel went black. Nixie groped for Taro's arm, a movement so automatic it shocked her, but the bone disciple was gone.

Necrotic light sliced down the middle of the archway. The spread-eagled skeleton bucked, spraying flecks of desiccated viscera at the floor. It writhed from its bonds and clattered to the ground, then poked the remainder of its dried guts back inside its body.

It looked at Nixie, who was too shocked to move.

When am I? it rattled. Its voice came not from its gristly tongue but from somewhere deep inside Nixie's head, as though it had simply deposited the words there. Its skull was too large for its body, its eye sockets deep and black.

It waited for an answer. She looked for the others, but she was alone in a puddle of light.

'The reign of the ninety-eighth Thaumaturge has ended,' she said hoarsely. 'He was … probably after your time.'

The skeleton drew breath through the nasal slots in his half-face. It had no lungs for the job, so the air billowed out through its mouldering robes.

You have entered Dagmar's chapel, it stated, as if it could only think if it spoke aloud. *The curse is still on Fourspires. I can smell the Desecrae.*

'The curse,' Nixie repeated. Her mouth was sticky. 'You think it's real.'

The corpse stared as though she had stated an obvious fact. A dark thrill crept up Nixie's spine. She hadn't let herself believe it until now. She thought she heard muffled spluttering behind her, as though the others were trying to shout, but the skeleton lowered its face towards her, and she couldn't break from its gaze.

You're here for the Blackspire skull, it said.

'Yes.' There seemed little point in lying.

You wish to break the curse.

'Yes.'

You should not.

Nixie surreptitiously wiped her palms on her robes. The knife was still in her pocket, but it felt paltry in the face of this … thing.

'Why shouldn't I break it?' she asked. She needed time to work out her next move, but her mind was blank with panic. Had the Ghost purposely sent them into a trap? Taro always said not to trust the dead bitch. The skeleton's dehydrated eyes rattled in its sockets, but it didn't answer her, so she fumbled for another question. 'The curse to destroy Sobweb was laid by Hallow Myre. Did he put you here?'

The skeleton cocked its head as though she had asked something inconceivably stupid. It gestured to the cushioned skull.

My instructions were given to me by Dagmar of Blackspire, head bone arcanist during the reign of Sobweb, it said.

Violence hummed between them.

'What instructions?' Nixie asked. The air between her and the corpse was as fragile as a sheet of glass.

I think you already know.

The skeleton flung itself at her, smashing her into the floor. Nixie's head cracked to the side and she saw, through red stars, the silhouettes of Taro, Alis and Elliot strung halfway up a wall. The skeleton's overlarge, undead head dangled over hers, its loose tongue flapping from its mouth. Nixie kicked and writhed, but it was too heavy to fling off. The handle of her knife jammed into her shin as the skeleton lowered its face towards hers, working its jaw in anticipation of chewing the rind of her nose.

Nixie clawed one hand along the floor, stretching her fingers to the knife. The skeleton wrenched its jaws apart to close them over her face. Nixie twisted the knife and stabbed it into the skeleton's hip bone.

Its pelvis cracked with a noise like tombstones grinding past each other. Nixie shoved the skeleton off and rolled to her feet, the knife in her fist, breathing raggedly.

She had saved herself for now, but her arcania wouldn't be any good against this thing. And none of her violent, anxiety-fuelled fantasies had prepared her for a physical fight with something already dead.

I do not stop, the skeleton agreed. It was in her head. It clicked its broken pelvis into place and rose. *I will put myself together as many times as it takes to dismember you.*

Like hell it would.

Nixie lunged with the blade. It was a good attempt, but all her practice had been against her very stationary bedpost. She missed. The skeleton caught her hair in both fists and pulled in two directions. Beads scattered. Nixie screamed furiously and stabbed again. This time she caught the collarbone and slashed downwards, cleaving its middle. The skeleton staggered back and she lunged again, stopping just short of the bloody line under the archway, ignoring the throbbing in her scalp and the ringing in her ears.

You can't do this for ever, the skeleton opined. It swiped for her shoulder, but Nixie ducked and plunged the knife into its eye socket. She twisted hard, and its skull wrenched to the side. Its words jumped into her head with a huge cleft in the middle.

Nobody   will have it.

Nixie landed more blows, insatiable with fury. She stabbed the skeleton apart until it was a torso on legs, all its power in its chomping teeth and spidery legs.

I am   bound to   protect.

More blows.

You will   not   undo   Black   spire's

good

work!

Nixie kicked it in the ribs. It fell and shattered.

I h a t e b o t a n i c a r c a n i s t s, it lamented as its teeth rattled away. Nixie kicked each squirming splinter of the skeleton into different corners of the chapel.

She bent over to catch her breath, but she knew she couldn't rest for long. Its parts were already rattling towards each other to reassemble. She felt her way to the wall of skulls and, gagging, dug her fingers into a pair of eye sockets. She wrested from the mushrooms and coaxed the wall of fungi to life until their sickly glow filled the chapel again.

Taro, Alis and Elliot were attached to the wall by skeletal hands gripping their limbs and gagging their mouths. Nixie kicked Taro's bonds apart.

'You broke some perfectly good bones,' Taro said weakly as she slid down the wall. 'So the curse is real, then?'

'Yes. Get Elliot down.'

Nixie started to release Alis. Elliot snarled as Taro broke his bonds.

'You could have mentioned this part.'

'Eat your bones like a good boy.' Taro flicked a metacarpal in Elliot's face. 'You wanted proof the Ghost was right, and you got it. Satisfied?'

Elliot glared at Taro, but Nixie could see he was rattled.

The guardian of the skull was pulling itself together at the elbows. Nixie stamped on the joints, breaking them apart again.

'Keep this thing occupied,' she said. 'I need to get the skull *now*.'

'You heard the Ghost,' Taro said. 'I'm the only one who can touch it without, like, imploding. It's too bony.'

'So pick it up.'

'Head. Pumpkin.' Taro pointed at the shadow on the floor. 'Whatever spell killed that person, it wasn't just bone arcania. It was botanic and stone and blood too.' She shuddered. 'Imagine if Jon and Kellan and Geraldin and Morgan decided to set a murder trap together.'

They would sooner rip each other apart. No discipline ever worked with another; it was as perverse as mixing wine with milk.

'The Ghost said the curse keys were lost to time,' Taro added, lowering her voice. 'This is the only one she knew the location of. But this isn't lost, Nix. Someone hid it on purpose.'

Nixie touched the shard of mirror in her pocket. The emptiness of the netherworld sucked at her, and she wondered if the Ghost had been laughing at their gullability all along. But Nixie had come too far to quit. It whittled her options to a single sharp point.

'We'll dismantle the trap together,' Nixie said. Elliot and Alis snorted dramatically at the same time, then looked at each other sharply. 'We'll coordinate unbinding spells. Then Taro can pass through the arch and take the skull.'

'Oh, goody,' Taro said.

'I acquiesce,' Elliot said. 'Only because there's no way you'll do it without me, and I don't want to be responsible for your corpses.'

'Did you bring any blood vials?' Nixie asked.

'No.'

'No problem,' Taro said, and punched him in the nose.

Elliot staggered and clutched his hand to his face, scarlet dripping from between his knuckles. He was speechless.

'Sorry,' Taro said, shaking her hand out. 'Nixie, you can use those mushrooms. Alis, this whole place is literally just a lump of stone.'

Alis looked as if she was going to deliver Taro a bloody nose of her own.

'She can't talk,' Nixie reminded her. 'Shit. That means she won't be able to incant.'

Alis kicked a bone at Nixie's ankles, then used the attention to jab a finger into her own chest.

'She's in the room and she can hear you,' Elliot interpreted through his bloody hand, which resulted in Alis kicking a bone at him too.

'That's fine,' Taro said. 'If she wrests and everyone unbinds their parts, the stone arcania should unravel too. It's all interlocking, right?'

'According to who?' Elliot laughed unpleasantly.

'He's right,' Nixie said, trying not to look at the leaf-green of his eyes, in case she fumbled again. 'You've never done this before.'

'You're just agreeing with him because you have a thing for—' she cut off at Nixie's warning glare. 'Have I ever let you down?'

The obvious retort unfurled from that deep, rotten heap of feelings behind Nixie's ribs. Four years ago Taro had smiled innocently and thrown her into the deepest circle of hell, and she still hadn't admitted it. The blackness bubbled into Nixie's throat as everything cool and calm in her turned to vitriolic flame. She wanted Taro to suffer. She almost wanted Taro *dead*. Alis looked at her weirdly, and Nixie realised she hadn't replied.

'Never,' she said, and with that lie she choked the blackness down. She unclenched her fingers, breathing hard.

'Then let's go, babes,' Taro said.

Alis weighed a chunk of fallen masonry in her hand. Taro wrenched some decorative bones from the walls. Nixie dug her fingers into the fleshy deposits of fungi and rolled the rotting mess in her palms, feeling the damp life trickle through her fingertips.

Once, when she tried to describe to Taro what plant arcania felt like before wresting, she said: It's a buzz, like someone gently breathing on your neck. And Taro had just stared at her, because bone arcania was cold and dry and sometimes it made you want to vomit. This was always the part where Nixie felt most powerful. Before she started wresting and became aware of her mortality, before the pain and the cloying sweetness in her mouth, while her fingers were simply on the trigger of a terrible weapon.

'I hope you know what you're doing,' Elliot said, as if he completely knew that she didn't.

'Go,' Nixie said.

She pressed her fingers into the yielding flesh of the fungi. The air was perfectly still. Then Taro stepped through the archway and Nixie eviscerated herself.

The chapel pinwheeled away. Pain spread up her arm, then through her shoulders and neck, as she transformed the fleshy life in her palm. The knotty incantation of her unbinding spell made her tongue ache as she forced it through the thickness in her mouth. Taro was right; the botanic spell that had exploded the microflora in the trespasser's body was a rope winding through the arch. It snagged on the knots of bone, blood and stone arcania entwined with it. The snags came loose as Taro and Elliot released the same part.

The engulfing headache of wresting fixed its teeth on Nixie's temples. The further the pain spread the harder it was to continue, but she couldn't stop unpicking the cat's cradle without tripping everyone else over. Nixie tightened her fingers and raised her voice, forcing the pain into submission. They hit another knot. Taro was incanting in a deeply disturbing way, mixing the typical syllables of bone incantation with hard, round sounds like pebbles falling down a well. With every inch of the four-way spell that came undone Taro took another step towards the altar, toeing the line of death as it crumbled before her.

The headache crackled, pushing its teeth deeper into Nixie's brain. Her tongue stumbled, and everything shuddered.

Stop! Feeling! Things!

In the Torture Pit they were taught to go slack, to disassociate and let the arcanist take what they wanted. To accept pain as nothing but a simple bodily sensation, to watch it from the outside and float high above their writhing bodies.

But Nixie turned inwards, where memories flickered like dreams. Opening her eyes in the Pit, all recollection of her past life gone. Being partnered with Alis for training. Walking into the exam hall, willing herself to be clever enough to keep and too mediocre to be desirable.

A noise forced Nixie back to the chapel. Taro was screaming while she incanted, her head bowed as she staggered through the archway. Nixie's pulse rose in her ears until it reached a crescendo, and she went inside herself again, to the darkest places in her memory. The Unholy Mothers dragging her to the castle with Taro. She and Taro grasping each other under their cloaks, the nuns not registering it as a misdemeanour but as a useful way of consolidating their cargo.

Something smacked into Nixie's legs. She surfaced and found herself on her knees. Her tongue stumbled, and it took everything she possessed to wind the spell back into shape. Elliot grunted and spat something to extract himself from the tangle she had created. Taro skittered back a few feet. Every mistake made the barrier in the archway grow back like a fire.

Stop. Feeling!

Nixie rose to her feet. She tried to free herself again, but she had lost the ability to run from her pain. Elliot gasped something gory and final, and the blood arcania was fully untangled. The slack yanked at Nixie's tongue as Taro's voice rose, tearing apart the last few feet of bone and stone arcania. Taro teetered at the last set of ribs, sweating blood. Alis sighed and crumpled to the floor behind Nixie, her wresting done.

Nixie was the only one left. She fixed her sight on Taro's back, but the bone disciple was a fuzzy outline. Her fingers loosened on the mushroom. One knot left.

She stopped wresting.

As her vision dripped away in runnels, she heard Taro gurgle something that sounded botanical, and the last strand of arcania fell.

When Nixie opened her eyes again she was twisted into a ball. She forced her head up and saw Taro leaning on one of the giant ribs for support.

'Easy,' Taro wheezed. She was sweating.

Nixie looked around, each tiny movement a needle-stab through her pupils. Something was wrong.

The skeleton was no longer in pieces on the floor.

No, it agreed.

It stood behind the altar, at the foot of a window, the glass holding back a deluge of dead bodies and dirt and rotting vegetation. It looked her in the eye, and when it knew she had given it her full attention, it slammed its head into the bottom of the window.

'Grab the relic!' Nixie screamed, or tried to, because it came out as a garbled, numb-mouthed yodel.

Alis and Elliot hauled themselves to their feet as Taro threw herself at the altar. Nixie lurched to her feet and promptly fell over again. Taro sprinted to her with the skull under one arm and yanked Nixie to her feet with the other.

Nixie came face-to-face with the grinning curse key. Up close it seemed nothing special: small and yellow, the crack nothing more than a painted-on scratch, patterned with crusted blood on the back. It looked like writing.

'It says something,' Nixie said thickly as the skeleton bashed the groaning window again.

'This isn't the time, Nix.' Taro continued hauling her towards the door.

'*Read it.*' Maybe it was the sudden edge in Nixie's voice, but Taro dropped her and thrust the skull into the greenish light. The bloody pattern resolved itself into four letters.

It read: *Ha. Ha.*

'I don't get it,' Taro said, because despite everything she was phenomenally slow.

'It's a trick,' Nixie said. She turned to Alis and Elliot, her voice hoarse. 'The curse key's gone.' The window bulged under the skeletal battering ram. '*Run.*'

Elliot grabbed the shoulder of Nixie's robe and, in a move that would live in her deepest and most embarrassing dreams, ran for the door while dragging her behind him. Alis, who had barely regained consciousness, stumbled after him. Taro yelped and sprinted *in the opposite direction*, towards the skeleton, spewing filthy words.

'Stop it,' Nixie shrieked, but Taro didn't hear.

The window shattered. The chapel inhaled the noxious sludge as the air turned black. Elliot yanked Nixie out of the chapel, followed by Alis. For an excruciating second there was nothing but the sound of breaking glass and falling stone. Then Taro shot through the hole, her heels barely through the door as the tide of death rushed towards them. She had the skeleton's head under her arm. Elliot swore and dropped Nixie.

With superhuman effort, Nixie dug her nails into the worts on the wall and spat an incantation through her teeth.

The squelching, minuscule tendrils of life exploded. The sides of the doorway collapsed inwards, cutting off the wave of dirt. Taro didn't waste time in wedging the new skull under her arm, grabbing Nixie under the armpits, and running – or attempting to run – away with her.

They staggered away from the chapel until the sound of collapse stopped, coming to rest near the mouth of the tunnel.

'The skull,' Elliot rasped. His chin was scarlet with blood. He reached for Taro, who kicked him away.

Taro was cradling the skeleton's head. Nixie had thought it was too large for the skeleton's body, and she had been right. The guardian of the chapel had put its own skull on the altar and placed the curse key on its neck, then poked its wizened tongue and eyeballs into the empty cavities. If Nixie had placed her hands on the skull as it bore down on her, the arcania might have killed her.

Their mistake was obvious now; there was something awful about this skull, as if it sucked all hope out of the air. But it was obvious that to Taro, the skull shone.

Taro gazed at it longingly for a moment. Then she snapped one of its teeth out and tossed the rest of the skull down the tunnel. They listened to it bounce for five long seconds before shattering at the bottom.

'What?' she said defensively. 'I can't carry the whole thing around.'

Nixie pulled herself into a sitting position against the damp wall. Her skull felt as splintered at the one that Taro had callously tossed. But there was something else inside her body, a spark that licked the back of her eyes and made her heart crackle.

'The Ghost was right,' she said. Nobody else was going to say it. They just looked at her. 'The skull's real. So is the curse. We can get out of here—' she stopped to cough and watched as a huge gob of blood hit the floor. Something moved in the corner of her vision. A ruby red beetle scuttled by her feet, making a trail through the blood before vanishing into the shadows. She forgot what she was saying and stared, fascinated.

'Nixie's right,' Taro said. She placed her foot squarely over the gob of blood, saving Nixie the embarrassment of having to acknowledge it. 'If we find the other curse keys, we can do it. We ambush the Slaughter, get in there before our arcanists, and break the curse at the top of the tower. Nobody has to die.'

'We're doing it, then,' Nixie said, and despite everything else, she felt a surge of righteousness that was ruined only by coughing up another bloody gob.

'She wrested too much,' Elliot said. He was, against all odds, lounging again; still beautiful, even smeared with dirt and sweat. 'I can't believe she exploded the chapel. Wasn't she distinctly average in the Pit?'

The memory of being dragged over the floor by Elliot was a punch to the stomach. Being called *average*, even though she had worked hard to maintain that illusion, was worse. Even while grievously injured, she was ashamed.

And strong enough to crush him.

'Your hair,' Nixie croaked.

'What?' Elliot looked at her as though she had spat on his impeccable boots.

'It's shit.'

She smirked and blacked out in Taro's arms.

Seven

Thirty-one hours until the Slaughter

Elliot ran his fingers through his grime-encrusted hair. 'She's delirious,' he said coolly. Taro clutched Nixie's limp body with one arm.

'You're both shitty people,' she snarled at him and Alis. 'You let her collapse the door by herself. She could have died.'

Sleepless agony pulsed through the base of Elliot's skull. He would have loved to give Taro a nosebleed, but he had spent too much of himself in the chapel.

'She didn't ask for our help,' he snapped.

Now the shock of adrenaline had faded he was spiralling back into exhaustion, his vision furring blood-red. His temples throbbed and his muscles ached. He desperately wanted to lie on the cool floor and sleep, but even trying would be tortuous.

'It's my turn now,' he said. 'You have to get me into Morgan's tower.'

'You leech,' Taro said in disgust. 'We barely got out, and you're already demanding payment.' She smoothed Nixie's hair. The unfairness of that adoration sickened Elliot. His mother had cradled him like that, before he was ripped away from her. The twist of the knife was that he alone knew what he had lost. The other familiars, coddled by the poison that had removed their memories, had nothing to mourn.

'The Slaughter begins in just over a day,' Elliot said through gritted teeth. 'I'm not helping you find the other curse keys until you've fulfilled your end of the deal.'

'I changed my mind,' Taro said. 'I'm not wasting my time helping you perve on Morgan, or whatever you're doing.'

'You don't even know if the curse is real,' he rasped. '*I'm* real. I'm dying.'

Alis looked at him curiously, but Taro was unmoved. She didn't even ask what he meant.

'You know the curse is real, and so are the keys,' she said. 'Look me in the eye and tell me Nixie stumbled on the location of a creepy arcanical artefact by accident.'

'No,' Elliot said, realisation dawning. He was dizzy with exhaustion, but his thoughts had never been clearer. 'You're making it up, aren't you? You wanted me to help you get this skull – whatever it is – so you can use it to destroy Redspire before the Slaughter. Because you know you don't have a chance of winning.'

Taro looked at him as though he'd announced he was the Thaumaturge.

'Get some sleep, you paranoid freak,' she said.

'I should have known better than to trust anyone outside Redspire,' he said. He laughed; if he didn't, he would break instead. 'A *ghost*. What was I thinking?'

'You bloodsuckers are obsessed with rivalry,' Taro snapped. 'Trust me, nobody pays that much attention to you.' She reached over Nixie's body and withdrew a fistful of cloth. She shook it out, and a shard of mirror fell to the floor. 'Look.'

Elliot picked up the glass. He saw his own face, and on top of it, a slice of death. A grinning teenager whose nerves were fully visible through her skin. She winked with an eyelid that did nothing to mask her eyeball.

'Hi, handsome,' the thing said.

Elliot threw the glass so hard it bounced.

'Satisfied?' Taro said. 'That's the Ghost. You can help us carry her around if you want. No? Didn't think so.' She wrapped the mirror up and put it back in Nixie's pocket; not, Elliot noticed, her own.

Elliot forced himself to breathe normally. Perhaps he *was* paranoid. But he knew full well the lengths people would go to to protect their disciplines.

'We still had a deal,' he said. 'My help for Morgan's tower.'

'Suck it, Elliot.'

Taro grunted with effort as she hauled Nixie back up the slope, towards the surface of the castle. Nixie's head lolled. It thumped against the ground, and something swelled inside Elliot, a breaking wave of deep panic that he barely held back. The smell of blood – of sweat – the sheen of Nixie's ashen skin – and he was there again, in his childhood home at the bottom of the Desecrae, with the sour smell of vomit in his nostrils.

The girl beneath his fingers was slack, too hot, delirious with sepsis. Elliot knew she was too far gone, but they were all watching him, the girl's parents and his own. Her faint and wild pulse was too broken to fix. He tried anyway. He knew his parents needed the money, and he needed them to acknowledge him. For his father to clap him on the shoulder, and his mother to cup his chin in her hands and smile. He felt his mother's breath on his shoulder as she hovered over him—

Alis slapped him. For a fraction of a moment Elliot was in two places.

Then the pieces slid together and he was fully under the castle, in the mould-furred passageway. It was clear that the ex-stone disciple had been studying him for some time. Without breaking eye contact, she produced a note she had written.

Do you think they're right about the curse?

Elliot tried to speak, but his tongue refused to cooperate. The sick girl's face was still vivid in his memory. She was his first and last mistake. The beginning of the end, when he was hiding in the chest with the useless knife between his fingers, and the Unholy Mothers were throwing themselves at the lid.

Alis considered him for a moment.

You're broken, aren't you.

Elliot couldn't work out if she was joking. Either way, he was preoccupied with remembering how to breathe. Alis observed the thin, hard line of his mouth and rolled her eyes. The gesture was another slap. It drew Elliot to his feet.

'If you tell anyone about this, you're finished,' he snarled. To fall apart in front of anyone was reckless, but to show weakness in front of a stone disciple was mortifying.

Elliot limped away. He would go to Morgan's tower alone, even if it meant dying under the gaze of the prodigal son of blood. Because if he didn't find what he needed soon, he truly would lose his mind.

Alis tapped his shoulder. She had written something else.

I'll come with you.

Elliot didn't know the castle well enough to avoid scrutiny, and he had to admit that having Alis here was useful. He followed her through the cramped servants' corridors, past dozens of menials on the night shift, none of whom paid attention to two more people with their hoods up. Alis stood aside for a man dragging a sack of animal carcasses to the kitchen, and Elliot took the opportunity to study her. He expected to find deceit in her face – something that would explain her motive for helping him – but like her discipline, she was unyielding. Elliot still refused to let his guard down. If she tried to move against him, he was ready to snap her neck.

She caught him staring and glared.

I've been screwed over by Taro too, she wrote, as if she could read his eyes.

It was clear that she and Taro were performing a long, complicated dance around one another, and that Nixie – if she was aware of it at all – was pretending not to see. Elliot knew their rivalry was pointless. They would all die in the Slaughter, probably at each other's hands.

'This doesn't make us allies,' he drawled.

Good. I would rather pull my nails out than be friends with a —

Alis's scrawl was so messy that Elliot couldn't read the last word, but he knew it was an insult.

The crooked passage uncurled outside Morgan's tower. Elliot ran his fingers over the locked door, smoothing them across the carved serpents with ruby eyes, painfully aware of the quick pulse at the base of his throat. Alis stood behind him, as silent as a pane of glass. It was deeply unnerving.

'Stand back,' he said softly, and pinched the cartilage of his crushed nose so a thin stream of blood splashed to the floor.

Even Morgan would break a sweat doing this. Elliot inhaled, drawing the blood inside his nose to the back of his mouth, and pressed his index finger against his wet molars. Wresting always started in the hands; only fingertips were sensitive enough to feel the locked-away power in blood, bone, stone or botanics. The blood mutated under Elliot's touch. The indescribable potential it held leeched into his body, where with excruciating pain it transformed. Another moment and it spilled back out of him, radiating from his skin, spreading up his arm until it soaked into the air. He removed his finger from the blood and breathed it in. *Arcania.*

Carving it was like shaping butter with his tongue. It was rich and thick and warm. His incantation gave the arcania direction and purpose; it sought the splatter of blood on the floor, which grew under his command. Cells divided and divided again, blooming ad infinitum until it was a towering spout. The spout of blood swayed beside his face like a writhing snake. It twisted and crept towards the lock. The scarlet stream slithered through the keyhole and played with the mechanism.

The door swung open, but Elliot was suddenly unwilling to stop. The cadence of the incantation was too sweet. He hurt, but there was something euphoric in the pain when he was using it for his own end. The sense of control was weirdly pleasurable. He twisted an utterance and darted the bloody snake back towards them. Alis flinched her body away from it, but the red spout had already split in two and lashed itself around their bodies. It yanked them inside and closed the door before disintegrating.

Alis retched.

'You're squeamish,' Elliot observed. His nausea was overwhelmed by triumph.

This is why you never had friends, she scribbled, as he felt around until he found a candle and matches.

Now it was Elliot's turn to snort. *Friends.*

Elliot lit the candle. The light was dark and warm and smelled like animal fat, and it poked deep shadows into the room, which bristled with the blood-soaked paraphernalia of a true Redborn. One wall was lined with thousands of blood vials, each neatly corked and labelled: leopard, magpie, dog, starveling. The others gleamed darkly with the things Morgan had stolen. Elliot recognised a set of teacups from the Redborn house. The edges were lumpy with human teeth.

'Look for a necklace,' he said, swinging the candle abruptly towards Alis. Anticipation lent an edge to his voice that he couldn't suppress. 'It has a pendant with an open eye, and there's a drop of blood under the glass.'

Is it the Redspire curse key? she wrote.

'Yes,' he lied.

Alis didn't look as if she believed him, but he could tell she wasn't willing to take the risk. She clearly wanted to impress Nixie by finding another curse key, and he would use that to his advantage. Anyway, would she believe Elliot if he told her what the necklace was really for? That it was his blood under the glass, and that Tamsin Redborn had contrived a curse that ensured he never slept? That the longer he existed without being unconscious, the more fissures appeared in the thin veneer of sanity he still had, and that he could no longer control what came through the cracks?

And if Alis knew what power it held over him … the thought of her holding it in her fist, crushing his sleep in her hands, made his jaw clench.

'Be careful,' he added shortly. 'I need it unbroken.'

Alis shrugged.

The first drawer Elliot opened was choked with stolen trinkets from the Redborn mansion. It was a game Morgan played. He came to visit; his parents didn't let him out of their sight; yet somehow Morgan always left with more than he came with. Like the molar-pocked teacup handed to him after dinner, or the five-pronged fork for the baked leopard, or the fourth gut-string from his father's violin.

Elliot caught glimpses of Alis as they searched the room. She worked efficiently, opening drawers and sifting through pots of knick-knacks in silence. Elliot found himself lagging, his eyes catching on her profile once, then twice. There was something about her that seemed … out of focus. Nothing literal. Just that he couldn't make sense of her, as though she was hiding something in plain sight. As she worked, her sleeves rode up and revealed flashes of the black ink he had seen in the library.

She saw him looking. It was too late for Elliot to pretend otherwise. She glanced around dramatically, then lifted her finger to her lips with a grin and pushed up her sleeves.

Black ships rode waves up her arms. The water swarmed with animals Elliot had never seen in the depths of the Redborns' menagerie. Planets clustered in the sky with blazing stars. It was storybook stuff that he had only seen in the ancient manuscripts Malachi collected, which he dissected for traces of blood under the leather.

She dropped her sleeves before he could say anything. The ever-present pencil stub, which seemed like an extension of her hand, danced across a scrap of paper.

If we're looking for your curse key, does that mean you're helping us in the Fifth Tower?

Us. Alis had already made her mind up about following Nixie into the Slaughter. But Taro had gone back on her end of the deal, and he gave nothing for free.

We'll die otherwise, she added.

Elliot closed a drawer.

'Just help me find the necklace,' he said.

Elliot left her to search the cabinets downstairs and went to the back of the room, towards a spiral staircase. He felt his way along the outside curve of the stairs, shuddering at the warm, sticky stone, until he was emptied into a long corridor.

Morgan's territory had expanded beyond the tower itself and into a high wing of the castle. It was cast in red light, a bloody aortal tunnel in the stone. Aside from the doors, the walls were completely obscured by junk: bottles of blood, mounds of books and hundreds of arcane treasures. Goblets with all the disciplines' mascots on them. Skull-shaped bread buns from dinner. Knives, forks, tapestries, keys and dead malefici that had been yanked out of the Desecrae. He heard that the people who lived down there hunted them sometimes. There was another maleficent mounted to the wall, a starveling with forks sticking out of its arm sockets.

Elliot walked straight towards the two doors at the end. He didn't believe in premonition or gut instinct, but there was something compelling about the darkness in front of him. As he approached, the feeling resolved into the sweet smell of ancient blood arcania. It seeped from the bottom of the right-hand door, which was locked. Elliot didn't waste time trying to break in. He knew what he was looking for, and as tempting as the smell of power was, the cursed necklace was nothing like this. The left-hand door was invitingly ajar. A suit of armour leaned next to it, holding an ostentatious black-jewelled dagger on a plum-coloured cushion.

A room with a threat. It was exactly where Morgan would keep the things he liked most.

Elliot slipped inside, his pulse loud in his ears. The darkness of this room was deep and purposeful. He raised his hands in front of him, losing the ends of his fingers in the gloom, and trod over a deep-pile carpet until he reached a window.

He twitched the heavy velvet drapes. A thin slice of moonlight fell over a table strewn with perfume bottles. A blonde hair lay over them like a strand of spider's silk; not Morgan's, but some visitor whose presence hadn't been erased. He slid around the table and felt along the wall, which was furry with damp wallpaper, his toes nudging more stacks of the interminable history books that Morgan read.

He was almost done with the deeply disappointing room when he knocked against something hard. Elliot ran his hand down the polished wood until his fingers met the yielding surface of a cushion, which he didn't realise was actually a mattress until the crucial moment that he touched Morgan Redborn's foot.

Elliot flinched into the sharp edge of the perfume-laden table. The bottles fell and shattered, slopping their bloody contents over his feet. The figure in the bed flickered upright, a shadow darker than all the shadows around it, a lithe nightmare that had sprung from *asleep* to *awake* so quickly that he must have been watching this whole time.

Elliot twisted away from the dresser, grasping for a weapon. A fist – a spell – a knife glittering with the Redborn crest. He heard a whisper of silk, like someone sliding a sword out of a sheath, followed by absolute silence.

Elliot's skin chilled as he held still. He couldn't tell where Morgan was standing, but he didn't want to give himself away. He stood motionless for agonisingly long seconds.

The door creaked. The shadows breathed out.

Morgan was gone.

He knew he was defenceless without his familiar, and he had decided to flee rather than fight the intruder in his room.

Elliot smiled to himself. He had almost forgotten in his exhaustion that he was so much more powerful than Morgan. He would rather steal the necklace back without making a fuss, but if he had to spill blood, so be it. He stepped from the room, bold now, and observed the empty corridor.

The suit of armour's hands were splayed wide, the plum-coloured cushion on the floor, the dagger gone.

So this was Morgan's game. He was behind one of the doors between the piles of junk, waiting to spring out and plunge the dagger into Elliot's neck. Or he had run to his familiar, ready to launch a violent spell when Elliot walked past.

Elliot pressed close to the shadows, easing along until he came to the nearest door. He took a deep breath, silently swung his body out, and wrenched the handle. It was locked. Blood roared through his skull as he worked back towards the staircase. His jaw was tense, but he wasn't scared. He had long trained fear out of himself.

'Morgan,' he said.

Nothing. Maybe Morgan had taken the stairs and found Alis.

Regrettable, but better her than him.

'Morgan Redborn.'

Still no reply. The blood arcanist was more cowardly than he had thought. That was the trouble with people who were born with everything; they had never learned how to fight for themselves.

'I know you're here, Morgan.'

Morgan clapped his hands in delight, and in that exact moment, Elliot realised that he wasn't hunting Morgan Redborn.

Morgan Redborn was hunting him.

They moved at the same time. Morgan charged from his hiding place between two groaning bookcases, the dagger glittering black in his fingers. Elliot scraped his nails over the wound on the back of his hand and screamed his incantation.

He pushed a tide of blood from Morgan's veins to Morgan's head. The arcanist fell against the wall and stayed there while his heart palpitated and tried to push everything back to where it belonged. It would have killed most people, but it only gave Morgan a nosebleed.

Elliot curled his fingers into the cuts on his hands and paused with his tongue against the roof of his mouth. He could do it again and finish the job. He could make Morgan's heart fail. He would be free to explore the tower and find the necklace, and he would be doing a good deed by ridding the world of a Redborn – not that he cared for good deeds. But Elliot's tongue stuck to the roof of his mouth. *Kill him*, he urged himself, but the same force that had stopped him from murdering Saul held Elliot still.

Coward, he hissed at himself. It wasn't true; cowardice had never been his problem. It was something else, and he liked it even less.

Morgan's dagger lay on the floor between them. Elliot picked it up as Morgan coughed and giggled, which made his nose blow red bubbles. The knife was merely decorative, as light as tin. If Morgan had tried to strike Elliot, it would have bent in half without breaking his skin.

'I wanted to see what you could do,' Morgan explained.

Elliot kicked the dagger against the wall, his face utterly still. Humiliation could wait for later.

'You have something of mine,' he said, his voice unsteady. It barely hid the undercurrent of rage.

'I know who you are,' Morgan said, wiping the blood from his nose with the back of his hand. 'You're Saul's familiar. Did he send you?'

Elliot met his laughing eyes with absolute coolness. Morgan was perfectly aware that Saul wouldn't have sent him.

'No?' Morgan said. 'But familiars aren't supposed to have autonomy. Or speak. As you well know, Elliot.'

It was the first time a Redborn had spoken Elliot's name aloud. It was as intrusive as having Saul rip his power away from him. He felt naked.

'You stole a necklace,' Elliot said, gritting his teeth. 'Tell me where it is before I expunge your blood through your skin.'

'Ah.' Morgan rolled his neck and began to lever himself from the floor, then stopped and said, with swaggering deference: 'May I?'

Elliot showed Morgan his bloody palms, ripe for wresting.

'Understood.' Morgan put his own hands in the air as he stood. Only now could Elliot see the full length of his body, the fine silk clinging to his chest, his hair falling over the front of his shoulders. He smelled of sweat and faint traces of the blood-covering perfume still warmed by his pulse. 'This necklace. I assume it's the one with a very ... cursed aura. The one I stole from my mother last night.' He grinned wickedly. 'What does it do?'

Elliot held his silence for long enough that it sounded like a sneer before answering.

'Your mother stole my ability to sleep.'

'Hmm. Let me guess. You can only be relieved when you're wearing the necklace, correct?' Elliot quirked his head in the same way Morgan had, which was supposed to be mocking, but it made Morgan smile. 'I'm sure she loved wearing it in front of you.'

He had moved closer without Elliot noticing. His teeth were very white, and his lips were preternaturally red. Hundreds of years of careful breeding had kept the Redborns looking like vampires, and Morgan was the pinnacle of their creation.

'You've broken a dozen rules to be here,' Morgan said softly. 'I could execute you right now.'

'You could.' Elliot's sense of self-preservation was telling him to back away, but there was something pleasurable in the danger, like biting down on an aching tooth. He had never spoken so openly about his own treachery before. 'But I would fight back. I'm good at it.'

'Let's say you killed me,' Morgan agreed, his voice soft as silk, still low. 'You still wouldn't have what you want.'

'I would find it.'

'Before the Slaughter? Probably not. And then the Slaughter would be won by another arcanist. Which means that, in the unlikely event of you getting away with my murder, you would be dispatched by the nuns in two days anyway.'

Elliot didn't react. The truth of his statement hung between them like a knife. Morgan stepped forward, and before Elliot could move, he pushed a curl of Elliot's hair behind his ear. Elliot shivered under his touch. Morgan's fingers were teasingly gentle as they grazed his skin.

Why wasn't Elliot running?

'What happens next?' Morgan asked.

Elliot couldn't think. His vision was fuzzing around the edges again. *Not because of fear*, he told himself. Not because of the touch. It had just been so long since he'd slept. So long since he'd healed. He felt like the walking dead, and his body was betraying him.

Morgan clapped his hands, and Elliot flinched away.

'Elliot, you're wonderful!' Morgan said. 'Uptight and humourless and *full* of adorably useless rage. Of course I won't hurt you.'

In a flash Morgan was halfway towards the stairs. He grabbed a fur stole and slung it over his shoulders.

'Drink with me!'

He slipped into the curved throat of the tower, clothes as pale as exposed bone against the dark flesh of the stone. Elliot stared after him. This had to be a mistake. A deeply textured hallucination borne of his insomnia. Surely he had not faced Morgan Redborn and lived.

Elliot steeled himself before following in Morgan's wake, descending towards the deep and crowded belly of the tower. He was almost at the foot of the stairs when a hand lurched from the darkness and yanked him into a grimy window-well.

Elliot hit his head on the glass and spat through his teeth. Black stars burst over his retinas. Alis crouched before him, eyes narrowed, teeth bared. Bloody flesh, she was good at hiding; even Morgan hadn't seen her lurking in the shadows on his way down.

'What the hell are you doing?' he hissed. Alis's nails dug into Elliot's wrist as she scrawled on the wall in a thin slip of moonlight.

Rescuing you.

Elliot yanked his arm away.

'I don't need rescuing,' he said. 'And if Morgan sees you he'll rip you to pieces. You were stupid not to run when you heard him attack me.'

Alis was stubborn.

What are you doing, Elliot?

'Manipulating him,' Elliot said. He glanced down the staircase, desperate to follow Morgan. 'He has the necklace. He'll slip up and tell me where it is.' Alis looked incredulous, but he was desperate, hanging on by a thread; he would walk into the jaws of a panther if it meant a chance of getting it back, however slim. 'You need to leave, Alis.'

I'm not in the habit of abandoning people to their death.

Elliot narrowed his eyes. This was outside the parameters of their deal. She had already come to the tower with him, and she had every right to leave him to his fate. Part of him ached to accept the rescue. The other part, the one that had kept him alive all this time, knew that her offer was self-serving; she only wanted him alive to keep looking for the curse keys.

'I'm staying,' he said coldly.

Alis stared at him, long and hard. Then she rubbed the pencil off the wall with her sleeve and climbed the stairs. He didn't know how she intended to get out, but he knew better than to ask, because her expression said: *Go impale yourself.*

Then she was gone.

Morgan was draped over an armchair in the circular room downstairs. Despite being half-dressed, he had furnished himself with several diamond rings and a gold coronet.

Elliot leaned at the bottom of the steps, his arms folded. He wouldn't speak first and concede ground in whatever game they were playing. Morgan didn't start either, and they stretched the moment into a long, uncomfortable minute before Morgan sighed and said, 'Come *in,* Elliot.'

If he had heard Elliot whispering to Alis, he didn't show it.

A low table was already set with a jug of black wine and two goblets. Morgan gestured to the opposite chair, which Elliot ignored.

'We could both be very happy, Elliot,' Morgan said, unperturbed. 'Drink?'

'No.' Elliot wasn't stupid enough to be poisoned.

Morgan filled both goblets anyway. He swished the dark liquid around his cup and ran his eyes over Elliot's face. Elliot returned the intrusion, a tiny part of him glad of the excuse to nakedly stare at Morgan's face. To study the crimson cut on his lower lip, the smooth plane of his cheeks.

'You're good at arcania,' Morgan said, casually, as though Elliot didn't already know he was phenomenal. 'I knew it the moment I smelled you lurking outside the tower. Even better, your bravery cancels out your stupidity.'

Elliot remained silent. As much as he wanted to fling himself at Morgan, dig his thumbs into his neck and strangle the location of the necklace from him, he knew the only way to find it was with excruciating patience. To find out what Morgan wanted without giving any of himself away, and use it to extract information from him. He loosened his tensed jaw.

'Come *on*, Elliot,' Morgan said. 'Aren't you curious as to why you're still alive?'

'Deeply,' Elliot said flatly. This made Morgan laugh. Nobody had ever laughed because of something he'd said. It was unnerving.

'You're fun,' Morgan said. 'All right. I'm going to give you what you want.'

Elliot smirked, putting all of his ugliness behind his expression.

'And what do you want in return?'

'You're so cynical.'

Morgan swung his legs over one arm of the chair and dipped his head over the other. His jewelled locks brushed the carpet as he smiled upside down.

'You're right. I do want something. Or the opposite of something. Did they teach you about Sobweb at the wyrdo school?'

Elliot didn't flinch at *wyrdo*, which was a victory.

'He was the first thaumaturge,' Elliot replied. He didn't add: *And the last to reign before the Blackspire skull was lost.* The skull they had stolen from the skeleton in the chapel less than an hour ago.

'But do you know his vices? I do. My parents supplemented my education. Sobweb was eccentrically murder-driven, and he was highly imaginative. He created the nuns. He was unbelievably talented.'

'History bores me.'

Morgan raised an eyebrow, but Elliot wasn't worried. This was part of the game. Morgan was playing with his food, seeing how many rules it would break, and Elliot was willing to make that number high.

'*Sit*, Elliot,' Morgan said, and this time Elliot did, but with forced laziness, as slowly as possible. He wouldn't let Morgan see his desperation for answers. 'I'm explaining my parents' desires. They want me to be the kind of thaumaturge Sobweb was. One who makes the history books. Their expectations were always high. They even thought I might be undisciplined, like Sobweb. That's how he made the nuns. You know it's no normal form of arcania driving them, don't you? I had terrible headaches as a child. Sweet Mummy and Daddy thought they were arcanical.'

Elliot looked at him blankly.

'You don't know what undiscipline is,' Morgan said.

'I can guess.'

'If you're undisciplined you can wrest from stone, bone, blood *and* botanics. It died out a very long time ago, much to my parents' disappointment. They thought I might be a prodigal throwback, but alas, I only deal in blood. Drink?'

Elliot unthinkingly touched the goblet, then remembered the black vial he had seen hidden in Morgan's sleeve the previous night. The one that had most likely poisoned the Thaumaturge. He pulled back.

'To the context, then,' Morgan said. 'I'm not here to please my family, Elliot. I'm not here to make them powerful. I want to win the Slaughter. And I will, because I'm an incredible arcanist. But I also want to have fun. What's the point in living otherwise? And I think you could help make things very fun indeed.' He reached out, still draped over the armchair, and pushed the goblet across the table with his index finger. 'You really don't … ?'

'No.'

Morgan shrugged. He drained both goblets in quick succession, still upside down. A drop of red clung to his mouth like blood from a freshly bitten lip.

'There's a flaw in your plan,' Elliot said softly. 'I'm not fun.'

'Maybe the word I'm looking for is *interesting*. You're planning a coup, no?'

Elliot's bones turned to water inside his skin.

'I have little eyes all over the place.' Morgan reached behind him and, so quickly Elliot barely saw what he was doing, grabbed a handful of red beetles from a bowl on the floor. He flung them on to the table, where they skittered away like long-legged rubies. 'I don't know what the plan is, but I do know that four familiars, from different disciplines no less, have been lurking underneath the castle together. And just a night after the Thaumaturge's murder, too.'

'I suppose you weren't involved in that,' Elliot snapped, desperate to change the subject.

'Me?' Morgan said sweetly. 'Of course not. But you're *definitely* plotting something.'

Morgan poured another two goblets of wine, and Elliot watched closely. Then he drank. The wine was as thick as tar, as cloying as blood.

'You must know that it would be impossible for a group of familiars to win the Slaughter, even together,' Morgan said. 'You would have to face whatever's in the tower and kill every arcanist who tried to take you down. You'd all be dead in minutes. And if you won, who in Fourspires would respect your power? You would have the crown, of course, and control of the nuns. But people would despise you. And you would have to learn how to share with each other.'

Elliot looked deep into his cup. Morgan obviously didn't know about, or didn't believe in, the supposed curse. Certainly not that Nixie was trying to remove the Desecrae and crack the world open like an egg. Even Elliot wasn't certain the curse was real, despite what he had seen in the chapel.

'Here's the alternative,' Morgan said, mistaking his silence for concern. 'You join me, and we win together. We could rule Fourspires for decades. I would let you speak freely and practise arcania, within limits. And,' he said, his lazy smile growing wide as he trailed a finger around the rim of his cup, 'I would give you your necklace.'

Elliot forced another gulp of the wine, but he tasted nothing. The promise of sleep was so achingly close he could almost touch it, yet even through that excruciating desperation, the promise of *more* was sharp and sweet. Not just freedom from his own curse, but real power. Control over not just his own body, but everyone who looked down on him. Other familiars. Arcanists. Even his parents, who had loved him, but who in their weakness had let the nuns rip him from their hands.

But even now, with Morgan dangling this over him, he wouldn't concede easily. Morgan wanted Elliot to fall at his feet in gratitude. He would have to work for it.

'How did it feel,' Elliot said, 'to win the raffle and go to the University? Do you hate knowing that you're only here because of luck?'

'What raffle?' Morgan said, unperturbed by the subject change.

'The one that decides who gets to be an arcanist or a familiar. Who goes to the Academy, and who goes to the Pit.'

'Oh.' Morgan yawned. 'I didn't *win* it. My parents paid the University off. Most arcanists' families do.' Elliot's disgust was bland; he realised he wasn't surprised. 'I was always destined to be great, and you were always destined to be used by me.'

Elliot hoped his lack of reaction was deeply disappointing.

'You already have a familiar,' he said, changing tack again. 'You don't need me too.'

'He's not you. And he's not—' Morgan cut himself short. He stared at the ceiling as though seeing another world, and Elliot knew he had found a weakness.

'He's not your fourth familiar? Rhys?' Elliot said. Morgan remained silent, but Elliot could see that his clenched hands were bloodless. Morgan's romance with his familiar had been an open secret, but Elliot had assumed it had all been in service of embarrassing his parents. This was … something different.

'Not all men can be as fascinating as Rhys,' Morgan said finally. His hands relaxed.

'You don't find me fascinating?' The wine was making Elliot bolder. More dangerous.

'A little,' Morgan conceded. 'And relentless. Unafraid. And you're quite beautiful. Maybe that's why I want you.'

Elliot locked eyes with him. He would not smile or be visibly thrilled. Nonetheless, he felt the sharp and hungry pull of that word: *want*. He swirled the bloody liquid around the bottom of the goblet.

'The others are relying on me,' he said. 'They want me too. In fact, I would say they need me.'

'They just need a blood arcanist. I want *you*.'

Morgan was unashamedly enjoying himself. He knew he almost had

Elliot in the palm of his hand. Elliot would get everything he wanted and more. It was far more compelling than the promise of a world beyond the Desecrae, which likely didn't exist. With Morgan on the throne Elliot could even persuade him to spare the other familiars from death. Elliot would be doing them a kindness by betraying them. The only question was one of trust: how could he know that the blood arcanist wasn't lying through his teeth?

Morgan leaned in.

'I know what happens to familiars,' he said. 'I know how they're torn away from their parents, and their memories are wiped, so they have nothing to miss. Nothing to look forward to except pain.' Elliot tried to swallow, but his mouth was too dry. He felt his mother's touch again; her hands cupping his face, her sad smile and quiet love. 'We're not that different from one another, you and I. I learned the only way to survive is to look after myself. I don't think the other familiars are looking after you, Elliot. They don't deserve your help.'

Morgan was right. They didn't deserve him. Taro had gone back on her promise to help him get into Morgan's tower, and Nixie hadn't lifted a finger to stop her betraying the deal. And Alis – well, god knew what she wanted.

Even if Elliot helped them, and they made the Desecrae patter to the ground like gory snow, he wouldn't have what he needed. Without the necklace he would live in wide-eyed agony, slowly falling into the pit of his own memories until he was a powerless, gibbering wreck.

Yes, he meant to say. *Yes, Morgan. It's a deal.*

But something pinned his tongue to the roof of his mouth.

Where was the clarifying compass of selfishness he had lived by? Why did it always fail him at the crux of the matter, right when he should go for the kill? It wasn't cowardice. It was something small and nagging that he had tried to stamp out long ago, something borne of morality, that stupid thing invented by people who feared others hurting them.

He wanted this, and he didn't. And no matter what he told himself, he knew the next words to come out of his mouth were simply a way to stall until he had gathered the strength to betray the other familiars.

'Show me how much you want me.'

There followed a long, dark silence, and Elliot wondered if he had asked too much.

'That's fair,' Morgan said. 'I'll do that.'

Elliot put the goblet down, the tension draining from his shoulders. The wine had already gone to his head. *Maybe it's poisoned after all.*

Morgan tipped his own goblet and drank deeply. Black wine dribbled down his chin and into the fur around his neck, making it look as though his throat had been slit. Behind him, somewhere in the shadows, his pet leopard Peridot growled. Elliot realised with a lurch that it must have been there all night, watching him and Alis from the shadows. Morgan had been expecting him.

Elliot stood. The room swirled around him. Morgan watched interestedly, tapping the rim of his goblet with a long, gold-painted fingernail.

'You'll get used to the wine,' he said as Elliot clutched the back of the chair. A swarm of red beetles scurried around his feet like a bloody whirlpool; or perhaps there were only a handful, and he was drunk. One darted up his leg and vanished into his pocket, but when Elliot felt around for it, he couldn't find anything.

Morgan smiled and raised his goblet as Elliot waded towards the door.

'To the future,' Morgan said, and Elliot nodded.

'The future,' he repeated coldly.

Eight

Twenty-four hours until the Slaughter

Dawn broke over Fourspires in grey clumps. Alis was on her fifth cigarette, tapping her foot while she stared through the window at the courtyard. She hadn't pulled an all-nighter in months, or at least since she'd figured out how to bind her chest and spent hours strutting through the towers of books. But after the chapel and Morgan's tower, no part of her could rest. Every time she almost fell asleep she remembered the skeleton in the chapel, and jerked awake.

They really were under a curse. There was something beyond the Desecrae. Maybe there, she might not be a freak for having the wrong body.

Then there was Elliot, who was probably either dead or dying. She didn't know for sure because she'd left him with Morgan. Elliot was technically a mortal enemy and kind of an ass, but his demise would put a massive crimp in the whole curse-breaking thing. Which was the third thing keeping her awake: she was planning to commit extreme treason.

For Nixie's attention, her sly inner voice said.

Nope. It was because she worked in the library and had waded through hundreds of ancient books. Fictions that, despite being thematically diverse, agreed on some weird fundamentals, like the concept of a blue sky and a sun so hot it literally burned people, instead of the grey orb that shone weakly from – or maybe it was actually *through* – the Desecrae. She'd always thought they were elaborate lies.

But maybe a small part of her had also wondered at their truth.

That's not why you're going to help. You'd follow Nixie to hell to make her like you again.

Alis angrily ground the cigarette stub into the windowsill. What she really wanted was to drop it into a pile of books. *Two seconds until absolute carnage*, she thought again. One paper-thin decision and the library would go up in flames. That would shut the voice up.

Sleep wasn't coming. She had a curse key to find.

Alis rolled her sleeves up and walked into the gloom. Books were a vast but finite resource. It was simply a matter of opening the right one, and she knew exactly where to look. Since the curse was unimaginably old, and the mascots of the four towers older still, she could discard the library's more recent acquisitions. Of the ones left, half would be eaten by bookworms and mildew. The rest of the oldest surviving manuscripts would be in the Librarian's office.

The stacks drew her along. Alis breathed in time with the pulse of the library, letting the shadows roll off her back, ignoring the gentle shuffling of starving cats.

Then there was something new. A rhythmic *thump*, *thump* coming from the gravesite records. Alis hesitated and briefly entertained ignoring it.

My dying wish would be that no assistant after me hears a weird noise and must ask: What wants to kill me today?

Curiosity was always her vice. She turned from her path and followed the noise. The further she walked the more the books sagged, their thousands of thick, handwritten pages unopened since the ink had dried. The thumping grew louder. When Alis turned the corner, she almost forgot her dead tongue and spat a curse out loud.

A nun was trying to walk through a wall, stepping and knocking into the stone face-first, shivering backwards, then trying again. *Thump.*

Thump. Thump. It didn't react to her, which meant its ears were blocked with dry rot, a common affliction for Unholy Mothers who escaped the maintenance cycle. Sometimes they got trapped in the squashed bits of castle underground and resurfaced when something truly compelling happened; this one must have answered the call of the Thaumaturge's murder and become lost.

Thump.

Alis observed the nun with macabre interest. They were aeons old, and she knew that the tiny piece of brain they had could grow like a tumour until the nun became a big, muddied parody of an autonomous thing. Sometimes that piece of brain was knocked loose to reveal something – a small, undead nugget of memory – that it wasn't supposed to.

Alis chewed the inside of her cheek. She should put it out of its misery. Or leave it for the Librarian to deal with. And yet …

She touched the nun's shoulder. It surprised her how solid the Unholy Mothers were, given their propensity to glide from the tops of buildings. She closed her fingers over its gnarled bones and turned it so she was looking directly into its bruised and vacant face. She thought she was prepared. She still shuddered.

Hello, she mouthed, making the word absurdly big.

The nun stared right through her. Alis wondered if it was following its fundamental instructions not to interact with anyone unless absolutely required, or if it was so broken it couldn't see her.

Do you know about the curse keys? she mouthed.

Still no response. Alis sighed and wondered how to dispatch it. Throw it from a window? Let it beat itself to a pulp?

Tell me where they are, she said, as she imagined children were spoken to. *The mascots of the disciplines.*

The nun's eyes rolled into the back of its head, revealing a tangle of greenish-pink veins. Its mouth cracked open with a sound that made Alis's jaw twinge.

M-M-M-ASCOTS, it puffed. *SOBWE-B-B-B HORR-RR-OR A-A-A-GAIN.*

Alis wrestled her revulsion down. When the nuns broke down they were prone to bleating random words, but she had never seen one look so … horrified. As if the fragmented soul moving the body felt something. A disturbing thought arose, one that she sometimes chewed on in the dead of night: that the nuns weren't the product of any normal arcania, but a fabled undiscipline that had been systematically wiped out.

Why are you scared? she tried, but the nun was no longer looking at her. Its body was shaking as if it was trying to break itself apart from inside. *Sobweb*, Alis repeated, trying to plant herself right in the path of its eyes, but they were rolling like marbles.

The Unholy Mothers didn't feel pain, but this one was too human-looking to disregard. Alis grasped the nun's face between her hands, closed her eyes, and twisted its head.

Its neck was the texture of dry pastry. Its head broke off and the nun slumped to the floor, spilling grey powder. Alis dropped the head and wiped her hands on her legs, suppressing a shiver. She left the corpse for the cats and went back to her path.

It was disappointingly easy to break into the Librarian's office, presumably because the Librarian knew that few people were insane enough to try.

The first time Alis had stepped into the small, oak-lined office was to have a staple removed from her leg. Her flesh remembered the pain every time she crept across the threshold.

A shelf of bottles glinted like wet ice in the greylight from the window, tight-lipped and deadly, along with delicate surgical instruments and cosmetic equipment: tongs, pins, a small knife inlaid with bleeding hearts. Alis thought of Elliot for a moment before pocketing the knife. There was something compellingly awful about the moody, pissed-off vampire that stuck in her head, even though he deserved none of her brain space, let alone her charity.

She turned to the books littering the desk. They were mostly full of the Librarian's notes, like punishments paid to over-loud borrowers and observations on the taste of different papers. One contained calculations for a potion that might undo the effects of ingesting cyanide. The books lining the wall were similarly disappointing, ancient and precious, but full of obscure incantations rather than useful histories. It was possible the ones she wanted had succumbed to collapse somewhere, and were now part of the bedrock, along with Alis's chance to do something impressive for Nixie. *Not that she should get my help*.

Alis wished she wasn't so invested in someone who didn't care about her.

As she ground her teeth, her eyes stopped on a familiar greyish-pink vessel. The vessel was full with a sickly elixir that had been her first taste of punishment in the Pit. Alis remembered her jaw loosening, the rush of dizziness, the delirium as the elixir entered her bloodstream. The class had stifled their laughter as she flopped over the teacher's desk and babbled, rolling her head and laughing. He asked for her most humiliating moments, and she had talked until Nixie dragged her back to her chair.

The door handle rattled. Alis darted through the curtains over the alcove window. Her heart thundered as the Librarian glided in.

Shitshitshit.

Alis pressed into the alcove and tried to breathe. If the Librarian was starting her skincare routine, she would be here for hours. Bottles squeaked and clinked as the Librarian moved around, singing book classifications under her breath. After a few long minutes Alis's heart settled. Growing bored, she gazed at her self-inked arms, wondering what to add next. Drawing on herself was like decorating a room so it felt more like home; it was one of the few things she could control. Unlike her hair, which wouldn't stop growing. She ran her hand over the fuzz and wondered at the reflection in the windowpane, feeling the sudden, disquieting sense of unease at seeing a total stranger.

The Librarian yanked the curtain aside.

'Alis, poppet,' she crooned.

Alis flinched as the Librarian dug her fingers into Alis's elbow and worked them as if she were tenderising a piece of meat. Alis was paralysed.

She could only process the Librarian's fingers rubbing over her bones. 'Soft arms. Female.'

May you die unloved in a corner of the library where nobody finds you in all the centuries after.

'I've been waiting for you to come out, sweet creature.'

I beg that the Desecrae collapses and crushes you under its molars.

'You're finally interested in my potions,' the Librarian said, stroking Alis's right eyebrow. 'Or did you want to view the great ugliness outside?'

I'm going to burn this eyebrow off.

The Librarian twisted Alis towards the courtyard and rested her chin on top of Alis's head. Alis could see nuns fluttering on the walls of the Fifth Tower like fruit flies on a decomposing pear. They watched the arcanists and familiars and ordinary people who scurried through the seething city. She saw the great open wound of the verdant Ulcer and the Mothers that hovered around its edge, keeping the starvelings in by eating anything that came close to the edge.

'I hear Geraldin,' the Librarian murmured in her ear, pointing at the ground. 'Was it lovely being her familiar? Were you jealous when they sent the prodigy from the Academy for her to test?'

I pray that your teeth fall out so you can no longer maul your dinner, Alis thought, but the universe, in its infinite cruelty, made her look down. Geraldin moved swiftly towards the great iron gates that split the castle from the city, with her familiar, Cassia, in tow. Cassia's blonde hair was woven tightly behind her head, making her face look even more strained. Alis felt a surge of jealousy. Cassia should have been the one to suffer a wrench clamped around her tongue. Not that she would have survived it; she wasn't as strong as Alis.

Or as good at telling lies.

'There were teachers in my library that day,' the Librarian said, running her nails over Alis's shoulders. 'They said she could wrest ten times more power than you.'

I implore the library to fall on your head and crush your spine like an accordion.

'Were you afraid of her, angel?'

I entreat the universe to— No, I wasn't afraid of her!

When Alis had met Cassia in Geraldin's tower – for the first time since they had been classmates in the Pit, anyway – the girl was a rigid pillar of anger. *Another poor sad sap who doesn't want to be here*, Alis had thought. It was only later that Alis realised she had fatally underestimated Cassia.

'I remember when we used to cut out *all* familiars' tongues,' the Librarian said. 'Wyrdos couldn't do things behind your back then.'

Half of them also bled out, Alis thought. They only stopped mutilating familiars because it was a waste of resources. When she didn't react, the Librarian wrapped her fingers over Alis's cheeks and gripped hard. It would have been thrilling for Alis to reveal her secret then, just to see if the shock would finally kill the old woman. But she wouldn't risk being wrung into a nun's goblet, even if she could speak.

'Why won't you write me a note?' the Librarian hissed.

Alis had caught the Librarian's sniffing around the scraps of paper Alis left in her wake. The Librarian desperately wanted her to write *You're the mother I never had,* or *I want to be moulded in your great and terrible image*. Her prolonged silence made the Librarian dig her nails in harder, and Alis was half a second away from biting her hand before she saw Jon crossing the courtyard.

The lanky arcanist was marching in the opposite direction to Geraldin. Their paths wouldn't necessarily end in collision should one of them move, say, three inches to the right, but that would mean one of them making a concession. Taro trailed several feet behind Jon, and, apart from a mysterious limp, she looked violently well-rested considering she had been fighting for her life under the ground a few hours ago.

Geraldin smirked as they approached. Alis had seen that expression before, usually a few seconds before she did something incredibly awful. Horror clutched Alis's throat.

She knew with cold certainty that Taro was about to die.

Jon swerved at the last minute, but Geraldin had already anticipated his defeat and stepped into his path. They stood nose-to-nose with their familiars behind them. Geraldin seemed calm, but Alis could see that Jon was aggravated.

What Jon didn't notice, and what Taro couldn't see either because she was busy rolling her eyes at Jon's back, was Cassia pinching something between her thumb and forefinger: a tiny, needle-thin glint of silver.

Alis twisted away from the window and out of the Librarian's grip. She vaulted over the desk. The Librarian shrieked, but Alis was already gone. She ploughed over her own footprints in the damp carpet, burst through the library doors, and raced through the intestines of the castle. If she thought too hard about why she was running, she would have uncovered the squirming thought: *Nixie will be so disgustingly grateful that I've done this.* But even brushing against the idea made her cringe, so she ran faster instead.

The smooth stone flags squealed under her feet. Alis had never travelled at more than a casual saunter, but now she grabbed hold of the walls as she swerved around corners, sweating heavily through her robes. Nuns detached from the ceiling and dropped to the floor behind her with an awful slapping sound, but she didn't stop.

At the last corner Alis tripped over a broken flagstone and slammed into the floor, biting her tongue so hard it bled. Another *slap* behind her, then the rapid squeak of a nun dragging its feet across the stone. Alis wondered if she should abandon Taro, who was an asshole that had never given Alis a second look, and who had caused Nixie more pain than any arcanist had to their familiar.

But if Taro died the whole plan was undone. The Slaughter would go ahead and it would kill Nixie. The appropriate response to that was: *Why do you care? She was a shitty friend.*

And yet.

Alis rolled on to her back. The nun bent at the waist to collect her, its mouth open so Alis could see its jagged molars. Alis kicked it in the stomach with both feet. They crunched through something deep in the nun's robes. It scudded backwards, screeching through its teeth in a siren call to every other half-dead thing in the castle.

Alis scrambled to her feet and ran into the courtyard. She hadn't been outside in months. The air was thin and cold, the greylight blinding. She sprinted towards Cassia, her panicked brain ignoring the Mothers trickling down the walls like spiders. Cassia was the only person who didn't turn to look at her, because she was busy sidling towards Taro with the needle between her fingers.

Jon saw Alis careening towards them and threw his arms over his head. Taro goggled as Alis barrelled into Cassia and grabbed her around the waist, throwing her to the ground. Cassia tried to shove her away, but Alis grappled with her until she dropped the needle, then there was nothing else to do because the sky was black and the nuns were on top of her.

Three of them picked her up and dragged her backwards. *Do something, you ass!* Alis screamed internally at Taro, trying to communicate the strength of her fury through gritted teeth alone, but the bone disciple was unstoppably stupid.

She was moments from being disassembled. Her whole world shrank to a pinhole: the grey cobblestones, the nuns' mottled feet, Cassia's venomous stare. She shouldn't have got involved. She could literally have done nothing, and her dream of Taro vanishing would have come true. But Nixie would be unbearably grief-stricken, and she didn't want to be responsible for that.

'Stop!' Jon shrieked. At first Alis didn't realise he was talking to the nuns, and neither did they, because they dumped her on the ground and one of them straddled her chest, its knees crushing her ribs. Jon marched over the cobblestones and poked his finger into the nun's back, his voice high with indignation. 'You're bound by the Thaumaturge's crown to keep order until the Slaughter,' he said. 'This girl just derailed a plot against me. As one of the competitors, I order you to leave her!'

The nun on Alis's chest creaked its terrible head around and stared at Jon's face, which turned from red to deathly grey. He twisted his fingers together.

'Please?' he said.

The nun hissed and billowed away. Its index finger had fallen off, and its nail was caught in Alis's robes. She tore it out and threw it across the cobbles. The other nuns floated backwards gently, their eyes wobbling like dumplings in soup.

'Explain yourself,' Geraldin barked at Alis. She turned the full force of her pale eyes on her, and Alis was suddenly back in Greyspire, flinching as Geraldin thrust a book against her chest. *You're not allowed to read*, Geraldin had said. *You stole this. Now eat it.* Alis had never forgotten the taste.

Jon swooped at the needle and thrust it in Geraldin's face.

'You were going to murder my familiar.' He had recovered from his brush with the nun, and his voice was shrill with excitement. 'That's foul play!'

'There's no such thing as foul play in the Slaughter,' Geraldin snapped, swinging her leonine head towards him. 'Haven't you studied the rules, Jon?'

'I have allies everywhere,' Jon said, tossing the needle. It landed close to Alis's head, its poisoned tip gleaming. 'They are always watching, and they will *always stop you*.'

Geraldin did something Alis had never witnessed: she laughed uproariously.

'Jonathan,' she said, 'nobody's rooting for you. Come, Cassia.'

She clicked her fingers at Cassia, and they strode away. Jon vibrated with indignation. As soon as he opened his mouth Alis could tell he was going to say something stupid. She just hadn't counted on just how bad it would be.

'I want a duel!' he screamed.

When Geraldin turned back, there was so much frost in her expression that Alis felt her blood cool. She got up slowly, trying not to draw attention to herself. It might not be too late to creep back to the library without them noticing her.

'You *have* been studying the rules,' she said.

'Because I'm sick of you using them against me, you bureaucratic hag. You can't decline. If you refuse, I can cut your familiar three times. I might go for the jugular.'

Geraldin smiled.

'Very well,' she said. 'I won't be accused of not following the law. Name the time and the place.'

'Wait.' Jon appeared to panic, and it took a moment for him to pull himself together. 'According to *the law*, I can choose someone to fight for me.'

Alis saw Taro pinch the bridge of her nose and felt something that almost bordered on sympathy for her.

'And your choice is?' Geraldin said, raising an eyebrow.

'Taro.'

Taro caught Alis's eye and mimed stabbing herself in the throat. It was incredible how her capacity for bad humour never failed.

'You're wasting a good familiar,' Geraldin said mildly.

'She'll tear you in half!'

'Not if I also use a proxy.' Cassia's face hadn't changed, but Alis could feel the hatred simmering behind her eyes. Alis hoped it burned her from the inside out.

'Good luck,' Jon scoffed. 'You won't get as far as the door of the Fifth Tower without your familiar.'

'You mean Cassia? I'm not as reckless with my possessions as you are, Jon.'

Alis felt thorns prickling at the back of her neck. She edged away, moving as slowly as the shadow of the sun.

'Who, then?' Jon said. Geraldin flicked her gaze up. It was like being slapped.

'Alis.'

Alis blazed so violently that Geraldin should have been swallowed by the blast. *May the nuns tear your face off*, she screamed, but the curse was lost in a storm of internal noise. *May the sun—*

'I know how furious you were when Cassia took your spot as my familiar,' Geraldin said, sweeping her eyes over Alis, stripping her down. 'Here's your chance to show me that I was wrong, and you're not useless. Do you accept?' She spoke calmly. As though she hadn't ordered Alis's death once. As though Alis even had a choice in the matter.

I beg that a mirror sucks your arcania up and twists you into a knot.

Alis had long suspected that Geraldin was annoyed by her escape to the library. She should have bled to death on a dungeon floor instead. The Librarian had done everything officially, with rubber stamps and gold coins, so Geraldin hadn't been able to protest. This was her way of finishing Alis off.

She expected Alis to protest. To try to find a way out. But Geraldin underestimated how strong Alis was, just as she always had. Alis had eaten that book as punishment, and she had done it whilst looking Geraldin in the eye, until even the arcanist flinched at her gaze. And Alis would take her revenge by surviving again.

If Taro got beaten up in the process, that was just a bonus.

'Do you accept?' Geraldin repeated, with a truly heinous grin.

There was something else that Geraldin hadn't accounted for. She might have been a stickler for the rules, which she wielded to get her own way, but Alis had learned all the same things. Everything Geraldin read, Alis had read too. The stone arcanist assumed it all flew over her familiar's head, but Alis was both very clever and extremely petty.

Alis reached into her pocket and withdrew the knife she had stolen from the Librarian's office. Looking into Geraldin's eyes, she drew the blade along the back of her index finger.

A sharp red line bloomed. She held the knife out to Geraldin. Geraldin took the knife and opened her skin with a hesitation so slight she almost, but not quite, hid it.

'You little bitch,' Geraldin murmured as they pressed their fingers together. Alis pretended not to hear. The ceremony was old and pointless, but she knew how much Geraldin hated blood, and equally how impossible it would be for her to refuse the ritual without the whole nomination falling apart.

'I'm not doing that,' Jon said quickly. 'Taro's my familiar, so I don't need to.'

Alis closed her fist, dripping her blood on the ground.

'We'll do it in the Fighting Hall,' Jon said. 'They'll keep attacking each other until one of them loses. Any physical weapon allowed.' There was a sick joke in Alis having to bludgeon Taro after saving her life. The universe had a dark sense of humour. 'Be there at noon, or forfeit and pay the price.'

He grabbed Taro by the shoulders and steered her away. Alis watched as the nuns rustled on the walls, as restless as flies, their tongues flickering at the promise of violence.

Nine

Twenty-one hours until the Slaughter

The room in which Taro intended to kick Alis's arse was deliciously macabre. The ceiling was a cosmic expanse of skulls, the door frames were studded with tasteful whorls of teeth, and the windows had shutters made of skilfully carved bone. Discreet grooves in the floor led to gutters at the sides of the room. At one end was a rotting canopy for the audience to stand under should they wish to avoid being spattered. A large bone-and-glass chandelier shivered on the ceiling, strangled by black ivy and hanging by a thread of rusted chain. Suits of armour slumped against the walls, each bearing an assortment of ancient weaponry. The room was a heady mix of elegant and foul.

'I have a mirror in my pocket,' Jon murmured to Taro. 'I'll get it out when you start. If Geraldin tries to use arcania she'll blow herself up.'

Knowing Jon's luck, he was more likely to release a violent maleficent from the netherworld on his face. If Jon weren't gripping Taro by the shoulders, and the clock on her back weren't making her distinctly aware of her own mortality, Taro would have enjoyed that image.

Kellan had come to watch the fight, his thin half-moon glasses on his nose so he could see better. This gave him the air of a kindly scholar, except his hand was on the back of Nixie's neck as if he was ready to snap it. Taro wanted to rip it off and break his fingers.

Only a minute pulse under Nixie's left eye suggested she wasn't calm. It made Taro melt inside, seeing how worried she was, but honestly, Alis had the muscle mass of a limpet. *Obviously* Taro was going to win. Then they could both get up, dust themselves down, and totter back to their respective holes in Blackspire and the worm-ridden library and continue their plot to destroy the patriarchy, yeah?

'She'll forfeit in a minute,' Jon muttered, drumming his fingers against Taro's shoulder.

Alis was late. The wait was winding up the spectators, mostly high-ranking bone and stone arcanists. The two disciplines leered at each other from opposite sides of the room, minutes away from starting a fight themselves. Even Malachi and Tamsin Redborn had wormed their way in with their arcanist, Saul. Only Morgan was separate, lounging on an ancient couch at the end of the room, apparently nursing a hangover. When Taro caught Morgan's eye he smiled brilliantly. If Taro ever developed an interest in men, she would one hundred per cent jump his bones.

'Will it slow you down?' Jon said. 'Your … toe?'

It was clear that naming any of Taro's appendages made Jon deeply uncomfortable. It had been worse for Taro; whipping her sock off and showing him the broken digit on her naked right foot almost killed her. But getting him to perform arcanical surgery was the only way she could conceivably have an aura of bone arcania hanging around her. She had to mask the deeply illegal, super-arcanical tooth she had in her pocket somehow. Plus, the look on his face had almost been worth slamming her toe in the door for.

She wriggled her foot in affirmation, and Jon looked hugely relieved.

Geraldin flexed her fingers. She had arrived at the stroke of midday, materialising at the door without so much as a glance at her pocket watch, with Cassia two steps behind her. She was clearly aggrieved by Alis's lateness. The ex-stone disciple had seconds to arrive before the match was forfeit.

Shame. Taro had been looking forward to being the centre of attention.

The doors at the end of the hall swung open. Alis sauntered in, exquisitely bored. Jon dug his fingers into Taro's shoulder blades as half the audience bristled with unrestrained hostility.

'Don't mess this up,' he murmured. 'I can't afford to go into the Slaughter with you maimed.'

Taro was immediately tempted to impale herself on a spike.

Jon shoved Taro into the middle of the floor, and the stone arcanists laughed as she staggered over the blood gutters. Alis stepped into the circle with an expression that suggested this duel was absolutely not worth her time.

Piece of piss, Taro thought, pretending not to be aggravated by Jon's absolute incompetence. *I'll just knock her down and sit on her until she stops struggling.*

'Who will arbitrate?' Malachi asked, having granted himself authority of the room. 'It must be someone who holds no stake in the outcome.'

Taro saw Jon open and quickly shut his mouth.

'Nobody?' Malachi said. 'If I may ...' he pushed his blond hair back in a gesture that was undeniably Morgan-esque. Unfortunately, unlike his son, he had the facial bone structure of a frying pan. 'It's the least I can do as a humble servant of Fourspires, and a devout slave to the new thaumaturge ... whoever they may be.'

'Announce the rules,' Geraldin said. Malachi gave her a freezingly polite smile.

'Of course,' he said, only *Of course* sounded like *Go choke on your tonsils.* 'One: arcanists will not help their fighters.' *Fat chance Jon would risk a hangnail for me*, Taro thought. 'Two: any manner of fighting is allowed, as long as it does not touch the audience.' Whacking Jon was out of the question, then. 'Three: the winner chooses their prize.'

Taro met Alis's eyes, which were deep and cold with something that should have been nervousness but was troublingly mercenary. Taro winked. *Don't worry, you idiot. I'm not really going to hurt you.*

'Four,' Geraldin said. Kellan steepled his fingers in rare and wicked delight. 'There are four rules. The fight ends when only the victor is left standing.'

Taro blinked. The last person standing didn't mean the last person alive, right? They weren't actually expected to *kill* each other?

Malachi gave the smallest scrap of an insolent bow.

'Begin.'

Taro and Alis circled each other. Suddenly Taro wasn't sure what to do. Should she just ... reach out and slap Alis? She had always envisioned herself being great in a fight, but she didn't officially know how to make a fist. What if she hurt her knuckles?

'Stop playing around,' Jon hissed.

'This is awkward,' Morgan said.

Taro raised her hands and shuffled towards Alis.

'Tarenteeno,' Jon raged. 'You delinquent dishrag, do something—'

Taro shoved Alis in the chest. The girl was wafer-light and went down like a domino. Taro plunked herself on Alis's legs and pinned her arms down, and, as the watching bone arcanists laughed, she lowered her mouth to Alis's ear.

'I'm going to hit you now, so close your eyes and groan, OK? Nixie can fix you up with some poultice later.' Then, her spite blooming under Alis's sneer, because Nixie was hers, and hers alone: 'You guys know each other, right?'

Alis's eyes narrowed. Taro drew her fist back, but before she could land a blow Alis shoved her in the stomach so hard she toppled sideways.

Taro clutched herself, stuck between shock and outrage. She knew she could just stay on the floor – she didn't care about winning for Jon, did she? – but something about Alis's brazen hatred made Taro boil. Alis stood up and brushed herself down, which made the stone arcanists titter.

She really thinks I don't know how weird she is over Nixie, the freak—

She grabbed Alis's ankle and brought her down too. Morgan hooted with laughter and clapped. Alis instinctively tried to kick Taro in the face, but Taro dodged and jumped to her feet. She put her foot on Alis's back, this time applying more pressure than was strictly necessary. Her eyes searched for Nixie, whose face was a silent mask of horror. Was she scared for Taro, or was she worried for the little weed under Taro's foot?

'I win,' Jon yelped. 'I get the pr—'

Alis punched Taro in the back of the knee. White-hot fire bloomed through Taro's patella as she hit the stone, but she had enough presence of mind to swipe for Alis's nose. She missed, but she saw the bitter expression on the library goblin's face and felt a great wave of contemptuous pity. It might have been enough to stop her from fighting if Alis hadn't immediately backhanded her, leading to delighted yelps from Morgan and jeers from everyone else. Taro grabbed Alis's wrist and twisted so hard the girl's eyes watered.

She could have stopped there, but Taro would be the first to admit she was an ass.

'I know you hate my guts,' Taro hissed, shielding her mouth with her hand while pretending that she was trying to twist Alis's ear off. 'But I didn't *steal* Nixie. She just liked me more—'

Alis punched her. It was a fantastic blow, the kind that would have made Taro scream with delight had she done it to another person – Jon, say – but she felt her brains slamming against the back of her cranium. It took all of Taro's willpower not to upchuck on the floor, and even that was only possible because Jon hadn't bothered to feed her today.

The part of her brain that dealt with self-preservation told her to stay down, but her body was taking orders from an idiot. She creaked to her feet, her head pounding. Alis was walking away. In another life Taro would have produced a fantastic one-liner, the kind that people would repeat at parties, but as her wit was entirely wasted in this shitty castle, she did the next best thing.

She took her right shoe off and threw it at Alis's head.

It landed squarely on the back of her weirdly shaved skull. Taro could have sworn she heard a gasp. Alis turned around, her face furiously white, and Taro grinned in a way she knew was antagonistic as hell.

Alis flew at her. Taro shoved her away ungracefully, almost throwing her over again, but Alis regained her footing and bounced back. As the girl lunged, Taro saw an unexpected flash of black ink on her arms, a nest of vipers and something that looked like a giant boat and the splayed pages of a book. Taro faltered, which gave Alis enough time to grab her neck and shove her to the floor.

This wasn't how it was meant to go at all.

Alis had a madly tight grip. Taro forced her head sideways so she could breathe. Through the pink clouds in front of her eyes, she saw a plaque carved into the floor. Her brain, which always hyperactively jumped to the least important thing in the room, decided that now was the time to develop laser-sharp focus on the plaque.

Praise be to the head arcanists under Sobweb who stopped the path of evil, and to whom this Hall is dedicated. Dagmar of Blackspire. Sabine of Greyspire. Gerold of Greenspire. ~~Aldous of Redspire~~.

The last name had an angry line gouged through it, but Taro was more bothered by Dagmar, who had set the skeleton to guard the chapel. If Dagmar was one of the head arcanists during Sobweb's reign, when the curse was laid by that jealous knob Hallow Myre, why had he hidden the curse-lifting skull in the chapel? If he really wanted to undo the *curse on your tits Alis, what the fu—*

Alis had let go too soon, so Taro rolled across the floor, stupidly and inelegantly, until she came up against Jon's feet. He kicked her back into the circle, hissing, 'Don't embarrass me, Taro,' then she was in Alis's grasp again. It turned out that even though Alis looked as though she had all the sturdiness of a meringue, she was quite hench under her robes, and it was Taro, actually, who had the physical integrity of a baked confection rather than, as she had assumed, the strength and speed of a motherfucking dragon—

Taro went limp.

If she was the weaker one, she was going to embrace it. She was going to be the most pathetic piece of shit Fourspires had ever seen. The city hadn't known anything like her. Neither had Alis, apparently, because she immediately dropped Taro. Nixie winced, possibly because she knew how Taro's mind worked.

Surprise, bitch, I'm not dead!

Taro jumped to her feet and ran towards Jon. He yelped and dived out of the way, but she wasn't aiming for her sack-of-shit arcanist, or any of his leering compatriots. She was going for the table at the end of the Fighting Hall, the one covered in tarnished silver and the remains of whatever blood-spattered celebratory feast had been held during the last fight a trillion years ago.

'Disqualification,' Malachi called over the rising voices.

'The rules don't say you can't leave the circle,' Geraldin said. Even when it didn't suit her, she couldn't bear not to correct him.

Taro grabbed a silver bowl from the table and turned back to Alis. The spectators automatically parted, finally looking uncertain, leaving a long corridor between her and her opponent. Except now Alis had something in her hands too, some kind of bronze staff with cobwebs fluttering from it. A statue behind her brandished its empty fists.

Alis walked towards her. Taro could see that her hands were trembling. She automatically raised the bowl to her chest, using it as a shield. It wasn't as great an idea as she'd thought, because a) the bowl wasn't that big and b) it turned out that silver was *really heavy.* But that didn't matter, did it, because this was all a show, right? Alis might beat her up a bit, but she wouldn't actually try to stave Taro's head in, haha, that would be really funny—

Oomph.

Taro crumbled. Alis stood over her with the dusty staff in her hands. She looked shocked at herself, but not as shocked as she should have, considering she'd almost snapped Taro's legs in half. Taro gaped at her. Alis gaped back, then looked down at the sceptre, and at Taro again.

Then her eyes narrowed, and she raised the sceptre once more. Her hands were no longer trembling.

Taro hurled the silver bowl at Alis's legs. Alis went down like a stone, and when she rose again she had honest-to-arcania murder in her eyes.

Taro scrambled to her feet. Alis swiped a splintered chair. Taro jabbed a fist at her, driving her back into the circle, until Alis realised Taro wasn't going to hit her and jabbed back with the chair legs stuck out in front of her. The audience closed around them as they circled each other, their eyes locked together, breathing hard. The silence was thick and expectant.

What are you doing? Taro wanted to scream. *We can't actually hurt each other, you lunatic. We're on the same side, remember?*

Alis charged.

As Taro weakly raised her hands she realised this was her last chance to tell Nixie everything, to remove the sharp barb of guilt before she went to hell, even if it meant yelling her confession across the room. The words crouched on her tongue: *I ripped your freedom away, and it was heinous of me, but I would destroy your life every day to keep you in my sight.* She opened her mouth—

And the chandelier fell.

Glass and bone spattered violently. The room reverberated with the three-ton catastrophe. Taro lowered her hands, electrified by the knife-sharp splinters bristling on her skin.

Alis was splayed on the floor, her robes like a puddle of ink, her head turned crookedly to the side. One of the arms of the chandelier, a twisted femur, had caught her on the back of the head.

'Taro wins!' Jon shouted. His fellow bone arcanists whooped and clapped like inappropriately bloodthirsty children. Jon strode over to Taro and, horror of horrors, *squeezed her shoulders* as though she was the champion of a wrestling match.

'The other one?' Malachi said.

The stone arcanists were already shoving through the doors, unwilling to pick Alis up or even look at her. To do that would be to claim responsibility for the body. Taro felt a hot wave of sickness.

She forced herself to move. Crunched lightly over the floor. Lowered herself and gently placed her fingers over Alis's mouth.

Alis was alive. Stone-cold unconscious, but respiring. Taro could see, now she was close, that the chandelier had only glanced off Alis's back. With luck she would only have a massive skull-ache in the morning. Which she completely deserved, by the way.

Everyone watched Taro rise. It was simultaneously the most terrifying and powerful moment of her life. She adopted what she hoped was a suitably sombre expression and drew her finger across her throat.

'Dead!' Jon shrieked.

'Killed by a chandelier, not your familiar,' Morgan pointed out.

'I'll allow it,' Malachi said.

Jon's triumph was embarrassingly palpable. 'I choose a prize,' he said. 'I want—'

'Actually,' Geraldin said, her voice as cold as an Unholy Mother's arse, 'it's your familiar's prize.'

Taro felt the ground wobble. *A prize.*

'There's nothing she wants,' Jon said.

'Nonetheless.'

Taro could have anything she wanted. She could have a cake the size of her head, or get a necropolis named after her. But instead …

God, I'm such a good person.

She strode over to Cassia. The people on either side sprang away from her. Even Geraldin stepped back. Alarm dawned on Cassia's face.

Taro was three steps away, then two, then she was right in front of Cassia, and—

Before the stone disciple could move, Taro knocked her to the ground with a single blow.

Cassia was no Alis. She folded like a towel and stayed there. Taro dropped to her knees and, her voice muffled by Morgan's explosive laugh, murmured: 'Tell me where Greyspire's mascot is. The real thing. It's a cube of stone, right? Is it in your tower?'

Cassia gawped. Maybe she thought Taro was joking. Taro raised her fist again, and Cassia quickly shook her head.

'It's not a cube,' she whimpered. 'It's a die. But it's not real. And we don't have it.'

Taro lowered her fist. It had been a long shot. If the relic was in Greyspire, Alis probably would have known about it. But she was still disappointed.

'Bitch,' Cassia hissed as Taro stood up, and then it was over, and Jon was dragging her away.

'You should have gone for Morgan's familiar, you idiot,' he said.

Taro nodded, but she wasn't really listening. *A die.* Where the hell were they going to find something that small before the competition began? They had more chance of Alis standing up and making a public speech.

On which note.

'Leave the body,' Malachi said to the servants at the side of the room. 'I'll send the nuns to dispose of her. The Librarian will be informed.'

Taro threw a look over her shoulder, but there was nothing she could do except pray the stone disciple woke up before she was devoured by nuns. Knowing Alis, if she did end up expiring, she would refuse to surrender her eternal soul and cling to the netherworld just so she could haunt Taro.

Yeah. Alis would be OK.

But finding a *die* in the labyrinthine castle? The raw flesh on Taro's back itched as the hand of the clock scraped closer to the Slaughter.

Twenty hours.

They were screwed.

Ten

Twelve hours until the Slaughter

Elliot slammed his foot into the door of the Redborns' quarters, putting the full weight of his fury behind it.

The door barely shivered. He twisted and slammed his shoulder into the wood instead, hissing through gritted teeth as new bruises were born. But the Redborns had sealed him in their rooms as thoroughly as a grave keeper seals a tomb. He couldn't use arcania on the lock, because Malachi and Tamsin would sniff it the moment they returned from slinking around the castle, where they were looking for opportunities to exonerate themselves from the Thaumaturge's murder. Meanwhile Elliot, who was little more than luggage, had been tossed in here to rot.

Every second he was stuck in the Redborns' purloined rooms, Elliot lost a chance to find the necklace. Morgan's offer to return it if Elliot became his familiar hadn't yet been fulfilled, and Elliot was sick with paranoia that it had all been a twisted joke. No. If he wanted to take his life back, he had to do it himself.

Elliot rested his head against the door, his heart fluttering with pathetic exhaustion. Deep evening shadows draped over him as the fireplace crackled.

The shadows moved. Someone was behind him.

Elliot didn't have time to turn before they clamped a hand over his shoulder. Elliot choked, his usual instinct to fight dying in a deep swell of panic. Someone had grasped his shoulder like this before. The memory bulged through the fissures in his brain, and it was more real than the door in front of him.

His mother grasped his shoulders, her nails pressing deep as someone howled on the other side of the wall: Your boy killed my daughter.

Elliot cowered by his mother's side, his confession stuck in his throat. When he had tried to heal the girl with sepsis he had known she was beyond help, but he'd always been so desperate to please that he couldn't turn anyone down. His parents needed the money, and the girl's parents needed their child. They all needed him. As the girl's father screamed, telling everyone in the street exactly what Elliot did in his spare time, threatening to call the nuns, his mother gouged her fingers deeper into his bones. Get in the wooden chest, *she said.* Take your knife and don't move. The Mothers will come.

Elliot gasped for air. His mind reconnected with his body and forced him back into the Redborns' room, into the cold and loveless now. He was slumped against the door. He'd been swallowed by that memory before, but it was getting harder to climb out. His skin was cold with sweat, his hands shaking. He had to remember that it was over now. The worst had already happened: he had been betrayed and torn from his parents, and the only thing he needed to do now was survive.

Someone huffed and shook his shoulder again.

This was real.

Elliot turned and swung his fist into their collarbone, and as they tried to punch him in return he blindly wrestled them to the floor. He expected more of a fight, but the person under his knees – he was sitting on them – had gone still. He looked at the blood-streaked face, the robes peppered with glass. *Alis.* A bruise was forming on her neck, and the top of her head was covered in scratches. Despite her ragged appearance and the fact that she was pinned to the mouldering rug, Alis's lips were quirked with disdain.

Elliot jumped up and backed away, his face burning.

'How did you get in?' he demanded, wanting something – anything – to make them both forget that he had more or less straddled her. 'There's only one door.'

Alis gave him a look that meant *Evidently not, you simpleton*, and got up. Elliot flexed his aching hand.

'What do you want?' he snarled. 'Here to beg me for help again?'

Alis was in front of him in half a second. She grabbed his jaw with surprising strength and forced him to look at her. Her tightening hand said, *Say that again.* Elliot sneered.

'Does it hurt?' he said through clenched teeth. 'Not being able to speak?'

Alis dug her nails into his face before releasing him. The pencil appeared in her hand.

Does it hurt, she wrote, *being a cursed insomniac?*

Elliot faltered.

I've seen sleep deprivation before, she scribbled. *You're barely functioning. What a weird thing to be cursed by.*

She flicked the scrap of paper at him and sauntered to Malachi's makeshift office. Elliot crumpled the paper and stalked after her.

It had taken mere hours for Malachi to stock the room with quills and parchment and ink. He was embedded like a tick; he meant to stay after his son was crowned. Alis leaned on the desk and studied Elliot.

'You're a mess,' Elliot said, for want of a better insult.

Alis removed a pre-prepared scrap of paper from her sleeve and shoved it at him.

I knew you would be too stubborn to ask what happened. I was forced to duel for Geraldin. I got beaten up and crushed by a chandelier. Taro told everyone I was dead. I spent three hours hiding while the nuns looked for my body.

Elliot read it twice. His chronic headache made it difficult to keep the words straight.

'Why are you here?' he said finally.

Alis stared at him deadpan, perfectly communicating that his response was catastrophically underwhelming, before picking up her pencil.

To make sure you're still going to help us.

They all knew they were screwed without him. Elliot felt a faint thrill that they so desperately needed him. Just like people had when he was a kid. Alis reached into her pocket and dropped a bag of purple sweets on the desk, along with another note she had already written.

I want you to hex these.

Elliot picked the bag up. The sweets were old and fluffy and smelled like rotting flowers. Alis tapped the last note. Elliot flipped it over.

Anticipated questions:

Q: Why should I do this?

A: Because I came to Morgan's tower with you, which was very kind.

Q: Why do you want them hexed?

A: Revenge.

Q: What kind of hex?

A: I will accept vomiting, rash or a semi-violent trapped spirit. Nothing deadly.

Elliot smiled faintly. He could give her what she wanted in a second, but given her lack of gratitude, he wouldn't make it easy.

'Ask Nixie. You're clearly infatuated with her. That's why you're helping her, right?'

Alis's face crumpled with disgust. Her scrawl was angry and almost illegible.

I like Nixie even less than I like you.

Elliot snorted at her blatant lie. It helped cover the tiny twinge of hurt he felt; as if he should care what his old classmate felt, who had barely exchanged one word with him even when she could speak.

'I don't like you either. You're a lost girl who got her tongue cut out and thinks it makes her interesting.' Alis flinched at the word *girl.*

Elliot, tasting victory, leaned forward. Stone disciples hated blood disciples, so he would give her exactly what she expected from his kind. 'Was there a lot of blood?'

This is why you never had friends, she scribbled viciously.

'I had friends.' But she was still writing.

Everyone thought you were weird. Instead of talking to people you carved things with that stupid knife. You cried when they took it away.

'I didn't,' he hissed. 'And I don't need friends.'

He read Alis's scrawl upside down as it formed.

Because you're oh-so-damaged and moody? You're a walking cliché.

'I thought you wanted my help,' he snapped.

She looked at him long and hard before reluctantly nodding.

'Fine,' he said magnanimously.

Alis shoved the bag at him. Elliot uncorked one of Malachi's blood vials, dipped his thumb in, and touched his bloody thumbprint to each of the sweets.

He was so exhausted he could barely stand, but he refused to fail in front of a mere librarian's assistant. He dug through his frayed memories for a sickness that he could put into the sweets, found the remnants of an incantation, and put his finger in the vial again. His skull pulsed, but he forced himself to ignore his instincts of self-preservation with the difficulty of swallowing a glass of somebody else's phlegm. He began wresting, and choked out the three syllables before tipping over and hitting his head on the desk.

When he woke up a few dark, sticky seconds later, he clawed for the remnants of his blackout. But the nauseating fuzz slipped away like a curtain being pulled away from a bright window.

Alis had dropped to her haunches and was studying him. She flicked a note at him. *It was too much for you.*

'Too much for *me*? You're the one who fainted in the chapel because wresting was too much.'

Alis coloured, red splotches growing on her cheeks. She suddenly looked dangerous.

I collapsed, she wrote, *because I haven't wrested for years.* Her hand faltered as she dug for words, and Elliot found himself holding his breath until it moved again. *But you have no idea what I can do.*

'Is this how you say "thanks"?' He pulled himself up with effort. 'You needed me.'

Alis sucked her cheeks in, as though she was seriously considering hitting him. Then, to his surprise, she fished something from her pocket. A tiny penknife. Blunt, notch-edged, with an ugly motif of bleeding hearts. There was a scrap of paper wrapped around it.

Payment for the hex, it said. In smaller letters, underneath: *No catch. But maybe doing something you enjoy will make you less unbearable.*

'I don't want it,' he said. Alis dropped the knife on the desk.

Just find your curse key, Elliot.

She swiped the paper bag from the desk and left.

'How did you get in?' he demanded. His hands clung to the desk even as he commanded himself to march after her. 'Tell me!' When he finally mastered his legs and strode into the drawing room, she was gone.

Was he completely broken? Were his intrusive memories now intrusive hallucinations? His toe nudged the screwed-up notes on the floor, but he was terrified that the paper might be blank. He hurled them into the fireplace.

The knife.

Elliot slowly walked back to the office. The knife fitted neatly in his palm as he gently screwed the point of the blade into the desk. He had almost forgotten the satisfaction he'd once felt from making shapes in wood. Somehow, Alis had remembered. Elliot didn't know if he felt exposed or grateful. Either way, he hated her for it.

A key turned in the outer door. Elliot froze. There was a moment of silence before it creaked open with deliberate slowness, followed by the gentle patter of claws clicking against wood.

Elliot turned, careful not to make a sound. The door to the Redborns' quarters was open, revealing the slick throat of the castle. Malachi's key was swinging from the lock.

Elliot already knew who it would be.

Morgan lounged against one of the four bedposts in his parents' bedroom, flicking an exquisitely decorated dagger between his fingers. All two hundred pounds of his coiled-up killing machine, the leopard Peridot, lay by his side.

'Hello,' Morgan said pleasantly. 'I stole the key from my father. He was busy watching your friends fight.'

Elliot recalled the glass peppering Alis's arms. He chose not to answer, and instead leaned against the wall himself, his arms folded. Unbothered. Not the least bit interested.

'Don't worry,' Morgan added, his eyes trailing over Elliot's face then, with insolent slowness, down his body. 'My father won't mind. Stealing things is a Redborn tradition. One of my ancestors betrayed the whole of Fourspires for the Thaumaturge's crown.'

Elliot attempted a lazy smile. 'I wasn't worried,' he said.

'No?' Morgan tilted his head, his hair brushing his mouth as it swung over his face. Not that Elliot was looking at his mouth. 'You should be worried by *me*.' Morgan let his eyes settle on Elliot's midriff, just long enough that Elliot shivered. Morgan saw this and grinned, as though Elliot had given him exactly what he wanted. 'But I'm not here to deliver threats. You wanted proof that I really want you as my familiar. I have it.'

'I don't see anything,' Elliot said, as flatly as he could considering the hitch in his breath.

'It's coming in a minute.' Morgan waved the dagger. 'By the way. I got bored this morning and played with your necklace. It's well cursed. Completely unbreakable.'

He dipped his hand into his pocket and withdrew a gold chain.

Elliot couldn't hear anything above his roaring pulse. The unmistakable pendant swung in the air, its enamelled eye wide, Elliot's own blood dancing behind the glass of its sclera. Every fibre of Elliot's being screamed at him to grab it, but showing his desperation could be catastrophic.

'You look pale,' Morgan said, tilting his head. 'Do you want it? You could take it. But if you're not fast enough, I'll stamp on it.'

Elliot's desire to snatch the necklace choked him. He would have gouged his heart out to put it around his neck. But he didn't think Morgan was bluffing.

'You don't want to try?' Morgan leaned forward with the necklace. The gold pendant bumped against Elliot's chin. He trailed it over Elliot's lips, his nose, his forehead. Elliot forced himself not to breathe, scared that even catching the scent of the necklace would break him.

Monster.

When he was able to speak, his voice was hoarse.

'Why are you here, Morgan?'

Morgan pulled his hand back and pocketed the necklace, looking disappointed.

'What's so bad about being awake?' he said, as though he hadn't just tortured Elliot. 'You could be doing things so much more carnally interesting than sleeping.'

They all knew about Morgan's proclivities. It hadn't just been his old familiar, Rhys; Morgan was famous for vanishing from the castle and not coming back until morning. The implication was clear in the way Morgan angled his body towards Elliot, the way his gaze lingered on Elliot's face. Elliot imagined leaning in to the small gap between them, and the part of him that still desired, that hadn't been crushed by his exhaustion, glimmered in his core.

'It's excruciating,' Elliot said softly. Morgan's eyes widened by a fraction, and Elliot smiled. 'Not sleeping, I mean. My body is killing me.'

Elliot imagined reaching out and running his thumb over Morgan's lips. He knew Morgan would allow it. The rush of power almost swept his headache away.

'I'm fascinated by you,' Morgan said. He dropped back, lounging against the bedpost again, hands clasped in a grotesque parody of innocence. The room breathed again. 'Anyway. Your gift. I thought about it for *ages*. I said: what would prove to Elliot how much I want him? What would make him trust that I won't feed him to the nuns?' He glanced at the door. 'Here it is.'

Saul strode into the Redborns' chambers. His shadow clawed at the bedroom door.

'Morgan?' he said. His voice was a mix of exaggerated obsequiousness and barely hidden dislike. 'I have the books you demanded. Except for the ones you clearly made up.'

Morgan winked, and Elliot knew what he was saying. He hesitated for only a second.

'Come in, Saul,' Elliot said.

The arcanist spidered into the doorway. When he realised the voice was Elliot's, who he had never heard speak, he choked.

'Cousin!' Morgan said delightedly. 'Can we help you?'

Saul's eyes travelled between Morgan and Elliot. He looked as if he wanted the floor to open and suck him into the heart of the mountain.

'Are you ... *fraternising* ... with my property?' he said, after an intensely uncomfortable pause.

'We were just having a chat,' Morgan said.

'He's not allowed to talk!'

'Seems like a stupid rule to me,' Morgan said. He idly drew a vial of blood from his pocket and played with the cork. 'Traditionally we don't let them talk because we don't want them uttering spells. But I can only imagine that it makes them very angry.'

Saul's mouth opened and shut a few times. He tried again.

'Your parents will be back—'

'I don't care,' Morgan said. 'I'm more interested in you.'

He flipped the lid off the vial and languidly poured blood into his palm. A deeply primal fear raised the hairs on the back of Elliot's neck.

'Do you know I've always loathed you, Saul?' Morgan said casually. 'I mean, *really.* You were the worst cousin. Have you ever found anything likeable in him, Elliot?'

This was a test. There was only one answer.

'No,' Elliot said.

'Shame,' Morgan said.

He drew his fist back so fast he sprayed the walls with blood. Morgan screamed an incantation, and Elliot didn't have time to parse the spell before Saul was slammed into the wall. Sticky red ropes bound Saul's arms to his sides, and a large black clot bulged between his teeth. His eyes flickered as he screeched through his own saliva.

'Did you see that?' Morgan shrieked, turning wildly to Elliot. 'I wrested!' The blood on his fist had already dried and cracked like glaze in a fire. He clutched his arm as though it burned. He could have killed himself. 'If you have arcanical ability you can wrest *and* shape it, yes? You've certainly done both. It's only tradition that decrees we do one or the other. I tried it the other day.'

Elliot tried not to appear shocked.

'If you can do that,' he said, his mouth dry, 'why do you need me?'

'Because wresting is horrible,' Morgan said. 'It feels like my skeleton is turning inside out. I would much rather you be in pain than me.' He smiled terribly. 'And now you know what I'm capable of, I doubt you'll betray me.'

Saul fell silent. He only just seemed to understand what was happening. Elliot looked his arcanist up and down, expecting to feel a fraction of pity, and finding none. He turned to Morgan, who was watching him intently. Waiting.

'Is that all you can do?' Elliot said.

He didn't know why he pushed Morgan. Maybe to see how far the blood arcanist would go. Or because Elliot knew exactly how far he could go, and he wanted to hasten it.

Morgan crushed the vial in his fist. It cut into his hand, its contents mixing with his own blood as he spat his incantation. The spell was short and barbaric. Saul jerked as something ruptured. He slumped sideways and heaved once, twice, then went still.

Peridot pattered over and sniffed Saul's outflung hand, deciding whether he was worth eating. Elliot instinctively turned away. He wanted to feel something over Saul's death, but he only experienced a bleak numbness.

'So, you'll be my familiar?' Morgan said, as though he hadn't just murdered his cousin. 'You can refuse and go back to my parents' service, but I think they might be quite furious. And I've already let my last familiar go, so it would be *very annoying*.'

This brought Elliot back to himself.

'You killed your familiar?'

'No!' Morgan said, affronted. 'I threw him into the street and gave him a five-minute head start before telling the nuns.' He gave no indication that he was joking. 'What's your answer, Elliot?'

Elliot fixed his eyes on Morgan's bloodied hand and the glittering shards of glass in his palm. He only pretended to think about the decision. He had known the answer since the first time Morgan had smiled at him.

It was easy to turn his back on Alis and Nixie and Taro. Aside from when it froze his tongue on a killing spell, Elliot's conscience rarely bothered him. The supposed moral good in helping them was nothing weighed against what he would gain: the oblivion of sleep and the relief it would give his tortured mind.

Elliot deserved this.

'I'll know if you're about to double-cross me,' Morgan added. 'And I'll make it hurt.'

Elliot knew his answer, but in this last moment, this knife edge before he verbalised his decision, there was still a scrap of power in his hands. He could delight or disappoint with a single word. Elliot held it in his mouth. Tasted it. He tilted his head, regarding Morgan with utter nakedness as the blood arcanist held his breath. The world was still.

'Yes,' Elliot said.

Morgan's shoulders loosened, and his swagger was back.

'Say it with some ceremony, you gorgeous idiot,' he said. 'Let the tower know what it needs to do.'

'All right. I am yours.'

'More.'

'I belong to you.'

'You have to mean it, Elliot!'

Elliot stepped closer to Morgan, and the blood arcanist clutched himself delightedly.

'I submit to being used by you,' Elliot said. He could see the want in Morgan's eyes, and it was only half to do with Elliot's power; it was also *this*, having Elliot at his mercy, body and mind. The twisted desire struck something in Elliot too. It made him ache. 'I put my life and my body in your hands. Use my power to your own ends.' He dropped to his knees sarcastically, and Morgan clapped gleefully. 'I give you the only thing I have ever called my own. I do it willingly and I suffer gladly, and if you ask for my last drop of blood I will squeeze it from my finger and tip it into your mouth, because you are my master.' He looked up and raised a smirk. 'Enough?'

Morgan laughed.

'I accept!'

Morgan's lips had barely parted before Elliot felt a searing pain on his back. It radiated from the middle of his spine, as though someone had plunged a knife between the discs and was rotating it to separate the vertebrae. He bent in half and clutched his chest – as though he could really save himself from something this ancient and beyond comprehension. His fingers were wet with blood. The pain swept across the backs of his ribs, the invisible knife scraping away layers of skin, giving him the same bloody clock that Taro and Nixie and Cassia had.

He was now the familiar to a head arcanist. He would help Morgan perform the Suppression in the morning to stop the castle drowning in blood; but he was also caught in the teeth of the Slaughter. He would fight with every breath to help Morgan win the throne. There was no turning back.

Elliot collapsed, but before he could hit the ground, Morgan was beside him and holding him. His cool hands supported Elliot's body, one on his chest and the other on his soaking robes. The blood drained from Elliot's head, and his skull, suddenly too heavy for his neck, hit Morgan's shoulder. The blood arcanist cradled Elliot like a child, and by some obscure arcania that Elliot couldn't fathom, this made water spring from Elliot's eyes.

He had done something incredible. Why wasn't he filled with joy?

Morgan gently rested a hand on the back of Elliot's head, and Peridot came to his side. The leopard ran his rough tongue over Elliot's hand like a house cat.

'Poor Elliot,' Morgan murmured, holding him. 'Poor, tired Elliot.' And as Elliot passed out for the second time that evening, not falling asleep but entering something black and dangerous and close to death, he thought he heard Morgan call him by his long-ago familiar's name, Rhys. Then the room was gone, and he was just a body, and he was nothing.

Eleven

Twelve hours until the Slaughter

Nixie writhed on the floor by Kellan's feet, her body stuck in a spasm of pain, the clock on her back bleeding as her dress snagged on its ragged edges. When her muscles had exhausted themselves and only her fingers trembled, Kellan turned back to his notebook and *tsk*ed.

She knew that the duel in the Fighting Hall hadn't satisfied his capacity for enjoying pain. It had only whetted his appetite for experimentation.

'You're getting weaker,' he observed. 'I believe you're coming to the end of your life. You won't be much use to me on the throne.' He looked at her over the top of his glasses. 'Do you know what's happening inside you, Nixeen?'

Nixie didn't respond.

'When I was a student, we studied the anatomy of familiars who had reached the end of their usefulness.' He paused, making sure she understood. 'Your bones are turning black. Your blood is getting thinner. Your flesh will turn to honeycomb. Approximately two months before you expire, your gums will loosen and your teeth will fall out like leaves from a rotting tree. You won't be able to hide it. And then you will develop wresting rot.'

Nixie counted her breaths: three seconds in, seven seconds out.

'When you get wresting rot,' he said, 'the degradation won't just be internal. The blackness will creep over your skin, from your arms to your collarbones, and envelop your heart. You will see it coming. You will be able to count the hours until you expire.'

Nixie breathed deeply and used the exhalation to raise herself. The verdant room, hot and humid with freshly watered plants, swirled with a constellation of red pinpricks. If Kellan wanted her to wrest any more he'd have to tie the plants to her hands, but to her surprise he placed his notebook face down on the table.

'Do you know why I'm telling you this?' he asked.

Because you're a psychopath.

'It's because I want you to know that I'm waiting for you to die.'

He held up a sliver of glass. It was the same deep cobalt as the bottle of poison Nixie had drunk to wipe her own memory. Her heart somersaulted.

'I found it this morning,' he said.

Nixie didn't usually deal in regret, but she wanted to strangle the version of herself that had stolen the potion.

Kellan regarded her blank face, oblivious to her rage, then sighed and eased himself into his chair. He clasped his hands under his chin and waited. The thick brown scars running from his hands to his elbows made him look sewn-together. It was so awful to be stared at by those bright, unblinking eyes that if she were prone to melodrama, Nixie would wonder how it didn't kill her.

'I will only ask once,' he said. He didn't sound angry, but that meant nothing, because he was habitually as expressive as a frozen pond. 'Who helped you?'

Nixie couldn't speak, which meant he was waiting for her face to betray guilt. So she didn't even blink. Her temples throbbed, and she used her pulse to count the questions he was really asking: *Did you kill the Thaumaturge? Are you a traitor to Greenspire? Are you a traitor to me?*

His eyes still hadn't left her face. Nixie very, very slowly pressed her hands into the sides of her robes to stop them shaking.

You will survive this.

'Well?' Kellan said.

He won't kill you. He can't afford to.

Kellan stood. His monolithic calm fell from his shoulders like a cloak. His lips parted in a snarl.

'Alone or not, you single-handedly destroyed decades of peace,' he said. 'I wasn't ready to make my play for the throne, but I will not let another tower get in the way of Greenspire rule. So if that means fighting for the crown, I will. But know that I blame you, and even if I win, *you will not survive.*'

He truly believed she had murdered the Thaumaturge. A deeply academic part of her was flattered that he thought her capable. And in fact, she was more than capable. But why would she? It didn't serve her. It wrecked her long-planned escape. The only reason she would have killed the Thaumaturge was if Kellan had ordered it.

She prodded the dark space in her memory where the dinner should have been, but it was hidden like the pith under the skin of a fruit. Memory loss was an art, and she wasn't an artist, but she had done a good enough job of winging it.

'I want a new familiar,' Kellan said. 'Luckily for you, there are rules against outright murder. Geraldin would have me hung. But accidents happen.'

Nixie bowed her head slightly. It was the tiniest fraction of submission without admission. He would not make her show fear. She knew this disappointed him.

'Continue,' he said.

Nixie went to the propagator and bound ivy around her fists. When she stroked a leaf with her thumb it filled her with wakefulness, a kind of sunrise behind her eyes.

Then she wrested.

Nothing wanted to give up its power, and wresting meant stealing it by force. Heat dug its nails into her skin and wriggled its fingers through the bloody holes, spreading fire through her muscles and into the grey skein of nerves. Kellan incanted faster than she could wrest, and in doing so pulled everything towards his mouth, doubling the pain.

Nixie tried to sink into herself. To go back to the most deeply ingrained memory of the Pit, when she had hidden in a cupboard with Taro, breathing in her oily lipstick and dark make-up, skin to skin and breath to breath.

Then the nuns came to bring you to the castle, and you knew what she had done—

Nixie screamed. She was on the floor again. Every breath was a fork being forced down her throat. Kellan didn't blink as she rattled on the stone with her mouth open and her tongue lolling back into her throat. She could hear howling. Was it her? No, because she never made any noise. It was the sound of her blood screaming through her ears.

Wresting was killing her, but every mote of self-preservation prevented her from cutting off the power. To do so would be catastrophic. It would kill her and blow the glass out of the roof.

When she opened her eyes again the dull grey moon had shifted, and the room was warm with lamplight.

She was lying on her side, her chin sticky with dried spit, the piece of glass from her haunted mirror digging into her thigh through her pocket. A reminder that the Ghost was waiting. She tried to roll over, but she found she couldn't move.

Kellan observed her from the other side of the room. He was in a chair, one finger resting at the centre of a book. She could tell he had expected her to never wake up.

He waited until Nixie had crawled away from the scorched ivy before coming to her. He dropped the book by Nixie's head. The noise sent a bolt of pain through her skull.

'Take this back to the library.'

At least she would finally know what had happened to Alis. Nixie grasped the sap-stained book. She raised herself, inch by inch, to her feet. Kellan reached out to – what, hit her? – but instead he lifted her hair and dabbed something cool on to her temples.

It was soothing, like a balm. This iota of unexpected care was enough to make her panic deeply.

'Go,' he said, and Nixie found the strength to run.

Despite the late hour, the castle rustled with tongue-flicking, eye-swivelling nuns. They swirled behind Nixie like leaves in a breeze, reaching out to touch her and drawing back when she turned to look at them. They knew she wasn't fair game, but they were ravenous. The looming Slaughter excited them. She imagined wresting for Kellan as he exploded ivy from Taro's eyeballs, or Jon bending Nixie's spine backwards until she broke. She shoved the image down, but it was irrepressible. It was her future if they didn't find the rest of the curse keys.

Twelve hours left.

A servant hurried the other way, and Nixie was grateful when the nuns fluttered after him instead. When the Mothers were out of earshot Nixie squeezed into a dusty alcove and pulled the mirror shard out of her pocket. She rapped on it hard to get the Ghost's attention.

'Show yourself.'

The Ghost flickered into view as though she had been waiting for Nixie to call her.

'Hi,' the Ghost said sweetly. Nixie briefly entertained the idea of reaching through the glass and yanking her hair, which was now in plaits. 'Have you made any progress?'

'We have the skull,' Nixie said. 'Part of it, anyway. But in the name of expediency—'

The Ghost bared her teeth, which was largely ineffective because her lips were already translucent.

'I told you, I don't know where the others are,' she said. 'I only knew about the skull because I grabbed a dead guy before he slid behind the veil, and that was centuries ago.'

'Was that Dagmar?' Nixie said. 'Or Sabine, or Gerold?'

The Ghost hesitated, and Nixie knew she had hit a nerve. *Interesting.*

'I saw their names on the Fighting Room floor,' Nixie said. 'They were the head arcanists when Sobweb was the thaumaturge. Another name was gouged out.'

'Aldous,' the Ghost said. She had recovered enough to toss her plaits over her shoulders. 'Scumbag, incidentally.' She paused to think. 'You should look into them.'

'Those head arcanists?'

'Yep. They were looking after the curse keys when Sobweb died. Before they all got lost. Get your nerd friend in the library to dig. Figure out where they liked to stash stuff.'

'You could have told me this two days ago,' Nixie said hotly, digging her fingers into the glass. 'Is there something you don't want me to know?'

'Just do it before time runs out,' the Ghost snapped.

'I wish I had never turned the mirror around.'

'But you did,' the Ghost said. 'And I made your life better. Because now, when you're free, you won't just be stuck in the city with the bone muncher. You'll have a whole world beyond the Desecrae to explore.' She winked. 'And it would be so easy to lose her then. You could even make it hurt. Imagine leaving her on some forsaken hill in the middle of the night.'

'I wouldn't do that,' Nixie said, but she didn't know if she was lying to herself.

'No?' the Ghost tilted her head. 'I thought you hated her. Don't you remember our tragic late-night chats?'

Nixie had needed to unload on someone. It was the only way to quell her sickness at the memories. Memories of Taro holding her hands, and looking into her eyes, and saying: *You can trust me with your life*. Or of the moment Nixie realised Taro had stabbed her in the back, and continued to do so every day, with every lie and every omission. How stupid did Taro think she was?

'You want her to suffer,' the Ghost goaded, and again Nixie thought of the ivy spewing from Taro's eye sockets. She shoved the image away again.

How could Nixie explain their relationship to the Ghost? That love was a splinter in her chest, and she felt it even as she was overcome with loathing? That she hated Taro, and tried to squash that hatred so she could continue functioning, but that a stupid part of her also wanted to hold Taro and never let go? That the last thing she needed was *feelings*, but that hers were so squashed and tangled that love and hate felt like the same thing?

'I'll see you in the Fifth Tower,' Nixie said coolly, and shoved the glass back in her pocket.

But the Ghost's words had punctured the wall around her feelings. A thin squeeze of anger trickled out, and when she tried to stop it, she found that it took more effort than usual. She felt very tired, as though the rotting, roiling pit of fury behind her ribs was syphoning her energy to keep itself alive. The bloody tattoo on her back throbbed in time with her chant: *You're fine, you're fine, you're fine.*

Sometimes she wondered what would happen if she stopped.

Nixie was scared of seeing Alis. She was even more scared of not seeing her.

The library doors whispered open. The cavernous wing was chokingly silent. The heinous Librarian was nowhere to be seen, but the books bore down on Nixie as though they were watching for intruders in her absence. Nixie went to the returns desk, meaning to leave a note, but as she searched for a pencil she saw the ripped-out page of a book lying on the floor. It was a dog-eared copy of the handbook familiars were given when they first woke up in the Pit. Alis had doodled intricately in the margins and scrawled angry, unintelligible notes everywhere. One of them read, over and over: *My name is Alix Alix Alix Alix—*

The library door snickered shut.

Nixie whirled to see Alis standing with her back against the wood. Nixie lowered her hands, which she realised were clutching Kellan's book as a shield.

'You're alive,' Nixie said, and once the words were out of her mouth she realised how cold they sounded. Taro had always laughed at her bluntness, her lack of emotional affect; she should have been a stone arcanist,

Taro said, because of the way her exterior seemed totally unconnected to the turmoil in her brain. It would have been more appropriate for Nixie to fling her arms around Alis and say what she felt, which was: *I was worried about you.*

Alis's face hardened. She strode forward and flicked a pre-written note in Nixie's face.

I know you dropped the chandelier on my head.

Alis waited for a response, then when Nixie didn't deny it, she shook her head in disgust. 'I had to stop it,' Nixie said sharply. 'You were going to kill each other.'

You could have dropped it on Taro instead, Alis scribbled.

Nixie wavered. She *could* have dropped the chandelier on Taro. Why hadn't she even considered it? She blamed it on the sentimental scrap that clung to her ribs. But she didn't know how to say that.

'It was easier for you to fake your death,' she said finally.

Alis bristled.

Because nobody cares about me?

'That's not what I meant.'

Alis scrawled again, her hand heavy with rage.

I don't know how you can stand her. She as good as destroyed you.

Alis alone had the power to expose Nixie's secret with the ease of peeling an apple, and Nixie loathed her for it.

'I told you that in confidence,' she said, her voice low.

Why? It's not like we were friends by then.

The last full stop broke Alis's pencil. Nixie felt a stab of irritation. Deep down she knew she deserved the barb, but she was also sick to death of being in the middle of Alis and Taro's fight. She hated stone and bone arcania, which were the antithesis of freedom. She felt like a plant trying to reach for the sun, but her roots were tangled around their trash in the ground, all these pebbles and bone shards and the dead things their disciplines worshipped. Alis and Taro had been pulling her down since they had all met in the Pit. She wanted them both to go to hell.

'You're so …' The word *jealous* fell dead in Nixie's mouth. Alis twitched the splintered pencil stub. Nixie could sense her frustration at not being able to say what she wanted.

Go on, Alis wrote finally, *finish your sentence. It's not healthy to hold everything in. You're really emotionally constipated, you know that?*

Nixie grabbed the paper out of her hand and threw it as hard as she could. It wafted to her feet in lazy arcs.

'Go eat a book,' she snapped.

Why are you here, Nixie?

'I came to see if you were OK.'

Not because the Librarian is ex-Greenspire and you think she knows about the curse key?

'Would you believe me if I said "no"?' Nixie touched the glass in her pocket and forced herself to cool down. She had a job to do. 'But since we're talking about it, the Ghost thinks the mascots – the curse keys – were still held by the head arcanists when Sobweb died. Maybe they wrote something down.'

So you __do__ want something from me. Alis looked at her as though she was despicable. *Everyone thinks botanic arcanists are harmless, but you're weeds who crowd everyone out to get what you need.*

'And you're cold and unfeeling like every stone arcanist who came before you,' Nixie said. 'I just want to *live*.'

Alis wrinkled her nose as though she was about to accuse Nixie of smelling bad. *Child*, Nixie thought, but Alis only pulled back and fingered the pencil stub.

Are you wearing perfume?

'I threw up on myself,' Nixie said. 'It's vomit.' She flinched as Alis jammed an ink-stained finger over her lips and sniffed the air. Before Nixie could protest, Alis grabbed her sleeve and towed her into the cramped space between two shelves.

'Where are we going?' Nixie hissed.

Alis just pulled her through the passageway, out of sight of the returns desk.

'If this is a game—'

An odorous cloud rolled after them. Nixie detected the sweetness of rotting flowers, the brackishness of vase water that has turned to slime. It hit her seconds before the Librarian billowed into view. Nixie had only seen her from a distance and had always thought her young. Up close, she could see the Librarian's wrinkles had been smoothed by the tight clipping-back of her hair, giving her forehead the texture of deeply crumpled then aggressively ironed paper. The woman drummed her knife-blade nails against the shelves as she walked towards Nixie and Alis.

Alis shoved past Nixie and stood in front of her, but the Librarian, in her infinite knowledge of the library, had already detected the intrusion.

'Who are you hiding, Alis?' Her voice was too smooth and pleasant for her face. Nixie stepped back. The Librarian's nostrils flared as the air stirred, and she swept past Alis, her robes crashing in torrents around her ankles. Her clouded eyes swivelled, looking for Nixie.

'Cyanide,' she said. 'A Greenspire speciality.'

Nixie touched the spot on her temples where Kellan had applied the sweet, almondy ointment. She took another step back. The Librarian matched her without hesitation.

'Kellan sent you here,' the Librarian said. Her knuckles popped as she curled her fingers. 'I told him what would happen if I saw him again. You're his emissary. How low he sinks.'

I want a new familiar, he had said. *Accidents happen.*

Nixie ducked as the Librarian lunged. The passage of books was narrow, and her razor-sharp nails tore through Nixie's sleeves, just as they must have done when the Librarian split Kellan's arms wide open. Anger surged through her.

No more.

Nixie yanked a dictionary from the shelf and threw it at the Librarian's head. The Librarian fell back, hissing, a scrap of Nixie's green robes fluttering from her nails. She drew back for another blow, but Alis barrelled into her from behind, giving Nixie enough time to turn and run.

She didn't know the library like Alis. Every turn looked the same. The Librarian clawed along behind Nixie until they reached a tunnel of manuscripts that rose on both sides and met over her head, their pages tangled together like hands. Nixie kicked the shelf in front of her, but it was ancient and immovable.

Stay calm. Find a weapon.

Nixie scrabbled at the spine of an encyclopaedia, but the book was wedged tightly between its sisters. She grunted and pulled as hard as she could. It slid out by an inch. The drumming of the Librarian's nails slowed as she strolled towards her. Nixie gritted her teeth and leaned back with all her weight.

The encyclopaedia came loose and slammed into her neck. Nixie fell against the opposite shelf, momentarily breathless, pain radiating from her collarbone.

The books around the encyclopaedia toppled inwards to fill the gap. The library moaned. Everything on either side of those fallen books tilted inwards, slowly at first, then with gathering pace. Hefty quartos toppled off the shelves, and the books above those sagged into the new spaces like water splashing into a cup, then the ceiling was groaning and everything was raining inwards—

The Librarian vanished under a shower of folios. For two seconds the world was a confusion of hard noise and blunt pain and darkness. Nixie dropped to the floor and curled into a ball as huge tomes smacked into her back. She couldn't believe this was how she would be killed. Not at the hands of a furious arcanist or by some monster in the Fifth Tower, but under a crush of words in the library.

When the world stopped shuddering Nixie unwrapped her hands from her head, her arms throbbing with nascent bruises. She could feel the floor shifting, and she thought it was a concussion before she realised the ground was sagging. She jumped to her feet and tried to run, spilling books from her back, but the floor was already tilting towards the

Librarian, who had vanished into a sinkhole. Nixie slid after her. She dug her fingers and heels into the splintering wood and bowed her head as falling books hit her on the back of her neck.

With a gentle, papery sigh, everything stopped moving.

Nixie cracked her eyes open. The falling books had broken right through the library floor and into the subcutaneous layer of Fourspires. She was plastered to the side of that funnel like a wasp inside a wet cup.

Nixie slowly tilted her face up until she could see the lip of the hole. She was only a few feet from the surface of the library. If she was *very* careful …

She pushed herself up by her heels, her fingers searching for cracks and knots in the near-vertical wooden floor. A stray book detached itself from the side of the funnel and bounced into the hole. Vicious cursing came from the bottom; unrepeatable words that she had never heard before but which Taro would have absolutely loved.

A hand grabbed her shoulder. Nixie almost flung herself back down the hole before realising it was Alis. Nixie scrabbled her heels against the vertical floor, until she finally breached the edge and hauled herself over the top.

'Thank you,' Nixie said, after probably too long a pause. Then, because that didn't seem adequate: 'I'm sorry about the books.'

Alis shrugged, and Nixie sensed that they had reached a stalemate in their argument. Her relief was deep but ashamed.

At least we don't have to worry about the old hag any more, Alis wrote.

'Someone will notice we've destroyed half the library.'

Alis cut Nixie off with a wave of her hand and scrawled something in huge block capitals on the back of a book.

THE LIBRARY IS CLOSED. ENTER AND BE FOREVER CURSED.

She shoved the book into Nixie's hand and pointed in the approximate direction of the door.

'That won't work for long.'

We only need until noon tomorrow. That's when we start smashing shit, right?

‘Theoretically,’ Nixie said, suddenly aware of the clock on her back, the pain of which she had almost successfully turned into background noise. Alis raised her eyebrows, and Nixie added, ‘*Yes.* Because our plan is going to work.’

Good. Now we're going to find the Greenspire relic.

‘How?’

Alis smiled as she wrote, and Nixie saw a flash of her old friend. The one she used to laugh with, before it all became awkward and wrong. Before, if Nixie was being brutally honest with herself, she completely and unequivocally fucked things up.

By torturing a prisoner.

Twelve

Ten hours until the Slaughter

Alis looked into the void and the void stared back, blackly seething with books. Alis could hear the Librarian at the bottom of the sinkhole, licking her nails and planning Alis's dissection.

Ten hours until the Slaughter. Ten hours before the four head arcanists fought in the Fifth Tower and raced for the crown.

Nixie came back from the library door, having deposited the makeshift warning. She twisted a braid around her finger, clicking a green bead against her front teeth in a way that had always been truly maddening. Alis huffed and yanked it out of her mouth.

'Ow!'

I thought you'd grown out of that.

'It's a better habit than smoking,' Nixie shot back. It was funny how they slipped back into old habits. In the Pit, Alis would slap Nixie's hand when the clicking drove her insane, and Nixie *tsk*ed when Alis scraped her hair back so hard she gave herself a headache, then redid it for her. It was one of the hundreds of infinitely tiny intimacies between them, like swapping dirty books and estimating how long Elliot spent arranging his curls each morning.

They'd driven each other mad, too. Sometimes they hated the sight of each other. But they always came back together, and it had been that way until Alis had said the most stupid thing of her life.

'Alis,' the Librarian said, her voice unfurling from the void like a damp streamer. 'Why am I here, pet? Is it because you're jealous of me? Are you sad you cut off your gorgeous hair? We can fix that.'

Alis ignored Nixie's sidelong glance and hurled a book over the edge. The Librarian hissed as it smacked into the floor.

'That won't help,' Nixie said. Alis rolled her eyes, because it was better to appear derisive than admit Nixie was the only person who made her feel like a monster. She pointed at the sinkhole: *I'm going down.*

'You're not,' Nixie said. Alis suppressed a smile at the hint of protectiveness.

Bite me.

Books slipped beneath Alis's feet as she inched down the side of the hole. The library floor had stretched into a wall of shredded wood, buckled shelves, and ripped books. She landed on a cracked stone floor that hadn't seen greylight in centuries.

The Librarian was perched on a self-made throne of books. One mottled leg hung awkwardly by her side. Alis swiped a large splinter of wood from the floor and dug it into the soft flesh of a bookcase, carving with the deep timbre of a threat.

Where is the Greenspire curse key?

It was too dark for the Librarian's poisoned eyes. She ran her fingers over the words. Alis knew from the crook of her smile that the Librarian knew the answer. Her instinct had been correct: the Librarian knew everything about the history of Greenspire and its head arcanists. If any one of them had stashed the mascot somewhere and left a trace in the books, she would know.

'You sound angry,' the Librarian chided. 'You'll get wrinkles, and then none of the boys will like you.'

One day Alis was going to shock her by answering back.

She flicked the splinter around so it pointed at the Librarian's face.

‘A painful subject, I gather,’ the Librarian said. She traced her fingers over the words again. ‘I don’t know what a curse key is.’

Alis gritted her teeth. She knew the Librarian was being difficult on purpose. She wished she had the ability to just open her mouth and talk back. Instead she had to write, like this.

Arcane relic. Greenspire mascot.

‘The pretty sapling stitched on your friend’s robes,’ the Librarian said. ‘Now *there’s* a story. But I won’t tell it to a dirty stone arcanist, even one who was expelled from their tower.’

Alis didn’t know whether to feel relieved that she was getting somewhere, or deeply worried by the snicker in the Librarian’s voice.

‘I smell mutiny in the castle,’ the Librarian said, smiling indulgently. ‘I recognise the signs. I’ve consumed all the books in this library, even the ones that go all the way back to when everyone was equal and nobody knew their place. If you upset things, you’ll unbalance the system, and everything will grow wild before choking itself.’

Alis ignored the shudder in her abdomen and thumped the words again.

Where is the Greenspire curse key?

‘Bring me a bottle first. The red one with the diamond stopper.’

Alis scoffed, but the Librarian looked at her plainly.

‘I’m not joking, Alis,’ she said. ‘I want my potions. I have dry skin.’

Fine. Alis would play.

She climbed out of the pit. The ascent was tortuously hard. Nixie offered a hand at the top, which Alis ignored.

‘What potions?’ Nixie asked, because she couldn’t bear to know less than anyone else.

Alis waved her hand: *Stay here.*

The Librarian’s office hadn’t been disturbed since her last visit. Her potion bottles winked in the moonlight, full of promises and poison. Alis hovered her hand over them and hesitated. Perhaps the Librarian was bluffing. She had been a high-ranking botanic arcanist once, but that didn’t mean she knew everything. Until recently Alis hadn’t even known the mascots were real, let alone that they had the power to break a curse.

'Alis.' The Librarian's voice whickered through the books.

Suck your nails, Librarian, Alis thought.

'I know you can hear me. Don't you want your answer?'

Choke on your toes.

'Bring me the bottle, sweetie.'

I hope bookworms bore through your skull.

'Ugly girl,' the Librarian hissed.

I pray that your curiosity devours you. I entreat the universe to keep you eternally unsatisfied. I hope to be an enigma that keeps you awake for ever.

'Alis!'

There had to be another way. She dumped the contents of the Librarian's desk drawers on the floor, sending up a cloud of pencil shavings, each one sliced away with a vicious thumbnail. She pushed the contents around with her foot, hoping for the clatter of a key, or a map-shaped *deus ex machina*. Anything that might help them find the Greenspire curse key without Alis having to give the Librarian anything she wanted. She opened a crumpled piece of paper and froze. There were staple marks and rust-coloured stains on one corner. Sweat crawled down Alis's neck.

Execution order for the attempted murder of Geraldin, head arcanist of Greyspire.

Alis instinctively touched the scar on her upper thigh, where half of the staple was still curled beneath a red gnarl. She hadn't seen this document since the Librarian had tried to pick it off her. Alis had bitten and kicked, but the Librarian had held her down like a squirming kitten and used her nails to scrape the staple out of her flesh. *I wouldn't bother for a boy*, the Librarian had said, *but we don't want your leg ruined. We'll get you fixed up, my sweet.* That was when the Librarian was still trying to be motherly.

Alis's thumbs creased the paper. It spelled the end of her time in the Greyspire tower, when she still had a voice and she hadn't been screwed over by Cassia.

That night was a black stain on her memory, and she had never been able to erase it.

Cassia had been dragged up from the Pit for Geraldin to test the following morning. She was supposedly a prodigy, but Alis wasn't worried, because she was too good a familiar for Geraldin to replace. Until, roused from sleep in the Greyspire tower, she had opened her eyes and seen Cassia's face right next to her own.

Alis screamed. Cassia stuffed the corner of the duvet in her mouth to stop her. Alis choked and struggled until Cassia said, 'I'm not trying to murder you, idiot.'

Alis stopped flailing, and Cassia removed the duvet from her mouth.

'You're not supposed to be in here,' Alis said, her heart thumping in the base of her throat. Alis, being a poor idiotic lamb back then, thought that Cassia had wandered into the wrong room.

'I know,' Cassia said, with all the warmth of an icicle. 'Don't you remember me?'

Alis pushed herself on to her elbows.

'Not really.'

Cassia's face twitched. For half a second she looked angry, but her lips smoothed out again. They would have crossed paths in the Torture Pit, but it was hard to remember your classmates when you were busy being torn apart.

'What do you want?' Alis said brusquely. It had been so long since she'd spoken to another human she couldn't remember any niceties.

'I want your help.'

'My help?'

'Does repeating everything help you learn faster? Yes, Alis, your help.*'*

Alis flinched at Cassia's raised voice. Geraldin rarely slept for more than a few hours, and the chances of her creeping around the tower were high.

'What could you possibly need help with?' Alis hissed. 'Geraldin said you're the best disciple in twenty years. You'll get a good placement.'

'I won't,' Cassia said.

'I read the letter. It said you almost destroyed a building.'

Cassia snorted.

'I barely wrest enough for a teacher to crack a brick. I'm virtually useless. You know what they do to people like that, right?'

'Of course,' Alis said coolly, one eye still on the door. 'They get killed and chucked into the Desecrae.'

'Bingo.'

'If you're so useless, how did you get sent here?'

'Because I'm clever,' Cassia said. She had the temerity to look pleased. 'I got my classmates to wrest for me during assessments. They were close enough I could pass it off as my own arcania. Bribery or blackmail can make people do anything.'

'You idiot,' Alis said softly.

'What would you have done?' Cassia leaned in, and Alis realised too late that she was trapped. 'It got messed up. One day this boy produced too much. Or maybe he screwed me over on purpose, I don't know. But I cleared all the tests in one go. I melted a wall. They thought I was a late-blooming prodigy.'

'I bet,' Alis said, keeping her voice steady.

'Are you enjoying this?'

'No.' Alis dug for a spark of sympathy to cling to. 'But I don't see what you need me for.'

Cassia's fingers tightened on the bedsheets.

'Of course you do,' she said. 'I need you to wrest for me tomorrow. Not enough to make me valuable, but enough to stop me being found out. I need them to think the wall was a fluke. I know you're clever enough.' She lowered her voice and gritted her teeth as though the word hurt her. 'Please.'

Even then, back in the Greyspire tower, Alis was familiar with desperation. She felt it every time she was twisted on Geraldin's floor, silently begging her to stop. She looked into Cassia's face and finally felt a deep squirm of pity.

'It's not that easy,' she said gently. 'You might have fooled the Academy, but Geraldin's too clever not to realise.' Secretly she suspected the Academy hadn't been fooled either, and they had sent Cassia up here as a morbid joke. 'She'll find out, and we'll both die. You can't get out of this.'

Cassia's face hardened, and Alis's pity fled again. She wasn't sending Cassia to her death; the girl had signed her own warrant when she decided to cheat. That was how she would justify it to herself in the long hours before dawn when she saw Cassia's face, white with fury and betrayal, every time Alis closed her eyes.

Cassia leaned in, gripping the edge of the bed, until she was so close Alis found herself pressed against her headboard.

'You will help me tomorrow,' Cassia said. 'Or you'll regret it.'

'Yeah? Why's that?'

Cassia sat back triumphantly, and Alis realised she had walked right into it.

'Everyone ignored me in the Pit, but you know what? I was listening all the time.' Cassia laughed at Alis's bewilderment. 'You really don't remember me? Unreal. We literally shared a room. But I was just a lump in the corner to you and your tedious friends. You barely looked at me. You always thought I was sleeping. But I heard what you said to Nixie, Alix.*'*

Alis stopped breathing. Her body was stone. I beg the universe, *she began, but no incantation had followed.*

'Geraldin won't like it,' Cassia said. 'She's very traditional. Notice she's only ever had women in the tower? Some old rule, I believe. You know what she's like.' She stood and smiled coldly. 'I expect she'll give you some of that tongue-loosening stuff. You'll tell her everything then. Sleep on it.'

Alis couldn't force her jaws open until Cassia was at the door.

'You won't do it.'

Cassia turned and sneered.

'Why not?'

But Alis didn't have an answer.

'You should have learned to keep your mouth shut,' Cassia said. 'Even Nixie wished you hadn't told her. I saw her face.'

Alis let her leave. It was probably the most foolish thing she had ever done.

Given the opportunity to go back, Alis would have killed her instead.

'Alis …'

The Librarian hissed at Alis from her hole. Alis, standing in the

Librarian's office, dropped the execution note. Her palms were damp. She wanted to run and curl into a ball and scream all at the same time.

You should thank Cassia. You got out. You won.

But she wished she could go back in time and rip her own tongue out. From blabbing her darkest secrets after being forced to take truth potion in the Pit, to finally confiding in Nixie about who she really was, all opening her mouth had done was hurt her.

That night in Greenspire was another moment in the birth of the deep black lie. The lie that had started with Nixie's betrayal, and which Alis now held, in all its sourness, between her gritted teeth.

'I'm drying up, sweetie.'

Her eyes landed on the Librarian's potions. She saw the purple-coloured vial with the same thick, oily liquid that had forced her to spill her guts in front of a whole class.

Sometimes the universe answered prayers.

Alis uncorked the bottle and breathed in deeply. She would never forget that smell: bitter, like orange peel. It gave her strength. She rifled through the other bottles until she found the red container with the diamond-shaped stopper, and without hesitation she upended it on to the carpet, where the liquid spread like the blood of a newly opened wound. She eased the bitter purple elixir into its new home.

Let someone else betray themselves with their tongue.

Nixie watched intently as Alis lowered herself into the hole. Nixie clearly thought she was doing something incredibly stupid. She also knew better than to stop her.

'Good girl,' the Librarian said, which made Alis's stomach lurch so hard she almost threw the bottle at her.

Instead she rolled it towards the throne of books. It flashed red-black in the lone shaft of moonlight. As the Librarian removed the stopper with her teeth, Alis's deceit felt huge and obvious. She quickly rapped her knuckles against the question carved into the bookcase: *Where is the Greenspire curse key?*

'None of your business,' the Librarian said, and sucked the mouth of the bottle.

It barely passed her lips before she dropped the vial and spat furiously. 'Bitch,' she hissed, scrubbing her mouth with her hands. Alis closed her eyes. 'Filthy wyrdo!'

After a long minute the Librarian fell quiet, and Alis cautiously opened her eyes. The Librarian was slumped sideways. Her mouth lolled open, and when she met Alis's gaze she giggled. Alis mimed tapping her temple: *Tell me what you're thinking.*

'I wanted a daughter,' the Librarian said. 'Like a best friend. You disappointed me.'

She chortled and rolled over, crushing her purple leg beneath her. Alis grabbed the Librarian's robes and tried to pull her back up, but she immediately tipped over again. So Alis got down with her, pressing her cheek to the scattered books, bringing them eye-to-eye.

'Why don't you like me?' the Librarian whispered.

Shadows moved above them. Nixie was listening. Seized by the ridiculous urge not to let her down, Alis took the Librarian's hand, lacing her fingers between the nails with great care, and pressed her palm to the message on the bookcase.

Where is the Greenspire curse key?

The Librarian smiled ruefully and pointed at the ceiling. Alis stared into the shadows above, at the vast expanse of sagging stone. Then she realised what the Librarian was showing her: the long, petrified tree trunk that stretched the width of the library and held the walls apart.

If I only ask for one thing ever again, it's that this is a joke.

'The Greenspire mascot is a sapling,' the Librarian said, 'but saplings grow. It was planted in the Ulcer so nobody would find it. Its bark was so dark it was almost black, and it was so big it almost touched the Desecrae. I wanted to take something of Kellan's. I traced it through the history books, then I chopped it down and used the trunk to prop up the library, then I burned the rest.' She grinned lopsidedly. 'It has no power now. Botanic arcania is about life, and that thing is dead.'

Alis looked at the ceiling again.

By the rotting bones of the library, don't make it so.

The Librarian took advantage of the silence and lurched for Alis, but Alis jerked out of the way and the Librarian fell back into her prone position. Her nails left a line of blood in the flesh between Alis's thumb and forefinger.

'Why do you want to know, sweet?' the Librarian asked, smiling sloppily.

Alis didn't realise that someone else was watching until Taro's shadow fell over her face.

Thirteen

Nine and a half hours until the Slaughter

'What,' said Taro, 'the actual fuck?'

Taro thought it was a fair question, but Alis looked at her as if she'd just pissed over the side of the hole. She was clutching a sticky bottle and her eyes were bloodshot and weighed down by purple shadows. The Librarian rolled around by her feet, giggling.

'Look, Alis,' the Librarian said. 'A friend. Is she the one who plasters her hair back like a balding man?' She belched gently. 'Why does everyone want to look like a boy now?'

'Wow,' Taro said. 'OK.'

Alis scowled, and Taro realised she'd made a fatal mistake in creeping away from Jon and coming to check if Alis was alive. Alis dropped the bottle and scrambled up the edge of the hole, climbing between broken bookshelves like a rodent. There was death in her eyes.

'No hard feelings about the fight,' Taro said. Alis tilted over the edge of the hole and shoved past Nixie. 'We both got some punches in, right?'

Alis stopped dead in front of her and pulled a bag of sweets from her pocket. They were sticky and they smelled like rotting apples. She proffered the bag, her eyes locked humourlessly to Taro's.

'Uh. Thanks?' Taro said. She wrestled one from the distinctly homogenous mass. She waited for Alis to look away, but the stone disciple didn't even blink. 'I'll, um …'

She raised the sweet to her mouth.

'Alis!' the Librarian croaked. Alis looked back at the hole, irritation flashing across her face. Taro dropped the sweet and kicked it under a bookshelf with her heel.

'What the hell was that?' she whispered to Nixie as Alis pulled faces at the Librarian.

'Leave her alone.'

Taro felt a deep, irrational stab of hurt that Nixie was spending any of her kindness on Alis, and not lavishing it all on her.

'I'm just *saying*.' Taro waited until Alis had turned back, then loudly said, 'Delicious!'

Alis watched Taro as though she was expecting her to turn green or something. What a freak.

'Why are you here, Nix?' Taro added under her breath.

'We know where the Greenspire relic is.'

'You— What?'

'It was a tree in the Ulcer, but it got chopped down.'

Taro's irrepressible fantasy of escaping with Nixie in her arms blinked out once again.

'So we're screwed.'

'No.' As usual, Nixie was three steps ahead. 'There might be something left. Remember how you took the tooth from the skull? If something's growing where the tree used to be …' Taro could see her working it out. 'Yes. It might be possible.'

I'll come with you.

Alis wrote so quickly Taro didn't have time to formulate her own answer.

'Is nobody going to ask why I'm here?' Taro said instead. She knew she sounded like a dick, but she also didn't care. 'I got information about the stone mascot. I could have had myself immortalised in a portrait or asked for a cheese fountain, but instead I spent my one and only request on punching information out of Cassia.'

'That's what you were doing?'

'Yup.' She left a sufficiently dramatic pause, then added: 'The mascot isn't a cube of stone. It's a die. I'm surprised you didn't know that already, Al.'

Alis turned a delicate shade of puce.

'Sorry. I mean *Alis*,' Taro said graciously.

'Are you sure about that?' Nixie asked. She didn't even wait for an answer. 'At least it's something. We only have until morning. But, Alis, if you look for the die while Elliot works out where the Redspire curse key is ...'

Taro and Nixie would escape. To whatever was out there, which Taro didn't give a shit about as long as they were together.

Alis was already scribbling. She shoved the paper towards Nixie's hand, but Taro got there first.

Go to the Ulcer. I know where the die is.

And just as quickly as it had been snuffed out, Taro's dream of escaping the Desecrae with Nixie was alive again. Their freedom was so close she could almost touch it.

And by the grace of the holy bones, their new life wouldn't involve Alis.

Taro clamped a hand over her nose as she and Nixie squelched through the lowest floor of the castle, which was little more than a sewer weaving between kitchens and workshops. Here animal fat was transformed into stinking candles, bones were carved into cutlery, and gristle and vegetable scraps were collected for familiars to wrest from. None of the scuttling servants stopped Taro and Nixie, because nobody who wanted to escape would come here. The only way out of these basements was down the long, narrow steps that snaked into the Ulcer.

And the Ulcer *really* sucked.

It was an ancient hole ripped open during a fight between a stone and a botanic arcanist. It was an open wound in the side of the city, where for centuries it had simultaneously festered and flourished. The land between the castle and the Ulcer was a tilted field of broken stone and rotting scrub and ankle-deep skeletal remains, ending at a sheer drop into that miserable garden. When they reached its lip, Taro got on her hands and knees and crawled around the edge, digging furrows through the gnawed bird bones and rabbit skulls.

'You're being dramatic,' Nixie said.

'I'm trying not to break my neck, babe.'

'Don't call me that.'

'OK, schnugglemuffin.'

Nixie muttered something under her breath, but Taro knew she loved it really.

After an eternity of controlled sliding along the perimeter, Taro peered over the edge. The vegetable matter at the bottom looked softish. She glanced up and saw a nun drifting across the steps they had just left, its nose lowered to the ground.

Taro muttered a quick prayer to the dead, who she didn't believe were listening but who might as well be appeased, and slithered over the edge. It was a lot further than it looked. She smacked into the vegetation with a visceral squelch and heaved as orange slime spattered away from her.

'If I vomit,' she muttered, 'I will literally make this place smell better.'

She extended a hand to help Nixie down. Nixie took it, but there was a second – a tiny, hot fraction of a second – of hesitation, almost a *flinch*, before Nixie slid her fingers through Taro's. Taro's panic was hot and sharp. *She knows what I did.* But then the moment was over, and Taro relaxed, because there was no way that Nixie could know what she had done. Nixie's love for her was as obvious as greylight.

Besides, Nixie couldn't keep a secret that long.

'Let's go,' Taro said, a bit too brightly.

They picked their way towards the far edge of the Ulcer, where the sloping sides distantly met at another sheer drop. Taro went first, even though she in no way wanted to be this close to nature. The Ulcer reminded her of a corpse that had been left out in the rain: half-chewed, too soft, and all the wrong colours.

'Wow,' Taro said, mostly to fill the eerie silence. 'Look at that.'

The enormous plant looked like a closed eyelid with thick, tangled lashes. A dense jungle of weeds grew around it, obscuring their path. A dead Mother hung from the plant's mouth, its arms dangling.

'It's digesting the nun,' Nixie said. 'And no, you shouldn't touch it.'

'I want to know if it has bones.'

'It's a *plant*.'

'And now it's a plant with a skeleton inside it.'

'Do you ever,' said Nixie, 'get sick of coming back with one-liners?'

'Nope.'

Yes.

Taro's second deepest secret was that she lay awake every night, staring at the ceiling and replaying all the horrendously unfunny things she had ever said. Taro wanted to be one of those people who knew what to say when someone was upset, but instead she was a shitty clown who had scared away everyone in the Torture Pit except Nixie.

'You're upset,' Nixie said, because she could read Taro like an anatomy book.

'Nope again,' Taro said, and wiggled her fingers between the nun's ribs and the upper lid of the plant so she didn't have to meet Nixie's eyes. The nun flopped to the ground, revealing the plant's disappointingly toothless interior.

'No throat,' Taro said, putting her head inside. 'It must gum the bones until they're mush.'

'Get out of there.'

'Bet the nun was surprised.' As an afterthought, Taro reached in to poke the back of the plant's mouth.

The plant snapped shut. Taro panicked and swung her other arm into the plant's chin. It made a long elastic sound that in any other circumstances would have been delightful, except her fist had bounced off the rubbery flesh and driven her elbow into her ribs.

'*Umph*,' she screamed, and in doing so received a gobful of something cold and acidic. She was vaguely aware of Nixie pulling her waist, but she couldn't feel much because the bastard plant was cutting off the blood to her legs. She used her other hand to punch through the back of the thick, gloamy mouth, then ripped the hole apart and dragged herself through it. Taro grunted as she wriggled through the head of the plant, feeling her feet disappear through the thick eyelashes behind her.

Nixie was screaming somewhere on the other side of the dense foliage. All she had seen was Taro being sucked into the plant.

'Surprise,' Taro said, wobbling to her feet. 'I'm ali—'

The ground collapsed and Taro rolled like a sack of bones thrown off a cliff. The world rotated past her: jagged stones furred with moss, ivy blowing about like party decorations, all the life of the world's lousiest garden. Then rotting floors, slumped walls, and bits of the melting castle that had spurted out of the mountain when the Ulcer was formed. Her bruised ribs and the bloodied clock on her back slammed against the sides, over and over, until her fall was terminated by a grey stone slab.

She was in a rotten green hole, a deathly pit in a place that was already disgustingly pit-like. She had fallen through the garden and right into the subcutaneous layer of the mountain, which was packed with squashed bits of sunken castle and fetid plants. Taro, thanks to her deep affinity with everything morbid, could smell the remains of centuries-old bodies.

'Taro!' Nixie yelled, her voice thin and far away.

'Down here,' Taro croaked.

She saw a statue sticking out of the ground. Its face had been eaten by the weather, its robes smoothed into a lichen-speckled mound, one hand a stump covered in yellow moss.

Taro didn't know what made her scrape the vegetation away from the plaque. Concussion, probably. She hated reading. She picked the dirt out of the inscription and squinted.

Here lies Sobweb the Undisciplined,
who made our world what it is.

She tumbled off the burial mound. Sobweb! Shitting *Sobweb*! The thaumaturge that Hallow Myre had cursed! The old man at the beginning of everything!

Sick.

'Nixie,' she shouted hoarsely. 'I know you don't love corpses, but this is a really good one.'

Her eyes fell back to the insultingly terse epitaph. It was a funny way of saying 'Thanks for arranging the Suppression to control the apocalypse that happens every morning'. Maybe Fourspires hadn't always been so pompous.

Something uncurled from the statue's shoulder. Taro goggled. Fingers. Five of them, unattached to anything, with smooth stumps instead of knuckle joints. The fingers raised themselves into a sitting position – and they really were sitting, despite not having anything resembling an arse – and looked at her in disgust, as though she had interrupted their bath.

'Taro!'

Taro jerked her head towards Nixie, who skidded down the rotting slope with scratches on her face and mud on her arms.

'Don't *ever* –' she crashed at Taro's feet – 'do that again.' She panted for breath. 'Are you OK?'

'Uh, yeah,' Taro said. She looked around but the fingers were gone. Nixie grasped Taro's face and wrenched it from side to side. The warmth of her skin made Taro forget everything else.

'What's this for?' Taro said.

'You're bruised.'

'It's where Alis punched me,' she said gallantly.

Nixie huffed and dropped her hands. Taro caught them instinctively. Everything went still. When she touched Nixie, nothing, not even impending death, felt as important as *this*. She could feel Nixie's faint pulse through her fingertips; the way it sped up at Taro's touch made her skin prickle. She threaded their fingers together, and Nixie leaned in. Just a fraction, as if she was trying to deny her desire, or that fact that she had just flung herself down a hole for Taro.

'Hear that?' Taro said.

'If you say "the sound of silence", I'll kill you.'

Taro pouted.

'Fine,' Nixie conceded. 'It's quiet.'

Exactly. It was the first time they had really been alone since the Pit. Even when they skulked into each other's towers there was a horrified tension, the knowledge that someone could sail through the door at any moment. It always felt like they had left off in the middle of a conversation, one that had been disrupted when they were first brought to the castle. Nixie took a deep breath, as if she was going to speak, and Taro's eyes snagged on the smooth dip between her nose and the bow of her lip.

'What are you looking at?' Nixie said, but she was looking at Taro in the same way. The sweet idiot tried to play it cool, but Taro knew how much Nixie missed being held.

'Guess,' Taro said, and kissed her.

Nixie's hands tightened around Taro's, not exactly saying *Yes*, but *I remember you*. Their mouths still together, Taro slid her hands to the small of Nixie's back, taking care not to touch the clock. Suddenly the world was small and the air was close, as though the Desecrae had contracted and made them the centre of the universe. She could smell she sweet scent of sap and bruised leaves, indecently bright and alive against the death of bone arcania. Taro impulsively ran the tip of her tongue over the sharp edges of Nixie's front teeth, and Nixie, apparently without thinking, pressed back into her. And Taro gasped—

Nixie shoved her. Taro's legs gave way, and she slumped against the statue.

'Oh,' she said, her heart flip-flopping.

'This isn't the time,' Nixie said. She was breathing hard, and her fists were clenched.

'I get it,' Taro managed. Her vision was still mildly kaleidoscopic.

'Do you?' The way Nixie looked at her … she had always been hard to read, but Taro had lost her grasp on the language completely.

'The Slaughter. Impending doom.' Taro gestured weakly at the rotting garden. '*This*. But after tomorrow, if we get it right, we have for ever.'

Nixie regarded her with absolute stillness, and Taro's stomach twisted with fear.

There's no way she knows what I did.

Nixie pushed her hair behind her ears and cleared her throat. She busied herself reading the inscription on the statue.

'So that's Sobweb,' Nixie said, and Taro seized the change of subject gratefully.

'Yep.' Her heart started again. 'Apparently he was undisciplined.'

'Really,' Nixie said, raising her eyebrows as though she was trying to tell Taro something.

They didn't exactly teach undiscipline in the Pit. Arcanists who could draw power from multiple sources were very … not cool, because nobody was going to trust someone who could switch sides. People were so very cultish about their disciplines. Maybe that was why Sobweb had basically been forgotten; it was embarrassing to owe your continued survival to someone who couldn't stay in their lane.

Nixie sighed and rolled her sleeves up.

'Come on.'

They picked their way out of the hole, tearing through nettles and slipping in mud, following a trail scratched by malefici. Every time their hands accidentally brushed, a jolt went through Taro's body. She tried to focus on terrible outdoorsy things like thistles and wet moss, until finally the ground levelled. They met the grizzled far edge of the Ulcer, which hung above the white spires of the University where the arcanists trained.

'The relic's close,' Taro said. She could feel the plant arcania in the air, a kind of soapy, herby slipperiness that made her tongue itch. Nixie cast an impenetrable sidelong glance at her, but Taro was already walking towards the tree.

Technically speaking, the tree stump. It hung over the side of the Ulcer, clinging on by its gnarled roots, which spiralled from the tar-black mud and split the carpet of festering leaves on its surface. There was no mistaking what it was. Its rotten bark was as black as night. Its edges were ragged and scorched where it had been savagely hacked down and burned by the Librarian.

'It's gone,' Taro said, her stomach twisting into a knot. 'Botanic arcania only exists in living things, and this is *dead*. There's nothing left.'

Nixie knelt at the foot of the stump, and Taro resisted the urge to heroically pull her back from the edge. Nixie stroked a mushroom growing from the side of the peeling bark.

'It's absorbent,' Nixie said. She wasn't actually talking to Taro. 'A lot of fungi are. That's why you shouldn't wash them before you eat them.'

'Nobody should eat mushrooms. They're a crime against food. But that's not the point.' Taro watched as Nixie inspected the fungus. 'The Librarian destroyed it, Nix. We can't use it.'

'The stump's dead,' Nixie said, 'but there's a reason this place stinks of a botanic curse key. These mushrooms must have been growing on the tree for decades, even before it was chopped down.'

Nixie dug her fingers into the base of the mushroom and dislodged it from the black trunk. It was curly and as thick as steak. Orange-brown discharge oozed from the gills. Taro suspected it was deeply poisonous.

'You're saying a mushroom has become the curse key,' she said flatly. 'Because it's alive, and it … absorbed the properties of the tree before the Librarian chopped it down?'

'Yes. Do you have a handkerchief?'

'No, because I'm not an old man.'

Nixie gave her a charmingly withering look and tucked the mushroom up her sleeve.

'I'm serious, though,' Taro said. 'Are mushrooms even plants? I thought they were more like … mould.'

'"Botanic" is a misnomer,' Nixie said. 'If it grows but it doesn't have a central nervous system, it's part of the discipline. Your discipline isn't about bones either. It's about death.'

'I wish unrequited love was a discipline.'

'Excuse me?'

'Nothing.'

As Nixie cradled her prize, a little voice in Taro's head said: *Why did someone stick the tree all the way out here if it could break a curse?* Someone needed hanging for losing it. If Taro had something that powerful she would—

Something scuffled over the ground behind them. It sounded damp and metallic. And hungry.

Taro pulled Nixie into a clump of trees. Nixie started to protest but Taro jabbed a finger over her lips and hissed, 'Those scrap-brained fork-wielding junk-heaps have been following us.'

She was furious with herself for not paying attention. The malefici that crawled around by the edge of the Desecrae were one thing, but everyone knew the Ulcer crawled with a particularly odious subspecies. They took any shape – flat, bony, semi-humanoid, bird-like, inside-out, organs stuck to the outside of their skeletons – but their one common feature was that their bodies formed around broken crockery and cutlery. These malefici were a mishmash of organic and man-made trash coagulated into animals. The starvelings.

The dirt erupted by Taro's ankles. Taro threw Nixie into a ditch as a starveling flopped out of the mud, shoving its fork-fingers through the air where Nixie's legs had been, its approximation of a mouth unhinged to grasp her kneecap.

Starvelings were clumsy and stupid, but they were also aggressively hungry and single-minded. Their modus operandi was to dismantle any kind of flesh they came across, dead or alive, with the cutlery protruding from their bodies. Like all malefici, they were thought to have oozed out of unguarded mirrors; but the starvelings were so abominable, and so well equipped for a full dinner service, Taro highly suspected they had been coaxed out by university students as a prank. The Unholy Mothers kept them confined to the Ulcer, but sometimes one made it to the kitchens and took the leg off a cook.

Taro felt around for a stick.

'Are you going to hit it with that?' Nixie asked.

'No, darling, I'm going to start a game of fetch.'

She jabbed the stick at the starveling, which reluctantly lumbered to the rest of its pack in the trees, its three gummy eyes rolling in the back of its head. Taro hauled Nixie out of the ditch and pulled her close. They were standing back-to-back, for all the good it would do them.

Another starveling detached from the group. It had eight finger-thin limbs that looked like – yeah, they were turkey legs. Nice one. Whatever sicko had come up with that needed to be thrown in prison. He – and Taro knew it was a 'he', in fact knew specifically that it was a teenage boy, because this was exactly the kind of shit they would come up with – had given it a massive pig's head with the lips torn off, so you could see all its bone-pulverising teeth. Within its ribcage, floating in a miasma of pale goo reminiscent of the jelly inside a pork pie, Taro saw the remains of a badger.

I swear by my guts I will never do a bad thing again if we get out of here alive.

Taro's pockets were empty of bones, but arcania wasn't an option anyway. Directing more power at creatures entirely propped up by arcania was more likely to beef them up than hurt them.

It lunged at Taro's face. She swung the stick at the gelatinous monster just as it was about to connect with her throat. The stick hit it with a wet slap that sent ripples down Taro's spine. Before Taro could draw her arm back for another blow the starveling was on her, and Taro was on the ground, and Nixie was squashed underneath her. The creature wrapped several of its legs around her waist and bore down on her. Nixie thrashed. The starveling wheezed excitedly as it loomed over Taro's face, wielding a fork with the prongs bent backwards. Taro could do nothing but repeatedly punch its midriff. Its arms were too short for its fork to stab her in the eye, but that didn't matter, because in a minute it was going to crush her. Despite being moments away from a really grim death, Taro felt a little ashamed that she wasn't going to tap out doing something more heroic.

'Someone's coming,' Nixie wheezed beneath her.

She was right. Taro could hear the unmistakable sound of footsteps over dead leaves. Shadows stretched over the ground, thrown from a copse of spindly trees. Another human was in the Ulcer with them, and they hadn't seen the starvelings. Yet.

'This is going to be fun,' said someone who sounded like—

Morgan Redborn?

Taro choked on her spit. She would know the soft velvet of his voice anywhere. The starveling stopped with its teeth a mere inch from Taro's face, its ears pricking.

Morgan was in the Ulcer. *Morgan* bloody *Redborn* was in the *Ulcer.*

'Do something,' Nixie snapped.

Taro took the distraction and drove her fist into the starveling's forehead.

The starveling fell off them, squawking and gobbling as it tried to find its footing in the slick mud. Taro grabbed Nixie's arm and pulled her upright. The other starvelings were looking towards Morgan, twitching and gibbering like turkeys. Taro knew they could smell blood.

'Taro,' Nixie murmured, gripping her arm. 'He's not alone.'

Yeah, because he wouldn't go anywhere without Peridot.

Except.

Except.

Except now he was with *Elliot.*

Just visible through the trees, hidden by a cage of dead branches, was the venomous little shit from the Redborn mansion. Except now the skinny creep was dressed in Redspire robes, jewelled drops of blood glinting on his shoulders. He held a jagged bone knife, which he twisted impatiently in his hand.

Morgan withdrew a vial from his pocket and threw it to the ground, splashing its dark contents over the soil. The starveling by Taro's feet hissed and ran towards them, its insides pulsing with excitement.

'Run.'

Nixie was pulling at her arm. Taro let herself be dragged away, but she couldn't hear anything else Nixie said over the rush of blood in her ears.

'We got what we came for,' Nixie said, yanking her along. 'Move, you idiot. The nuns are coming.'

Unholy Mothers flickered overhead. Taro finally tore her eyes away from Elliot and ran after Nixie, stumbling through the rotten undergrowth to the place where they had entered the Ulcer. They crouched in thick mud as the nuns converged on Morgan's shrieks and the smell of blood.

'Taro,' Nixie said, her voice tight. 'This is bad.'

'I know.' Taro's stomach was clenched like a fist.

'If he's changed sides – if he tells anyone—'

Taro's whole life centred on Nixie. Every good and terrible thing she had ever done was to save the botanic witch. Taro would throw her own soul away if it meant being a hero for her.

There was no way Elliot was getting close to Morgan just to find the curse key. The odious bloodsucker looked too happy. He had obviously been drawn into Morgan's orbit like so many other familiars: lavished with praise, showered with gifts, then used like a toy. And he had never bothered to hide his disdain for Nixie's plan.

No. Elliot wasn't going to help them. He was a blood arcanist, and blood arcanists were the slime at the bottom of the pond.

'I'll deal with it,' Taro said. 'You know I'm mad enough.'

There was no question in Taro's mind. Elliot had to die.

Fourteen

Nine hours until the Slaughter

Elliot walked in Morgan's crepuscular shadow, his eyes trained on the back of the blood arcanist's neck.

The boots Morgan had given Elliot dug into his ankles as they walked through the Ulcer. The bitter black Redspire perfume imbued in his clothes lent a new edge to the ache in his skull. His back was still moist with blood, his skin raw where the ancient arcania had ripped the clock into him. His blood soaked into the gold-piped coat Morgan had given him, mixing with the red droplets embroidered on the fabric. The inside was lined with red silk and had a dozen pockets filled with delicate glass vials. It was a murder coat, a relic from more lawless days when the second or third blood thaumaturge reigned. Of course Morgan wanted to mark his territory by making his new familiar wear it.

'Tell me what you're thinking,' Morgan said without turning around. His tone was playful, but Elliot could feel the undercurrent of danger. It traced its fingers along his jaw and made his teeth ache. Elliot may have been dressed well by Morgan, but he was a mere possession, and he had to give Morgan whatever he wanted.

It was the only way to make sure Morgan gave the necklace back.

'I'm imagining your parents finding Saul,' Elliot said. 'They'll brand me a traitor.'

Morgan turned. The moonlight limned his cheeks.

'Are you worried?'

'No. Because you're more important than them.'

Morgan threw his head back and laughed. Elliot didn't know what to do with this reaction, let alone the fact that they were speaking like peers. In another world, one in which Elliot had been taken to the University rather than the Pit, they might have been colleagues. They might even have been rivals for the blood-drenched Redspire tower.

'I have something for you,' Morgan said.

They stopped under the black trees, feet sinking into the moist detritus between a scattering of dead rabbits that had been torn up by starvelings. Morgan handed him a package wrapped in red velvet. Inside was a dagger with a warm bone handle. Elliot dropped the velvet in the mud, where it lay like a puddle of gore.

'You could just hunt with arcania,' Elliot said drily.

'It isn't as fun.'

Elliot ran his thumb over the bone handle. He hadn't touched a real weapon before; it was so much clumsier than the slim knife Alis had given him, or the one his parents had armed him with. This one was for killing. His eyes flicked to the inside of Morgan's wrist, the warm skin, the rivers of his purple veins.

'What do you expect me to do with this?' he asked.

'Learn how to use it.'

'Here?'

'On the starvelings.'

'You already have blood.'

'Don't argue with me.' Morgan's voice was light. 'I need it fresh for the Slaughter.'

It was a bald lie. Freshness made no difference. Elliot had the sense that he had failed a test by not falling at Morgan's feet in gratitude and giving Morgan what he really wanted.

He wanted Elliot.

'I think you're bored,' Elliot said carefully. Testing. 'You want to spend time with me.'

Morgan's jaw tightened, and Elliot feared he had gravely miscalculated. He squeezed the knife in his palm, wishing that he was trained in using it and knowing it wouldn't make a difference anyway. His palms were sweating as Morgan chuckled.

'I knew I made the right choice with you,' Morgan said. 'Fine. We're here because we can't talk inside. If they hear you running your tongue I might not be able to stop them killing you. And I'm sick of talking to Peridot.'

Elliot ran his thumb over the carved insignia at the top of the knife, the drop of blood. He slid it into his belt and walked by Morgan's side.

'Don't lie again,' Morgan added. 'Tell me what you're *really* thinking.'

'I'm wondering what you like about me.'

'I like your company, and I think we're similar.'

Elliot's pulse jumped. *Adrenaline*, he told himself, but a primal part of his brain disagreed.

'How are we similar?'

'You know how.'

The hairs on the back of Elliot's neck stood up.

'And?' he said carefully.

'And I want you to surprise me.' Morgan flicked his eyes across Elliot's body, just as he had in Malachi's room. The look was unmistakable and thrilling, and it made Elliot's breath falter. Then Morgan smiled again, and the tension was broken. 'Your turn. Ask me something.'

Elliot fingered the edge of the dagger in his belt. He had the sudden, almost irresistible urge to squeeze his hand around the blade, just to feel that danger again. Instead he jerked his head to the castle looming above them.

'How far would you go to become the Thaumaturge?'

'What do you think?' Morgan understood what Elliot was asking, but even in the seclusion of the Ulcer he wouldn't admit to murder. Not until he was ensconced on the throne. 'Next.'

'What's in the Fifth Tower?'

'Ah.' Morgan glanced at Elliot. '*That* I don't know. I've trawled through every book I can find, but the interior has never been seen by anyone other than the thaumaturges and their familiars. It could be a lavishly appointed apartment, but I suspect not. In the Slaughter, the tower kills people and vomits them out as pulp.' A light pause. 'Now tell me about yourself.'

Elliot briefly considered plunging the knife into his own neck.

'Your earliest memory, for example,' Morgan added, and the images swept over Elliot with the aching familiarity of an embrace.

The house at the bottom of the city. His mother squeezing his cheeks. His father watching silently as Elliot mopped up his own nosebleed, which he had accidentally wrested from. His mother cradling him and telling him how clever he was. Her warm smell of tallow and sweat. The feeling of safety, even though Elliot knew the nuns hunted for people like him …

Elliot swallowed the memory, the sweet ache.

'They wipe our memories when we arrive at the P— the Academy,' Elliot said. It was true. Had been true for him, at first. 'Our first memory becomes standing in the hall with tags on our wrists.'

'A room full of gibbering babies,' Morgan said. 'And so the wyrdos are born.'

Elliot flinched.

'We know how to read and write. We know how to look after ourselves. But nothing autobiographical.'

'Your names?'

'They tell us.'

Morgan considered this.

'I would happily forget dear Mummy and Daddy,' Morgan said. 'When I was little they put me in a cage with a starveling and Saul's old familiar to see if I would use arcania.' When Elliot didn't answer, Morgan snorted. 'You don't feel sorry for me.'

'You went to the University. It's no hardship.'

'It was cold and horrible and the teachers were nasty old men who wouldn't die.'

'They helped you come into your power. They tried to kill *us*.'

Morgan saw a ragged bird and, quick as a sneeze, flicked his knife at it. Elliot heard the soft *thump* as the bird hit the ground.

'For Peridot,' Morgan said, simultaneously pocketing the carcass and ending the conversation.

Elliot's turn.

'Why do you have a leopard?'

'Why wouldn't I?' Morgan cracked his knuckles, bored of the subject. 'When you came to my tower, you told me that because you don't sleep, you remember things. What do you remember?'

Black fog rose behind Elliot's eyes. Morgan knew which questions would crack Elliot open and make him bleed.

'Fragments,' he said hoarsely.

'Such as?'

'I don't know.'

Morgan grabbed Elliot and spun him against a tree, quick as a breath, shocking Elliot into silence. He stabbed his knife into Elliot's throat – *no* – into the bark, nicking his skin. Morgan grinned at Elliot's horror, his face so close Elliot could see the minute gaps between his eyelashes. He tangled his fingers in Elliot's dark curls and pushed his head back slowly.

Elliot could feel his own pulse in his exposed throat. He half expected Morgan to sink his teeth into his neck; he wanted it, too. To give himself, and his blood. To feel Morgan's mouth in the crook of his neck. His body was lighting up in ways it hadn't since he was cursed, and he wanted more of it, even while he was disgusted by himself.

'Tell me before I cut you,' Morgan said, tightening his fingers in Elliot's hair. Elliot shuddered, and Morgan pressed closer, as though he was well aware of how much Elliot enjoyed it. Elliot could feel the blood arcanist's heartbeat through his shirt. 'Well?'

'I remember my family,' Elliot conceded hoarsely. He couldn't concentrate on anything except Morgan's touch. He hated Morgan, but Elliot was only human, and Morgan could clearly tell what he liked. The blood arcanist lowered his gaze to Elliot's mouth. 'They mended walls by the Desecrae. At first.'

Anything could happen now. Elliot only had to concede to Morgan, and the world would change.

But Elliot wasn't going to let him win the game so quickly.

Elliot gathered his will and shoved Morgan in the chest. Morgan conceded, grinning, and yanked the blade from the tree. He swaggered away as though nothing had happened.

'Were they scared of your power?' he asked.

Morgan's touch still burned on Elliot's skin. There were so many things he wanted to do. Things that transgressed the bond between familiar and arcanist, things that were wrong and dangerous and yet would render Morgan utterly helpless beneath Elliot's fingers. He knew exactly how he would make the blood arcanist fall apart. And god, he wanted so badly to do it.

'They encouraged me,' he said finally, his voice strained with the effort of not betraying his own desire. 'Everyone came to them for help. People paid them for it.'

Morgan looked at him closely, as though he knew what Elliot was suppressing and liked it.

'You weren't caught by the nuns?'

'They were good at hiding me.'

'Because they cared about you,' Morgan said.

Why did it suddenly feel like there was a rock in Elliot's throat? His useless body, his soft, traitorous shell, was infected by a mysterious weakness that he had tried to kill. His desire was dead. He wanted nothing more than to stamp Morgan into the ground.

'Yes,' Elliot said gruffly. He remembered how his mother had cupped her hands around his. The awkward touch of his father when he had done something particularly good. 'They needed me.'

'You were their livelihood,' Morgan said. 'And now you have attachment issues. How *passé*.'

'Excuse me?' Elliot said frostily, remembering what Alis had called him when he had placed the hex for her. He felt like everyone was telling a joke that he didn't understand.

'We're the same, Elliot,' Morgan continued, as though he hadn't heard. He started walking again. 'We're merely vessels for our parents' needs, which means they were always going to be disappointed when we didn't fulfil them.'

Elliot didn't reply. Morgan knew nothing about his parents. They hadn't fought the nuns for him, but only because they knew they couldn't win. They had needed him, but they had also loved him. He often wondered how it must have felt for his parents, having Elliot ripped from them, and whether they had the same hole in their hearts that Elliot did.

Elliot pressed the blade of the knife into his palm, feeling its cold bite. He didn't want to think about them any more.

'Did you feel anything when you killed Saul?' he asked bluntly.

Morgan stopped short, and just as Elliot braced himself for a dagger to the heart, Morgan flashed a wicked grin.

'You're worried I could do the same to you,' he said.

Elliot gritted his teeth. The blood arcanist could read him like a cadaver on an autopsy table. He knew exactly where to cut to lay Elliot's feelings bare; he could see the fear and doubt that Elliot worked so hard to conceal. Nobody had examined him so thoroughly and seen him so well, and it was both gratifying and terrifying.

It was also Morgan's greatest weapon. Elliot couldn't keep any secrets from him, and he would be a fool to forget it.

'Would you like to see something?' Morgan asked.

Elliot was in no position to refuse.

The buttons on Morgan's stiff collar shone like pomegranate seeds as he unbuttoned them, exposing a sliver of his long throat. When Morgan pulled the collar aside Elliot could see an angry scar. It was still lividly red and fathoms deep.

'When I was promoted to Redspire,' Morgan said, 'Saul tried to kill me. My own cousin. He genuinely thought he was going to be chosen. He believed he could leap from being my parents' servant to ruling the tower, and it was a nasty shock when he was judged not good enough.' Elliot watched the shallow dip in Morgan's throat as he buttoned his shirt again. 'I let him live, obviously. Having to continue bowing and scraping to my parents was a wonderful punishment.' He smiled ruefully. 'I saw you flinch when I killed him. I thought this would make you feel better about it.'

'Really,' Elliot said flatly, his eyes still caught on Morgan's collar.

'All right. I wanted you to see me unbutton my shirt.' Morgan flashed him a conspiratorial look, and Elliot knew that he was never going to know Morgan's truth from his lies.

They walked a little longer. Morgan stroked the head of the dead bird hanging out of his pocket, humming softly. Elliot knew something had shifted between them. Maybe that was why insanity seized him by the throat.

'I need the necklace,' he said. It came out too quickly, with a tinge of desperation. Morgan's smile died. It was too late for Elliot to erase his mistake, so he forced himself to sound calm. Bored, even. 'If I sleep tonight, I'll be more useful tomorrow.'

'Do you think you deserve it yet?' Morgan said. His voice was amused, but it also carried a warning: *Don't push, or you'll end up like the bird.* Elliot struggled to think of something that wasn't a humiliating plea for mercy. But pride was the only thing he had left to give away.

'Please,' he said through gritted teeth. Morgan let the word burn in the air before replying.

'Don't beg, Elliot.'

Elliot's humiliation was an inferno. Nonetheless, he would have fallen at Morgan's feet if he thought it would help. He would have buried his face in the ground and swallowed the worm-ridden dirt. Elliot loathed Morgan, even found him hideous in his power. And yet. And yet.

The forest darkened. Dried leaves clenched against the ground like dead hands. The Desecrae held its breath.

'I can smell them,' Morgan said abruptly.

'What?' Elliot gripped the knife in his belt.

'Starvelings.' Morgan drew a vial from his pocket and tipped the blood on the ground. 'This is going to be fun.'

The bone handle was suddenly slippery in Elliot's palm. He was in a toxic garden with a maniac who killed birds for his pet leopard in the middle of the night, who thought a dead body was a fantastic gift for a man he had strong-armed into being his familiar, and who hunted insatiable arcanic beasts for fun. And Elliot still didn't know how to fight.

Morgan threw another vial to the ground, splattering blood over the leaves. The first starveling arrived seconds later, its bloated stomach hanging from its spine, three mismatched eyes swivelling independently of each other. Elliot pointed the knife at it, but the knife now seemed very thin, and the starveling obscenely large. It stopped a few feet away from them, staring them down as it gobbled. Morgan regarded it with his head cocked.

The darkness belched out another creature. It came closer than the first, bringing the stink of rendered fat with it. Its organs spilled from an upside-down pudding bowl with a delicate pattern of violets around the rim. Together they slid forward, inch by inch, eyeing the splatter of blood on the ground. The trees produced another starveling, which became a dozen, then a dozen more. They bristled with dinner table accoutrements, forks with bent tines and rusty knives and skewers. Elliot's skin ached, anticipating the needle-sharp teeth. He felt more awake than he had since the dawn of his eternal insomnia.

The first starveling launched itself at them. It hit Morgan square in the chest, teeth-first, knocking him to the ground. They rolled over and over, fighting and thrashing, leaving a trail of black blood on the forest floor. Elliot backed into a tree, sure that Morgan was being torn to shreds in front of him.

Morgan jumped up. The starveling fell away. It gobbled for breath on the ground, dark fluid leaking from its gelatinous body. Morgan was covered in scarlet, but he wasn't even scratched.

'Go on,' he panted, jabbing his knife at Elliot. 'Show me how angry you are.'

Elliot's mouth twisted into a knot.

'I don't know what you mean.'

'Your life is full of pain and now I own you. Show me!'

The prone starveling suddenly struck Elliot with its whole body, legs crunching beneath it, thick blood spraying from its mouth. Elliot stabbed wildly. The knife hit something hard like bone. His arm twisted sideways, carried by the starveling's weight as it fell to the ground with a wet *thump*. Elliot couldn't see anything through the black fluid dripping into his eyes. He scrubbed them with his sleeve, and saw the starveling now motionless, shreds of flesh peeling away from its body.

Elliot clutched his aching arm to his chest, the bloodied knife still between his fingers. His hands were shaking, and his mind was revolted. But something else had come to life.

'How does it feel?' Morgan asked. His eyes roamed Elliot's face. His body. 'Can you do it again?'

The pack jerked around them. It grew noose-tight, filling the air with the sound of damp bones grinding against each other.

'I know what's in your heart,' Morgan told him. 'I know it's black and rotten. I think that you secretly loathe your parents for using you. You hate that you long to be wanted. And I know you think you've embraced your rage, but have you ever really let it out?' The bloodied knife shone. Morgan was dissecting him again, and this time he wouldn't stop until Elliot was fully exposed. 'Maybe it's time to find out what would happen if you stopped *thinking* for a second, Elliot.'

His name was honey on Morgan's lips.

The beasts surged, a nest of spiders exploding from the mother web. Elliot struck out in a moment of ice-cold terror, the roaring in his ears covering the sound of their feet slapping into the mulch. He caught a chicken-skulled starveling in the side of its head, but it kept moving and jabbed its beak through Elliot's sleeve before he twisted the knife through its eye socket. It slid off the blade; he gasped with the pain of its beak tearing his flesh. It was a different pain to that of wresting, somehow more pointed, fresher. Morgan dispatched another with the fork it held between its own teeth.

The starvelings gobbled around Elliot's feet, jabbing and slashing. This time Elliot was ready and struck three blows before a set of teeth broke through his boots. He kicked the starveling away and heard a *crunch* as something vital broke in its neck. Morgan hissed as he dispatched another and pressed a glass vial to its sopping wound, but the vial immediately slipped from his fingers. He didn't seem to care. They weren't really here for blood collection.

The rest of the starvelings struck as a single beast, flying for Elliot's face and chest. Elliot had no time to draw arcania from the wound on his arm, but something else was happening, a huge cleaving between the roiling darkness of his mind and the prison of his flesh. For the first time in his life, Elliot left his cage. His pain was abandoned. He was a mind piloting a body, wholly unattached to it, and with that puppet-body he held a knife and carried out his own instructions.

The bites and jabs were nothing. He would pay later, but for now he was racking up his debt, and he would until his body was destroyed. Elliot thrust and kicked and punched: *Four. Five. Six.* The ones not dead by the third strike retreated with their ribcages split open. *Seven. Eight. Nine.* Elliot became aware of the numbness crawling up his arm, but he forced his mind away from his body again, and it kept doing its work as the creatures came. *Ten. Eleven. Twelve.* Morgan was shouting, but the sound was part of another world. Elliot realised with glee that the starvelings were easy to kill as long as he wasn't afraid of them. They were stupid, and he was strong.

Thirteen.

It was over.

Heaving bodies littered the ground. The others scattered, leaving greasy footprints and scraps of meat behind them. Elliot didn't realise how hard he was breathing until pain bloomed in his chest.

Morgan was doubled over, panting. It was the first time Elliot had seen him suffer. Their eyes met, and Morgan quirked his lip.

'I killed the starveling,' Morgan said. 'In the cage, I mean. As a child.'

His face and his silk shirt were stained red, and his boots were in tatters, torn to shreds by teeth. There was a smear of blood on his chin, which could have been from a starveling, or might have been from his own tongue.

Elliot tried to slow his breath. Every inhalation was pain.

'Did I pass the test?' he said.

Morgan, still doubled over, grinned.

'There is no test.'

It might have been blood loss, or hysteria, or the adrenaline leaving his body, but Elliot was seized by the urge to laugh and scream. He struggled against his own hand, which wanted to keep slashing with the knife, then he threw it to the ground so hard it landed point down.

Morgan flinched as Elliot locked his fingers around Morgan's throat and walked him backwards. Morgan let it happen.

No more drawing it out.

They hit a tree, and Morgan melted against the bark. It was clearly acquiescence. Elliot kissed him, even though he didn't know how to begin. He knew he was doing it all wrong. Their teeth clashed, and Morgan was laughing. But it was delight rather than derision. Their lips pressed together with bruising force. Morgan's face was hot, and his heartbeat was wild under the corner of his jaw, and Elliot realised it was the first time he had enjoyed being in his own body. Here was someone who really wanted him. Someone who liked how awful he was. Someone who wanted to be putty in his hands, and who wasn't disgusted by him, someone who was now pulling him in urgently as though Elliot was the only thing that could fill a terrible void. Someone else who might need him.

Morgan gasped, 'Rhys.'

Elliot shuddered. His wild desire twisted and broke at the name of Morgan's most infamous familiar. The one Morgan had whispered in his ear on the floor of Malachi and Tamsin's bedroom. Elliot pulled away with a ragged breath, but Morgan didn't look abashed.

'Do you have a problem with that?' Morgan asked, his lip curling.

Elliot hesitated for a second too long. Morgan's face twisted into a sneer that didn't meet his eyes. He sheathed his bloody knife, which Elliot realised had been in his hand the whole time, just inches from his heart.

'You are not my equal,' Morgan said. 'You do not have the privilege of judging me.'

Elliot backed away. Morgan stared at him, his expression flat with disdain. The viscera soaking through Elliot's clothes suddenly felt very cold.

The shadows moved. Elliot looked up. The nuns had heard the commotion from the castle, had smelled the blood, and they were circling the Ulcer like vultures.

Elliot had the sickening urge to fall at Morgan's feet and beg forgiveness.

'Fill your vials. And don't let me down tomorrow.' Morgan turned away, leaving Elliot standing in the blood-slicked mud. His voice was cold. 'You know what I'll do if you change your mind.'

Fifteen

Nine hours until the Slaughter

Alis hunted her prey in the back stacks, tapping her fingers along the shelves, eyes narrowed at the shadows. The cats sensed violence and oozed away with their ears plastered to their heads. Alis dug her fingers into a shelf and scraped a furrow in the dust as she walked, which Fingers deeply hated. It was the only thing guaranteed to drag him from whatever hiding place he had been in for the last couple of days.

Let's play a game, Fingers.

It had been two hours since Nixie and Taro had left, but Alis knew how to be patient. She understood her quarry, and she knew its limits.

She pinched a gilt-edged book and pulled it out. It teetered delicately on the edge of the shelf before smacking on to the floor. She stalked to the next row and chose another victim.

Smack. Smack. Smack.

The Librarian heard what she was doing and moaned from the bottom of the sinkhole. Alis pulled out a hefty dictionary.

Crack!

The shadows stirred. Alis knew the movements of the library like her own heart. *Finally.* Something was picking the books up. The gilt-edged volumes scraped across the floor and squeaked against the burnished wood as they were dragged back up the shelves. Fingers only liked chaos of his own making.

Alis folded her hands behind her back and waited by the window.

The courtyard wavered in the moonlight. The nuns fluttered restlessly from their perches or drifted in circles around the tower, as though they wanted to go inside but couldn't find the door. A few truly ancient Mothers had crawled out of the bedrock, identifiable by the robes that hadn't been replaced since they were transformed, their skulls dented by burial.

A flurry of activity pulled Alis's eyes to the iron gate at the front of the courtyard. A dozen nuns were contorting through the bars, dislocating their shoulders to squeeze through rather than waiting for the gate to open. Something was happening outside the castle.

The Ulcer. Nixie was down there. Had Taro done something heinously stupid and drawn attention to them? She was the kind of idiot who destroyed everything in a breath, then strolled away from the aftermath picking her nose. If she had done something to Nixie, Alis would throttle her. She had been looking for an excuse for years.

The first time Alis had seen Taro in the Torture Pit – not just glimpsed her skulking at the back of a classroom, but really *noticed* her – was precisely the same moment that Taro had noticed Nixie. For weeks afterwards Alis had seethed as she replayed the bone disciple locking eyes with her best friend across the dining room. Crunching the boiled sweet she had been sucking between her teeth, decisively, in the same manner that one might crack their knuckles. Wandering across the room with false nonchalance. Sitting opposite them and tilting her body away from Alis, who clearly didn't interest her.

Alis had known right away that she was going to lose. This was long before she had blurted *Help, I feel like something's wrong with me*, long before she had tried to force intimacy where there was no longer any room for it. Once upon a time that intimacy had flowed between her and Nixie so easily: when they were put on gutter-cleaning duty and hid on the roof instead. When they sat outside Alis's bedroom and wrote stupid poems about everybody who walked past. When Nixie realised she was in love with Elliot's hair. But the moment that Taro came along, Alis felt the tiniest part of that intimacy slip away, and she knew it was the first pebble before an avalanche.

Soon every sentence coming out of Nixie's mouth started with *Taro said* and *Taro did*. She forgot to eat dinner with Alis, and she started using the same words and phrases as Taro. She brought Taro with her when Alis needed help, and for a while she even copied Taro's eye make-up. And Alis had realised that the most important relationship in her life was a practice run for Nixie, who was waiting for someone else entirely. Once Alis would have sworn blind that she would never be alone because Nixie wouldn't let it happen. It still took her breath away, sometimes, how wrong she had been. How pathetic it was that she still worked herself into gut-wrenching jealousy. When Alis looked back at their diverging paths she saw herself as a stone in the ground, and Nixie had her roots wrapped around her, pushing her further into the earth as she sprang towards the light.

She hated Nixie. She missed her even more. It hurt so badly to have all this room for someone and nothing to fill it.

A soft *scritch*ing brought her back to the library. The lump in her throat broke. Alis refocused her eyes on the murky reflection of the books.

Fingers was perched on a pyramid of manuscripts. His two smaller digits were streaked with dirt and slime. Alis tried not to stare as he casually tossed the stone die and caught it between his thumb and forefinger. She had only seen its burnished brown surface in glimpses, blurring as it rolled across the floor, always out of reach because Fingers picked it up before she got there. She had assumed it was made of bone, but stone made as much sense. And it wasn't ridiculous for Fingers to have something so important; he was a magpie, a trickster, a relic himself with a taste for old and precious things. For all she knew, Fingers was the one who had stolen and hidden the die in the first place.

Alis turned casually. She reached behind her ear for a cigarette, lit it with the last damp match from her pocket, and brought it to her lips. Too nonchalant?

Be normal.

Her fingers acted for her, flexing towards her boot, where she kept pre-written paper scraps.

Hello.

The die vanished behind the thumb as Fingers *tip-tapped* over to read the note. Alis drew on the woody cigarette, forcing her body to relax. Fingers produced a pencil from the unknowable space between his thumb and forefinger.

You put the Librarian in a hole, he wrote.

Alis nodded and exhaled, sending a plume of smoke to the ceiling. Her eyes flickered to the space behind his thumb where things appeared and vanished. Could she reach in and grab the die? What if she felt something else instead? She had no idea what was in there. A creature from the fifth dimension, or a brain, or old fingernail clippings, or perhaps the rest of his dismembered body.

Why? Fingers asked.

Best to tell a version of the truth. Alis took a pencil stub out of her boot.

She was annoying me.

Fingers was satisfied. He flopped on to his back and stretched out lazily, as though he was enjoying the sun instead of a patch of mildewed carpet. He twirled the pencil between his fingers.

I am concerned, Fingers wrote in a very unconcerned way.

Alis tilted her head in question: *Why?*

Because the Librarian is no longer there.

Alis listened. The Librarian had stopped moaning.

She crushed the cigarette and sprinted towards the sinkhole in the library floor. Fingers pattered behind her, elevated by the bookshelves he used as walkways, using her pencil as a walking stick with mirth emanating from his fingertips.

Alis skidded to the edge of the hole.

The Librarian had vanished. Claw marks covered the bookcases she had used as a ladder. She had been faking her broken body; either that or her desperation to reach her elixirs, or some side effect of the truth potion, had blunted the pain of her shattered leg.

Alis savagely kicked a book into the black depths.

'Alis,' the Librarian cooed.

Alis clenched her fists and turned to the voice. The Librarian's footprints led through the carpet to her office at the back of the library. Having the Librarian loose would seriously impede Alis getting the die from Fingers. The Librarian knew the familiars were conspiring, and all she had to do was raise the alarm to make hell rain down on them. She couldn't remain free.

The Librarian was standing lopsidedly behind her desk, propped up on her hands. Her knuckles creaked as they threatened to snap under the pressure of her grip. A jumble of open bottles rolled on the wood, her mangled leg shining with freshly administered oil.

Alis deliberately met her eyes. She had to prove she was unafraid and in control.

Barely.

'Sweet Alis,' the Librarian said. 'I've been tolerant and let you play dress-up. But you don't smile. You don't write me notes. You moon around, scribbling on my books and pulling faces at me.'

She walked her nails towards the bottle on the desk. There was still some purple liquid sloshing around in the bottom. It was the potion Alis had used to make the Librarian spill her guts.

'I've finished indulging you,' the Librarian said. 'I don't understand you, and I deserve to. I want to know who you are.'

Alis couldn't take her eyes off the Librarian. The moment she did, those nails might flash out and slice her open. There was violence in the woman's smile. Because Alis had left the Librarian in the hole, all the rules were broken. Alis steadied herself against the shelf by the door and her shoulder bumped into a thick encyclopaedia. A memory flickered through her panic.

The Librarian's lips twitched.

'Perhaps I don't need you to tell me,' she said. 'I see you quite clearly. You don't like your own kind, and you would mutilate yourself to be different. But you can't change your reality with bandages and scissors, dear.'

Alis's fingers were cold, but in that moment her fury became hot and sharp. She pulled the encyclopaedia off the shelf. A book of matches, hidden long ago, fell from between the leaves. The Librarian squinted to see what was happening, which gave Alis time to flip one into her fingers and strike it against the doorway.

For one glorious second Alis had the cathedral of books in her hands.

But she wasn't going to do it. It was just a threat.

Alis understood the power of threats. Cassia had taught her that, long ago in Greyspire. She had threatened to tell Geraldin Alis's secrets. And at the last minute, Alis had panicked. Wrested for Cassia. Gone too far and brought the stone down around their ears. An appalling accident that had got her excommunicated and almost killed.

The Librarian's eyes alighted on the match. Even she could see the bright flame against the bookshelves. She sucked her lips, surprised.

But then she continued.

'You won't do it,' the Librarian said. 'You're not capable of real malice. Poor sweetie. You've never been strong. Stone disciples have to be strong. No wonder nobody wanted to keep you.'

Alis bared her teeth and waved the match. It was already burning close to her fingers. *Get back in the hole, you haggard lump. Go choke on a bookmark.*

'You won't do it, gumdrop. Sweet goose. Silly girl.'

Alis hadn't thought this through. The Librarian knew Alis loved the library too much to hurt it. She spat at the Librarian's feet, which made the old woman's milky eyes stretch with righteous delight.

'You want more?' the Librarian said. She tapped the nail of her index finger against her own cheek and leered, and Alis didn't need to guess what was next. Her throat tightened. 'I know what's going on inside your mouth. I know you—'

Alis dropped the match.

The carpet went *woomph.* The Librarian screamed. She dropped the bottle and careened towards the inferno as though intending to squash it with her body, then flinched away from the heat and twisted towards Alis as flames licked her robes. Alis didn't think; she lashed out and pushed her back into the desk, and heard a short, bone-splintering *snap* as one of the Librarian's nails broke off.

The air was as black as burned toast. Alis dropped to the floor and backed away from the office, coughing wretchedly in the smoke. The heat had already dried the perpetually damp carpet inside the office, crisping the mould and baking the verdant wildlife that lived between its mud-coloured tufts. Tiny bodies crackled under her hands as she crawled away from the room.

'Alis!' the Librarian screamed. Alis wasn't sure if she was asking for help or threatening her.

It was too late to stop the fire. It had been ever since she'd struck the match. Everything Alis loved ended in catastrophe, and her reign over the library was no different.

And soon the whole world would know. The nuns would storm in and rip her to shreds. Nixie's stupid plan would be in tatters. Alis would be the cause of everyone's death.

'ALIS!'

Alis groped to her feet, tried to run, and hit a shelf. Smoke curled after her.

The Librarian limped to the flaming doorway. Her clothes and skin were wreathed in smoke. Only her white teeth and yellow eyes were distinguishable from her blackened skin. Her tongue flicked out, licking her lips, wiping a grey circle in the soot. Fire billowed around her ankles like a voluminous dress. She had never looked more striking, nor more awful.

And she was not alone.

The Librarian inclined her head, stroking the thing on her shoulder with her cheek. She smiled and cooed even as the flames crawled up her back.

Traitor! Alis screamed silently at Fingers.

The Librarian collapsed into the smoke, but Fingers was already moving, propelling himself from the Librarian's body, trailing sparks and soot. He came at Alis so fast she didn't see that he was holding the Librarian's broken nail.

She tried to kick him away. It was too late. He stabbed Alis through the foot, right through her middle toe, pressing the Librarian's nail through her shoe and deep into the floor.

Alis screamed from the back of her throat. The nail quivered in the floor. Fingers pranced away, laughing silently.

The fire danced closer, but the threat of being burned wasn't enough to make Alis's body override its aversion to pain. She gritted her teeth and tried to pull herself free, but the nail was stuck fast, and every movement brought a fresh wave of agony. Water streamed from her eyes. Each inhale made her feel as if she was being stabbed again. She just needed to lean down and yank the nail out of her foot, but her miserable body wouldn't let her do it.

Move, or you'll burn.

The nerves between Alis's brain and limbs were tied in knots. The smoke was thick and choking. The room shimmered and turned with dizzying heat as shelves collapsed and windows shattered, drowning out the sound of her panicked breathing.

Just move, Alis.

Alis.

Move!

Her traitorous body still wouldn't listen. Dark flakes swirled around her feet and tiny, charcoal-tasting particles tickled the back of her throat.

Move, you stupid, useless streak of a human being!

This was the end. The closing chapter of her entire shitty story. Nothing, she thought with chilling clarity, could make this conclusion to her life worse.

Which was precisely when the skeletons attacked her.

Sixteen

Six and a half hours until the Slaughter

The nuns swirled around the Ulcer like flakes of ash. The air thickened with rain as Nixie pulled Taro against the muddy wall below the terminated steps, close to where they had jumped in.

Morgan and *Elliot.* Together.

'If he's changed sides – if he tells anyone—' Nixie didn't know how to finish the sentence. If Elliot had already betrayed them, they were as good as dead before the Slaughter had even begun.

'I'll deal with it,' Taro said. 'You know I'm mad enough. Son of a corpse-muncher. I bet he never even looked for the curse key.'

'Deal with it how?'

Taro wasn't listening. She was flexing her fingers, as though she was practising scratching Elliot's eyes out.

'Don't do anything stupid,' Nixie said sharply. 'They don't know we've seen them, which at least puts us ahead of whatever game they're playing.'

'We don't want to be in their game. We have our own thing going on!'

Our own thing. But really, they were playing Nixie's

game, and she was already re-planning. To win they had to keep playing at speed, without pause or hesitation; overthinking would only open the door to her loathed enemy, panic.

'We'll find the Redspire curse key ourselves,' Nixie said. 'And we'll recruit another arcanist to take Elliot's place, even if it means holding them at knifepoint.'

A shadow swept overhead. Taro cringed into the mud as a nun passed over them, landing a few yards away and dragging its soggy toes towards Elliot and Morgan. Nixie could hear the inhuman shrieks and *crunch* of bone as the starvelings were slaughtered by the blood arcanist and his new toy.

'We need a replacement blood disciple,' Nixie whispered as soon as it had gone. 'We'll try the Torture Pit.'

'We have to deal with *him* first.' Taro's furious eyes were smudged with black rings. 'I'm going to do it. I'm going to kill Elliot.'

Nixie almost laughed. They had to stop Elliot talking before the Slaughter, but actual murder? It was the next logical step, but it was too huge and bloody to look in the eye.

'It wouldn't help us,' she said. Even she could hear the lie in her voice.

'It would if he hasn't blabbed to Morgan yet.'

'Why would he save it for later?'

'Because he's an asshole, Nixie.'

Nixie grasped for something more solid, but everything wilted under her fingers.

'We've never murdered anyone.'

'Everyone has their first time,' Taro said. 'And you know what? I'm glad it's Elliot. Blood arcanists are the scum of Fourspires. I've never trusted them, and this is *exactly* why.'

Nixie closed her eyes. Rain dripped over her eyelids. She was so, so tired.

'Do you really think you could do it, Taro? Could you actually stick a knife in someone instead of just talking about it?'

'For us to get through this together, yes.'

Nixie's skin suddenly felt very thin, the roiling darkness of her suppressed rage too big to be contained. *Together*. She sank to her haunches and put her head in her hands. *Push it down. Don't make things messy now.*

'I know you're scared,' Taro said gently, squatting beside her. She touched Nixie's back, right on the most tender part of the bloody clock. Nixie recoiled, but Taro misread it as the shudder of a sob and wrapped her arms around Nixie's shoulders. Caging her. Everything was too hot and too close. She tried to shake Taro off, but Taro only hugged her more tightly, because who wouldn't want to be held by the bone witch? Her hip pressed into the broken mirror in Nixie's pocket. The pain made her suddenly furious. The blackness rushed up her throat. Nixie grappled violently with Taro's clutching hands.

'You're having a panic attack,' Taro said.

'No.' Nixie did not do things like *panic*. She was furious because her plan to escape the castle was unravelling, even after she had accommodated the Thaumaturge's murder and the machinations of the Ghost. She was filled with rage because she had let herself become stuck with Taro, instead of telling the truth four years ago. And yes, maybe there was a bit of extra adrenaline coursing through her right now, and maybe this felt like the time she collapsed before an exam unable to breathe, and maybe she was exhausted because for her whole life she had trodden this incredibly thin tightrope of trying not to feel anything, and it was quite difficult, actually, but she was *not* having a panic attack because she was in control of her body at all times—

Nixie untangled herself. She clawed her way up the edge of the Ulcer, and when Taro sighed behind her, she imagined the bone disciple spattering on the stones like a rotten apple. She made it over the top. She didn't help pull Taro up. The darkness in her chest was so nauseating she could barely breathe.

Bury it, bury it.

But it was in her throat, oozing over the base of her tongue.

'Are you crying?' Taro said, beside her again. She was a parasitic vine – hooks everywhere, blocking out the sun.

Swallow it.

Nixie couldn't. She had been stupid not to recognise the spread of her repressed anger, the dark new life growing in the mulch. Every bad thought she'd never expressed, the opinions she had taught herself to hide, and the blows she'd absorbed all bulged around her heart.

'Don't worry,' Taro said. 'I'll always be here.'

And Nixie knew, too late, what should have been obvious: that nobody could repress their hatred for ever.

'And don't I know it,' Nixie snarled.

Taro reeled, but Nixie was already vomiting words.

'We're always *together*,' she said. 'Just how you designed it. Was it worth the effort? Did you ever feel guilty? Did you think it was clever, how I never knew?'

Taro had gone rigid. Nixie could almost hear her thoughts: *She's talking about something else*, then: *Fuck, she isn't.*

'I could have been sold to a gardener,' Nixie said. 'I was perfect. I made sure I was never good enough for the castle, and never bad enough to be disposed of. Do you know how much work it took? I limited myself in just the right way so I could spend the last years of my miserable life growing carrots. I could have lived into my thirties, and yeah, it's not exactly great, but it's the best anyone coming out of the Torture Pit was ever going to get. But *you*—'

Her heart palpitated. She dug her fingers into her cheek and pressed so hard she felt the slice of each nail. She wanted to force her body back into submission, but the words kept coming. '*You* were going to be sent up here, because you were really fucking good at everything and had too much of an ego not to show it. Then you heard Kellan needed a familiar at the same time as Jon. So you went into the headmaster's office, and I don't know how the hell you did it, or who you threatened, but you *changed my results.*'

Taro stuffed her knuckles into her mouth, trying not to cry.

'I always wondered,' Nixie said. 'I made a list of the possibilities. Did you hurt someone to make it happen? Did you break bones?'

She had imagined this moment over and over. In her fantasies, Taro had always resisted her, and Nixie had leaned her full weight into the accusation until she broke the bone disciple down. But Taro fell so quickly Nixie found herself overreaching and falling with her.

'How long have you known?' Taro snivelled.

So here it was. No grand confession. No more lies. Just the bone witch crumbling. The lack of effort was insulting.

'I've known for ever,' Nixie snarled, 'because I'm not stupid.' The truth was flowing out, everything she should have said the moment she realised what Taro had done. 'You wanted me to think I'd accidentally shown the Academy my full abilities. But I don't make errors like that. Your head's just so far up your own arse you don't think anyone can see through your shit.'

Taro wiped her nose on her sleeve and reached for her.

'Do you hate me?'

'What do you think?' Nixie stepped back from Taro's grasping hands. They made her feel sick. 'I waited for you to say something when we got here. You didn't. Then you were the only person I had left, and I was too scared to be alone. Then I—' she almost stopped herself, but there was bile left. 'Then I just needed you to help me get out, because it would be easier with two of us. That's all. I used you.'

Taro howled silently into the ground. Nixie felt a twist of pain, but it was just habit, nostalgia, that made her want to pick the bone disciple off the floor and hold her. No – it was *weakness*. She hadn't thought that expelling the dirt would leave her feeling like this.

'What are you actually upset about?' she asked, wringing more poison from her tongue. She wanted to be empty. 'Bringing me up here to be slowly killed? Or that I knew you were too much of a coward to come to Fourspires by yourself?'

'Stop,' Taro croaked. Nixie willed her voice not to break. She twisted her lips into a grimace instead.

'I feel sick when you come near me. Touching you is disgusting.' It was only a half-truth, but she couldn't leave room for mercy. 'I don't want to be with you. Do you understand?'

'You kissed me.'

Taro's teeth were pressed together, her lips an angry line, but her eyes were wet and Nixie realised with horror that she and Taro had moved closer and were almost clinging to each other. 'Literally, just now,' Taro continued, her voice rising. 'You love me.'

I was just lonely, Nixie wanted to scream. She had just wanted someone to touch her and make her feel as if she was on fire again.

'No. I hate you.' But Taro had found a path in the storm, and she wasn't going to turn back.

'You wouldn't have been OK by yourself,' Taro said, her voice rising. 'You secretly wanted to come to the castle with me.'

'You don't know that,' Nixie hissed.

'But I—' Taro choked. Snot was running down her face. 'This isn't fair.'

Fair? The idea that Taro deserved anything like *fair* was hilarious.

'Well done,' Nixie said contemptuously, hating her voice, hating herself. Hating Taro even more. 'That's the most honest thing you've said in months. Whining about *fair*. Usually it's crap jokes you think sound clever.'

Taro blinked, water dripping down her face and leaving runnels in her make-up. Her thin lips were pressed together so forcefully they were grey at the edges. Nixie closed her eyes, willing her anger to remain, but it was being washed away with the rain.

'Go to hell,' Nixie said finally.

'I would, for you, you know?'

Nixie snorted. Everything about Taro was so awful it was a miracle Nixie had ever liked her. She had a perpetually sarcastic expression like curdled milk, and stupid brick-coloured lipstick that she didn't realise looked awful on her. She was impatient and loud and she was rarely a good person. In fact, she was the worst kind of person: someone who every day, by dint of existing, stabbed Nixie in the back, who lied by omission every day they existed together.

So what drew her back towards the mess? What made Nixie sometimes enjoy the fantasy that she was still in love? And what would she do now it was gone?

'I won't apologise,' Taro said finally. There was something new in her eyes: righteousness. 'I've felt guilty for years, but you know what? You should be happy that I kept us together. I did it because I love you.'

Something snapped. The last final, bitter piece of Nixie's heart.

'Oh, fuck you,' she spat, screwing her finger into Taro's chest. 'If you really loved me, you would have put my needs above your own. You don't love me, Taro. You—' she choked. She could hardly bring herself to admit it. 'You never did.'

Taro was crying again, silently.

Nixie swept the water from her own eyes. Her lips were numb with cold. She was hollow and in pain and the only thing she knew how to do was to keep moving, to run away from this black, howling hurt.

She turned away from her monstrous lover and climbed back to the castle.

Nixie marched through the stinking kitchens with her hood up, the mushroom cradled in her sleeve, shouldering past servants and cooks. She needed to get away from Taro. She couldn't stand the thought of looking her destroyer in the eye.

As she stalked through the castle, she smoothed the crumpled edges of the plan in her mind. It was something solid to cling to, but if she was honest, she had lost her conviction that it would work. Their success hinged on the assumption that Hallow Myre's curse could really be undone: that the Desecrae could fall and reveal a new world. To do that, they had to find another blood arcanist and the last two curse keys, the bone die and the drop of blood. They had to fight through the Fifth Tower, disabling the head arcanists and whatever lay inside, and follow the Ghost's instructions – whatever they were – once they reached the throne.

Nixie had never enjoyed operating in the dark. Her comfort came from knowledge. She didn't know the *whys* or the *hows* of the curse or its keys. She hadn't been told why the relics were created, or how they were lost, or why it seemed like they didn't want to be found. Why the Ghost was trapped in a mirror, or how the Desecrae had formed, when both of those things seemed deeply arcanical yet didn't belong to one discipline.

She shouldn't let those questions gnaw at her in case she wavered. But it was better than thinking about what had happened in the Ulcer. It was certainly better than acknowledging Taro's presence behind her, because that would mean arranging her face and finding something to say.

The library, she thought. It came to her in a rush, and she grasped desperately at the unexpected crumb of relief.

Alis would know what to do. She always had.

Nixie knew something was wrong as soon as she touched the library door. A deep glow seeped through the keyhole. And smoke. The sound of crackling paper.

Her stupid cigarettes!

Nixie rammed her shoulder into the door. It burst open too easily, and she fell in. The air was black. She dropped to her knees and spluttered, pressing her damp sleeve over her mouth.

'Alis!' she croaked.

The whole library was a deep, dark orange, and the air wobbled with a wicked heat that lifted the water from her hair. As she looked for Alis a saucer-sized spider darted between her legs, fleeing the carnage.

Above the crackling of a thousand burning books Nixie heard a gasp and the muffled, mangled sound of struggle.

She didn't wait for Taro; there wasn't even time to think. She crawled towards the noise, almost blind, sweeping the carpet for obstacles with her hands. Her body had taken charge. She cleared the issuing desk, rose to her feet, and staggered towards the sound.

The library door groaned behind her. She looked back as Taro careered over the threshold. The bone witch took one look at the burning library and plunged her hand into her pocket, scattering fingerbones on the floor.

The bones stretched and plunged upwards, vertebrae spraying from pelvis, ribcage bursting from collarbone. Lumpy, misshapen skulls bloomed at the tip of each backbone. A dozen fully formed corpses, each one hastily assembled and only approximately anatomically correct, lurched away from Taro's epicentre. Taro already had another handful of bones between her fists. Her back was hunched under the unbearable strain of wresting, but she didn't stop. The skeletons threw themselves over the flames. They beat the burning desk with their fists. They smashed the windows to let the rain in, and one removed its skull to use as a bucket.

It was phenomenal.

It was *impossible.*

There was another strangled cry, and Nixie tore away from the gory spectacle. She ran at a half-crouch, her fingers clasped over her mouth.

Alis was backed against a shelf. She had something long and yellow, some kind of spike, sticking out of her foot. Two of the skeletons were beating flames out around her feet.

Taro ran into Nixie and gagged.

'Nail,' she said, before retching dramatically at the foot of the bookcase.

Nixie didn't understand until she had taken a few more steps. The thing pinning Alis's foot to the carpet was one of the Librarian's long, thick fingernails. Nixie shoved the flailing skeletons out of the way.

'I'll pull it out,' Nixie told Alis, even though they both knew Nixie had zero medical knowledge. She had just always taken charge in a crisis. Alis gritted her teeth and nodded. Nixie dropped to her knees and gripped the base of the jagged nail. She knew it would hurt, and if she thought about it for much longer, she would lose her nerve entirely.

Nixie yanked the nail so hard she elbowed herself in the face. Alis gasped and slumped to the floor. The soft leather of her shoe was dark with blood.

'Sorry,' Nixie choked. She dropped the foul nail and wiped her hands on her knees. The air shimmered with heat, burning the side of her face. 'Taro, check Alis's foot.' It was the first time she had addressed her since the Ulcer. Alis looked as if she would rather drink a cup of Taro's spit.

'Looks fine,' Taro said. She had lost her green tinge and her voice was bright again, if brittle. 'It missed most of the bone. You ready to go, Al? We're murdering Elliot.'

'Stop it, Taro,' Nixie said. Skeletons clattered around her, stamping on flames. 'We're not murderers.'

Alis looked at them sharply.

'That dickhead has his knife in our backs,' Taro explained. 'He's Morgan's new familiar. We should have known. Morgan's always had a wyrdo fetish.'

Alis threw a withering glance at Taro.

'What? We can't say the word wyrdo ourselves? The point is,' Taro said, 'he's in the perfect position to sabotage us. We need to get rid of him so he can't help Morgan win the Slaughter or tell anyone what we're doing.'

'No killing,' Nixie snapped. She didn't care if Alis was confused by her coldness towards Taro. 'It's dangerous, and you don't know how.'

Taro surprised her by turning to Alis.

'You get the deciding vote, stone witch.'

Alis tightened her hand around her shoe, blood welling between her fingers. Her eyes slid to the smouldering door of the office where the Librarian's corpse lay on the floor, oozing and charred. Nixie had to swallow bile. Alis pressed the soft lead of her pencil into a bookshelf.

Elliot dies.

'That's the spirit,' Taro said.

But you have to do it yourself, Alis added. *Fingers has the Greyspire relic. I'm going to catch him.*

Nixie stared at Alis's scrawl, wondering if she had misread it. What did she mean, *fingers*?

'That's decided, then,' Taro said.

Everything was going wrong. Nixie had exposed herself to Taro. The Librarian was dead. Elliot had betrayed them. The Greyspire relic had been stolen by a set of marauding fingers. The library was burning, and an army of skeletons was punching the flaming books. Nixie was trapped in a maelstrom that she couldn't control, and now they were going to kill someone. She felt her chest tighten as the room swayed and crackled. Was she panicking again? No. She never panicked.

Alis touched her shoulder questioningly.

Nixie opened her mouth. Shut it again. She felt heavy and hot, but also as if she needed to run around and scream. There was a huge stone in her throat.

'Nixie?' asked Taro.

'It's fine,' Nixie said, pushing down her rising panic. 'Elliot betrayed us. So he dies.'

'I already said that, Nix. But—'

Alis stopped Taro by slapping the back of her head, a gesture that Nixie would be eternally grateful for.

'—*Ow*. Fine.' Taro glared at Alis. 'We'll talk later. Alis, you get the curse key.'

'I'll come,' Nixie said quickly.

Alis looked surprised, but she didn't object. She pointed at a line of black dots. Fingers had left a trail out of the library.

'You're leaving me to deal with Elliot alone?' Taro said.

The bloody clock on Nixie's back throbbed, its invisible hand scoring her skin. Six hours until the Slaughter, when she had to fight the other familiars. Six hours to kill Elliot, hide the body, hunt for a die, and find the Redspire curse key.

She would be damned if she spent it all with Taro.

'Yes,' Nixie said. 'Don't mess it up.'

'Cool.' Taro turned to the skeletons. 'Oi, you lot. Finish putting this out before you self-destruct, yeah?'

She pinched a chip of bone from its hiding place in her collar and hissed between her teeth. Veins burst in the whites of her eyes as a heavy, bone-yellow sword grew from the inside of her wrist, bursting through her skin and extending past her hand. She wrapped her fingers around it and turned to Nixie. She looked sombre.

'I'm literally going to murder someone for you,' she said. 'I'll do it a million times if you need me to. You know that, right?'

Nixie didn't reply. Taro faltered, then she rallied and winked.

'See you later, suckers!'

She saluted with her free hand and strode through the smouldering doors of the library, leaving Nixie with the bleeding stone disciple and the tattered remains of the night.

Seventeen

Five hours until the Slaughter

Elliot demanded the one room he knew Morgan didn't want him to have. The one behind the black, ivory-inlaid door at the top of the Redspire tower, next to Morgan's bedroom. He desired it because its proximity to the head arcanist was horrifically inappropriate. It was his way of redressing the imbalance between them, of saying *I do not fear you* when the opposite was true. It was the room he had sensed something deliciously powerful emanating from when he first broke into the tower.

Elliot turned the key and thrilled at the reluctance of the lock. He could feel it already; the heavy quality of air thickened by blood arcania. The danger that ran its finger over the back of his neck, telling him to reach out and grasp it.

But he would not be rash. He regarded the room, his prize, which was plush with overstuffed and ornately gilded furniture. A tall window looked on to the courtyard, shielded from prying eyes by glistening red ivy. Unlike the rest of the blood-spattered tower, this room was spotless, as though a cloche had been placed over it when the last occupant had left.

Morgan was moodily drinking downstairs with Peridot

at his feet. When they had returned from the Ulcer Elliot had stood and watched, the blood cooling on his forearms, as Morgan uncorked a bottle of wine; then, realising that Morgan was giving him the silent treatment, he had sat opposite him.

'I want my own room,' he said.

'Do you.'

'Not the one your last familiar had. Something better.'

'And what am I supposed to do about it?'

Elliot didn't blink as he looked into the eyes of the most dangerous man in the world.

'I want Rhys's room.'

Morgan twitched. Elliot could tell he was livid, but Rhys's name also had the strange effect of rendering him powerless. He enjoyed the fleeting feeling of Morgan's helplessness.

'Don't touch his things,' Morgan said finally. He clutched his goblet so hard his fingers turned grey.

Elliot had taken a large ring of keys from the table, and Morgan didn't stop him. So here he was, inside the hallowed room, breathing in blood arcania as deep and old as the crushed heart of the mountain under Fourspires. Its feverish warmth was in stark contrast to their violent kiss, which was still cold on his lips.

Be patient.

The starvelings' blood remained damp on his skin. He stripped, cast the stained clothes to the floor, and searched for something new to wear.

The first chest of drawers was full of junk that belied the tidiness of the room. He fingered the chewed quills, embroidered handkerchiefs, and jewellery, trespassing on the minutiae of a secretly privileged life. In the next drawer were sheaves of handwritten papers. There were two sets of handwriting, one spidery and languid, the other thick and florid. Elliot glanced through a couple of pages before shoving them back. He did not want to read intimate notes between Morgan and Rhys.

He ignored the arcania that trickled from the shadows, and opened the wardrobe. It was filled with clothes that had lain untouched for years, along with several sets of Redspire robes for a familiar. Elliot was almost the exact size and stature of their last owner. He ran his hand through crisp white shirts, exquisitely made trousers, and embroidered jackets. A strand of blond hair drifted from the shoulder of a black velvet coat.

This room had been special. A gift, and a secret. And now Elliot was prising it open and taking what he wanted, just like Morgan had laid him bare and torn out his feelings in the Ulcer.

He scrubbed the dirt from his skin. He dressed in the clothes of the dead man, easing a brilliant silk shirt over the tender clock on his back. He re-equipped himself with vials of starveling blood. When there was nothing left to do, Elliot finally answered the call of power emanating from the corner of the room.

It was more of a taste than a scent, as if something had settled on the back of his tongue, dark and heavy and sweet.

Elliot followed it to a cabinet under the window. It was full of more blood vials, Rhys's tools for the Suppression. He slowly ran his fingers over the glass bulbs. They hummed gently, responding to something preternatural in their ranks.

Closer. Closer.

He trailed his hand over the fragile necks. It was a thrill to draw the feeling out.

Closer.

The hum made him ache.

Stop.

His teeth throbbed with a weird pressure that came up through his bones and into his mouth. He could sense how close he was. The two vials in front of it shimmered, the air bending to its shape.

Elliot eased the curse key from its place.

He now truly understood the way Taro had cradled the skull in her arms. But where the skull had only the dull itch of bone arcania, this power was for *him*, deep and black and singing with darkness. How sad that no other discipline would know the taste of that power: the sweet, the salt, the pulsing richness of life mixed with death. It set his skin on fire.

He knew instinctively that if he were to use this blood for a normal spell it would scorch through him. Even he, as strong as he was, would finally succumb to wresting rot. A black tide of death would visibly travel up his wresting arm, towards his heart. And Morgan had given it to his lover as – a gift? Some desperate show of affection, a token of trust?

Elliot didn't need the curse key. He wasn't going to give it to Nixie, because he was throwing in his lot with Morgan. He just wanted it with a desire that outweighed bland common sense. Perhaps he was jealous of the gift Morgan had given, but that wasn't wrong, was it? And why shouldn't he take what he wanted, now he was the familiar of the next thaumaturge? He might even find a way to use its power.

He slipped the vial into his pocket with the starvelings' blood and lay by the cold hearth. The clock between his shoulder blades squirmed and itched, a wound that had stopped bleeding but wouldn't heal. Only a few hours remained until dawn, when the other familiars would enter the Fifth Tower and realise that Elliot wasn't joining them.

He closed his eyes and breathed slowly. But the second his thoughts wandered and he started drifting away, his pulse jumped and his heart squirmed and his whole body shuddered back to wakefulness. He curled on his side, wrapping his arms around his knees, clenching his jaw at the writhing in his chest. Something dug into his thigh. The knife that Alis had given him. He pulled it out and turned it in the moonlight.

This was how he had hidden from the nuns who had searched for young disciples in the city: bundled on his side in the wooden chest, whittling tiny figures, working by touch while his parents feigned innocence. When the nuns had finally found him – after the girl's death, and her father's treachery – they hadn't searched his pockets. He had carried that knife into the Pit, and had found it again after his memory had been wiped. He had continued birthing creatures from wood, even though he had no idea where he'd learned the skill or where the blade had come from.

This replacement was old and blunt, but sitting with his insomnia was too painful an alternative. Elliot unflinchingly broke a wooden handle from a fine drawer and tried to pare it to a new shape. The wood was hard and combative, and the little enjoyment he might have felt was marred by the knife's origin. He did not like to be in debt to a stone disciple.

Still. He wouldn't need this distraction for long. When they had won the Fifth Tower Morgan would give the necklace back, and Elliot would sleep. His name would travel through the city. He imagined his parents hearing that their son held the Thaumaturge's ear, their quiet pride and joy that he wasn't just safe, but powerful.

Elliot flicked the tip of the blade into the grain. He just had to trust that Morgan would win without accidentally killing him. Whatever the tower held, and whatever came after, Elliot would have to wrest far more than Saul's anaemic little spells required. He couldn't imagine that Morgan was ever careful. He had, after all, killed Rhys – accidentally or not.

The floor creaked. A shadow slid past the door. Elliot paused with his knife against the wood, expecting – even wanting – the handle to turn. But Morgan slipped into his own room, followed by the tap of Peridot's claws, and the tower fell silent again. Elliot released his breath and pressed the flat of the knife to his bottom lip.

In his mind the kiss in the Ulcer extended, grew longer and more wrong and bloodier, and his insides squirmed with odious desire. He imagined leaving his room now and opening Morgan's door to continue it. Morgan wouldn't tell him to leave.

He would kneel on Morgan's bed. He would pull Morgan's hair back and pin him down. The blood arcanist wouldn't argue, although he might pretend to struggle, and if Elliot so much as loosened his grip, Morgan would press him down and kiss him instead. Later, after Morgan won the Slaughter, they would undress each other at the top of the Fifth Tower. And one day, when Morgan was asleep, Elliot would take his knife from under the pillow and kill Morgan for the crown.

His pulse quickened. He could do it. He was terrible enough.

The knife slipped on the unforgiving wood and nicked Elliot's index finger. The bite of the metal shocked him; a memory slipped through that fracture in his shield, and he was cramped in the wooden chest again, with his blade between his fingers and blood welling from his hand. The girl with sepsis was dead, and her father had screamed for Elliot to be taken by the nuns, and they were flinging themselves at his casket—

In Rhys's room, half conscious, Elliot raised his finger to his lips to quell the flow, but the taste of salt and iron opened the fracture further. And he *remembered*. In the casket, that last time, he had licked his blood from his finger lest the nuns should smell it. But they had already been ripping the lid open. And now he saw, with sharper clarity than his broken mind had ever afforded him, a sliver of what else he had forgotten: his parents' faces as the nuns had dragged him from his hiding place.

Neither of them would look at him. His mother's face was so clear Elliot could have cut himself on its sharpness: eyes still, mouth tight, every ounce of affection wiped clean as though she had already given up on him. Where was the remembered love he had clung to?

Elliot had been so good, and so useful. He had given everything to his parents. He had worked himself through pain and exhaustion, and they had shown him what it was like to be adored. They had raised him to be the stable force that held a world together. They had given him a curse wrapped as a gift by creating a need in him, by making him hungry to be wanted, and now they were letting him go without a struggle. He wasn't worth fighting for.

Something scraped the outside of Elliot's door. The memory slid away, leaving a rank betrayal that Elliot thought he had blunted. Elliot looked at his hands and saw that he had split the wood he was carving in two, right through the centre of Morgan's sneering face.

The door handle rattled. Elliot put the knife away and rose, his head throbbing, his eyes blurry with—

Exhaustion. Never tears.

'Morgan?' He lowered his eye to the keyhole. A shadow flitted past, too agile for a nun, too silent to be Morgan. Whatever it was, Elliot was all too glad to redirect his thoughts. He unlocked the door and stepped into the hallway.

Empty. He descended the stairs. The velvety drawing room was deathly quiet. No outside noise penetrated the thick, blood-soaked stone. Instead of returning to that silent bedroom he wandered the chamber, running his fingers over Morgan's high-backed chair, the wooden cabinets, the blunt swords and jewelled daggers. He pretended for a moment that it was all his.

'Hiya, bloodsucker. I see you have a new tattoo on your back.'

Taro dropped from the ceiling. Her black exoskeleton shattered on impact, spraying the walls with shards of bone. She cracked her knuckles, unhurt and unhurried. In her hand – coming *from* her hand – was a long white sword with a serrated edge.

Elliot immediately knew what this was. She was the worst third of the unholy trinity that was bone, stone and botanic arcania. They didn't want him to be part of their scheme any more, and Taro had been sent to dispatch him.

His first thought was mortifying: *But they need me.*

His second was: *Punish them.*

Elliot grabbed an ornamental sword from the wall. It was the only thing long enough to reach Taro's organs without putting him within her range. Taro slouched towards him, her hair freshly oiled, her eyes outlined in thick black and red eyeliner as though she had dressed specifically to scare the shit out of him. Her own sword – an extension of her arm, because it was a literal bone thrusting through her wrist – caught the firelight and glowed white as it sailed towards Elliot's heart.

Elliot ducked inelegantly, the weight of his sword dragging him down.

Taro grunted in annoyance and thrust again. Elliot swung his sword with both hands, throwing his whole weight behind the blade. It crashed into Taro's bone-blade and glanced off with a teeth-rattling *clang*.

'Morgan's not coming to save you,' Taro said, already breathing hard. 'Even if he wasn't drunk as hell in his room, he probably wouldn't give a shit about me killing you.'

She aimed her blade at Elliot's sternum. Her arm jerked and he ducked.

'Don't even try to hit back,' she said. 'I ate a whole bunch of knucklebones on my way here. I'm fast and strong and basically impossible to kill. I'm running on skeleton power, baby.'

She thrust again, and Elliot barely dodged in time.

'Stay still and it'll hurt less,' Taro grunted.

'Get out of my tower,' he rasped.

'*Your* tower!'

'What are you trying to achieve, Tarenteeno?' His arms burned as he held the sword aloft.

'Listen, Elliot,' she said, the tip of her blade wobbling at eye height. 'I know you betrayed us. And I've had a really bad day. I'm sad and I'm pissed off and I hate myself, so I'm going to take it out on someone who deserves it. I'm going to enjoy it. And I'm going to do it with my bare hands, because that's what will hurt you the most.' She jabbed her bone sword at him. 'And if it even looks like you're going to use arcania, I'll try a really fun new spell and crush your skull like a boiled egg.'

Elliot jabbed his sword at Taro. She jumped back, but the tip of it had grazed her belt buckle, which was in the shape of – obviously – a leering skull. She looked surprised. Then angry.

She lurched at him so fast he only had time to scramble out of the way, not parry her thrust. Even though he had the advantage of sheer weight in his hands, he had no idea what he was doing. And Taro was moving so quickly he didn't have time to gather his thoughts for an incantation, let alone draw enough blood for it.

Taro swung her sword like a scythe as she drove him towards the empty fireplace. She didn't necessarily know how to fight either, but all she had to do was hack at him until he ran out of blood. He tried to swing, but the deep cabinets on either side of him made it impossible.

So he lunged. He caught Taro's wrist with the broadside of the sword. She swore and dropped back. Elliot sidestepped, but then she was in front of him again and trying to poke new holes. She lopped off two of his buttons and smirked. Elliot jerked away, drew his arms back for another blow, and instead smashed the hilt through a cabinet. He yanked it out, vision misting red with exhaustion.

'Stop,' he panted.

Taro didn't answer. She was too busy looking for the best place to skewer him.

Elliot wasn't going to win on strength. He weighed his options and grasped his only advantage. Taro was stubborn and driven by fury, and she always used brute force instead of her brain. She was too reckless to know when she was being led into a trap.

He slid towards the tower door, looking Taro in the eye as she caught her breath.

'What's that smell?' she said, narrowing her eyes. 'If you're wresting, I'm going to pull your eyes out through the back of your skull.'

'You can see I'm not,' Elliot said raggedly, adjusting his grip on the sword. He shifted his weight.

'That scared?' Taro said, flicking her eyes to the door handle.

Elliot kicked the door open and ran.

The idea of fleeing rankled, but not as much as being beaten by a bone disciple. Taro swore. Her second of hesitation gave him a lead. He pounded through the castle, swerving through puddles, darting around corners and veering past rows of grotesque statues while Taro's feet hit the stone behind him.

'Corpse-muncher,' she hissed.

Elliot followed the stench of rot to a set of mould-blistered doors. He shouldered them apart. He had never seen the abandoned wing of Fourspires. These rooms were damp with moss and fungi, lichens and semi-sentient gunges. Geraldin's Suppression only did surface work here, and the floors were as stable as wet toast.

He tucked himself into the shadows, his eyes stinging with sweat. Taro lugged her sword past him. He lunged, swinging his blade, and drove her across the room and into a patch of ear-shaped mushrooms that smelled like rotten meat. If he drove her in the right direction, he could get her to fall through a rotten floorboard, right … *there.*

Taro was trapped, and she knew it. Her sword-arm dropped. She had run out of power. Elliot's arm went limp in relief.

'Psych,' she said.

Elliot had never felt such genuine hatred for another human.

Taro swung her sword in a huge, underhanded arc, hitting his blade so hard his vision vibrated. Elliot's fingers gave up and dropped the sword. It landed with a sad *thump*.

He had imagined many bloody deaths for himself. Malachi slitting his throat, Morgan stabbing him through the heart. Instead his life would end quietly, shamefully, at the hands of an insufferable bone collector.

'You would kill Nixie.' Her voice was low and soft. 'I don't care about Alis, and I can take care of myself, but if you betray us she would fall first.'

Taro struck him. Elliot flung his arm up. The blade sliced sideways into his skin, leaving a deep, livid line of red that wet the blade. Taro withdrew and readied herself for the killing blow. Elliot's gaze fell on the sword that would split him, and he saw that it was covered in his blood. Taro's mistake was so unexpected and fundamentally stupid that he almost hadn't seen it.

He clamped his hand over his wound and screamed.

Taro's sword snapped at the bloody mark, leaving a stump of splintered bone at her wrist. Taro shrieked and tried to kick him at the same time as he grabbed her shoulders and slammed her into the wall. They fell to the floor, the black buttons on Taro's shirt tangling with the holes in Elliot's clothes. She smacked his face and rolled him over so she was sitting on his legs.

'Say "hi" to the Ghost for me,' Taro said, and raised her arms to slam the stump of her broken sword into his forehead.

'I have the curse key,' Elliot rasped. Taro froze. The serrated bone stump wavered above his neck. Elliot hadn't planned this far, but now he had started he could only unroll the next words with a cold sneer. 'I stole it from Morgan.'

Taro lowered her arms, but she didn't release him.

'Oh yeah?' she said.

'You can't feel its power because you're a bone arcanist,' he said. 'But I'll happily find a way to verify it. It's real. I have it.'

'Don't patronise me,' Taro said. 'Obviously I can feel its power. I can feel all of the disciplines. It's the rest of you dumbasses who can't smell what's right in front of you.' She wrinkled her nose for dramatic effect and added, 'I just thought you needed a bath.'

'Get off me, Taro.'

'Give it to me first.'

Elliot reached into his jacket. His fingers slipped over the curse key in his pocket and closed around a vial of starveling blood, fresh from the Ulcer.

Taro snatched the vial and inhaled. Elliot doubted she was clever enough to know that the stench of power was still pressed close to his body, but if she was, he knew more than one killing spell. And there was already blood pooling in his hands.

'*This* is a curse key?' she said scornfully.

'Can you really not tell?'

'Why didn't you say something earlier?'

'We weren't having a conversation.'

'You literally could have opened your mouth at any moment to stop me.' Taro was gripping the vial so tightly Elliot thought it would shatter. 'You could have said, "Hey, Taro, I'm not betraying you, I just shacked up with Morgan so I could get the relic".'

'I was busy trying not to get skewered.'

'So, you were going to bring this to us,' Taro said flatly.

He held her gaze for a long time before answering, just because it would irritate her.

'Yes.'

Taro rose. She looked as if she was trying very hard to mask relief. Something fluttered in Elliot's chest, and for a moment he thought his curse had unstitched him so far that he was experiencing guilt. Then it was gone.

'You won't mind if I keep this until we get to the Fifth Tower, then,' she said.

Elliot shrugged. Taro didn't look entirely convinced, but Elliot already knew that the fire was gone from her. She didn't want to kill him because she wasn't really a murderer.

'Be ready for tomorrow,' she said. 'You know what to do. Alis will create a distraction, and you do … whatever you need to stop Morgan from entering the tower. And if you look for a second like you're going to turn your back on us, I'll snap every bone in your goddamned body like a – What?'

The floor squirmed. Elliot thought it was a new symptom of his chronic inability to sleep until he realised Taro could feel it too. They both stared as the floor sagged like a wet flannel. A black spot appeared in the centre, and Elliot didn't see that it was a hole until it very suddenly yawned, revealing a black throat and blooms of orange fungal goo.

'You've got to be kidding,' Taro spluttered. 'Why are there *so many goddamned holes* in this place? It's not even funny!'

They both scrambled for the door, but the floor had warped and jammed the door shut. Elliot gagged at the necrotic stench coming from the hole. The sound of collapse stretched and rose in pitch until it somehow resembled a scream.

'Nixie?' Taro said, turning stupidly towards it.

Her foot slipped. She hit the tilting floor. She tried to dig her hands in, but her fingers scrabbled uselessly on the gangrenous slime. Elliot wrenched the door handle again, pulling with all his weight.

'Not without me,' Taro hissed, grabbing Elliot's ankle.

He slammed into the floor and slid into the centre of the room with her, towards the hole, which was growing like a pool of spilled ink. He scrambled for a hold, but the only thing he could grip was Taro, which he did, desperately. They locked eyes. Taro bared her teeth at him.

Tangled like furious lovers, they fell.

Eighteen

Two hours until the Slaughter

Alis stalked Fingers into the rotten depths of the castle, following her prey's sooty fingerprints to a warped iron gate near the Fighting Hall, a loose scab over the subterranean passages. She snatched a lantern from the wall and sucked her breath in to squeeze through the black gap. She didn't slow for Nixie, who followed her bloody trail in silence.

The fingerprints turned from black to blue as they picked up smears of corpse-fed mould. The passages bowed under the crushing weight of the castle, the ceiling bending to meet the floor, the statues broken-spined. Soon Alis was deeper than anyone had dared set foot in two hundred years, where the air was tight and the darkness was absolute. She should have been scared, but her fear had morphed into something unrecognisable. It was hot and spiky and it dug its fingers into her throat, making her want to enact terrible violence on the castle. It drowned the throbbing pain in her foot. It screamed into her ears.

Elliot betrayed us.

Fingers turned on me.

Cassia destroyed me.

Taro stole my best friend.

Alis bared her teeth and pushed on.

The five digits were as fast as rats, twisting and vanishing into tunnels that were barely visible in the oppressive gloom. But Alis knew how Fingers moved, and she could see from the twitch of his thumb how alarmed he was. He hadn't expected her to follow this far. Like everyone else, he had underestimated her. Alis was limping and bleeding, but Fingers only had to make one mistake and the chase was over. She was going to wrench that die from the arcanical space between his fingers, and he was going to *suffer*.

Fingers twisted and jumped through a hole in a rotting door. Alis slammed her shoulder into the wood until it gave way. The new chamber had iron hooks in the rumpled ceiling. Bones with deep knife marks littered the floor, and a dented pot shivered in front of a clammy furnace. Mr Fingers coiled and sprang into an empty cupboard set deep in the wall.

Cornered.

Alis shoved the lantern into Nixie's hands and peered into the cupboard. Fingers scattered his digits, poking and scraping until he found a damp rope hanging from the back. He clumped back together and grabbed it. Alis cracked her knuckles.

'Dumbwaiter,' Nixie said flatly.

Alis yanked her head back just as Fingers snapped the rope. The cupboard plunged away, whistling for a few seconds before smashing far below. Grey dust puffed out of the service hatch.

The shock of Alis's almost-decapitation was brief, but her fury was infinite. She kicked the wall, forgetting her injured foot, and choked with pain. She doubled over as the room warped.

'We lost him,' Nixie said, unnecessarily.

Alis had been embarrassingly happy when Nixie decided to join her, but she already regretted it. Nixie had been like this during exam season in the Pit, too, when she had only spoken in detached monosyllables. She had often been irritated by Nixie, Alis realised, but she had suppressed those memories to … what? Injure herself more?

Alis raised her middle finger, her vision pulsing: *Like hell it's over.* She wasn't going to let a set of dismembered appendages get the better of her. She picked up a calcified knife, rendered white and bubbly by the indescribable ooze leaking from the ceiling, and weighed it in her hand.

'Alis?' Nixie said, finally sounding worried, but Alis was already striding over to the dumbwaiter. She gripped the edges and lifted herself in feet-first, bracing herself against the sides of the empty chute. '*Alis*,' Nixie repeated, and Alis ignored her, because if she stopped to think for even a second, she wouldn't be brave enough to do this catastrophically stupid thing.

She gritted her teeth and lowered herself down the chute. Wood splinters snarled against her hands and clothes. It was as black as the inside of a book, and within minutes her arms and legs were burning with the effort of bracing herself. *May the castle crush you*, Alis chanted through the pounding in her head. A bolt of pain shot through her foot, but she raised her internal voice to drown it out. *May all your nails be dislocated.* It wasn't just about Fingers, but everything else that was wrong with Alis's life, the betrayals and the bad luck and being trapped in a body that didn't fit. Fingers was a conduit for her anger – she knew this – but Alis, suddenly free from the library and never able to return, was dizzy for revenge. She heard Nixie scuffling above her. Loose stones fell and bounced on her head. Nixie muttered something under her breath, and by the time Alis hit the crushed remains of the dumbwaiter on the next floor, Nixie was coming after her.

They found themselves in an ancient wine cellar. Jagged bottles lined the wall, so dirty they were almost black. Most of them had cracked, leaking viscous, tarry liquid all over the floor. A skull gazed accusingly from a crusted puddle.

Nixie stumbled out of the dumbwaiter, cradling the lantern to her chest. Alis motioned to Nixie to stay silent and covered the lantern with her cloak.

Darkness folded over them. Nixie silently drew closer to Alis; she had never liked the dark. But Alis was used to the colour of absolute night, and the walls here absorbed almost as much sound as the millions of books in the library. In the darkness, as she was in silence, Alis felt at home.

Come out, coward.

They waited. And they waited. The walls and floor merged, and if not for Nixie's steady breathing Alis would have thought they were suspended in a void. At last, a couple of bottles clinked together. There was a light scuffling, which resolved into a gentle *tap-tap-tap* as Fingers padded out of his hiding place.

Scuffle. *Clink.* Scuffle.

Alis waited until Fingers was almost level with her and yanked the cloak away from the lantern. Light flared across the room, stretching the shadows of his digits into talons. She leaped at him with the calcified knife, her teeth bared, already triumphant—

And he was gone.

No. He's never gone.

Fingers dropped from the ceiling and landed on Nixie's face. Nixie screamed as he grappled with her head, his fingers splayed, his thumb pressed into her left eye socket. Alis flung the knife away and grabbed the thumb, digging her nails into its joint. She peeled him off, finger by finger, and flung each part against the wall. The digits bounced and scuttled into formation, and only then did Alis see that he was holding one of Nixie's hairpins.

Before she could hurl herself forward again, he lunged and jabbed Alis in her right tear duct. He dropped the pin and ran off again, and Alis followed, her hand clamped over her eye. She heard Nixie grab the lantern and stumble after her.

The ground slanted upwards, back towards the surface. But Alis knew they could be a mile from where they started, and there might not be a way to get above ground. Fingers vanished into a room with a groaning ceiling.

No going back.

Rock bubbled through what had once been wallpaper. A centuries-old mattress had become a garden for bristling fungi, and beside it was a hulking wardrobe with a tarnished brass key hanging from the lock. They were at another dead end.

Alis braced herself against the door frame, blocking it off as Nixie clattered to a halt behind her. She and Fingers looked at each other, waiting for the next move.

She wished she knew what he wanted. She desperately needed to understand why he had befriended her – if there had been any real kindness in it – and why he had turned on her. His betrayal was worse in its senselessness. He had helped the Librarian attack Alis, but he had also spent the last two years waving the die in front of her face as though he wanted her to know about it. He could have blinded her with two jabs of Nixie's hairpin, yet he had missed. Did he have a motive, or was his function purely chaos? And had she really cornered him, or was she doing exactly what he wanted?

'There's something in the wardrobe,' Nixie said, gripping Alis's elbow.

The wardrobe door trembled. Something scratched from the inside.

I place a thousand gory curses on whatever this trap is, because it will. Not. Be. Good.

Fingers' smallest digit leaped at the brass key, caught the ring, and swung it around.

The door opened to reveal an Unholy Mother on a coat hanger. Its robes had been eaten by moth larvae, exposing its slack grey skin. The hanger was caught around its neck. When the lamplight fell on its face its eyes popped open and its eyelashes scattered like petals.

Nixie dropped the lantern. It smashed against the floor, throwing a slick of burning oil towards the bed. For a second the room was so brightly lit Alis couldn't see anything but the silhouette of the nun, which writhed free of the coat hanger and sailed towards Alis with its mouth open.

Alis folded as the light sputtered out. Her legs just stopped working. All the terror she hadn't felt flashed across her skin. There was no time to fight. It was too dark to run. Yet as she hit the stone she knew her prayers to the universe was being answered; and it was laughing at her, because at the same time as saving her it was about to break her. She slapped her palms into the floor and leaned her weight into the impenetrable slate and screamed with all the hurt she'd never put into the world.

'Motherfucker!'

Her scream folded into an incantation.

The walls burst outwards. A bolt of stone punctured the nun and flung it backwards, pinning it to the wardrobe. Sparks flew as chunks of stone chipped past each other. They hit the pile of jubilant fingers and crushed them into the corners of the room.

Alis was slapped backwards by a sheet of light. The fall lasted for seconds. Was she dying? It felt like dying.

I hope you die I hope you suffer I hope your fingers never bend again—

'Liar,' Nixie said softly.

Alis opened her eyes to another layer of darkness. She was on her back, peppered with splinters of stone. Her arms burned from the wresting, eclipsing the pain in her foot. Her mouth ached, reminding her of what stone arcania had always been: a burden, something that you had to force your tongue around. A discipline for those who were hard and unforgiving.

She still couldn't believe she had spoken. But she was *not* a liar.

She turned over and crawled towards the bed, sweeping her hands over the floor until she met Fingers. He was spread far apart, each digit as still as a piece of meat. She felt the gaps between each one, lacing her own fingers between them until she felt something small and hard resting behind its thumb.

She huffed with laughter. Her throat was full of knives, and her tongue was twitching like a fish. But she had the Greyspire curse key. It was cool and heavy and it ached with power. It was all she could do to thrust it into her robes instead of swallowing it whole.

The nun twitched against the wall, dust pouring from its pierced stomach, the sound growing fainter until it died.

Then there was nothing. No light, and no hope of escape. If Alis or Nixie left the room they would shuffle in endless circles until the clock engraved on Nixie's back completed its countdown and flash-fried her heart, and Alis would simply starve. It was just them, a twice-dead corpse, and five disembodied fingers for all of eternity.

'Alis?' Nixie said. She was no longer expressionless. Actually, she sounded pissed off. Alis would have preferred to perish in awkward silence.

'*Alis*,' Nixie repeated when she didn't reply.

Alis knew what she should say – what she *wanted* to say – but the harder she tried to line the words up and get them out of her mouth, the tighter her throat got. She closed her eyes and practised the words in her head until they sounded meaningless. She still couldn't do it.

'I didn't lie,' Alis said instead. *Good enough.* Her tongue was thick and dry. 'You … assumed.' Her own voice was alien. Every syllable came with a pulse of anxiety that she had to smother.

'You knew what we assumed. You could have corrected us.'

Alis declined to answer.

'You don't get to ignore me now,' Nixie snapped.

I'm not ignoring you, Alis wanted to scream. *You just don't understand.* She couldn't see Nixie's face, but she knew exactly what her expression was: self-righteous and furious. Another thing that had always pissed Alis off. She automatically moved her hand towards her pencil, but it was too dark to write.

It took everything for her to force the air up her throat again.

'How didn't you notice I have a fully functioning tongue?' *That's not how you say 'functioning', you idiot.* 'You've seen me eat.'

'I don't spend much time looking at your tongue.'

'No, because you're busy chewing Taro's,' Alis mumbled, and immediately wished she hadn't. Conceding any hint of jealousy meant she lost to Taro *again*. Just as she had for years, over and over, every time she had missed her best friend.

'You went ten whole seconds without mentioning her,' Nixie said with genuine scorn. 'It's a record.'

Alis rubbed her temples. Her throat was raw, and her face felt hot, and everything hurt. She rolled the tiny stone die between her fingers, but it didn't bring comfort; it made her bones ache with the weight of its power. She screwed a piece of crumpled paper around it and crawled back to Nixie.

'Take it,' she said hoarsely.

'I don't want it.'

'It's your plan, so it's your responsibility.'

Nixie looked confused, and Alis realised she'd got the inflection all wrong. When Nixie didn't take the die, Alis shoved it in Nixie's pocket and forced herself to try again. 'If you don't, I'm going to throw it down a hole. I didn't want to be part of this. I just thought …'

'What?'

I thought you would be impressed. I thought you would want to be friends with me again.

She couldn't even begin.

'Doesn't matter,' she muttered.

'I heard they maimed your tongue when the Librarian saved you from execution,' Nixie said. 'To stop you sharing anything about Geraldin.'

'They forgot.'

Nixie snorted. 'They didn't.'

'OK.' Alis squeezed her eyes shut. *They're just words. You're a goddamned librarian. Words are your job.* So why did it feel like her heart was trying to squirm out of her ribcage every time she tried to make the right sounds? 'I knocked the surgeon out with a chunk of masonry before the Librarian picked me up. He was too embarrassed to admit what had happened.' She paused to breathe. 'Or he died. I didn't stay to find out.'

She wasn't joking.

Silence fell. After a while Nixie started clicking one of her hair beads against her teeth.

'Really. Why didn't you tell me?' Nixie asked finally. Alis put her head between her knees and tried to breathe through the tightness in her chest.

'When would I?' she said finally. 'We didn't see each other after the Pit.' *Although you clearly managed to stay in touch with Taro*, she added silently, before shouldering the thought aside. 'And it was safer. If I slipped up, someone would slice it out for real.'

Alis squeezed a piece of grit between her fingers, trying to make it hurt so she wouldn't have to think about how exhausted she was from talking. Or listen to the small, furious voice in her head that whispered: *Liar.* There was another reason she never spoke. It had nothing to do with fear of discovery. It wasn't even a choice; it was bound up in the deep panic she had started to feel every time she said something out loud.

'I don't believe you,' Nixie said. As if she had her goddamned tentacles in Alis's brain.

'OK,' Alis snapped. 'I like not accidentally saying things I might regret.'

'What does that mean?'

'Can't you think of an example, Nix?'

Fucking inflection again. It was humiliating.

'No,' Nixie said.

'*Sure.* OK.'

'Don't underdo the sarcasm, Alis. I almost didn't catch it.'

'Do you ever say shit like that to Taro, or am I easier to use as a punching bag?'

That shut her up. Alis hugged herself, triumphant and wretched at the same time. The silence between them thickened with unspoken accusations and insults, defences and comebacks, all the things they should have argued about for the last four years and had strenuously avoided. The things Alis wanted to scream felt like a maelstrom.

Alis was trembling. She thought her bottled-up anger had broken her body; then she realised that the wall was vibrating. The sound ran through the stone and into the floor, shaking the bed away from the wall and making the nun sway on its pin. Alis grappled for Nixie, and they clung to each other's elbows, not for comfort but because if they didn't, they would both fall over.

'The castle's collapsing,' Nixie announced, because even now, she had to be the cleverest person in the room.

Bones pattered down and rattled across the floor. Murky light poured through a fissure above their heads. Alis yanked Nixie into the open doorway as the ceiling burst open like a boil.

Layers of flooring, rotten wooden boards and scraps of liquefied carpet, slapped into the ground and released noxious mould spores.

Two bodies slammed through what used to be the ceiling.

'You're touching my butt!' Taro screamed.

She rose from the pile of debris, bloody and torn and nightmarish with fury. She glowered at the other body, which was scrambling away from her as though she had something infectious. A bleak hole whistled above them.

'I can't help where I land,' Elliot snarled. 'I don't want to be anywhere near you.'

Taro saw Alis and Nixie.

'Oh, hi,' she said.

I beseech of the universe to give me a fucking break.

Alis had to be dead, and this was hell, because the cosmos was playing a horrifying joke on her. The person she loathed most in the world had found her by smashing a hole through the castle and landing *right in Alis's lap.* A splintered shaft of bone, one side of which was serrated like a knife, protruded from Taro' wrist. Taro followed her gaze.

'Oops,' she said, wrapped her fingers around it, and winced as the bone retreated. Nixie was looking at Taro with a weirdly curdled expression that Alis couldn't put down to shock or relief. It was almost … disdain? Taro studiously didn't make eye contact with her. Instead she surveyed the room.

'Damn, whose party—'

'Stop,' Nixie said frostily, and Taro did. 'We found the die, then a nun tried to eat us, then the light went out. That's everything.'

Alis had no desire to be the third wheel to their spat, however gratifying it may be. Instead she locked eyes with Elliot, who was trying to disentangle himself from the rubble. His arm was dark with blood. It would be a shame to ruin that beautiful face, but someone had to do it.

Alis cracked her knuckles and strode towards him.

Elliot's concern turned to deep alarm when he realised that Alis was about to separate his spine from his body. He jumped up, holding a piece of wood like a shield.

'You don't understand,' he said loftily, which was possibly the worst thing he could have told Alis. She smacked the wood aside and kicked his knees. He dropped to the ground with an indignant splutter, his dark curls falling over his eyes. Alis grabbed a splinter of wood the length of her forearm and aimed it at the weakest part of his skull.

Taro leaped on to Alis's back and flung her spindly arms around her chest. Alis stumbled and fell with the bone disciple still stuck to her.

'He's on our side!'

Alis kicked Taro off, itching from proximity to her toxic make-up. Before she could swing at Elliot again, Taro caught the back of her robe and thrust something in her face.

'*Look.*'

It was a vial full of a liquid so deep and black it looked like a hole had been cut out of the world. Alis couldn't, as a rule, sense blood arcania, but at the same time it was impossible not to guess what Taro was holding.

'Yup,' Taro said. 'Our bloodsucking friend was cosying up to Morgan so he could get the last curse key. Lucky, huh?' She pocketed the vial and scowled at Elliot. 'I'm keeping this.'

Alis fixed her eyes on Elliot. He met her gaze with a curled lip, but Alis knew guilt when she saw it, and Elliot's face was lousy with it. She should go ahead and stab him anyway.

Nixie swore. They all looked.

Fingers was gone.

He was no longer pinned to the mattress, but Alis knew he wouldn't have gone far. Something pale darted through the doorway, followed by the sound of nails tapping urgently against the floor. Elliot looked at them incredulously.

'Was that a—'

'Yes,' Nixie and Taro said together.

Alis considered bolting after Fingers, but now she had what she wanted, the rage was gone. Fingers could wreak all the havoc he liked, but Alis had got Nixie what she wanted. She had proved her worth. They had the curse keys, they were all together, and their plan – what existed of it, anyway – was still unfolding in approximately the right shape. There were more dead bodies than she had anticipated, but still. They might actually be … *winning*?

'We need to get back to the surface,' Nixie said. She sounded businesslike again, but Alis knew her too well to think her minor breakdown was over. This was the lull before the storm of Nixie going absolutely batshit. 'It's almost morning. We need to do the Suppressions before anyone knows we're missing.'

Taro looked at the hole in the ceiling.

'I think we missed the boat on that one.'

'Why?'

'The Desecrae's already light. You can see all the way into the castle.'

'Shit,' Nixie said softly.

'The blood,' Elliot said.

'The vines,' Nixie said.

'The brain-eating, bone-munching, skeletal army of the dead,' Taro said.

Behind them, through the ragged doorway through which Fingers had escaped, was an endless jumble of pitch-black tunnels and deathly silent rooms. They still hadn't solved their problem. They would never find their way out without a light.

Alis looked at the greylight and remembered the bookshelves she had climbed to get out of the Librarian's pit.

I beg of the universe, not again.

Alis pointed at the skewered nun, which was still pinned to the wall by the shard of stone. There were plenty more horrors where that came from. Room upon room of terrible relics, poisonous plants, and dead bodies, all the way up through the abandoned wing of the castle.

'Rad,' Taro said. 'I'll go first.'

Good, Alis thought. *If anything's waiting to bite our heads off, you can let us know.*

Taro jumped on to the stinking bed, spread her hands along the damp, furry wall, and used the stake pinning the nun as a rung to the room above. She grabbed the edge of the hole she and Elliot had fallen through and pulled herself up, showering them with worms. Nixie went next, ignoring Taro's hand.

Alis rolled her sleeves up and climbed ungracefully on to the bed. The dead nun stared at her, grey dust still leaking from the hole in its chest, as she dug her heels into its shoulders.

'You're doing it wrong,' Elliot said. 'Spread your arms for balance.'

'Don't patronise me,' Alis said.

It was less than a whisper, but Elliot spluttered. Alis took the opportunity to kick some nun-dust at him with her heel.

'Holy shit, Al.' Taro's voice floated from above. 'You talk?'

Call me 'Al' again and you'll wish I didn't.

She wedged her foot into the nun's open mouth and began the ascent to the Slaughter.

Nineteen

Forty-five minutes until the Slaughter

Taro puffed with effort as she hauled herself to the next decaying level of the castle. The other familiars' voices floated below her, or to be exact, Elliot's did, with Alis offering a terse monosyllable when he took breath in his diatribe. Nixie … she was trying not to think about Nixie.

'That's how you got into the Redborns' chambers,' Elliot griped. 'You can still use arcania. You incanted and passed through the stone. You could have let me out of there, but instead you left me to Morgan.'

'Yeah,' Alis said, then after a heavy pause: 'It's how I got out of Morgan's tower, too. You didn't want my help then.'

This silenced Elliot, who was apparently struggling to come to terms with meeting someone who gave even less of a shit about being likeable than he did. Taro didn't know what to think of Alis's sudden ability to speak, aside from the small, shameful squirm of triumph at knowing Nixie had been kept in the dark too, which made Alis a truly shitty friend. Not that Taro was doing well in that department, *ha ha, oh no I feel sick*.

'You could have incanted in the chapel.' Elliot had found a new bone to chew on.

'Mmm.'

But Taro didn't have the luxury of revelling in Alis's deceit. The trickling greylight that spilled through the hole Taro and Elliot had made illuminated rooms that hadn't been seen in decades, each one alive with pale tendrils of new ivy. Its fingers crept over the walls like pinworms, flopping around for purchase, sprouting hair-fine offshoots every few seconds. It would only get stronger. There was a vast difference between the ancient ivy that crawled up the exterior of the castle and *this* stuff, which was usually suppressed. She brushed a hand over a pale tendril and it snapped around her finger, squirming its minuscule hooks into her skin. She swore under her breath.

'Hurry up,' she called with forced jollity. 'Five floors to go.'

'How are you OK with this?' Elliot rasped.

Taro's fingers slipped, and in that brief second of panic something awful made its way into her cranium. It was a small, whimpering voice that said, *This is scary and I want to cry.*

'Because I'm not a wimp, Elliot,' she said.

A yellow arm punched through the wall between her and Nixie. Taro automatically kicked down. There was a loud *thunk* as the arm detached from a shoulder, hit Nixie, and bounced past Alis and Elliot. Taro braced herself for more, but the walls only groaned.

The skeletons were still being held back by Geraldin's Suppression, which kept the walls from melting like wax. She would have been the only one able to perform it this morning; all the other head arcanists' familiars were down *here*. Taro had always assumed the head arcanists had some kind of backup plan, like a cupboard full of unclaimed familiars they could wheel out if theirs went missing. It hadn't occurred to her – although it was now painfully, tragically obvious – that they would be too proud to admit they had lost the source of their power. Even they, in the light of a huge failure, might not be safe from the punishment of the Unholy Mothers.

The next floor seethed with botanic and necromantic life. Crumbs of stone shivered away from the walls as dead people bucked and twisted inside them. Even with the walls holding steady, the undead were unrelenting and impossible to hurt, which meant they would never stop trying to break free. Far below, in the room with the dead nun, they were making a noise like gravel hitting the bottom of a well.

Taro smacked a yellowing hand away.

'Whose blood is this?' Nixie said.

Taro squeezed through the next Elliot-and-Taro-shaped hole and flopped down on the mouldering carpet. Nixie was right; something corpuscular was happening. She pressed her thumb into the floor and held it to the greylight. It was red. Moments later the same stuff bubbled out of the carpet. Taro had never seen Morgan's Suppression fail before, and it smelled worse than she had expected. Some people said the blood belonged to all the familiars who had died in service, in which case there would be enough to drown them all.

'It's just random castle blood,' she said brightly as Nixie climbed into the room. She raised her voice. 'Oi, Elliot. Anything you can do about that?'

Elliot said something that she couldn't make out, but he sounded irritated.

'No worries, blood boy,' Taro said. She wiped her hands on her robes and turned to Nixie. Her cheeks hurt from smiling. 'While we wait for the vampire to catch up, tell me what happened to Alis.'

'They forgot to kill her tongue. She went along with it.'

'And she didn't let us know?'

'I don't want to talk about it.'

Taro felt a lump swell in her throat, but she forced it down. Nixie was going to forgive her. She hadn't meant anything she'd said in the Ulcer, and everything would be normal once this was over.

Alis climbed through the hole in the floor, shortly followed by Elliot, and Nixie gave Taro a glance that very clearly said *Now shut up.*

They were only two floors away from the inhabited part of the castle. The greylight cast a pall over the whole room, revealing the fuzzy edges of moth-eaten tapestries and the blunted corners of rotten furniture.

‘OK, wyrdos,’ Taro said. None of them questioned why she was their leader, a role that Taro didn’t really want, but if she stopped now she was fairly sure they would fall apart. ‘I think we can get out of this door and use the stairs. Going by the giant scab on my back the Slaughter doesn’t start for half an hour, which means we’re not super-totally screwed.’

Without waiting for an answer, she flung the door open and walked into a wall of dead people.

They were white and yellow and their eye sockets were packed with centuries of dust. Their shoulders were covered in chips of stone and their legs were twisted from where they had wrenched themselves from the walls. They lolloped in a way that could, under very specific circumstances, have been quite charming but wasn’t because they were heralding the apocalypse and *now they were trying to grab her*—

Taro tried to slam the door, but the dead were already on top of her. They ripped the door off its hinges and almost flattened Taro beneath it. Taro wriggled away and tore a crusty sconce from the wall, then swung it hard at the first skeleton. The sconce lodged in its head but did nothing to impede its progress.

Nixie dug her hand into the moss on the wall. Taro heard the faint gasp of effort as she wrested, growing green tendrils of weed from the infested carpet and binding them to the skeletons’ legs. The skeletons ripped through them like wet tissue paper. Taro backed into Nixie, who backed into Elliot and Alis, and suddenly they were standing in a ring in the middle of the room, facing outwards, about to be completely and utterly decimated.

‘Do something,’ Elliot demanded, as though Taro was both responsible for this fatal mess *and* being lazy.

‘Do it yourself.’

‘I can’t,’ he muttered, and Taro realised how deeply in shit they were. Elliot was one nosebleed away from collapse, and Alis was so out of practice she probably couldn’t control her stone arcania without blowing them all up at the same time.

A skeleton in rotting servant’s livery swung for her. It still possessed a fair amount of flesh, so Taro grabbed the exposed forearm, yanked hard, and broke it from the torso with a wet *schlop* that made her stomach recoil. Its skin was loose, and when she shook the arm it peeled away from the bone like an oversized glove. Taro gagged. She liked them dry.

'Hold on,' she choked.

Bone arcania crackled through her hand. Taro almost dropped the bone and caused the kind of short-circuit that would take out not just the corpses but everyone within a two hundred-metre radius. She needed her concentration for the messiest, most explosive spell her memory could fetch from the drawer marked *Don't even think about it, idiot.* An anti-bone marrow, corpse-sucking death spell that Jon didn't even have the wherewithal to pronounce.

All the moisture left the skeletons with a loud *whoosh*, hitting the ceiling in great globules of red and pink and grey. Fleshy rain pattered back down on the bones, which had turned into soft, grey hummocks of ash.

Nobody moved for a few seconds. Taro released her breath, feeling light-headed.

'Easy,' she said to the others, then remembered to turn around and check that they were alive and she hadn't, you know, pulverised them as well.

They were all staring at her. Alis and Nixie both had rocks in their hands, which was sweet, because they would be zero use in a fight. Alis hadn't even chosen a sharp one. Elliot's fists were bunched as though he planned to defeat the walking dead by cuffing them around the ears.

'What?' Taro said.

'How did you do that from one bone?' Elliot said. 'You should be on the floor.'

'*Boo-hoo*. You just can't stand someone being better than you.'

Alis was still giving Taro some serious side-eye, as though she agreed with Elliot but couldn't bring herself to use her newly found power of speech to concede.

'Righto,' Taro said. She was shaking, but she'd rather let the reaper take her than let the others see. She shoved some more bones inside her robes. 'We'll go to the stairs and get out of here ASAP. Yes, Chatty Alis, you have a concern?'

Alis, now she had her hands free, had inexplicably gone back to her pencil.

There's a pile of eviscerated bodies in the way.

'We'll climb.'

They scaled the hillock of dead bodies outside the door and slid down the other side. The walls and floor were riddled with holes where the dead had removed themselves from their penultimate resting places, and splattered with chips of bone and gobbets of flesh. Taro's range, she was starting to realise, was pretty phenomenal.

'Nuns,' Elliot said sharply.

'Go eat a noseblee— What?'

Six nuns were staring at them from the end of the hall. These ones looked as though they had been asleep for decades, hibernating so far from the surface that they hadn't heard the countdown to the Slaughter. But this – the implosion, the apocalypse, the familiars trampling through their graves – was too much. They peeled away from the stone and drifted, tapping their fingers and toes along the walls, nostrils quivering. Taro automatically raised her hands, showing them her empty palms: *No wresting here.*

If they understood, they didn't care. They probably hadn't been fed in years, and here were four familiars stinking of arcania, creeping around the belly of the castle while the world ended. Taro stepped back and heard the others do the same. She didn't dare take her eyes off the nuns in case her gaze was the only thing holding them back.

'Get back into the room,' she said to the others, trying not to move her mouth.

'It's still blocked up with bones,' Elliot said from the back.

'Climb over them, you ass.'

'Then what? We won't get through the ceiling in time.'

'I don't know why you bothered to open your mouth if that's the grand total of your contribution,' Taro snapped.

The corpses rustled as Elliot and Alis climbed back over them. Taro backed down the corridor, begging herself not to trip on anything.

'Nix, can you do something botanic?'

'Yes, I'll grow flowers at them,' Nixie said, choosing the absolute worst time to develop a sense of humour.

'Alis? Stone?'

She was back at the doorway with the moistureless corpses.

'If we bring the ceiling down we'll kill ourselves too,' Elliot pointed out.

'OK, bloodbag, how are *you* going to help?'

Nixie scrambled over the pile of bodies in the doorway and helped pull Taro over, which was surely a concession that she didn't want Taro to die, even if she did dig her nails in too hard. The nuns had traversed half the corridor, and now they were so close Taro could count their fingers.

'Any ideas?' Taro said. 'No?'

She gripped the pile of knucklebones in her pocket. She had sometimes wondered if running a spell backwards could undo the damage it had caused. She didn't think anyone had tried, but … by throwing in the same amount of energy it took to dissolve the walking dead, maybe the gobbets of viscera on the ceiling would spring back into the spongiform bones and the skeletons would come back to – er – life? Even better, if she could funnel it through the doorway without catching any of the bodies still in the room, the familiars wouldn't be trapped inside the melee.

Theoretically.

Even Jon hadn't attempted something as gross as re-resurrection. Taro closed her eyes and tried to untangle the spell in her head. She could almost see the slice of her words and how they would intersect with the wresting. Her tongue fidgeted as she ran it over the imaginary grooves left by the imploding spell.

Taro dug into herself for one more bolt of pain. She tightened her grip on the knucklebones. She opened her mouth. The flipped-over words tumbled into the darkness.

And vanished into a great gloomy silence.

'What was that?' Elliot said. Taro didn't even have the urge to punch him. Nixie pressed something into her hand: a chunk of stone. Suddenly smashing things in the face didn't seem like such a bad idea.

'Sorry, Nix.'

'What for?' Nixie said frostily.

'For us being stuck here.'

'Here right now? Or in the castle in general?'

Taro shifted uneasily. She knew what Nixie wanted her to say. She knew, without a flicker of doubt, that she had done the right thing by changing Nixie's results and bringing her to Fourspires. That Nixie had secretly wanted her to do it, and that Nixie still loved her. But if Taro had to decide between Nixie dying angry at her, or Taro swallowing her pride—

'I mean stuck under the ground,' Taro croaked, nodding towards the apex of their loveless home. One of the nuns drifted closer to the barricade, and Taro's palms started sweating.

'Not good enough,' Nixie said softly.

The room shrieked. The air was vacuumed out of Taro's lungs. For a moment she was blind and breathless and as helpless as a single solitary metacarpal, then—

Dust particle knitted to dust particle. Bone welded to bone. The bodies of the restless dead, hastily and grossly reassembled, built from a blueprint that no longer existed, towered in front of them. Toes crunched together at the ends of arms. Fingers sprouted from eye sockets. Teeth bristled from sternums.

Taro, queen of bones and lover of all things cartilage, almost destroyed her bodily assemblages all over again. Her creations defied everything that was good and natural. The only thing that remained from their previous incarnation was their blind hunger.

The Unholy Mothers unhinged their jaws and spurted grey powder as the skeletons lunged towards them. It would haunt Taro's nights for as long as she lived. A hundred disjointed bodies with malformed jaws ran towards the nuns, and the two sides met with a high, ear-rending shriek.

Unholy Mother and unholy corpse tore into each other with inhuman speed. Bone cracked and flesh ripped. In three heartbeats the noise fell dead and the air swirled with floating scraps of skin tissue.

Taro lowered her hands, which she hadn't realised were in front of her face. Something was missing.

You need to breathe, idiot.

She dropped the stone with a *clang* and sat on the floor, which was now pockmarked with extra holes like a honeycomb.

'Move,' Nixie snapped.

The ceiling caved in like a wet chocolate pudding. Thousands more bones pattered down, along with the details of ancient domesticity: tin spoons, broken plates, bent coins, buttons, pins, beads, tobacco pipes and teeth. Alis shouted something unpronounceable. All the stone-based detritus bounced off her as if it was hitting an invisible shield. Elliot and Nixie ducked into her orbit, then Nixie grabbed Taro and dragged her in too.

Ploing! The last piece of junk hit the ground and rolled away.

It was a long time before Taro could bring herself to move. Or perhaps it was only a few seconds. Every moment stretched like toffee. She crawled out from under the shield and elegantly choked up a wad of bone-flavoured phlegm.

'OK,' she said, wiping her mouth. Alis lowered her arms, and the last bits of stone fell harmlessly at their feet. Alis looked as surprised as Taro that she had pulled the incantation off. Taro nodded to Alis with respect, and Alis didn't scowl, which was almost the same as receiving a warm embrace. '*Now* we can go up there.'

Taro adjusted the stinking hood over her face, curled her fingers into claws, and generally tried to appear dead.

The nuns' robes were thin enough to let a trickle of greylight through, turning the world into a vague series of humps and shadows. The hood stank of mildew, bad breath, and now supernatural castle blood. It was all she could do not to gag. The others shuffled behind her with varying levels of commitment. Nixie was standing too straight, Elliot couldn't bring himself not to swagger – did he literally have a dislocated hip? Was that it? – and Alis wasn't even trying.

They needn't have bothered. The nuns had all been sucked into the courtyard, and the remaining servants looked away the minute they saw the robes, desperate not to make eye contact. It was easy to shuffle through the labyrinthine halls, following the thrum of thousands of bodies packed into the amphitheatre around the Fifth Tower.

'How long until everyone realises the apocalypse is happening, Nix?' Taro asked. Nixie was cold, unmoved by Taro's desperation to start a conversation.

'Historically, an hour after the missed Suppression.'

'There's still time to fix it,' Elliot said, as if Taro had a wet mop for a brain.

'That means facing our arcanists, you idiot,' Taro said. 'The last thing we need is them asking where we've been.'

'What's your suggestion, Taro?'

'We'll assemble that skeleton when we get to it.'

'You make those expressions up,' Elliot sneered. His velvety voice, Taro considered, only made him more exquisitely punchable.

Her brilliant response died in her mouth when she heard Jon's shrill voice through the wall.

'*—begins in five damn minutes!*'

Taro stopped dead, causing a small pile-up and much eye-rolling from Alis. Taro flipped her middle finger at the stone disciple and walked towards the sound. It came from a room at the side of the hall, just a few yards from the iron doors that opened on to the courtyard. Taro crouched in front of the keyhole.

'… none of your business where she is,' Jon said. He couldn't hide the hysteria in his voice.

'You've lost her, haven't you?' Morgan said lazily.

Jon and Kellan stood in opposite corners of the cramped antechamber, which had recently been resplendent with bowls of fruit and jugs of wine. This luxury was now scattered across the floor in the aftermath of a brawl. Jon stared at Kellan, his arms braced in front of him as though he expected the botanic arcanist to lash out with a razor. Kellan, breathing hard, had fruit pulp spattered up his legs. Only Morgan, standing in the middle, looked mildly amused.

'All right,' Kellan said finally. 'If none of us killed each other's familiars, it must have been Geraldin. Or they ran.'

'They wouldn't,' Jon said. He didn't lower his fists. 'They know they'll die if they don't take part. The spell's already in their blood—'

'It seems to me,' Morgan interrupted, 'that whoever's to blame, we're in a bit of a pickle. I assume that, since you don't have your familiars to wrest for you, you gentlemen haven't performed the Suppression this morning? No? Me neither. I think this means the end of the world is bubbling beneath our feet.'

'You don't seem concerned,' Kellan observed flatly.

'I have a feeling my familiar will turn up,' Morgan said. 'He's no fool. In the meantime, as I suggested, we should perform the Suppression with trainees.'

'No,' Jon said sharply. 'The Slaughter starts in five … four minutes. Geraldin would go into the tower unopposed.'

'Which is why you should have listened to me before.'

Jon grabbed a peach from the floor and hurled it at the wall. God, he was embarrassing. And he was willing to let the army of the undead run riot through the castle for the chance to be called the Thaumaturge.

Kellan snorted with derision. 'Any danger is still under the ground. Nobody needs to know what's wrong until the Slaughter is over.'

'Monsters,' Morgan said, untroubled. 'Both of you.'

Kellan ground his teeth.

'We still need familiars. We can tell the Academy to hand over their best.'

'And let them know we've lost the ones we have?' Jon snapped.

Morgan shrugged and strolled to the window. He twitched the velvet drapes aside, revealing a sliver of the courtyard. What Taro had assumed was rain smashing into the glass was the sound of a thousand people crammed into the amphitheatre. The city had overflowed like a boiling pot, spilling them into the castle. Taro had never seen so much humanity in one place.

'Get away from the door, Taro,' Elliot said. 'Jon and Kellan will kill you if they see you.' He was leaning against the wall, somehow deigning to look bored. 'Literally. They already think you're up to something.'

'Why aren't you concerned about yourself, bloodclot?' Taro said, drawing away from the keyhole.

'Because Morgan likes me,' he replied. He looked pleased with himself, as though he didn't know he was just Morgan's latest plaything. As though he was any better than Taro, who felt more and more like a worm in the face of Nixie's disgust. 'I can't help noticing, in contrast, that nobody has a good word to say about you. You even seem to have pissed Nixie off.'

Taro was on him in one second. She grabbed him by the collar and hauled him away from the wall. She was smaller than Elliot, but he was weak and easy to move.

'I've had it with you,' she hissed, pulling his face in so their foreheads were almost touching. She knew she wasn't really angry with him. She was furious at herself for the terrible way she had hurt Nixie, but she didn't know how to turn the shame inwards and stay alive. 'We get it. You think you're strong and clever and we're just stupid women who got hauled off to the castle while you landed a plush job with the Redborns. But you're not safe, Elliot. You just think you are because Morgan wants to fuck you.' She thrust him away. The castle was spinning, but she wasn't empty yet. Guilt was a terrible and unending fuel. 'No wonder your parents threw you away.'

'What?' Elliot's face went still.

'I've seen your records. In the Pit. They make notes on everyone, and yours are *hil-ar-i-ous*. Everyone knows because I told them.'

'Taro,' Nixie said warningly. Oh, so *now* Taro had her attention.

'Your parents were using you as a healer to get money,' she jeered. 'Then you messed up and a girl died, and the nuns hauled you to the Academy. You ended up there because of your own shitty mistake.'

'I ended up there because the dead girl's father turned me in,' Elliot spat.

'What? You think it was the *girl's* family?' Taro could have stopped right there. She did think about it, for a moment. But she wanted to see someone hurt as much as she did. And Elliot was standing right there, and god, sometimes he was just asking for it. 'It wasn't her parents, dumbass. It was *your* parents. They got scared of being found out, so they told the nuns to come and get you before someone else ratted on them.'

Elliot looked as though someone had drained the blood from his pretty face. Nixie stared at Taro as if she was a monster, which hurt so much she could only twist the knife more. 'The minute the nuns came to your door, Mummy and Daddy pointed at your hiding place,' Taro snarled. 'They didn't really love you. And you know what happened when the door closed? The nuns killed them anyway, which was probably a kindness, because how were they going to stay alive without you to leech off?'

Elliot wasn't breathing. A shred of shame curled through her. *Dick*, hissed the small voice in the back of her head.

She was good at ignoring it.

Taro bent to the keyhole again and refocused on the courtyard. Four burnished crosses were set into the flagstones around the door of the Fifth Tower: black for bone, green for botany, red for blood, grey for stone. Geraldin was already on hers, unmoved by the crowd at her back. Cassia squatted behind her as if she was ready to break into a sprint, her fists clenched around polished blocks of marble. Taro looked at the nuns grinding their jaws with anticipation, and the swirling mass of people pressed around the walls. She felt the loose thread of an idea tugging at the back of her skull.

She didn't like the idea. She didn't like any part of it. But they had about sixty seconds before the Slaughter began and their options were severely limited.

'Alis,' she said. 'The original plan still stands. Get into the crowd and distract the nuns.'

Alis gave a single, stony nod. Elliot's eyes drilled a hole through Taro's forehead. She did her best impression of not noticing it. 'Nobody knows we're gone except our arcanists. They can't kill us if we don't give them a choice.'

'Meaning?' Nixie said.

But Taro was already striding towards the iron doors.

She didn't let herself think. If she gave herself one moment to consider the insanity of what she was doing she would throw herself back into the guts of the castle and let the apocalypse take her instead.

Taro cast the Unholy Mother's robes from her shoulders. The great iron doors that led to the amphitheatre were five steps away. Three. The noise of the crowd rocked them. Two. One.

Taro flung the doors open. Greylight flooded her eyes, so bright after the deathly gloom that she saw nothing but brightly coloured splodges. The roar from the amphitheatre took on a new urgency, rising until it almost lifted her from her feet. Taro rolled her shoulders back and blindly marched to her mark.

Towards death.

She crossed her arms over her body and reached inside her blood-spattered clothes as she walked.

She pulled out two totally gnarly bones.

She thrust them into the air like swords.

And the crowd went wild.

Twenty

Five minutes until the Slaughter

In his mind, Elliot threw Taro against the wall so hard she gasped. He took his knife and turned her into a pile of bloody ribbons, and he felt nothing but crystalline calm, the balancing of a universe in which heinous people were punished and he was the agent of justice.

In that world Elliot had control over his body. In this one his mortification suffocated him, and he didn't move even though his hands screamed to inflict violence.

Your own parents threw you to the nuns.

He almost crumbled. But he couldn't. Not with everyone watching. Not when it would give Taro so much satisfaction. She could be lying, but he didn't really believe that. Maybe it had always lived in the back of his mind, something so painful he couldn't even look at it. *That's why they didn't try to save you. That's why they couldn't look you in the eye when you were dragged away.*

It was the look on Taro's face that twisted the dagger. That spiteful triumph, the sneer always hovering at the edge of her lips. Elliot thought he had buried the indignity of his capture, but Taro had wriggled her fingers under his skin, pinched the shameful memory between her nails, and watched as he bled.

Then she was walking away, and the doors were flung open, and the courtyard was screaming. None of them could do anything about it. They were in Taro's show.

Your parents didn't really love you. And now they're dead.

The greylight burned his eyes. He followed it, a feather caught in the snarling wind, his feet carrying him across the courtyard. This was so much of Elliot's existence: a passenger in a corpse, wanting one thing and doing another. Sometimes, in the dark of night when he realised how alone and unloved he was, his body cried while he stood by and watched with disgust.

Elliot's body walked. It raised his face. Everyone screamed and clapped for him, the new familiar in the Redspire robes. They sensed that something terrible had happened to bring him here, and they loved it. Their voices swelled again, and some of them laughed, which meant that Morgan had walked out behind him and was making obscene hand gestures.

'I told you to walk *behind* me,' Morgan drawled, loudly enough for the front rows to hear. 'Is your brain damaged?'

More laughter. Morgan placed his hand on the back of Elliot's neck and steered him towards the red cross on the cobbles. If he squeezed any harder Elliot would pass out.

'Clever,' Morgan murmured. 'Walk into the Slaughter and force us to follow or lose face. Jon's gone a very interesting colour.'

The voices ebbed, but Elliot could feel their eyes scraping his clothes, his hands, his face, hungrily watching Morgan pinch the back of his neck. Wondering what they were to each other, the new boy and the blood arcanist with infamous predilections. Elliot felt too faint to look up and too proud to look down, so he fixed his gaze on the Fifth Tower. Its cold, white face suddenly made the other four towers look trivial.

Elliot felt sick as he walked, and he realised with horror that his waning humiliation was edged with guilt. At what? At planning to let the others bash their arcanists over the head while he stood there with Morgan? He had nothing to be sorry for; they weren't ever going to win. And when Morgan rose to power, Elliot could ask him to save them.

Not Taro, though.

They reached the burnished red cross, and Morgan pulled Elliot's hand into the sky. The voices rippled and swelled into another delighted jeer. Nixie reached her cross next. Kellan had his hand on her back, his jaw pulsing as he ground his teeth, pressing his nails into the place where the bleeding clock was.

Nixie would thank Elliot one day. They all would.

'Tell me where you've been,' Morgan said, barely parting his lips, his mouth still bright and smiling.

'Busy,' Elliot said.

'How mysterious. I look forward to prying your secrets out of you.'

'I look forward to you trying.'

'Flirt.'

'Renegade.'

An arrow struck Elliot's back, its point splitting the dent between two vertebrae. Elliot buckled and writhed. The blood arcanist had decided to kill him after all.

'Stay calm, Elliot,' Morgan said. 'It's just the clock.'

The nuns flipped their mouths open and screamed. Taro and Nixie and the other familiar, Cassia, were jerking like landed fish, mouths open, blood spreading through their robes. Their arcanists dragged them towards the tower while they spasmed. Morgan caught Elliot before he could collapse, and shook a tiny black bottle from his sleeve. It was the vial Elliot had seen him carrying on the night of the Thaumaturge's murder, the poison that had caused this mess.

'Drink it,' Morgan said.

Elliot tried to shove the vial away. Morgan, misreading his panic, shrugged and downed the bottle. His pupils swelled, and he smiled loosely at Elliot's shock.

'Liquid courage. I stole it from Kellan to put in my food when I think someone might try to kill me.' He giggled breathlessly, just like he had in the dining hall.

Morgan didn't kill the Thaumaturge.

But the truth was irrelevant. The Slaughter had begun, suddenly and with little fanfare, and all that mattered was winning. Elliot's legs kicked helplessly. His arms were slack and his head lolled forward as fire spread through his back. Alis was supposed to be doing something. Destroying things and distracting people before the familiars actually had to start killing each other. Perhaps he wasn't the only traitor.

'We need to move,' he gasped. Geraldin, Kellan and Jon had given up trying to haul their familiars and had dumped them on the ground, screaming at them to wrest. So much for disarming the arcanists; none of them could move.

'Do you want me to drag you like a sack?'

'No,' Elliot grated out.

'So I'm letting you recover first.'

'They'll get to the tower before you.'

'Probably. But I was hoping to see your friends do something spectacular.'

The amphitheatre exploded. The middle tier fell inwards like a broken pie crust. Alis's work was huge and uncontrolled. Chunks of masonry hit the ground and exploded into smaller pieces, which exploded again and again into clouds of dust.

Elliot threw his hands over his head, but Morgan was ready. Blood sprayed from a vial between his knuckles. A sheet of red plasma arced over their heads. The exploding debris hit it with a wet slapping noise and coagulated at their feet. Morgan hissed between his teeth, his lips white with pain.

'Your turn next,' he said. 'That's how we do it – together. Keep up.'

The blood shattered into a fine mist, smearing across Elliot's vision. Alis's explosion had torn a hole in the amphitheatre and through the walls of the courtyard itself, exposing the greasy descent of the city. There were people mixed up with the stone, crooked-limbed and pink with viscera.

Spectators pushed to get away from the ragged hole, some falling and hitting the stone below; everywhere else, the crowd surged against the upper back wall. The nuns swept in, but they were unable or unwilling to discriminate between the living and the dead as they methodically threw bodies aside so they could find where the blast had come from. Arcanists used spells to get out of the crush, but the nuns latched on to them and, not knowing who was an arcanist and who was a familiar, covered all bases by wrenching the heads off everyone who used arcania.

Elliot jerked towards the tower, but Morgan held him back.

'Let them clear the floor,' he said.

Taro was suddenly on her feet. Perhaps she had never really been unconscious. Jon grabbed her by the cheeks, and from the way Taro was laughing at his bulging eyes Elliot knew she had spoken to him. Jon didn't think to take hold of her arms; she swung a long, thick bone at the side of his head. It connected with a nauseating crack. He crumpled at the knees – for a moment it looked as if he was praying – then his head smacked into the ground. Taro strode towards the tower door, still wielding the bloodied bone, grinning manically.

Cassia was back on her feet and running alongside Geraldin, whose huge strides swallowed the cobblestones. Elliot looked for Nixie and found her transformed. She had a sling around Kellan's throat, made from the empty sleeve of her robe. She was leaning back with all her weight, but Kellan was twice her size and he barely flinched. Nixie should have used arcania, but either she wasn't capable or she had panicked and done the wrong thing, and it was too late to change her mind. Kellan let her struggle. Then he turned so fast Elliot barely saw it. They were simply facing each other, with Nixie still attached to Kellan's neck. She let go of the ligature, but Kellan was already pressing his thumbs into the soft hollow of her throat.

Elliot's hand moved to his arm, which was sticky with blood from Taro's sword blow. He dug deep into himself. The arcania was sour and reluctant, his blood overused. He forced the incantation between his teeth. There was very little power to carve from, but Elliot was good. Kellan crumpled as Elliot's spell crushed an artery in his neck. He twitched on the stones just like the familiars had. Nixie wavered for a few moments before stumbling over his body and running after Taro.

Morgan ran his own thumb through the curls at the base of Elliot's neck, where he was still holding him. Possessive, and a threat.

'We aren't supposed to help them, Elliot.' He sounded amused. 'It's a fight to the death.'

'We want your rivals out of the way,' Elliot said. He didn't want to examine his own moment of – what? – concern? *Sympathy?* As if knowing his parents had given him up had torn a hole in his armour, and now he was weaker. He refused to be pathetic. The only thing left in his life was for him to win the Slaughter.

'So you weren't helping from the goodness of your heart?'

Elliot knew that Morgan was poking his weak spot. His lightest comments were his deepest barbs, and they fed the deep swell of Elliot's self-disgust.

'I have no heart,' he said.

'You haven't met a real villain,' Morgan replied. 'Pray you never do.'

Nixie vanished into the tower, through the door that had been smashed open by Geraldin. Elliot wondered if Nixie knew her plan had gone wrong yet. Imagined, without pleasure, the ice cold shock of it hitting her. Nixie, Taro, Alis and Elliot were all meant to be in the Fifth Tower with their curse keys, having killed their arcanists. They were supposed to run to the crest of the tower together, then follow the instructions of the Ghost in the shard of glass to somehow break the aeons-old curse on Fourspires and flee from the Desecrae.

But Elliot was standing here with Morgan, with the Redspire curse key in his pocket. Geraldin and Cassia, still alive, were inside the Fifth Tower instead. Alis hadn't even emerged from the rubble. Elliot twisted his shoulders for a better look, but a cloud of dust immediately hit the back of his throat and made him choke. He could only see vague shapes through the thick air, gaping faces and twisted limbs struggling to unbury themselves. The nuns swarmed over each other like pigeons converging on bread, fighting to find the illegal arcania at its epicentre. It would only take seconds for them to realise the collapse had been a distraction and the familiars had gone rogue.

'You seem tense,' Morgan said. Elliot wanted to scream. The tower was so close: and that meant winning the throne, and getting the cursed necklace back from Morgan.

'Do I?' he said, barely holding himself back.

'Do you think I got to where I am by being the strongest?' Morgan said. 'I *am* the strongest. But that's because I let everyone powerful enough to compete with me kill themselves first. Ambition is only helpful if you know when to deploy it.'

He was still holding Elliot's neck. Elliot could feel the blood pulsing through his fingertips. He considered shaking Morgan off, but he couldn't make himself. Morgan was the only person who touched him with anything other than cruelty.

'You've surprised me today, Elliot,' Morgan said. 'Perhaps you are more terrible than you think.'

Elliot felt a dull twist of fear.

'Why?'

Morgan already held the Redspire curse key between his thumb and forefinger. Elliot's hand flew to his empty pocket. Morgan, opportunistic and light-fingered, had taken it from Elliot when he was writhing on the ground.

'I would ask why you've been carrying this,' Morgan said, 'but everyone's entitled to their little magpie moments. I assume that you just liked it. Or perhaps you thought it would be helpful to us later.' He looked at Elliot pointedly.

There was no point in fabricating a noble motive. Morgan was too clever.

'I don't know why I took it,' Elliot said, suppressing the urge to snatch it back. 'I just wanted it. Nothing belongs to me except for what I steal.' He forced himself to remain calm. 'You know what that's like. You do it too.'

Morgan looked surprised, and Elliot realised with satisfaction that he was just as good at manipulation as Morgan was.

'Oh, look,' Morgan said, after the shocked pause. 'Our gender-transcending friend is back.'

'Our – what?'

'Never mind, Elliot.'

Alis staggered out of the dust, coughing her lungs up. Her robes were shredded and her face was torn, but she had crawled past the nuns unscathed. The air was too thick with the tang of blood and rampant arcania for them to follow her trail.

'I've always liked the library,' Morgan said to himself. He put his hand on the dagger at his belt. 'And I always thought the assistant had something wonderful about her. She radiates anger. The fun kind, not your self-indulgent blackness.'

Alis looked up, straight into the crossbeam of Elliot's stare, and took in his stance: too close to Morgan, the blood arcanist's hand resting intimately on his body. Her face twisted in recognition of his betrayal. The whole world shrank away from Elliot, leaving him with nothing but Alis's merciless eyes.

'Taro was right,' she said. Her voice was gravelly. She wiped her mouth on the back of her hand, smearing dust and blood further over her face. 'We shouldn't have trusted you.' She laughed bitterly, which made her cough again. Pink phlegm landed on the ground.

The knife she had given Elliot dug into his thigh. He started forward, but he didn't know what he intended to do, only that he was seized with the sudden need to stop her searing gaze. Morgan yanked him back.

'Let her go in. She can deal with Geraldin.'

Alis ran towards the Fifth Tower, her torn robes fluttering behind her. Before she was swallowed by the blackness she paused in the doorway. Her face didn't move, but Elliot perceived the awful change behind it, like air pressing down before a storm.

She had seen what was inside. She knew she was going to die.

Then she was gone.

Elliot slid his fingers over the knife again and was stung by the hypocrisy in its bite. Alis had remembered his habit of carving figures in the Pit, but instead of using it to torment him, she had turned it into a gift. Morgan used his knowledge of Elliot to cut and drain and manipulate him. Elliot had even begged for the only thing he really wanted, the necklace, and Morgan had responded by humiliating him.

Elliot had only ever known cruelty. He had never considered that kindness could undo him too.

'Are you ready?' Morgan said. 'The throne waits for us, my bloody prince in training.'

Elliot barely heard him. His voice was detached as he said, 'I'm ready.'

He felt as if he had taken his own kind of poison. His mind was calm. He saw himself act as though he was watching a fish move under the frozen surface of a pond, and he didn't know which part was really him: the part that observed, or his body as he turned to Morgan.

'You're beautiful,' he heard himself say, his voice eerily serene.

'You're telling me this now?' Morgan pretended to be careless, but Elliot could tell he was delighted.

Elliot turned and curled his fingers around the back of Morgan's head. Morgan held his breath between his teeth.

'Truly,' Elliot said. 'Especially when you murder.'

'So that's what you like,' Morgan said softly. 'I should have known—'

Elliot wrenched Morgan's head to the side. The blood arcanist screamed and fell to his knees. Elliot – Elliot's body – grabbed Morgan's dark hair and pulled his head back, exposing his throat. So much for Morgan's strength. Elliot felt little horror as he placed his knife at Morgan's throat. In the violence of the competition for the throne, the rabid fervour of the arcanists and their desperation to win, the spilling of Morgan's blood was nothing.

'The vial,' Elliot's mouth said.

His blade wasn't long, and it wasn't sharp, but he could push hard enough to open a vital artery. Morgan's pulse trembled through the knife. Something about the sheer intimacy of holding the blood arcanist's life in his hands made Elliot snap back into his body. The noise of the amphitheatre roared through his ears, and he was doubly aware of every sensation: the cold stones radiating through the soles of his shoes, the dust coating his hands, his shirt damp with sweat. People had noticed what was happening, and those who hadn't been caught in the avalanche were starting to shout. Elliot pressed the knife harder.

'Now,' he said.

Morgan reached into his pocket and fumbled with the relic. Elliot let go of Morgan's hair to grab it. Morgan stayed where he was, his throat taut, the knife biting into his skin.

'Now the necklace.'

Morgan retrieved the cursed necklace from his pocket. The chain dripped between his fingers like molten gold. Elliot snatched it and shoved it deep into his robes, fighting the urge to tug it over his head. He ached to squash it between his teeth, to swallow it, to make it a part of himself even if it ripped his insides to shreds. But putting it on now would be debilitating. It would leave him at Morgan's mercy.

'Go.' He shoved Morgan roughly. The knife slipped, leaving a thin red line that swelled and ran down the arcanist's throat. 'Don't try anything. You know I'm faster than you. It would take no effort to make blood pour from your eyes.'

Morgan had nothing to say. His lips parted, but his mouth was empty. He suddenly looked very young, like a teenager who had been left in charge of something that he didn't really understand. Morgan reached up to touch his neck.

'Don't,' Elliot said sharply. 'I've spent my whole life learning how to wrest and incant at the same time. You've tried it once or twice. Do you really think you can do better than me?' Morgan's hand fell, and Elliot was surprised by the spite in his own voice. 'Your tower and your university can't help you now.'

'What are you going to do?'

'I –' Elliot broke off. The knife shook in his hand. He strengthened his grip and thrust the blade in Morgan's direction. 'I'm going to help them.'

'Why?'

'Because –' He took a step back, then another. The blade was still pointed at Morgan. Why *was* Elliot helping them?

He wasn't. He was only helping Alis.

A nun's head jerked towards them. Its eyes darted between the knife tip and Morgan's throat.

'In your tower,' Elliot said. 'The first time I went there. Someone … tried to help me.' He struggled to put his words in order, because all he could see was Alis: Alis with the knife. Alis crouched on the stairs of Morgan's tower, teeth glittering, ostensibly there to rescue him. He'd said her reasons were selfish, but he also knew the taste of a lie when he told it to himself. 'I don't know why she bothered. But sometimes –' he hated himself. He hated this weakness. He also couldn't stop. 'Sometimes I think I would like to be rescued.'

He didn't need to explain anything to Morgan, but he wanted someone to hear him. How he had always been saving his parents, but they had never helped him. How that lack of care was even worse at the end, now he knew about their betrayal. How nobody had *ever* attempted to help him, but that he wanted it so badly his whole body ached. It ached with the same desperation as his need to sleep. 'I want to know what it's like. But I need to help her first. Even if I regret it for the rest of my life.'

'Let me come with you,' Morgan said. Elliot's hand faltered.

'What?'

'Are you going to make me say it?'

'Say what?' Elliot flicked his eyes up. The nun was walking towards them now.

'I won't.'

'Say *what*?' Elliot's voice rose. He was young and bewildered again. He was not the man he had spent so long turning himself into.

'I don't want to be alone,' Morgan said. His hands were clasped tightly. He was begging. Elliot felt the world tilt. 'I don't want the crown. You can have it. But I don't want to be alone.'

Elliot's grip loosened on the knife. Morgan closed his eyes and tilted his beautiful face towards the greylight.

'I had Rhys,' he said, his voice cracking. 'I killed him. Not on purpose. But he made me promise—'

The nun shrieked from the back of its throat. Elliot looked up to see that it was flying, and now others were coming from the rubble behind it, having found their foul play.

Elliot had time to slice Morgan's throat open. The nuns would devour him, which would give Elliot more time to reach the tower. Yet Morgan's plea made his hand weak. *Do it!* he screamed at himself, but the nerves to his wrist might as well have been sliced. He had failed at being abominable.

Elliot shoved the knife in his pocket and ran towards the Fifth Tower.

He was a few paces away when he hit a loose cobblestone and fell, cracking his jaw against the ground. All of that – all of this – and then a *cobblestone.* He forced himself up and saw the nun sailing towards him, its fingers hooked in the air as if to strangle the wind.

He scrambled for the knife in his pocket, but his hand was too slippery with blood. Not from his fall. Tiny dots of blood had appeared on the surface of the smooth cobbles. They shivered and rolled, making the ground appear to tremble and blur. Scarlet bruises appeared all over the courtyard. The apocalypse was coming, and it smelled of metal.

He launched his body at the tower door. The world was tilting and he swerved with it, his head ringing, bile rising in his throat.

He thought he had outpaced the nun until it bit him.

It ground its teeth into his left shoulder. They hit bone. Elliot gasped and twisted away, but instead of releasing him, it dragged its teeth through his flesh. Pain bloomed outwards.

Elliot contorted his arms so he could reach his pocket, but the mere act of shifting his muscles was agonising. The nun's bite radiated into his neck. He clutched the hilt of the knife in his slippery fingers and twisted around again. This time the movement cast a black shadow over his vision, eclipsing everything but a fraction of the nun's starved face in which one eye, too small and dehydrated for its socket, rattled at the end of a gristled muscle.

Why did you do this?

He wanted nothing more than to save himself and break his curse, yet some weak and stupid part of his brain had decided he should throw in its lot with the familiars. He fumbled with the knife and drove it sluggishly into the nun's collarbone. The nun's teeth ground against his shoulder bone as he sawed the knife sideways through its neck, grunting and sweating until its body fell away and slumped to the ground. The head remained attached to his shoulder, its teeth hooked into his flesh.

Elliot looked for Morgan, but the blood arcanist had vanished. Nuns were crowded around the place where he had been standing, dismantled limbs hanging from their mouths. Maybe they were Morgan's. Maybe he had escaped, and the Mothers were devouring a random corpse. Either way, they would soon finish their carrion feast and come for Elliot.

With the nun's teeth clamped into his flesh, Elliot ran into the Slaughter.

Twenty-one

The Slaughter

Alis's vaulted library was minuscule compared to the monstrous height of the Fifth Tower. Its emptiness was stark: as hollow as the crown, as grey as the everlasting, never-ending teeth in the sky.

She raised her eyes to its peak, through the wrought-iron floor of the uppermost room, to the faint smudge of greylight emanating from the hole in the roof. The height made her dizzy. She felt as if she was falling backwards out of her body until she squeezed her eyes shut.

'It looks bigger on the inside, doesn't it?'

Alis's eyes snapped open. Taro was clutching the wall next to Nixie, who was practising breathing exercises with her gaze fixed solidly on the floor. Taro was correct. The problem with the tower was that you could see how tall it was, whereas the sky gave the impression of knocking around just over their heads.

Alis reached for her pencil and the soft scraps of paper up her sleeve.

Nuns, she wrote with a shaking hand.

'They're not coming in. It must be against the rules.' Taro was putting a lot of energy into being flippant. 'Nice distraction, by the way. Bigger than I expected.'

You underestimated me, Alis scrawled.

'I thought you could talk now,' Taro said, which Alis chose to ignore.

'There's nothing here,' Nixie said abruptly, emerging from her breathing exercise.

That wasn't true. The circular floor was covered in deep scratch marks. Two staircases climbed the walls, spiralling in opposite directions and crossing several times, both covered by a latticework of stone painstakingly carved to resemble lace. It was impossible to see through the latticework from here, but anyone pressing their eyes against it from the stairs would have a clear view of the tower floor.

There was no beast guarding it, Alis realised. Puzzles and tricks weren't necessary. The arcanists would burst through the door and realise there was nothing in their way except each other and their own killing spells. There wasn't even anything to stop Alis, who was no longer a high familiar, from entering. It felt like a nasty joke: anyone who was hungry enough to kill their way to the top could seize the crown, if only they were desperate enough to come in.

But even that's not cruel enough.

Alis touched the stone wall and tried to wrest. She felt nothing but a low, pulsing headache. She pressed her fingers harder, trying to draw something from the tower, but it was like trying to melt ice by glaring. So, this was the Slaughter: four arcanists and four familiars, all facing each other with nothing but their pride and shit-all power between them. No way to wrest or incant, and no way to win but with brute strength and viciousness.

'Damn,' Taro said softly.

'Nothing changes,' Nixie said bluntly. 'When Elliot gets here, we'll climb the stairs and wait for the Ghost's instructions.'

Alis beckoned to them and wrote, ignoring the shame of not having been fast or murderous enough. Ignoring, too, the fact that Geraldin was physically stronger than Jon and Kellan and Morgan, and if Alis had remained in Greyspire, she could have made it to the throne with her. It wasn't what she wanted. But still. That power could have been hers.

Geraldin and Cassia already came in. They're on the stairs. I can't see them at the top, so they've stopped to watch us.

Taro automatically adjusted her hair.

'OK,' Nixie said quietly. 'And Elliot?'

Alis's fingers tightened on the scrap of paper. She wished she was digging them into Elliot's eyes. Her silence was answer enough: he had stayed with Morgan. *Bastard. Traitor.* Alis didn't know why she felt a deep pang of disappointment, but she could bury it easily and completely in malice. *Vampire. Coward.*

'That's fine,' Taro said, with absolute bullshit confidence. 'We just need to disarm Geraldin and Cassia before they get to the top. Which Alis was meant to do five minutes ago, by the way.'

I was destroying the courtyard for you, asshole.

'Don't start,' Nixie said. She pinched the bridge of her nose and muttered under her breath. Probably making an interminable list of pros and cons. 'Taro's right. You need to catch Geraldin before she gets to the top.'

Me?

'We'll make sure Morgan and Elliot don't follow you,' Nixie said.

You want me to commit double murder while you two stand here?

'Yep,' Taro said.

I'm not talking to you, bonelicker.

'Stop antagonising each other,' Nixie snapped, but she was looking at Alis when she said it. Alis felt her cheeks flush. This was not the right time – this was the worst time for anything except saving their own lives, in fact – but screw being sent off by herself.

Tell your girlfriend to back off, Alis scrawled. She knew how much that word – *girlfriend* – would rile Nixie.

'She's not my girlfriend,' Nixie said without thinking.

'Ouch,' Taro said. 'Only because of a technicality.'

Alis dug her pencil into the paper.

It's so sweet that you're with her even after

Nixie snatched the pencil from her hand. Alis was too shocked to move. Nixie looked appalled at herself too.

‘You’re so –’ Nixie broke off, but it was too late to stop the ghost of the sentence.

‘I’m so what?’ Alis, pencil-less, flinched at the sound of her own voice, which was low but furious. She suddenly couldn’t stop. She stepped forward, which made Nixie back away. ‘You wanted to say it when we were under the castle. You were going to say *jealous*, weren’t you? You think I’m jealous of Taro.’

Nixie blushed. Taro stared, goggle-eyed, as Alis – at the end of the world, at the centre of the actual apocalypse – went absolutely pyrotechnic.

‘Excuse me for feeling bitter,’ Alis hissed. Her words were low and fast and out of control, but she was tired, she was *exhausted*, and here was the one person she had always trusted, who had always listened to her, and who had now turned against her. The space between them was tiny; small enough, somehow, that Alis could fill it with her vitriol without wanting to die. ‘Funny that I didn’t enjoy being shoved away because you became obsessed with a bone witch. Most people can have a girlfriend and still acknowledge their best friend’s existence, but apparently you can only focus on one person at a time, and they’re the centre of your goddamned life. It’s fucked up.’

‘You’re wrong—’

‘It’s true.’ Alis leaned in, and Nixie, already backed against the wall, pressed further into the stone. ‘But I’m leaving something else out, right? Because the thing that really put the nail in the coffin was me telling you who I really am. Don’t look away. We both remember it.’

‘I don’t—’

‘I told you it was killing me. I was begging for help. I only wanted you to be able to see me, because I felt like I was going mad, playing this role that fucking suffocated me, being a girl and drowning in it. But you pulled away. You *physically stepped back.* You asked if I was *sure*. Then you never spoke to me again.’

‘I was surprised,’ Nixie said. ‘It came out of nowhere—’

‘And the day after that? And all the other days? I wanted to fling myself out of the window. I felt like an aberration.’

'Shit, Alis,' Taro said. 'That's rough.'

Alis's guilt at embarrassing Nixie barely reared its head before her rage crashed over it again.

'So no,' she said. She stepped back from Nixie, and Nixie finally breathed out. 'I'm not just *jealous*. I'm also angry that I still love you, even though you were a shit friend. I'm furious that I would come running back if you showed any interest in me, even though I know you would dump me again the second someone better and less complicated came along.'

'Alis,' Nixie said, but that was all.

'Jealously has a bad reputation,' Alis snarled quietly. 'But you know what? It's normal, and so is being incredibly fucking angry at someone who deserves it, and I'm sick of – I'm sick of holding it inside me and pretending I don't care.'

Alis hadn't realised how tightly her body was clenched until this moment. Or how many times she had silently rehearsed her outburst, teeth gritted, in the night. And now her rage was out in the world, and it had its own life in Taro and Nixie's hands, and she couldn't take it back. She had exposed her truest self again, just like she had the first time she told Nixie how she felt, all the way back in the Pit.

She snatched the pencil back from Nixie. Nixie flinched, and Alis wondered if she had gone too far. Whether Nixie was right, and Alis was just a confused, attention-seeking prick who didn't know what she wanted. It was excruciating to know herself so well and at the same time have all this doubt.

But then she met Nixie's eyes and juddered at the pity in them.

'You were always so hard to be with,' Nixie said. 'It's why you didn't have any other friends. I couldn't be your babysitter for ever, Al. That's all you wanted – someone to take your problems away from you. You didn't give anything back. You were exhausting and self-obsessed. I was just your dumping ground.'

Even Taro looked shocked. Alis's face contorted into a weird half-smirk that she had no control over. She didn't know if she was laughing or grimacing, only that she wanted Nixie to know how little she cared. Nixie shook her head sadly, and for a moment, Alis truly considered pushing her out the door for the Unholy Mothers.

Something moved on the stairs above them. Alis heard a wet cough, then the sound of meat hitting the floor. She tightened her fist around the pencil.

We're wasting time, she scrawled. *I'm going up*.

Her foot peeled from the stone with a noise like an apple being pared. The toes of her shoes were red. She thought her wound was leaking until Taro lifted her own foot and gagged at the blood oozing out of the stone. Green fingers of ivy curled around the doorway, prying it apart as the floor wept. Alis saw gnarled humps of bone pushing through the ground outside, and someone using a chunk of stone to beat a clump of tendrils to a pulp. More sprouted from its place. The apocalypse was coming.

Alis backed into the centre of the tower. Taro pulled Nixie away from the door, and they clutched each other tightly, pathetically dependent on each other despite whatever had happened between them. Alis desperately wanted someone to clutch hold of. The yearning was so strong and unexpected that her eyes stung.

A grey arm slithered through the doorway, followed by a torso, then a skull with lush greenery bursting through its eye sockets. It thrust itself through the vines that were knotted against the eyehole of the tower and lolloped towards them with ivy curling around its ankles. Its feet splashed against the darkening floor.

Burn in hellfire.

This must be what hysteria felt like: anger and frustration and horror mixed into the bloodcurdling desire to take a swing at something. Alis marched towards the corpse. She didn't know what she was doing, only that it had to be something violent or she would burst out of her skin. Taro said something urgent to Nixie but Alis was too far away to hear. She swooped on a chunk of stone that had fallen away from the door. She hefted it into both hands and smashed it into the skeleton.

Its ribs cracked like sugar brittle as it collapsed on top of her. Alis crashed backwards, landing so hard on the wet floor that her lungs were knocked empty. She shoved the corpse away, but another had risen behind it and was climbing on top of them both, its hands breaking through the remains of the first skeleton's chest cavity.

Alis punched at their skulls, but her rage was quickly draining, leaving a smear of panic in its place. Her blows only made the skeletons pause for a second before they dug their hands into her arms, pinning her to the floor with such force Alis was sure their fingers would burst right through her skin and into the stone.

'Do something,' she grunted, twisting her head awkwardly towards Nixie and Taro. 'Fucking come and help me—'

They ran away.

Alis shuddered, bracing against the skeletons as they stumbled towards the stairs. Nixie was pulling Taro, yanking her into the dark mouth of the iron latticework on the left. Taro looked back at Alis, and for a second she was hesitant.

Then they vanished.

They had *left* her.

They were playing the tower's game. By leaving her, they were as good as murdering her. They were no better than the arcanists who had fought here before, ensuring that they won their lives by taking someone else's.

Alis screamed and drove her knees into the corpses. She rained blows on their skulls. She thrashed like a trapped rabbit. She was going to break them into tiny pieces and grind those pieces into dust and throw them across the chamber like immortal confetti. She was going to make them wish they'd never been born, wish they'd never died, just so they could avoid their eventual resurrection and the damage Alis would inflict. But her strength was not as infinite as her anger; her arms were jelly and the dead were still smashing her into the floor with unchanged and inexhaustible determination.

It only then occurred to Alis that she didn't know what they wanted. Did they wish to dismantle the living? To eat them? Or did they want to crawl inside their skin and experience mortality again? Did they *want* anything at all?

Stupid philosophical question, Alis thought as she struggled with the writhing mass of bones on her torso. *You're going to die. Pray you don't come back.*

The skeleton that was pressed right against her, which was trying to chew through her nose, felt lighter now. Maybe this was the famed rush of adrenaline before death. Alis laughed hysterically. She pushed the two tangled skeletons upwards, and they buckled. She kicked hard – OK, so her feet weren't severed – and they tumbled sideways with a shriek of bone against bone. It was as easy as kicking a duvet off. They flapped around together, their ribs interlocked. Alis spat at them. They slid backwards under the force of her ire.

She rolled on to her front and crawled away. Something gripped her ankles and yanked her towards the door and the skeletons. She clawed at the slick ground, trying to get to the stairs. Her nails left sticky trails in the red floor as she slid backwards. Leaves unfurled from the bloody mess, cigarette-sized tubes opening to reveal perfectly green hearts that stroked her exhausted cheek. For a moment she thought Nixie was saving her. Then a tendril jabbed her tear duct, and she knew that she was being dragged into the ground by the apocalyptic ivy.

She pedalled her legs and heard the vines snap, but for each breakage another tendril lashed around her. She flipped over again, twisting the stalks into a rope. The green fingers of the apocalypse bulged through the doorway, creaking as they multiplied. Alis jerked her legs towards her chest once, twice, three times, stretching the tendrils until they snapped and sprayed her with sap. The skeletons were in pieces, greenery bulging through the holes in their craniums, their torsos sheathed in bristling flora, each a clump of bones jerking fitfully as they were dismantled.

Alis rose to her feet and ripped a cluster of leaves from her ear. When she yanked the tendril from her tear duct she saw that it was growing a new stalk. She stamped on it.

I beg of the universe that you drag yourselves to hell!

Something scraped above her head. Instinct made Alis look up. A face pressed against the stone lacework of the second staircase jerked away.

Alis flexed her fingers, and before she could make a plan, she was striding towards the open mouth of the staircase. She didn't care why Cassia hadn't already climbed to the crest of the tower, or whether Geraldin was still with her, or what she would do once she reached them. She would play by the Slaughter's rules. She would be merciless in her violence. She would plough through them; she would climb the tower; she would reach the chamber before Nixie and Taro; and maybe, if she was feeling really special, she would put the crown on her head and make them pray for the day that Alis would die.

The sounds of writhing life and restless death dropped away. Alis limped up the stairs with her teeth clenched and her hands bunched into fists. She didn't hide as she climbed around the spiral.

Cassia stood over Geraldin's body. Her blonde hair was streaked with dried blood, her robes damp with perspiration. Geraldin's arms were flung over her head, which hung limply down the stairs. The arcanist's back was crooked, her spine bent in a sideways V-shape. Her face was sullen, as unreadable in death as in life.

Cassia looked up. Her mouth was bent into the smile of someone who was trying very hard not to scream.

'We can't use arcania here,' Cassia said. Her voice was higher than Alis remembered. Perhaps it was fear. 'I don't really care. I'm sick of it anyway. You know why bits of the castle keep falling down? It's because I can't do the Suppression properly.'

Alis leaned against the stone latticework, trying to look unperturbed even though her heart was racing. Her grand delusion of fighting drained away in the presence of a very real death. She tucked her pencil into her fingers, making slow, exaggerated loops, instinctively knowing that a sudden movement would be fatal.

I see, she wrote. Cassia relaxed, as though the fact of Alis's silence made her less dangerous. Alis nodded at Geraldin. *Was it planned?*

Cassia's fingers twisted together.

'No,' she said. 'I just got scared. I've been scared for ages.' Her breath was ragged. 'I didn't want to belong to a thaumaturge. I wouldn't last. So I-I did it.'

Maybe it was exhaustion, or fear, or pain from her foot, but Alis just ... ran out of anger. She had been spending it for years, and had squandered the last at the bottom of the Fifth Tower, and now, looking at Cassia's face, she felt only a deeply tiring pity for the girl who had locked herself into a mortal contract with Geraldin. Given a longer tenure, Alis might have staved the Greyspire arcanist's head in too.

Climb the tower with me, she wrote. *We'll see what's at the top. It's got to be better than this*. She gestured at the chamber floor, where a new corpse was hacking at the greenery with frenetic energy. It appeared to have two heads.

Cassia's gaze sharpened.

'Why help me? I blackmailed you.'

Alis shrugged.

Your choice. I'm going with or without you.

Cassia moved so fast Alis didn't have time to flinch before her head was slammed against the stone. When she emerged from the pain, Cassia already had her thumbs pressed into Alis's neck. Alis grappled with her, but all she could do was dig her fingers into Cassia's armpits as hard as she could. Cassia faltered, but when Alis took advantage and drew a gasping breath Cassia panicked and pressed harder.

Cassia was no villain. She was crying hard. She had just broken under the weight of the tower, and Alis was the nearest target. If the smallest thing had been different, like a change in the wind or a warmer breakfast, she might have embraced Alis and howled into her shoulder instead.

Curtains drew over Alis's eyes. They were spangled with white stars. Through a narrowing slit Alis saw the end of the scene: Cassia's snot-streaked face, and below her, the corpse with two heads climbing the tower. It was a limping abomination covered in blood and dirt; then it was Elliot the Traitor with a nun's head hanging from his left shoulder, which was much worse. His dark, curly hair was stuck to his head with sweat. What a shitty hallucination for Alis to die with.

The curtains swept shut on the vision. Even as the pressure increased on Alis's neck she thought that maybe it wasn't so bad, dying here, on the steps in the Fifth Tower. Life had already been mind-numbingly long and painful, and she would be happy to leave it.

A thump. A grunt. The pressure vanished from Alis's throat, but she could still feel the thumbprints radiating blackly into her neck. Her eyes opened, but the curtains didn't draw back until hands closed over her shoulders and shook her.

'*Ow*,' she said, and when that didn't work she spat directly into the face of the nun-bitten vampire who had the gall to save her.

Elliot thrust her away, cursing.

Cassia was halfway down the stairs. She held herself up by lacing her fingers through the stone latticework; her right foot was twisted to the side, and she was sobbing without making any noise.

'Get up,' Alis rasped. Her voice sounded like wind blowing through a gutter, but there was no time for the pencil. Cassia slid down the steps on her knees, pulling herself along with her fingers. 'They'll rip you to shreds.'

Alis was faintly appalled that she was trying to save her almost-murderer. In any case, her plea didn't work. Cassia slid down the stairs and into the darkness. And then she was gone.

'Alis.'

Alis was glad to have something else to focus on, even if it was this idiot.

Well done, Alis wrote. Her sarcasm cost dearly; a trail of blood followed her pencil across the page. *You screwed us over then changed your mind. Did Morgan not fuck you adequately?*

Elliot flushed red in a very satisfying way. Hopefully he was dying of an infection.

'I'm here now,' he said coldly. At least he didn't ask for gratitude. 'I don't know why. I should have stayed with him.'

Yeah, you should. The anger she knew she should feel was still absent. It had all been spent, and she was so, so tired. *I guess you're coming to the top with me. Nixie and Taro will already be there. If they try to kill you, I won't stop them.*

She had to give him credit for not rising to the bait.

'Can you give me a hand first?' he asked.

Elliot gestured at the Unholy Mother's head attached to his shoulder. It looked like a giant tick, its long rabbit teeth dug deep in his flesh. The remains of its dehydrated brain leaked from its ragged neck. Alis realised that Elliot's face was covered in a thin sheen of sweat. It was astonishing that he was still standing.

You're about three seconds from collapsing, aren't you? she scribbled.

'Probably.' His throat bobbed. Maybe he really did have a deadly infection. 'I think I've lost hearing in one ear, and I can see two of you.'

You're joking.

He sat down. He was not joking. Alis waved the paper scrap at him, but his eyes couldn't focus on it. Of course he was going to force her to speak.

'Elliot,' she said with difficulty. Elliot looked up, clutching his shoulder. His face was greasy and pale, and he had never looked more unattractive, which was a real achievement. He closed his eyes.

Madness gripped her. Alis thought she had followed Nixie into this mad scheme because she didn't want to die. Then she thought she just wanted to make Nixie like her again. But now, looking at the messed-up ground, she knew that she had been waiting for the world to crumble. Praying for it, actually. Because she didn't belong to any place where she was still called Alis, and this might be her last chance to tell someone. And even though she knew who she was, she didn't know if she would feel whole unless somebody else witnessed it.

'You're all getting it wrong,' she said. The words tumbled out of her; Elliot was half dead, and he surely wouldn't remember this. 'I'm not a woman.'

'Huh,' Elliot mumbled. Blood oozed from under his fingers, and Alis had the sudden impression that he already knew. Arsehole.

'I don't want to be called Alis,' she said. 'That's not my name. Someone gave it to me when they thought –' she stopped. *I beg that the universe collapses under the weight of its own inadequacy that it put me in this body.* 'I want to be Alix. I mean, I am Alix. But I'm not a man either. I'm not either of them. If you don't like it, too bad. If you think I'm wrong, your world is tiny and I pity you.'

Elliot didn't say anything for a long minute, and she thought he might have slipped away.

'Good,' Elliot said. He eased his torso to the floor, sighing in relief as his arm met the cold flagstones. His face was a really funny colour now. Almost grey.

'Is that it?'

'It's the least weird thing I've heard all week, Alix.'

'Right,' Alix said. They sat down. *Alix.* They hadn't heard anyone say it out loud before. The madness swelled again. There was power in words. They had always known it. Man – woman – wyrdo. Putting those words back in their own mouth neutralised them, then made them sweeter.

'Hey, Elliot,' Alix said, sweating, soaring high. 'There's something else.'

'What?'

'We're going to be friends.'

Elliot paled.

'Friends?' he said.

'Starting from now.'

Alix tried not to retch as they gripped the nun's skull and worked it loose from Elliot's shoulder. He gasped as the head rocked back and forth, until its teeth slid out with a wet sucking noise. Alix tossed it down the stairs. Elliot breathed shallowly, but he was no longer rigid. His shoulders melted against the floor.

'No time to rest,' Alix said. They grasped him around the torso and tried to hoist him up, but he was too heavy to carry. 'We're going to beat Nixie and Taro to the top. We're going to dismantle them. Then we're using the relics and getting out of here.'

'No,' he said.

Good job they were besties, or Alix would leave him here to rot.

Alix rolled their shoulders and dug their hands into Elliot's armpits, bracing themselves against the stone latticework. Elliot's body was unwilling. He didn't have the simple heaviness of a book pile, but an unyielding weight that fought against them.

'Help me out,' Alix grunted, but Elliot had gone silent. His head lolled into his chest. Alix swore and punched him in the shoulder. The sound of the apocalypse bubbled up the staircase, the clattering of bone and rasping of strangling vines becoming more frantic. Green tendrils embroidered with droplets of blood felt their way around the corner, dragging themselves up each step with pale fingers. The staircase became a maw, the tunnel its throat, the writhing bones its teeth. Alix stood at the bloody beast's lip.

Damn you to hell, Alix screamed at it, silently, rage-filled. The tunnel exhaled the stink of its victims. *Damn you to the depths of the netherworld, monsterfucker.*

The curse fell flat, and the apocalypse opened its jaws.

Twenty-two

'She's fighting the skeletons,' Taro breathed. 'What the hell is wrong with her?'

Nixie realised she was still clutching Taro. The vines bursting through the door of the Fifth Tower flowed towards Alis's legs, and the skeletons on top of her scrapped like dogs. Nixie knew she would be swallowed if she got close, but horror had dismembered her impeccable logic. Horror at the awful things she had said to Alis, and that the foetid tangle of cruelty she kept pushing down had driven Alis into the arms of the undead.

Nixie couldn't even get their name right. *Alix*. Not Alis. Alix had told Nixie their real name years ago, and Nixie had blanked it out and run away. Because it was awkward. Because Nixie hadn't known how to respond. Because it had felt too heavy, and Nixie hadn't wanted to deal with it. Alix was right: she had been the worst kind of friend.

She started towards Alix again, desperate to show she wasn't useless, but Taro caught her.

'Don't even think about ploughing in. We have to get up the stairs *now*.'

'I shouldn't have said—'

'You were a dick. You don't have to be a dead one.' Taro tugged her urgently. 'She'll be fine.'

'They.'

'What?'

'Alix. Not Alis. They.'

'I – fine, whatever. They'll be OK.'

Nixie wanted to be free, didn't she? She was so close. She'd always known she would do whatever it took to live. This was the very last step: turning her back on Alix and walking up those stairs.

But she hadn't reckoned with this guilt. She was doing the same thing she had done in the Pit, turning her back on Alix and going with Taro. Nixie looked back at the stone disciple. She hadn't expected Alix's eyes to be on her. They were bleak with fury. A vine lashed around Nixie's ankle, and she was glad for something else to rail against. She wrenched her foot away and pulled Taro roughly up the steps. The action was automatic; she couldn't stop herself trying to save the bone disciple, and it sickened her.

When they were safe Nixie let go of Taro and started back down, thinking she could pull Alix out too, but Taro caught her robes.

'You'll die,' Taro said firmly.

Nixie struggled to get free. It wasn't too late – she could make it – but because Taro was holding her the precious seconds were being chewed up. She fought until she was weak.

'I'm sorry, bunny,' Taro said.

Taro had done it again. Made a decision for Nixie, supposedly for her own good. Stolen her autonomy. And now it meant the death of someone who used to be her best friend.

Push it down.

Nixie climbed, her breath ragged, her chest aching. She looked back in time to see a ravaged body fall and slam into the bottom step. She stumbled a little further, and the body disappeared from view.

'They can't climb stairs,' Taro said. She sagged against a wall to catch her breath. 'It'll take them a while to work it out, anyway.'

But ivy would still grow up the walls, the stone would weep blood, and they would reach the crest of the tower with half their party. And Nixie had abandoned Alix for Taro, who now looked totally unconcerned by the fact that Alix was probably fighting through a heap of angry corpses, if they weren't dead already.

A lump swelled in Nixie's throat.

'What now?' Taro said. 'We don't have Elliot or Alis – Alix. When were you going to tell me about their name, by the way? Actually, I don't care. I'm saying we don't have all the curse keys, so we're screwed.'

Stick with the plan. Don't look back.

'We can do it ourselves,' Nixie said. Speaking was difficult, but she forced herself to be calm. 'You took Elliot's curse key, didn't you? Well, Alix gave me theirs. So we use them.'

They just had to pray they wouldn't meet Geraldin on the way. Nixie counted the steps as they waded away from the tower floor, leaving bloody footprints that dried into smears. Fifty. One hundred. Two hundred. The climb became her heartbeat. She could smell burning toast, but she didn't have the capacity to wonder what it was, or why it screamed *Run!*

'We can't use them,' Taro panted, struggling to keep up. 'The Ghost said we need blood and stone disciples too. We can't break the curse alone.'

'Why can't you see what's in front of your face?' Nixie snapped.

She surged ahead. It felt like she was running away.

'See what?' Taro ran up beside her.

'Use your brain.'

'I accept that you hate me, but say what you mean instead of being a cow.'

Oh, she was asking for it. Nixie stopped dead.

'You're not a bone disciple,' she said. Her words had the clarity of iced water. 'You're undisciplined. An aberration. If anyone knew, they would chop you into pieces and throw you into the Desecrae. I could have written a note and slipped it under someone's door, and they would have dragged you off years ago.'

'Undiscipline doesn't exist any more,' Taro said, but she sounded uncertain. And too calm. Almost like she had already thought about it.

'Wresting by sticking a dead mouse in your mouth, when you're only meant to be able to use your hands? Incanting for Alix in the chapel? Spells can't just unknot themselves. You were doing something to the stone part too. Drooling every time you're near one of the curse keys, even though you're only meant to feel your own?'

Taro only looked shocked for a moment before pulling herself together.

'Cool,' she said. 'I'm special. Always knew I was good.'

'That's it?'

'What else do you want me to say?'

'Don't you realise how big a deal it is?'

Taro smirked, and Nixie fought the dark, squirming urge to shove her down the steps. 'Whatever,' Nixie said. As she began the climb she struggled to keep her voice level. To not feel anything. 'We're going to finish what we started, just the two of us. I'll use the botanic relic, and you'll use the others. Then I'm walking away, to whatever's out there, and you can find someone else to latch on to.'

'Don't say that—'

The staircase opened into the apex of the tower. As soon as Nixie crossed the threshold she felt the air loosen, and without brushing her hand over a stretch of ivy – normal this time – she knew that she could wrest again. The floor was a wrought-iron grid. In the centre was a circle of polished red stone. At the opposite end of the chamber, flanked by great columns of stone with the burn marks of wresting, was an iron throne, and in front of it – dislodged from the Thaumaturge's skull – was the crown. Four Unholy Mothers stood sentry around the chamber, wreathed in clothes that hadn't been touched by mould, their hands clasped to their hearts. They didn't move as Nixie stepped up and pressed her index finger to one's cheek. Neither would they until the crown was worn.

The old Thaumaturge – Lord of Clockwork, Master of Fourspires, Two-Hundred-and-Tenth Stone Arcanist of His Bloodline, Emperor Against Time, His Frozen Highness the Tick-Tock King – was sprawled in the centre of the room. One bone-thin arm was outstretched, grasping for the throne. His cheeks were as hollow as if the flesh had been spooned out, his thin hair spreading like a rotting halo. He gazed blankly at the hole in the roof through which the blue-black smoke had poured after his death, his mouth agape and stained the same colour, the smell of burned flesh lingering in the air.

The last bleak truth oozed from the box where Nixie had hidden everything.

The memory had always been there, hissing at her through the cracks in the wall she had put around it, trying to break free of the poorly administered potion she had downed in Greenspire. She had shoved it down with all her feelings, but it hadn't been hidden well enough.

She had committed this murder.

Nixie laughed. Then she heard she was laughing and stopped. This did something to Taro, who was balanced on a knife-edge between good humour and hysteria. She recognised Nixie's breaking point, and she broke with her. Taro fell to the ground and clutched Nixie's robes. Nixie tried to push her off, but weakly, and Taro only tightened her fingers.

'I fucking love you,' Taro said, and Nixie knew that Taro was not OK at all, had been shoving everything deep into her guts almost as hard as Nixie had. 'I'm obsessed with you. I bent people's bones to be close to you. I did terrible things to get your results changed in the Pit.' Taro grappled with Nixie's robes. Nixie knew she should kick her away, but the vestiges of the blackness that had choked her for years escaped from her eyes in hot streaks. *Don't go*, she begged, but it did, and then she was on the floor, and Taro's face was in her hands, and her face was in Taro's hands, and they were grappling with each other as if they were trying to pull each other apart, because they were both angry; but they also wanted to be one thing, one line of sight and one stupidly convulsing heart. They were both pieces of shit. Nixie had walked away from Alix because she didn't know how to cope with their pain, and Taro had forced Nixie into the castle because she didn't want to be alone. They deserved nothing better than each other, and Nixie, for all her snarling, had never even sought anyone else. She had thrown the world away for the bone witch.

'I love you,' Taro said again. 'I'm sorry and I love you. I'll pay for everything I did, and I love you. I'd go to hell for you, and I love you. You don't even have to love me back.'

Nixie tried to detangle herself, but her fingers kept crawling towards Taro's mouth. Her thumbs searched for the corners of her lips. The remains of Taro's make-up rucked under her nails.

For years Nixie had pressed down her vile disgust towards Taro. But there was always something she couldn't destroy, which she needed and loathed in equal measure. That silver thread that she thought was nostalgia but was really too alive for her to bear. Love, probably. But it was nothing compared to the anger that had brought them here.

'I killed the Thaumaturge,' Nixie said.

She choked back another hysterical laugh, because she couldn't believe she'd been so reckless; but the memory was blasted wide open, howling for her to see it. Her words were running away without her. 'I didn't want to run away with you. I couldn't stand the thought of being stuck with you for ever. I didn't plan it. I just snapped at dinner. I left the room, and I broke the Unholy Mothers' necks and pushed them through the window. I went to the kitchen and self-wrested. I poisoned his food.'

Taro sobbed.

'You didn't,' she said.

'They don't think any of us are capable, but it took five seconds to make the soup toxic.'

'I don't believe you.'

'I knew the Slaughter would stop us running away,' Nixie said. 'You looked at me over the table with that stupid expression, and I knew I couldn't wake up every day and see your face next to mine and not go insane.'

Taro's body heaved as she wept.

'I didn't plan beyond that,' Nixie said. It was a perfectly crystalline memory, unbattered by overthinking, cruelly preserved by the potion that had locked it away. 'When the Thaumaturge died, I panicked. So I blocked out the memory with one of Kellan's potions. I think it stopped working a while ago, and I was just forcing myself not to think about it. But it was me. I did it because I needed to get away from you.'

'But you love me. You kissed me.'

'Because I'm weak.' Nixie peeled Taro away from her, limb by limb. She couldn't breathe like this. 'I hate you, but I keep helping you. You don't deserve it.'

'What are you doing?'

'Get off me.'

'No. I love you. And you love me.'

'So?' Nixie said savagely. She finally managed to extricate herself from Taro's grip, which made the bone disciple sob again. 'I don't trust you. We can't make it whole again.'

'We can,' Taro said. 'I can show you—'

'You can't make a gesture and expect everything to be fine. Do you understand?' Taro was staring at her with wide, helpless eyes, a nauseating look of complete surrender on her face. She would do anything. She would throw herself into the roiling sea of bones for forgiveness. She would perform heroics until her flesh burned, because she was Taro, and Taro thought she could earn forgiveness by grandly prostrating herself. But Nixie didn't see regret for what she had done. Only sorrow at being discovered.

'You don't understand,' Nixie said. She wished so badly that she didn't love the bone witch, because it would make hating her easier.

She couldn't look at Taro any more. If their eyes locked together Nixie might try to comfort her and say *I didn't mean it, everything's fine*, because she wanted to stop her crying. But it would be a lie. Nixie hated Taro so much that she had killed to get away from her, and in doing so had damned hundreds more familiars to death.

You're a murderer. And you would do it all again.

Dark rain spattered against the windows along with bone-splitting howls from the courtyard. The screams yanked Nixie out of her self-loathing. She had to help whoever was left. It was time to do what she was best at; pack as much of herself away as possible and do the work required to survive.

She drew the shard of mirror from her pocket. She had followed the

Ghost's instructions to the letter, without questioning anything, like what deep and awful arcania kept the Ghost tethered to reflections. She had been perfect, and this was her reward: the saving of the world. She unwrapped the glass and set it on the stone circle.

A slice of the Ghost's face appeared. Nixie thought she saw hungry delight.

'We have all the curse keys.' Nixie had no room for niceties.

She threw down the crushed handkerchief containing the mushroom and the stone die. Taro, hiccuping as she tried to stop sobbing, followed suit with the yellowed tooth. Then she drew the blood vial from her pocket.

'What's that?' the Ghost said sharply.

'The blood curse key,' Taro said. She wiped her snot on her sleeve and tried to recover a fraction of dignity. 'You can thank me later.'

The Ghost shot her hand through the mirror and mashed her incorporeal fingers through the vial. Nixie immediately knew what was wrong. It had been too easy. She shouldn't have trusted Taro, who was as perceptive as slime mould, to get the real curse key from Elliot.

'Idiots!' the Ghost screamed. Vomit rose in Nixie's throat, because this was it, the fuck-up of all fuck-ups. 'This isn't the curse key, it's trash!'

Ice sharp anger stabbed Nixie's ribs. All of this for nothing. Scrabbling through the underbelly of the castle. Hurting people and being hurt. Leaving Alix to the apocalypse. Nixie savagely kicked the vial over the edge of the chamber, where the stairs converged and boiled with the approach of the apocalypse, and imagined the heinous castle might finally choke on it. It shattered against the stone.

Someone kicked the glass back.

Alix staggered into the room, supporting Elliot.

Ivy and bones and blood followed at their heels. Piecemeal corpses made the frothing sea of death buck and heave. Alix dropped Elliot and left him slack on the floor.

'You,' Alix said, pointing a trembling finger at Nixie. It wasn't funny or overdramatic; it was a terrifying gut-punch. The Ghost stopped shrieking with fury and shrieked with laughter instead. The blood vial had come to them.

Alix raised their hands and shook grit from their bleeding fingers. They screamed at the door. The floor buckled. Stone rained from the archway as the stairs fell, the stone latticework crumpling, ripping the fingers of apocalyptic ivy from the chamber with a long, wet sucking sound.

The cacophony of chewing and ripping was far below them now. Nixie took an automatic step towards Alix, wanting to embrace them even more than she wanted to shake the curse key from Elliot's limp body. She did neither.

'You're alive,' she said blandly. She didn't know how to express her soul-crushing relief.

Alix shook their head in disgust. They had been scratched and stabbed and wrenched at, and they probably hadn't eaten or slept in days, and they had wrested so much power the average familiar would be comatose; yet here they were, on their feet, withstanding the end of the world. Nixie had forgotten how powerful Alix was; it was one of the things that had drawn her to the stone disciple in the first place. Nixie had always liked people who half killed themselves in the pursuit of brilliance.

Alix clamped their pencil stub between their bloodied fingers as the Ghost wheezed with breathless laughter.

You left me there, Alix scrawled. Nixie felt her insides shrivel with deep black shame. *What were you going to do? Somehow break the curse yourself and skip into the sunset with Taro while I was chewed up?* They stepped closer and placed an index finger on Nixie's chest. *I shouldn't have given you my curse key. It was the only thing that made me valuable to you.*

'That's not true,' Nixie said hoarsely.

If I still had the die, would you have left me there?

'It wasn't a choice—'

Alix slapped Nixie so hard she felt it in her teeth. Nixie's hand flew to her jaw; it hurt in a beautifully bright, clarifying way.

Don't lie to yourself.

Elliot groaned and raised himself to a sitting position. His shoulder was stained with rust-coloured gunk, and he looked as if he was about to pass out.

'Why is he here?' Nixie asked, grasping for anything to divert Alix's scrutiny.

He didn't leave me to die. Alix eyed Nixie meaningfully.

'Are you stupid?' Taro spluttered. 'He betrayed us. He gave me a fake curse key, then he just *stood* there with Morgan. I'm going to put a goddamned spike through his heart.'

Elliot coughed up pink spittle.

'You're welcome to try,' he said. 'But you need something I have.'

He opened his hand, revealing a vial. It was ancient, the fluid as black as Taro's pupils.

'Did you really think I'd just hand the curse key over?' he said.

'Monster,' Taro spat. She shoved past Alix. 'If you hadn't changed your mind and come into the tower at the last minute, Nixie and I would be absolutely *fucked.* I hope you cough your guts out of your mouth!'

'What are you going to do? Snap my neck? You can't use the curse key without me anyway.'

'Turns out I can, you jumped-up little vampire—'

'Stop!' Nixie yelled. Taro halted mid-snarl. Alix and Elliot looked at her too. Nixie hadn't planned to take charge, but she wanted to hold everything together. She had brought them here. She had tied them all to each other. She might also be the only person level-headed enough to get them out again.

And there was something else. It was a small, cloying lump in her throat, something hard to identify because it was so unfamiliar to her. It tasted a little bit like hope. Oh *hell.* She was going to make a goddamned speech.

'I know we all hate each other,' she said, and she knew Alix was going to snort before they even did it; Nixie's eyes fluttered closed as she resisted the urge to bite back. 'But we're all here for a reason. We want to escape

Fourspires. But if we want to make it happen – if all any of this is going to be worth it – we need to help each other.'

Alix's lip twitched with derision.

'Alix actually came here to kill you,' Elliot drawled. He coughed again, his chest rattling, and Nixie knew he was being sardonic to cover the fact that he was probably bleeding to death.

Nixie met Alix's eye. The stone disciple held her gaze.

'But I'm not dead yet,' Nixie said softly. 'Which means you don't really want me gone. Because the Alix I knew would have slit my throat without a second thought if they meant it.'

Alix stepped towards her, their fingers crooked as though they wanted to strangle Nixie right there in the chamber. Nixie stepped forward too. If anyone was still alive in the city, they needed Nixie to make this work. How shameful that it took *that* to make Nixie speak, when she should have done it years ago. She forced her teeth apart.

'I'm sorry,' she said. Her voice cracked under the weight of her shame. 'I was a really bad friend, Alix. I don't expect you to forgive me. But we need to work together. Just one last time, so we can get out of here. Then we can fight, OK? I mean it. I'm *sorry*.'

Part of her expected Alix to crumble into her arms and say, *Of course I forgive you. I've missed you so much. You don't even need to apologise.* But Alix only sucked their cheeks in, thinking long and hard, before nodding stiffly.

And that was it.

Nixie felt empty. But she didn't have the right to hope for more. And all of this, the mess and the sadness and the fury, could be dealt with later; now they had to get what they came for.

'Elliot,' she said. 'Are you in?'

'If Taro stops grimacing at me.'

'Fine,' Taro said sulkily. She looked at Elliot blackly, her lips twisted. 'But this isn't over. Once we've broken the curse, I'm coming for you. I'm going to kill you for lying to me.'

If you come for him I'll push you off the tower, Alix wrote. *What's a little more murder?*

'Try it. I could do with a laugh.'

Alix stared at Taro with daggers in their eyes, not breaking contact as they wrote.

Do what you need to, Greenspire.

Nixie swallowed. The city was writhing beneath them. Ivy forced itself through every crack in the world, sprouting through gutters and stone slabs, whispering as it crept up walls, pushing tiny tendrils into minuscule fractures, dragging itself up by its fingertips. A shoot by itself was nothing, but like drops of water, its gathered mass was suffocating. People were fighting piles of bone and wading through streams of blood. Perhaps some arcanists were using their familiars to hold it back, but it wouldn't be enough. Even Nixie and Taro and Alix didn't know the right spell for the Suppression. Of all the incantations they had stolen, the one preventing the collapse of the world should have been first. But it had seemed so foundational that learning it had felt as pointless as learning how to breathe.

'You know what to do, right?' Taro said. Her face was full of hope. Nixie felt a deep swell of fear that Taro was living in a different reality to Nixie. One in which Nixie had forgiven her, and the only thing standing between them was a big enough apology, when Nixie knew that every tiny part of their relationship was broken.

'Yeah,' she said. She went to the shard of mirror and picked it up. The Ghost had her translucent fingers hooked over the edge of the glass.

'That was a vomit-inducing reunion,' the Ghost said. 'Are you finished?'

'Tell us what to do.'

The Ghost drew back into the netherworld so they could see her full face, from her sinuses to the roots of her teeth. The muscles in her cheeks pulled her lips into a grim smile.

'Put me in his mouth,' she said.

'What?'

'Feed. The glass. To. His. Mouth.'

'Kill me,' Taro muttered, but Nixie was already approaching the Thaumaturge's body. Elliot muttered something dark as she pushed the shard between the body's dry lips, working it between the front teeth.

'Further,' the Ghost said, and Nixie wriggled it deeper still, until a flash of the Ghost's hand made her stop. She drew away, her fingers itching. Greylight fell from the hole in the ceiling and smeared across the body, spangled where it was thrown by the glass.

'Now the curse keys,' the Ghost said.

'Aren't we using them to wrest?' Nixie asked.

'Give them to the body.'

They decorated the Thaumaturge's corpse with their macabre loot. Nixie slipped the mushroom between the old man's fingers. Alix placed the die on his chest. Taro pushed the yellowing tooth into the dip at the base of his throat. Elliot, still on his hands and knees, worked the stopper from the vial, and daubed the blood on the Thaumaturge's forehead.

'Now what?' Nixie said. A hot sickness gripped her. Everything felt wrong. But none of them could stop this, because there was no other way out of this tower.

The Ghost pushed her right hand through the glass. Nixie expected her to ooze back in, but she kept stretching, expanding into the smear of light that was reflected across the corpse's body. She wriggled out face first, her skull buckling as she pushed through the shard, and when her head was at the old man's toes she turned over, swimming up to fit the length of her body to his. Her right arm bobbed up as she crawled. She was missing all five fingers. Alix and Nixie looked at each other sharply, clearly thinking the same thing: *Mr Fingers*. Who was not, in fact, male at all.

The Ghost eased herself into the Thaumaturge's corpse, shivering in the ice bath of his flesh. She pushed her remaining fingertips into one of his hands as if it were a glove. Her face drifted into his skull, her pert nose disappearing under his, her high cheekbones bobbing above the surface of his clammy skin, her hair drifting through his shoulders.

For a long while nothing happened, and Nixie felt faintly stupid watching a dead person trying to wear another dead person like a coat.

Then the Thaumaturge smiled, and the whole world went to shit.

Twenty-three

The Ghost's voice became the Thaumaturge's moan. Her new lips stretched open and Elliot saw a translucent tongue flicker before it snapped into the old Thaumaturge's real one, dark and dried out.

The Thaumaturge – the Ghost – rocked to her feet, leaving swathes of dried skin on the ground like rifts of snow. The mirror shard fell from her mouth. Her eyes flickered around the room, her ghost-irises moving just a fraction of a second before the Thaumaturge's caught up. She inclined her stolen head, which made the neck crack, and gazed at Elliot.

'Redspire,' she said. Her voice was full of crevices. Elliot's torn-up shoulder thrummed as he raised his chin. He didn't answer. It might have seemed like obstinance, but the pain radiating through his jaw meant he could barely open his mouth. So he screwed his eyes into hers, and she looked back pitilessly with something close to disgust.

Taro coughed. The Ghost swivelled and stared at Taro through her two sets of eyes.

'… hi,' Taro said. 'Are you … happy … with your new body?'

'It's necessary,' the Ghost said. She seemed to be having

trouble with her tongue. Her voice was both that of a young woman and an old man, the two lapping at each other thickly. 'A non-corporeal tongue can't—' she choked, jerked her head forward, and spat her tongue back into her mouth '—can't shape arcania any more than the ghost of a body can wrest it.' She looked down at herself, and the shadow of eternal adolescence briefly haunted the old man's face. 'It's not fun, if that's what you're asking. I'll improve it later.'

Elliot imagined her cracking the bones and reshaping them. Shrinking the oversized teeth to fit over her phantom mouth. Punching the body into shape like wet clay. The haunting of the Thaumaturge's body was deeply impressive, and if he hadn't been watching the end of the world, Elliot would have crawled at her feet and asked: *How?*

'But thanks for getting me here, babes,' the Ghost added. She curled her tongue experimentally, then added: 'You're totally fucked, by the way.'

She said it so casually Elliot thought he had misheard. The Ghost pushed her nose around her face as they processed that.

'Excuse me,' Taro said finally, 'but how are we fucked? We did what you asked. So now you're going to lift the Desecrae and stop this apocalyptic bullshit, right?'

'Sure,' the Ghost said. 'After a little more destruction.' She dug her fingers around her mouth and spat out a tooth. 'If I'm going to rule, I want to start with a clean slate.'

The silence was heavy. They were all thinking the same thing: *Something's wrong*, and *Please don't let this have been a mistake.* Elliot felt a deep, terrified pressure in his lungs. It was hard to speak.

'We brought you here to save us,' he said. 'You didn't say anything about ruling.'

'There's a lot I didn't say.' The Ghost looked at her right hand, which hung limply at her side. She picked it up with her left and massaged the knuckles. A nail fell off, revealing a strip of rotting skin. 'I can't believe this is what I have to work with,' she added with disgust.

The Ghost was enjoying herself. She knew something they didn't, and she was waiting for them to catch on. She was having fun in much the same way as Malachi played with the big cats before sending them to slaughter, chucking them under the chin and smiling as his zookeepers sharpened their knives.

'People are dying outside,' Nixie snapped.

'I said *wait*.' The Ghost's tongue flopped out, and she pushed it back in with her fingers. 'Let the weak ones die off. I suspect the people without arcanical ability will be the first to go. It will be good for the strength of the kingdom. God knows it's been diluted since I was booted out.' Her two voices were beginning to slide into each other. The body was becoming her home. 'Go on. Gasp at my prowess in haunting corpses. Ask who I was before I died.'

The kingdom. A noiseless laugh wracked Elliot's body. The command in her voice told him everything he needed to know about who she was. They had played into the hands of a deathless tyrant.

'Tell us what's happening,' Nixie demanded, her voice almost cracking, and Elliot felt a deep wave of pity for her. She didn't have a clue, and instead of understanding in one cold, bottomless moment like he had, she would face the iniquity of Elliot telling her.

'The Ghost tricked you,' he said. The Ghost looked at him curiously, almost impressed. 'She didn't need the curse keys to lift the Desecrae. She needed them to resurrect herself. And she needed us to bring her into the tower with us. Presumably because she couldn't do it by herself.'

'Why?' Nixie said. Her eyes kept going to the window, where the sounds of slurping and tearing and screaming bounced against the glass. Every sound made her twitch.

'Poor baby,' the Ghost said.

Alix flicked their eyes towards Elliot, and their eyebrow quirked, just for a second. It was an infinitesimally small twitch, but a purposeful one, and Elliot knew what Alix meant. His apparent ability to interpret the stone familiar was disturbing. He loathed the idea of some bond, instinctual or otherwise. Nonetheless—

Elliot tried to grab the crown on the floor. The Ghost moved at the same time. She was stiff, but she moved in short, sharp jerks, and she got there faster than he could. Elliot twisted away, his body automatically flinching from the standing corpse instead of ripping the crown from its fingers. Alix's eyes burned with disappointment.

'Oh boy,' the Ghost said. 'I haven't had this much action in centuries.' She flexed her left fingers around the crown, listening to the bones pop. 'I think my joints hurt, but I haven't settled into the pain receptors yet. I can feel things breaking, but I kind of don't need my bones to be whole, you know? As long as I can move things.' She delicately sniffed the crown. 'Greasy,' she said.

Gore pattered against the outside of the window as something, probably a huge, bloody boil, exploded.

The Ghost put the crown on, her eyelids fluttering as the cold ring settled on her naked forehead. The nuns at the edges of the room blinked, and the Ghost smiled at them. It was the first real joy Elliot had seen from her.

'I can almost understand why Aldous took the crown,' she said. 'Nothing else feels as good.'

'Sorry, but does everyone have a different script to me?' Taro said. 'Why the *hell* are we talking about the old head of Redspire? Why has this spectral blob put on a new meat suit, and why are we still balls deep in the apocalypse?'

Nixie put a hand on Taro's elbow, and the bone disciple fell silent.

'Elliot,' Nixie said with the calm of someone who knows they're already dead. 'You said she tricked us. Tell me what you think you know.'

'Morgan told me about Aldous Redborn,' Elliot said. 'He was the head blood arcanist when Sobweb was in charge.'

'Why does Sobweb matter?' Taro snapped.

Elliot jerked his head at the Ghost, who was trying to smother a grin even as another fingernail peeled off. 'Did you really not ask her name?'

'Stop it,' Taro said. 'Sobweb's a man.'

'Says who?' The Ghost flicked her head, momentarily forgetting that she had very little hair. 'You just assumed he was a man. Everyone did after I was gone a while. That really pissed me off.'

'You're not Sobweb,' Taro said, jabbing her finger at the Ghost. 'Sobweb's—'

'Dead? Uh-huh,' the Ghost said. She nodded at the nuns. 'Mothers. If you will.'

Elliot shuddered as an Unholy Mother embraced him from above. It respirated into the back of his neck, the smell of its rotten tongue tickling his nostrils. It lifted him from under his ribs, its fingers digging into the flesh between his bones. The pain in his shoulder made him pulse with a rage that was only matched by his helplessness. Alix was in the air next to him, hissing as the nun grasping them scraped its nails into their cuts and grazes.

Sobweb watched hungrily. Elliot knew that she found a weird pleasure in their suffering. He had seen that hunger from teachers in the Pit, and from Tamsin when she had cursed him. But Sobweb had an army of Unholy Mothers at her fingertips. This was a despot who could twist her hand and turn the promise of pain into something very real. And they were the ones who had given her a body.

Elliot had long ago tried to kill empathy in himself. Being responsible for his fate, and his fate alone, had given him the strength to stay alive. But something had happened at the bottom of the tower, right at the moment he had decided to follow Alix. He had leaned on them, and now he felt part of the world leaning on him. They couldn't let Sobweb win. No world with her in charge was worth having.

'Sweet Mothers,' Sobweb said. She lolloped towards Elliot and poked the cheek of the nun with her index finger. 'One of them is my actual mother. But it's so hard to tell them apart, you know?' The nun holding Elliot tightened its grip. Every breath Elliot took drove its fingers further into the sensitive flesh between his bones. His vision furred.

'Your mother,' he repeated weakly. Sobweb moved to the nun holding Nixie and tilted its head to the light to better inspect its face. She *tsk*ed and dropped it.

'They're not really nuns,' she said. 'After their creation I forgot which one gave birth to me, so I called them all Mother as a joke. The name stuck.

The robes are just practical.' She came back to the nun holding Elliot and dug her finger under its chin. 'Up,' she said, and the nun lifted its head. 'I think she had a birthmark here,' Sobweb added. 'Something they don't tell you is that after a few hundred years, your memories become formless. You mostly just remember what you desired.' She sighed and moved away, and Elliot released his breath. 'I'm surprised the Mothers have lasted. And you lot – I would have expected a revolution. Familiars could have killed their masters a million times over if they'd used their brains and banded together. Which suggests that you deserve to be here.'

'The world's dying, asshole,' Taro croaked. 'Lift the curse!'

Elliot prayed for Taro's teeth to fall out so she would stop antagonising the dead tyrant. He glared at her, expecting her to feel the depths of her idiocy, but when she caught his gaze she smiled archly as if they were co-conspirators.

Sobweb stalked lopsidedly to the window to watch the world writhe. The city bubbled with movement, but it was clear that the fight was dying out.

'Almost there,' Sobweb observed. She peered down her nose at the ground. 'What do you think? Ten minutes for good measure?'

It took Elliot an embarrassingly long moment to realise that Nixie was prying herself from the arms of her nun. Its bones were jammed in place, its eyes dull and its mouth slack. Deadlocked. It sometimes happened to ancient nuns who hadn't been mobile for a while; they either started thrashing or froze with overwhelm. Nixie was trying to break its arms at the elbows. It cracked its mouth open and released a puff of stale air, emitting a wheezing, oozing sound. Sobweb turned to look.

'Let us go,' Elliot barked, and was only half relieved when Sobweb turned her attention to him instead.

'Unoriginal,' she said.

Nixie had prised the arms of her nun open by a few inches. Dust trickled from the corner of its lips and spilled into her hair. Nixie sucked her breath in and tried to wriggle towards the floor, her robes snagging on its elbows. Elliot fought the urge to scream.

'You look upset by the destruction, Elliot,' Sobweb observed. 'But Fourspires is a speck of gilded dirt on a colossal dinner table. When I was alive – the first time – the world was as flat as a plate, and it went so far on all sides that you couldn't see past the horizon. Do you know the word "horizon"? No, I suppose not.' Something new spattered against the outside of the windows, the viscous sap of ivy. 'Fourspires was just the heart of the kingdom. I could look through the window on every side and still not see the whole world. There was no Desecrae above us. There were so many people. So many cities and so many things to eat.' Her hand fluttered to her cheek, her tongue perhaps remembering sugar. 'It was a mess before I inherited the throne. Few people used arcania to its full potential. I popularised the use of familiars. Made it mandatory. Arcanists can do a lot more when they aren't limited by pain. Whole economies sprang up. The general growth in wealth was phenomenal. I travelled with my nuns and people cheered for me everywhere. Some hated me. Others were jealous. But no one opposed me.'

'Hallow Myre did,' Elliot said. 'The man you told Nixie about. He sealed Fourspires and the city under the Desecrae and made it destroy itself. Not because he was jealous. He wanted to stop you.'

Sobweb sneered.

'Oh, he was definitely jealous.'

Nixie turned her head sideways to squeeze it through the nun's arms. The nun began to judder. She reached up and tried to pry its arms wider before they crushed against her head. Elliot could see she was starting to panic.

'He saw you for the tyrannical piece of shit you are,' Elliot said. He was playing a stupid game, but they needed enough of a distraction for Nixie to free herself. Sobweb left the window to shove her face in his. The stench of her insides oozed through her mouth.

'Hallow Myre was the ultimate do-gooder,' she said. 'He was so insufferably moral even priests avoided him. And I'm not just saying that because I lack virtue.' She touched Elliot's hair and *hmm*ed under her breath. 'So soft. But yes. Mr Moral had a thing for me. They said it was righteous hatred, but it was the kind of obsession that makes me suspect he wanted to jump my bones. I wouldn't let him. So he did the next best thing, and chatted up all four of my head arcanists and persuaded them to kill me. He said he thought the system with the familiars was unconscionable, and I needed to go.' She twirled a lock of Elliot's hair around her stiff, stolen finger. 'He was nothing if not exacting. After they stabbed me, they used some truly horrendous arcania to split my soul apart and ram it into four objects. Did you know that the flavour of your soul is the same as your arcania? Mine was like a buffet – too much of everything. They carved it into four sections, bone and blood and stone and botanic, because that was all they could see between them, and squirrelled it away in their little keepsakes, then shoved *those* away where nobody would find them.'

Elliot looked at the swirling Desecrae through the hole in the roof. Up here, closer to the sky than he had ever been, he could see individual molars bobbing in the grey gore. Nixie wrestled with the nun's fingers.

'And the curse?' Elliot said. He tried to hold Sobweb's gaze, to ignore her breath on his face. He just had to keep her occupied.

'As soon as the arcanists crept off to murder me, Myre put the Desecrae over the city and threw in the apocalypse for good measure. It was insurance to make sure they got the job done. All they had to do was destroy the crown after killing me, and the curse would lift.' She brought her lips to Elliot's ear. 'Guess who messed up?'

Elliot smiled the briefest, coldest smile.

'Aldous Redborn,' he said. 'I know the family.'

'He was always a little weasel,' she said. 'The other three left him in charge of destroying the crown, but the whole thing was too tempting. He would rather be the king of a necrotic little bubble than a nobody in Myre's democracy, so he waited until the other arcanists had disposed of my soul, murdered them, and put the crown on his own head.'

'He kept his quarter of your soul as a souvenir,' Elliot said. He nodded to the vial, which was unstoppered on the floor with a drop of blood hanging from the lip.

'It doesn't surprise me,' Sobweb said. 'He was arrogant. His arrogance didn't serve him well, because he hadn't considered what he was going to do once he was on the throne. Nobody was powerful enough to break the curse. He had to get some new arcanist pals to deal with the apocalypse pretty quickly. I believe knives were held to throats. That's how the Suppression began. Aldous always had a knack for ritual. He's the architect of the Slaughter, too.'

'Nice legacy,' Elliot said, and Sobweb smiled. She thought they were both in on the joke: *that's Redborns for you.* 'And on the off chance you were still clinging to existence, he hexed the tower so nobody could bring you in.'

'Couldn't bring me in *knowingly*,' Sobweb said. 'He was sloppy.'

She withdrew and looked at herself in the shard of mirror on the floor, dispassionately taking in the liver spots and sunken cheeks.

'Any questions?' she said. 'We've got time. I can still hear people screaming.'

'No,' Taro said, then flicked her eyes at Nixie, who was still struggling. 'Actually, yeah. Why were you perving on my girlfriend through her mirror?'

Sobweb's mouth didn't so much as twitch with humour.

'You mean how did I manage to stay in the netherworld when everyone else passes through? Because I'm clever, you unimaginative little shit.'

'Oh, I get it,' Taro said. 'You expected someone to come and rescue you. Unbelievable. As if anyone would want you back.'

'Oh, *sweetie.* Your so-called girlfriend did,' Sobweb said. She moved closer to Taro and cupped her chin. 'She's so easy to sway. Every night I told her to murder the Thaumaturge. And bless her, she thought she was immune to me, but when crunch time came she took my suggestion. I didn't expect her to wipe her memory afterwards. That was a surprise. But I still got my way.'

'She didn't know this was going to happen,' Elliot said.

'Boo hoo, daisy chain.'

Nixie's nun was straining to move, but Nixie had squashed through its fingers and fixed her hands around its neck. She pressed hard, trying to break its upper spine. She grunted with exertion. Elliot kicked his feet in mock rage and Sobweb sauntered back to him.

She inclined her head so their noses were almost touching. Elliot knew her dead, milky eyes were bobbing behind the Thaumaturge's pupils, but as she leaned in, all he could focus on were the old man's dry lips and rancid breath. Sobweb kissed him lightly. Elliot closed his eyes and felt Sobweb's eyelashes tangling with his own.

'Just like I remember,' she said softly, and drew upright. 'I'll be sad when you're used up.'

Elliot willed the taste of dead flesh to drop from his lips.

'You won't use me for anything.'

'You're an important part of the takeover, silly,' Sobweb said, girlish again. 'You're all going to help me lift the curse, and I'm going to do it without destroying the crown, because I want to keep control of my Mothers. I'm the only person clever enough to incant for the four disciplines, so I need you to wrest harder than you ever have in your sad little lives. First, I'm going to stop the apocalypse, and when I've done that, I'll take down the Desecrae. Then I'll swarm the land, do a bit of conquering, and be Queen again. Got it?'

'All to sit on a fancy chair,' Taro said. 'How boring.'

'Only people at the bottom of the pile say that,' the ghost-piloted corpse sneered.

Nixie was behind Sobweb. She was so fast Elliot didn't see her moving, just as he hadn't noticed her sweep the shard of mirror from the floor. The glass sailed towards Sobweb's neck.

'No,' Sobweb said.

Nixie screamed and collapsed. The glass clattered to the floor with her. She writhed on the cold stone, her fingers clawing at her leg.

'What are you doing?' Taro shrieked.

'I broke her kneecap,' Sobweb said. She parted the fingers of her left hand – the Thaumaturge's left hand, grey and wrinkled – to show a chip of bone. The right still dangled by her side; she had given up on trying to save it.

'You couldn't – You didn't *say* anything—'

'Undisciplined,' Sobweb reminded her. 'And tongue work is so basic. You don't really need it to incant. Standards have really slipped in the mortal realm.' She turned Nixie over with her foot. 'Still conscious? Good.' She clicked her fingers, and the Unholy Mother that had been holding Nixie sailed across the room. Its neck was crooked where Nixie had broken it. It bent over with a sharp *crack*, grabbed Nixie by the shoulders, and hauled her upright. Her left leg dangled underneath her body.

'Die already,' Elliot snarled. He did not, as a rule, shudder at other people's pain. But he couldn't stop himself.

Sobweb forced his chin up. Elliot was reminded of the slow, sweet way Morgan had done the same thing.

'Would you die for these people?' she said. She squeezed his cheeks so hard he felt her nails on his teeth. 'Would you let me snap your bones if I promised to let them go?'

Elliot spat in her face.

Sobweb froze. The bright white gobbet slid down the dead Thaumaturge's left cheek. Through the roaring in his ears, Elliot was dimly aware of Alix squeezing their eyes shut.

Without breaking eye contact, Sobweb wiped her stolen face on her shoulder. Then, with the slowness of melting ice, she pushed Elliot's head back so he was looking at the vaulted ceiling. And she kept pushing. And pushing. Her fingers slid down his neck and dug into the soft part under his chin, forcing his tongue to the roof of his mouth. Elliot couldn't breathe. His legs kicked, but Sobweb was immovable. Fire burst behind his eyelids. He heard his own breath rattling in his throat, then the sudden, guttural stop as his airway closed.

'Well?' Sobweb whispered in his ear.

Elliot couldn't move his tongue. Sobweb released the pressure on his neck, and he emitted a low, ugly wheezing sound. Alix's shoulders slumped.

'What's that?' Sobweb said.

'No,' Elliot said. He swallowed and coughed. 'I don't want you to snap my bones.'

'Right,' she said. She dropped her hand and walked away. Elliot's head flopped forward, and drool spilled to the ground. His face was numb. 'Gather your materials, children. You're going to wrest, or the nuns will tear you in half.' She glanced back at Elliot. 'All of you.'

Elliot couldn't look Alix, or Nixie or Taro in the eye. He realised with disgust that Sobweb was right. He would wrest for her because he would rather do that than die. All it took was for someone to put their hands to his neck and he would break, because he didn't want to be killed.

Why did that realisation about himself matter? Acting in his own best interests had never been a problem before. He had never questioned his right to self-preservation. But the world was ending, and here – right at the last hurdle, the termination of all existence – he realised that something was forcing a change in him. He was suddenly ashamed of his inability to withstand a threat to his life, because it meant that he was just as bad as his parents.

His shame meant that Elliot, slave to the bloodiest family dynasty under the Desecrae, up to his eyeballs in curses and close to death, wanted to be good.

Twenty-four

The familiars were propped up around Sobweb, limp in the arms of the Unholy Mothers. Nixie's eyes were squeezed shut, legs twitching several inches above the floor. Haplessly gorgeous Elliot was staring at the ground, his left shoulder slumped forward where a chunk had been bitten out of it. Alix looked like they were going to kill someone by spitting fire at them. Red mist squalled through the hole in the roof.

Oh, goody, Taro thought. *It's coming out of the sky now.*

As Sobweb closed her eyes – the eyes of the corpse, anyway – and readied herself, Taro uneasily turned a finger bone in her palm. Rotting hands scraped the outside of the windows. The corpses had built a literal tower out of themselves to reach the chamber. If Sobweb was going to stop the apocalypse, she needed to hurry the hell up.

'You don't need to restrain us,' Taro said. 'We want this to stop as much as you do.'

Sobweb ignored her.

Taro glanced anxiously at Nixie. Her face was a weird colour and her lips were wobbling as if she was trying not to cry out. Taro needed to get her out of this mess, but plans had always been Nixie's thing.

I'm undisciplined! she shouted into the ether, as though the plant disciple would sense her if she thought loudly enough. *That's huge, right? I was being flippant earlier. Tell me how to help.*

Taro had always known she was shit-hot at arcania. When she had woken up in the Torture Pit she had seen the black cross on her arm that meant she was a bone disciple, but she'd been able to do other things. Explode stones in the wall and give people nosebleeds, for example. She'd assumed everyone could, and that they were just sticking to their nun-given disciplines because of the rules. By the time she'd realised that Nixie couldn't, for example, raise a skeleton, she'd figured it was because she just hadn't practised. And the fact that Taro *could* haphazardly use the material of any discipline was because she was, like ... better than everyone else? Just a bit?

It struck Taro, standing on that red floor with a scarlet tempest raging outside, that her parents, whoever they had been, might have told the nuns she was a bone disciple for her own good and hoped she'd keep her own secret.

Sobweb's eyes opened. She flipped the sliver of mirror face down with her toe.

'Wrest,' she said.

Taro only had a second to brace herself as Sobweb sucked the remnant arcania from the room, that invisible fuzz of the curse that carried the apocalypse, before she latched straight on to the familiars. The bone arcania Taro wrested was ripped away from her in skeins. Elliot had anointed himself with the blood from his shoulder; he clasped the seeping wound with his hand, sweat rolling down his nose. Alix flopped like a broken kite, the stone beneath their fingers crackling like firewood. Nixie exhaled through her teeth as the ivy Sobweb had shoved into her hands crisped and drifted away.

Kill me, Taro screamed inwardly as her fingers burned white hot, but in truth she had known worse. Wordless agony was a familiar's constant companion, and this was only a little worse than the Suppression. To say that the ghost of an all-powerful thaumaturge puppeting the dead body of another thaumaturge was using her to break a centuries-old apocalyptic curse, this was actually … fine.

Then it really started, and Taro screamed.

The windows shook under the force of flying blood clots. Skeletons bubbled past the glass like scummy water frothing over the edge of a saucepan, the oldest bodies with honeycomb bones bobbing to the top. The windows groaned under the pressure of holding them back, but this was a moot point, because they could have been advancing towards her with scythes and Taro wouldn't have moved, because each of her nerves was being individually crushed with a tweezer. The room flew into pieces around her, and for a terrifying second Taro surfed high above her body, cresting the wave of corporeal agony and finding herself, like a marble flung high into the air, motionless at the top for a moment that felt like infinity. *Welp*, she thought blandly, then she plunged back down and it started again.

Blood filled her ears. Taro accepted that her brain was leaking out. Her mind flew up to the ceiling and back again even as her body stuck to the floor like a wet mop – had the nun dropped her? Had she wrested too hard and started sucking from its bones? – and it was from this vantage point, with her vision split in two, that she realised they were all going to die.

A truly powerful spell necessitated arcania so colossal it liquefied the poor sap wresting for it. Sobweb was going to suck the familiars dry to undo Hallow Myre's curse. Taro tried to scream this at the others, but it turned out her mouth was open and she was already screaming. They probably already knew, and she had been the last to work it out because she was stupid. It was why they were being held by the Unholy Mothers, because even though the wresting was going to fry them – they would literally be seized by wresting rot, their arms and their hearts turning black – it was impossible not to keep doing it when an undead creature was bending your bones out of shape.

Her skull cracked open, and for a second, with the red light seeping in,

Taro experienced utter clarity. It arrived without language. It was a simple calculation that was born fully formed and went straight to the front of her head, skipping all the tired filters of sarcasm and fear and her impeccable good humour. It said: *You can be the hero.*

Yeah, she would be helping Sobweb to win. But Sobweb was going to win anyway. If she did this, at least the other three might survive. At least Nixie might see the new world.

She wound her tongue into a shape she only half knew, a cleaving of two spells that awkwardly locked together. The arcania she used for this was a trickle diverted from the torrent she wrested for Sobweb, and if the dead girl noticed, she only thought it was Taro's life flickering. Taro bent her tongue; she took the undead arms holding Nixie and Elliot and Alix, slipped inside, and worked with their grip.

She choked the familiars. It was easier to make the nuns pull their limbs tighter than it was to make them fight their orders, and if Taro hurt them enough they would have to stop wresting. Sobweb's eyes were rolled to the ceiling, the incantation pouring from her mouth in a tangled, knotty mess of braided-together disciplines. Taro knew that as long as the power flowed uninterrupted, she wouldn't care where it came from.

Nixie screamed hoarsely. Taro ignored the cracking of her heart as she slipped her power into the nun's fingers and moved them towards Nixie's face. The effort it took to hold Nixie's jaw closed without breaking it was nauseating. She was concentrating so hard on silencing the botanic disciple that she overbalanced the nun holding Alix. Alix slipped backwards, dragged down by the weight of the nun on their back. They crashed through its ribcage, which engulfed their torso, the sound of breaking bones drowned only by the roaring air; or perhaps that was the blood in Taro's ears. She couldn't trust her senses. Elliot was struggling face-to-face with his nun, twitching weakly as he tried to punch his fingers through the nun's eye sockets. They all thought Sobweb had ordered the nuns to do this to them. Taro crushed them all tighter. The pressure in the room shifted as their wresting flickered. Nobody could create much power when they were fighting for their lives.

Making it impossible for them to wrest was the point. Taro had the ability to do it all herself. It might kill her, but if it meant nobody else died, she would take the risk.

Alix was the first to black out. The room wobbled, or seemed to wobble to Taro because she was reluctantly attuned to every horrific drop of power. In the second that Alix stopped wresting, Taro leaned into the gap and picked up the slack, her fingers pressed into the stone floor. It was just like being in the chapel with the skeleton: a moment of confusion and overwhelming nausea; the sense that her eyeballs had turned inside out and she was looking into the back of her own head; then a single, soaring moment of ecstasy when she was spinning two plates at once and everything was flooded with sunshine.

Taro's spine curled backwards as though a rope had been strung between her head and toes and wound tight. Then – *snap* – she went limp again, a second of relief in a sea of red screaming before her vertebrae tightened and she curled again, each oscillation longer than the last. The world shuddered for minutes at a time. Taro realised that it was her teeth clattering together, driving the side of her head against the floor. Her vision narrowed to a slit between the bars of her eyelashes as something wet and hot collected in the corner of her mouth. Blood from her tongue.

Elliot was next. This time she was ready. The vampire had never been as strong as he pretended, and he was already half dead. *You should leave him to it*, she thought, but the impulse to abandon him was absolutely theoretical, and she was already sucking the blood from her own mouth to wrest for him.

Nixie was still trying to shout. Taro didn't dare adjust the pressure of the nun holding her jaw in case it accidentally snapped her; changing any part of the spell now would be like trying to poke a thread through the eye of a needle in a hurricane. *Give up*, Taro tried to scream, but her own jaw was clenched. All the same, while her body cried and bucked on the floor, the better part of her was deeply proud of Nixie for outlasting Alix and Elliot. She had always been ludicrously strong, but her stubbornness was even greater and could outlast epochs. Taro inched her fingers along the floor to a smeared, half-pulped tendril of ivy. Then she grasped for the bones of the nun holding Nixie, and with all the delicacy she could muster – which wasn't much – dropped her so hard she hit the back of her head and went silent.

The transfer of power was instant and absolute. It was no longer ecstatic. Taro's body snapped rigid. She was a conduit for agony and nothing else. But she was finishing what she started. She was wresting with every part of her body, for every discipline, and she was doing it all by herself. Even in the middle of total disintegration, the weight of power made her giddy. Her eyes rolled and fixed on the ceiling, and she saw the Ghost standing over her, spittle flying as she incanted, transfixed by the sheer impossibility of what Taro was pulling off and simultaneously unable to stop, because that would mess everything up too. Taro's eyes shuddered to the window. The bones pressing against the thick glass were unknitting themselves. The blood left the stone with a long, ear-rattling slurp. Cold air poured through the hole in the ceiling, thick and so fresh it made Taro's molars ache.

Then something went *pop* between Taro's ears. She no longer had control over her body. She had been wrong. It was too much. She wasn't an infinite fountain of power, she was a wretched piss-stream, and if the whole thing didn't blow up in her face it would, at the very least, sever her spinal cord and flash-fry her. Sobweb was standing over her body and droning, basically using a teaspoon to scrape the very last of what Taro had out of her bones. She was a pumpkin being gutted, and the next few seconds would end her.

And she couldn't stop if she wanted to. Her body was a deep groove carved by the flow of arcania, and as its conduit she was powerless to divert it. Her head rolled sideways. Behind Sobweb, Alix was awake again and had forced open the arms of their nun – Taro must have broken the joints by squeezing too hard – and was for some reason using a fallen thigh bone to lever Nixie out of the grip of her own Unholy Mother. Elliot, still trapped in the arms of his nun, was wrenching its head sideways as though he was trying to separate the skull from the neck.

Sobweb loomed over Taro. Taro's heart was beating so hard in her ears she didn't realise that Sobweb had finished incanting. She touched Taro's cheek with the back of her stolen hand; it was corpse-cold, and Taro was burning up.

'Remarkable,' Sobweb said.

Taro opened her mouth to say something truly hilarious. Drool slipped down her cheek instead. Sobweb wrinkled her nose.

'You understand I can't leave you whole,' she said. 'You could be very disruptive. I am sad, though. Look at you; you didn't even start rotting.'

The miracle of Taro's survival felt empty. Behind the corpse queen, Nixie, Alix and Elliot were raising themselves from the floor with all the grace of the skeletons. The only explanation was that they were making good on their promise to kill each other: unhinged Alix in their vendetta against Nixie, and Elliot in his eternal quest to piss off Taro. Sobweb would laugh as they finished each other off, turning Taro's amazingly grand gesture into a sad, wet whimper of an ending.

Nixie silently picked up a curved rib bone. She flicked her eyes at Alix, who returned her gaze with a total lack of warmth. Elliot rolled his hand into a fist, the other injured arm hanging limply by his side, oozing brownish fluid. Nixie spat a broken tooth out and jerked her head at Sobweb.

Oh.

'No,' Taro tried to say, but her tongue had the strength of a wet shoelace. Sobweb pushed Taro's sweaty hair away from her head, almost maternally.

'Yes, sweetie,' Sobweb said. Water streamed from Taro's eyes. She wanted to howl for the familiars to stay away, but there was no strength left. She hadn't done all this to see them get killed. Not that she would mourn Alix or Elliot, but her sacrifice had to mean *something*.

Nixie narrowed her gaze, an avenging shadow with a blood-streaked chin and bruised eyes. She threw herself at Sobweb's back. Taro screamed as Sobweb's necrotic nose mashed into her own. Nixie swung the curved bone against the front of Sobweb's neck, gripped both ends, and leaned back. Sobweb kicked backwards, catching Nixie in the stomach. They both fell, and Sobweb, with her nails caught on Taro's robes, dragged Taro down with them.

Taro writhed and screamed until she found the presence to roll away. Nixie raised herself to her knees, pulling Sobweb up with her, still braced against Sobweb's neck. Sobweb punched and kicked, and she would have opened a vein in Nixie's neck if Alix hadn't flung themselves in. They put their hands over Nixie's and pulled back with her. Sobweb drove her elbows into them both, tearing and scratching, until Elliot finally decided to do something – of course he waited until the last minute, the floppy-haired psychopath – by piling on top of Sobweb and crushing her.

They were an unorganised mess, but they were – in the sense that they were sort-of getting the result they wanted – effective. Sobweb squirmed under their weight. Taro could only watch, limp as a glob of porridge, as the weak familiars squeezed the life from Sobweb's stolen body. It was an awkward, embarrassing murder enacted by three exhausted people who didn't have a plan and were not, when it came down to it, very good at being violent. They did not like working together; they didn't know what they were doing; they seemed to be trying, variously, to suffocate Sobweb and dislocate her neck. Taro commanded herself to reach out and help. Nothing happened.

'You'll die without me,' Sobweb croaked. Her two voices were sliding further apart, the overlap creating an echo. 'You gormless idiots. *You need me.*'

Taro had thought Sobweb would kill them. She thought that a centuries-old ghost with the power to possess corpses and manipulate Nixie through a mirror was undefeatable. But what made the familiars useful to arcanists was the same thing that made Sobweb weak. Like them, Sobweb now wore the despairingly mortal, easily-bruised flesh of a human body. She knew how to pass her pain and hurt on to others, but she didn't know how to stand it herself.

None of the arcanists had. As Taro watched purple blotches appear on Sobweb's face, she imagined that every person who had taken power from someone else, from the heads of the towers to the weakest servant in the Redborns' mansion, was dying with her.

Taro found her tongue. She pulled her lips into a smirk, which set her face on fire. It was worth it.

'Bye,' she said.

Nixie yanked backwards, hard. Something cracked. Sobweb's corpse-body went limp. Nixie yelled in strangled triumph, but Alix clapped a hand over Nixie's mouth and pointed. Something unholy was happening to the flesh.

Sobweb – the real Sobweb, ectoplasmic and milky – was rising from the Thaumaturge's body. She was being forced out by its second death, but she was half stuck, having merged her skin with his. When she raised her head Taro only caught a glimpse of her childish face before she forced it back down, and the Thaumaturge's face spasmed instead. The corpse was possessed, a joke and a nightmare. Its limbs jerked and its fingers twisted and its eyes rolled as Sobweb tried to get back into the body before she was expelled.

Taro raised herself to her elbows, a gargantuan feat of strength, and met the Ghost's eyes.

Sobweb had grossly misrepresented herself. She had never come back to life. She would only have been piloting a dried-up puppet, keeping herself from decaying by … spraying herself with perfume? Sewing chunks back on when they fell off? Trying not to slip out of her skeleton every time she sneezed? How pathetic.

'Oi, blood boy,' Taro said to Elliot. 'Go wild.'

Elliot dug his fingers into his shoulder. He closed his eyes and spat savagely, and something awful happened to the body of the Thaumaturge. Something internally explosive. A short, violent incantation that turned its eyes into scarlet puddles and its mouth into a hole.

The body went limp, Ghost-less.

Elliot flopped over and retched. Nixie rolled away from the body, her injured leg splayed awkwardly beneath her, trying not to look at the Thaumaturge's broken neck. Taro didn't want to know where Sobweb's ghost had gone, as long as it was far away. Back to the netherworld, perhaps, and maybe this time she hadn't found the strength to cling on before she was sucked through the veil to oblivion.

Taro fought a shudder. She felt like she should say something – thank everyone, maybe – but everything felt flat. Alix crawled over and checked her pulse by prodding her neck.

'Suck my dick,' Taro's mouth said. 'I'm alive.'

But it took a monumental effort for Taro to keep breathing. Her ears appeared to be leaking blood. She slumped forward, considered being sick, then realised she hadn't eaten in more than a day.

'You still got those sweets, Al?' she slurred.

'No.'

'I can see them in your pocket.'

'You don't want them,' Elliot said from somewhere in the detritus.

'Screw you too.'

The chamber was silent. Taro hadn't realised how loud the apocalypse was until this moment, with all the writhing and the bubbling and the grinding of bone finally gone. All she could hear was the distant wash of the Desecrae, millions of grey teeth gently clinking together as they swirled in eddies of bone dust and gummy plasma. The apocalypse was undone. They would never need to perform the Suppression again. Not that there was anything left to save; they were stranded in a room high above the ruined city, the stairs gone, no way down, grievously injured and with nothing but a bag of half-sucked sweets to sustain them.

'Idiots,' Taro said thickly. 'Now Sobweb can't lift the Desecrae.'

'She was going to murder you,' Nixie said sourly.

'I thought the wresting was going to kill me anyway. That was the whole point. I put my neck on the chopping block for you lot, and now you've ruined it.'

'You're pissed because you didn't get to be a martyr,' Elliot said.

'I'm pissed because I have to spend the remaining hours of my life with *you*.'

Alix looked as if they wanted to kill everyone. Instead they scrawled heavily on the floor.

Do you think anyone's alive?

'No,' Elliot replied bluntly.

I feel like we killed them. Alix pressed their fingers into their grimy forehead. *It was all pointless. And now we can't undo it.*

The stone disciple was being dramatic, but they were also right. Time and bad decision-making were the only truly irreversible forces. Even arcania could be undone – Taro had unknitted it under the ground, when she reverse-exploded the skeletons – but mistakes? Permanent.

Taro's fingers knew the answer before she did. They crept towards the iron crown beside the Thaumaturge's head. They brushed the ice-cold metal. They grasped one bent tip and pulled it towards her, and as she watched herself act, Taro cracked a rueful smile.

Arcania *could* be undone. The problem was, she was the only one with that ability. And the only one with a debt left unpaid.

She had screwed up a lot. Over and over, from the moment she had decided to force Nixie into Greenspire by changing her exam results. But she could fix the whole thing right now, and she could be a good person again. She could show Nixie how sorry she was, and how much she meant it. She could save them all and pay her dues in one fell swoop.

'Anyone need this crown for anything?' she said.

'Don't you dare put that on,' Nixie said.

'As if.' Taro groaned as she raised her body, climbing first on to her elbows, then her hands. 'I'm just thinking. Hallow Myre put the Desecrae down as a temporary measure, right? It was meant to lift when the head arcanists destroyed the crown. Except Aldous Redborn came back and stole it.'

'Yes, Taro,' Elliot said. 'We heard the same thing you did.'

'Are you stupid?' Taro tightened her grip on the crown with incredible difficulty. Her fingers were as stiff as matchsticks. 'If we destroy the crown, the Desecrae lifts. We don't need to disassemble the Desecrae itself, we just need to get rid of this stinking piece of metal.'

Alix looked up sharply. They knew Taro was right.

'OK,' Nixie said. 'So we chuck it over the side of the tower and smash it.'

'Might work,' Taro said. 'But we want to be sure. Do something really permanent. Good job you've got me.'

'Stop it,' Nixie snapped. 'Don't be an idiot. It's metal. You're more likely to blow us up.'

'I'm undisciplined,' Taro said. 'Didn't you hear the way Sobweb was talking? Like there aren't just four disciplines. Like, if you're undisciplined, it applies to loads of stuff. Maybe everything. Like metallurgy. Come on. How else does the crown control the nuns?'

'There aren't any incantations for metal,' Elliot said.

'I'll improvise.'

That's stupidly dangerous, Alix wrote; but they didn't, Taro noticed, try to dissuade her.

Taro bared her teeth in a bloody smile. She had wrested for all four of them. She had probably pulled off the biggest wresting in history, and she was *still alive*, without even a trace of wresting rot. She was perfectly familiar with the concept of a Chosen One and she'd be damned if she wasn't that person. Special powers? Unparalleled strength? A face-off between her and an enemy who was literally just evil for no good reason? Check, check and *check*.

Taro rose. Detritus from the fallen roof poured from her shoulders. The chamber rang with a silence so thick she could have put it on a plate and carved it into slices, decorated only by the steady drip of Desecrae-water falling from the eaves of the tower.

'Let her try,' Elliot said. 'I give her three seconds before she realises it's impossible and blows her eyebrows off.'

'Don't encourage her,' Nixie said. 'She's not in charge.' But Taro was already running her fingers over the valleys of the crown, searching for a way in. It wasn't the same as pulling from bone, let alone the other disciplines; she knew the shape of their doors, and they were easy to open. But if she searched hard enough, and led with the assumption that an opening was there …

Hi there.

It was almost too easy.

Later, if asked, Taro would say: *I guess I was exhausted and hurt and it pushed me over the edge, y'know? Like when you're nearly asleep and your brain does some weird-ass stuff like falling through the bed or showing you fireworks, and you remember something you haven't thought of in years and didn't need to see again. I just went to the right place. I got lucky.*

In the moment, it was more a do-or-die thing.

She ate the crown with her fingers and she saw the universe inside it. A map of stars opened behind her eyes, and each one was a tiny building block that made the whole. She had been wresting blindly before – they all had – doing without understanding, fumbling through the dark. Now she wrested with intention. The map of stars fell apart. When the power gathered in her hand and flowed over her skin, it wasn't anything to do with the metal itself but the gaps between every infinitesimally small particle. As the power radiated into the air it looked for a new home, new particles to wrap itself around. She gave it direction. She pushed with her tongue. It rushed back to the crown and began to prise it apart, blooming between its motes at her command, even as the remaining metal unknitted itself to be wrested in her.

Taro's knees hit the floor, which she observed only distantly. Stupid bodies. So weak and dependent on equilibrium. As the space rushed through her, going in and flowing out again, it dragged life from her: and her body weakened and shrivelled and mewled piteously in response because it didn't understand what Taro's mind did. That wresting was perfect, it was glorious, it was power, and her body should be happy to be used for such incredible ends. So what if it was sucking her life away? What did a life matter if it wasn't being used to change the fabric of the world?

The room turned gold around the edges, and Taro could no longer feel her legs, but she wasn't scared because she was overthrown by ecstasy. No sorrow or hate or sarcasm left. Just her with her fists around the crown, and poetry coming from her mouth, whatever curse was tied into it breaking the roof over their heads. And when she was done, she would take Nixie by the hand and they would walk away and never come back.

Her eyes skipped to the botanic disciple, her face their always-resting place, her body Taro's home. And Taro's joy snagged on the thorns of her cool eyes, twisted and struggled in the thin set of her lips and the disgust in her eyes.

Nixie stepped towards her, fists tight, cheeks dark, and hissed between her teeth.

'I said *no*.'

Nixie grabbed the crown. Taro dug her fingers in and shrieked. Nixie didn't understand – she couldn't see what Taro was doing – she couldn't see that Taro was making everything better. They struggled for control, pulling the crown into their chests, its spikes digging into their skin. Taro's fingers, already weak, screamed under the pressure.

'Nixie,' she croaked, and she couldn't see the universe any more, only the green storm of Nixie's robes and the black implosion of her fury. She was losing the incantation. The air bulged and crackled. Horror fell through her like a fist through a glasshouse. 'We'll be together after this.'

'Stop saying that.' Nixie's voice was a dagger. 'We haven't talked about it.'

'I'm doing it.'

'Stop making decisions for everyone,' Nixie said, twisting the crown. She had never sounded so bleakly vicious, her hurt this open. She couldn't know that she was ruining the spell; or maybe, horrifically, she didn't care. She just wanted to break something that Taro had, no matter the consequence. 'You think you can fix us by doing something big, but I don't want you to.'

'We need this,' Taro gasped, and they both knew full well that Alix and Elliot weren't factored into the equation. 'I'm doing it for us.'

'You're being selfish—'

'It's for your own good—'

'You don't get to decide that,' Nixie screamed. '*That isn't love*—'

She wrenched the crown. It left Taro's hands, and the universe of gaps folded. Alix screamed, or maybe Nixie screamed, or maybe they all did because it felt as if every drop of water in their bodies was suddenly unknitting itself from the rest. Taro was the epicentre and untouched, but only because the destruction needed somewhere to come from and a home to return to. She fell back into her body and smacked into the pain waiting for her, the black twist of her heart and the curling of her bones and the blood pouring from her chewed tongue, and then she slid into the throat of darkness.

It spat her out again. Her eyes wrenched open. She was on her knees, still facing Nixie. The chamber walls had cracked open and slumped outwards, revealing the – *No*. Not yet. She fell on her hands and crawled forward, through the stone now littering the floor, towards Nixie. Alix whimpered beside her, and Elliot heaved.

Taro reached for Nixie's body.

She was too heavy to move. She bristled with thousands of needle-thin metal splinters, the abhorrent remains of the crown. Her face was warm but her lips were grey, and Taro knew before grabbing her wrists that there wouldn't be a pulse. She yanked Nixie's shoulders and screamed at her to move, and she didn't stop screaming until Elliot came up behind her and clapped a hand over her mouth. She bit it, and he swore, and then she stood up and tried to wrest again – to put back what was broken, to knit the Desecrae together again – but she didn't know how.

Alix saw what she was doing and tried to wrestle her down before she could cause another explosion. Taro struggled like a nun in a glue trap. She kicked and bit and screamed but Alix's arms were tight, and then Elliot was holding her too, and they both kept squeezing until she couldn't breathe.

The fight left her body. She went limp so fast they dropped her. Taro hit the floor with a wet *thump*, but before she lost consciousness her head rolled as though something – someone – was pulling her eyes towards the gaping ceiling, saying: *Look what you did it for, then.*

And the sky was – blue –

Twenty-five

Taro's fuck-up was the end and the beginning of everything.

When Elliot opened his eyes he was on the floor. The roof and walls were split like an eggshell, revealing a decadent shade of blue that was blazingly bright and impossibly expansive. The Desecrae, the *world*, had shattered, and he was sprawled on a column of rock with a new sky bearing down on him.

Taro was slamming her fists into Nixie and screaming. Alix was groaning through gritted teeth, nursing their right shoulder, a mirror to Elliot's torn flesh. He tried to say *Alix, stop moving*, but his ears were ringing and he wasn't sure if he had spoken. He rolled over and dry-heaved with vertigo. He needed the swirling of molars to orient himself. He struggled to stand, flailing pathetically. At last he threw himself upright with his eyes closed, and he didn't open them again until he had crashed into Taro and pinned her down.

He hated Taro. It was clear that Alix also hated Taro. But they were the only people left in the world, and it felt crucially important that they all stayed alive.

Taro bit his hand. Elliot swore. She fought free of

his arms and rasped incoherently, fumbling ashy bones between her fingers. She was trying to wrest again. Elliot lost his balance again – the goddamned sky – and failed to lock her arms to her sides until Alix slammed into her too. For a brief, confusing moment they were all on the floor, wrestling beside Nixie's body, then Elliot and Alix somehow had Taro sandwiched in the middle of them, and they held on until she hiccuped and went limp.

They lay in queasy silence while the world rotated. When it stopped, Elliot raised his head and immediately wished that he hadn't.

The sky was everywhere. Its depth was infinite. It poured over a meaningless plane with no edge, but at the same time it crushed him. He tried to follow the ground to its natural end, where it should have met the Desecrae, and its absence was the coldest, most brutal definition of emptiness. There were no stairs or mansions or bridges or ramparts, just a great openness with vast lumpen features that were nonetheless dwarfed by missing boundaries. It made Elliot feel small, but it cruelly didn't shrink his pain or lessen the chill of cold sweat inside his clothes.

'Alix,' he said, tearing his gaze away. Taro's eyes snapped open. 'Is Nixie—'

Alix nodded, and Taro shuddered with her whole body.

Elliot released his grip on the bone disciple and levered himself to a sitting position. A hot wave of nausea rolled through him. He leaned over to empty his stomach again, but nothing came out. The nun's bite radiated stiffly through his shoulder and into his collarbone, and he knew with terrifying certainty that an infection was sweeping through his blood. He had never been this ill, but he was too weak to do anything about it.

'I might die,' he said.

Alix untangled themself from Taro and regarded him evenly. Their lack of denial was cutting.

'Listen,' Elliot said. 'If there's life outside, people will come. If we're lucky they won't want to kill us. Tell them to fix me.'

Alix thought about it for a moment, then twitched their broken pencil and scrap of paper from their pocket.

Why would they help us?

'Get leverage. Hurt them.'

Alix laughed bitterly.

I'm five foot two, they wrote. *I have a hole in my foot. If I wrest again, I'll have an aneurism. What do you expect me to do?*

The nausea hit him again. He bowled over and gasped. When the feeling passed, he reached into his pocket and wound the gold chain of the cursed necklace around his fingers, searching for comfort. He prayed he would remain alive to know sleep.

Alix wrote faster.

Don't leave me alone. There's already a body, and Taro's lost her mind, and there's no way down from here.

Elliot forced his head up. Darkness welled from a black spring inside him.

'Do I have to say it?' he asked.

Say what?

'You know.'

I don't.

Elliot gritted his teeth.

'I … need your help.'

Alix looked at him evenly.

'Please,' he said.

Alix thought for a moment before looping their pencil across the scrap of paper. Calm now. Sarcasm in the bend of their knuckles.

Is that, Alix wrote, *supposed to make me attracted to you?*

'Damn it, Alix,' Elliot said, and more or less died.

Elliot slumped face down like a discarded book. Alix punched his shoulder to wake him up. His eyes remained closed. *Rude.* Alix cracked their mouth open reluctantly.

'I won't leave you here to die,' they said scratchily, 'but I hope you know this is a shitty start to our blossoming friendship.'

Elliot didn't answer.

‘This isn’t the time for your first nap. I’m not joking. Elliot. Wake up.’

Alix looked up and saw the gold chain of the necklace wilting from Elliot’s hand. Not around his neck.

He isn’t asleep.

‘Elliot, you asshole!’

The gossamer-thin veneer of Alix’s calm disintegrated. They savagely kicked a chunk of stone off the side of the chamber floor. It fell silently for a few seconds before smashing into the ground and triggering a cascade of distant rockfall. *Asshole!* they wanted to scream, but their throat was wrecked. *I hope you implode! I hope you get burned up by the sun! I hope the universe hurts you so much your soul evaporates through your nostrils!* Alix was alone at the top of a tower with no stairs, and more corpses than living bodies.

Including—

Alix hadn’t looked at Nixie yet. They’d managed to keep her in their periphery, but she was growing in size, demanding to be seen, and now she blotted out half the sky, even with Taro’s face buried in her robes, heaving and sobbing. Alix turned their head and gulped down a sob that hurt their chest. *Don’t cry, you coward. There’s nothing you can do now.*

They dropped their eyes to Nixie’s face. She didn’t look bad. Just dishevelled. It was the stillness that Alix couldn’t get over. They hadn’t reckoned with the fact that even sleeping bodies were full of life, and that the dead were, by comparison, utterly empty. Alix tried to read Nixie’s face as having an expression other than total absence. She had never been that still; had normally, in fact, been smiling, at least when they had first met. Alix and Nixie had almost killed themselves laughing once; they had talked about Elliot’s beautiful cheekbones from across the classroom, and grinned at their ingenuity in learning to incant. And even though Taro had taken Nixie away from them, Alix realised that they had never stopped thinking of Nixie as their best friend. Their separation had always felt to Alix like a brief and temporary absence. Alix was always going to forgive her. They should have said that out loud when Nixie told them *I’m sorry*. They shouldn’t have sneered as though their heart wasn’t aching, shouldn't have assumed there would be a million more chances to close the book.

And now the sky. The silence. The hugeness of the world. The impossibility of knowing what to do next, when the only obvious option was to sit here and starve or wait for someone to find them.

Something smashed in the corner of the room, and Alix whipped their head around. Mr Fingers froze guiltily. He was covered in bloody grazes and streaks of dirt, but he was still very much – miraculously, infuriatingly – alive.

Alix dove for him. They landed on Fingers and squashed him to the floor.

Alix didn't know what Fingers wanted, only that Sobweb had been missing her right hand, which meant the haunted cluster of digits was probably born from her ancient flesh. They had developed an independent mind and variously helped or hindered Alix depending on which way the wind was blowing. Fingers grappled with Alix, but Alix wasn't playing. They held the writhing, fleshy lumps down with their heel, breathing hard while they scribbled.

What do you want? they scrawled.

Fingers squirmed and flopped. *Why are you here?*

Alix moved their foot, just slightly, to see if he would magic a pencil from between his fingers. Instead, he pointed at the edge of the tower. Alex scowled: *What?*

He gave Alix the thumbs up.

You're wrong, Alix wrote. *This isn't what I wanted.*

Fingers squirmed mirthfully, because they both knew Alix was lying. Alix had outwardly wished to be saved from possible execution; secretly they had also been throwing themselves after Nixie; but what they had really wanted, deep in their soul, was a new world. The one they had found between pages in the library, the one they had drawn on their arms with indelible ink, where nobody knew them or their old name. And they had won, hadn't they? Now Alix could be whoever they wanted.

Not like this, Alix wrote.

Fingers wrenched himself free. Alix let him. He scuttled to the middle of the floor, realised he was trapped between Alix and the edge of the ruined tower, and paused. For a moment they stared at each other, breath bated. Then he darted back towards Alix, so fast they instinctively threw their arms in front of their face.

He swerved to a halt in front of them. He grabbed the shard of mirror out of which Sobweb's ghost had come and held it to the light, catching the sun.

Then – *whoosh* – Fingers was gone.

Alix stared at the spot where he had vanished. There was nothing but a smattering of fallen stone and the sliver of mirror, the too-bright sun smearing it across the floor.

Taro sat bolt upright. Alix had almost forgotten she was there, crying into Nixie's body.

'Where did it go?' she demanded.

Don't know. Don't care.

Taro lurched forward and gripped Alix by the shoulders, feverish.

'Did it go into the mirror?'

Alix shook their head: *Of course not.* 'The Ghost came out of it, though,' Taro said. 'She was dead, and she came out of the glass, and now those weird fingers have gone *in*, and the mirror's still there—'

Alix realised what Taro was saying.

It's not a door.

'Says who?' Taro shot back. 'Nixie's right next to it. Her ghost has to go somewhere.'

You're not a ghost. You're alive.

'So are the fingers.'

The streak of light wavered. Taro squeezed Nixie's limp hand, muttering under her breath.

You can't do it, Taro.

Taro snatched the paper from their hand and screwed it up.

'You won't even try,' Taro snarled. 'You're pathetic.'

Alix resisted the very strong urge to punch her.

Then they glanced out and stopped short. The vast plain outside Fourspires was churning. Alix screwed their eyes against the horrific sun and saw the ground swell with tiny specks of grey. Termites? No.

People.

Taro was already on her feet, and there was madness in the curve of her mouth, and Alix knew they had already lost her.

Taro did not like the new world.

She had never interrogated her assumption that it would be an extension of Fourspires, namely, black and grey and mostly made of stone with the occasional rotting hole of vegetation. Instead she was served a noxious shade of green criss-crossed with bright threads of metallic water and huge swathes of bristling forest, and over there, near where the ground was grey and shimmered like water, a sparkling lump of *something* that might be an obnoxiously huge city with a castle at the edge. Except, against all Taro's understanding of cities, it wasn't on a hill. How did they know who was important if there was no top and no bottom? How did they decide where the city ended without a Desecrae? Nixie would have known. Nixie knew everything.

Alix paced through the rubble, looking haggard, scribbling.

Safest to assume they're aggressive. We can either surrender or hide. Fighting isn't a viable option.

Taro arranged Nixie's hair around her face and folded her hands over her stomach. Nixie liked to be neat.

'I need to go fetch her,' she said.

Alix pinched the bridge of their nose. They looked a million years old.

You're in shock. We need to save Elliot and not get killed by whoever's coming for us.

'I'm not in shock.'

Two minutes ago you couldn't speak.

'That was before I realised everything's fine,' Taro said.

Alix shook their head, but Taro strode over and grasped them firmly by the shoulders.

'Here's the deal,' she said. 'When Elliot wakes up, he's going to use his gross blood magic to keep Nixie's body warm, and he's going to continue doing that until I come back with her.'

Alix plucked Taro's hands away, slowly and deliberately, their eyes saying: *No.*

'Yes,' Taro said.

Nobody can bring back the dead, Tarenteeno.

'Get Elliot fixed,' Taro said, and now her voice had the timbre of a threat. 'When those people get here, look after her, and tell Elliot to keep her warm. Do it until I say otherwise, or I'll snap every bone in your body.'

Taro saw Alix hesitate. The stone disciple could probably do something heinous to her right now, like crystallising the minerals in her body until they poked out of her in huge spikes, but Taro was willing to bet they were too scared. They had seen what Taro was capable of. They had no idea that she was on the verge of collapse, or that another second of wresting would break her in two.

I hate you with nearly every fibre of my being, Alix scrawled, *but I really mean what I'm about to say*. They genuinely seemed to be struggling. *For some reason, I don't want you to die.*

Taro didn't have time to explain. She had work to do. She knew how to repair every shitty thing that had ever happened, every bad thing that she had done. All her regret and sorrow was swept away by the huge, wonderful realisation that she could absolutely and irrevocably redeem herself, and then nobody could be angry with her ever again.

'Keep a seat warm for me,' she said to Alix.

You're traumatised.

Taro knelt by Elliot's side and inspected him. He was a lot less annoying when he was unconscious. If he'd had a decent night's sleep in the last few years, he might even have been bearable during the day. She felt his pulse; still there, quite weak. He would live. Probably.

He didn't stir as she went through his pockets.

'Bye, loser,' she whispered, and before Alix could catch on she strode towards the light cast by the mirror. The refraction slowly tightened like a healing scar. There was a curl of iron lying among the rubble, and on impulse she picked it up. It was blunt and notched and was probably only good for clubbing people over the head, but she couldn't afford to be picky.

She stood before the light. There was a whiff of arcania about it, the remnant of whatever power Sobweb had used to prise it open. If she sharpened her focus she could almost see something on the other side. Shapes. A floor. A room. Guess this was it, then.

She opened her hand to reveal Elliot's cursed necklace. She flashed it at Alix, who baulked.

'You dick,' they said, their voice cracking. 'Elliot's part is over. He's *done.*'

'Wrong,' Taro said, pocketing her insurance. 'Good luck out there. Hope it's everything you asked for.'

Before she could change her mind Taro swung the iron bar over her shoulder, rolled her neck, and strolled into hell.

A Brief Introduction to Mirrors and the Netherworld for New Familiars, Who Upon Having Their Memories Erased May Require Reintroduction to Important Facts

You do not need to know about mirrors. It is none of your business.

The following exists only to impress upon you that the destruction of mirrored glass is a necessity, and to emphasise the safety and comfort of the world in which you are allowed to live. To be generous, then:

Mirrored glass warps arcania. We do not know why, but that is beside the point. Wrest or incant in front of a mirror, and you will suffer. Your bones will warp and sprout from your cheeks; your skin will erupt with fungus; your blood will freeze or boil; you will calcify and choke on your own teeth. Furthermore, the mirror may spew forth a creature known as a maleficent.

Malefici are varied in appearance but uniformly violent and hungry. Thanks to the universal destruction of mirrored glass malefici have been largely exterminated, with two exceptions: those loose in the Ulcer (known as starvelings, kept at bay by the nuns) and the rare maleficent that seems to come through the Desecrae (usually dealt with by the closest citizen with a pitchfork).

To address a popular myth: some academics insist that mirrors are also a gateway to the 'netherworld', the space between life and death. According to this myth, before you leave this mortal plane and slip through the veil into oblivion, you may linger a moment in the netherworld. The netherworld looks significantly like our own, but monstrously twisted and stuffed with the aforementioned malefici. Believers suggest that a small minority of people, upon death, choose not (or are unable) to slip through the veil, and instead cling to the netherworld in the form of a ghost.

It is also suggested that the netherworld is briefly visible through mirrored glass, but *only when* a ghost is looking out from the other side. This is obviously nonsense. Ghosts are not real.

This is a digression. The point is: you will not play with mirrors. Should you find one undestroyed, you will report it to an arcanist immediately. You will not touch it. You will not 'try to see into the netherworld'. You will not, under any circumstances, attempt to enter it.

An exquisitely painful death awaits if you defy these instructions.

ACKNOWLEDGEMENTS

These Shattered Spires has been years in the making, even before I started putting pen to paper. I still can't believe the permutations it's been through. Here's the secret: no book comes from nothing, and it definitely doesn't get anywhere without a lot of help.

So thanks to the very first people who read this book and gave their invaluable feedback: Holly Walton, who I am very proud to have a similar brain to; Lucy Foster, who also gamely stalked my writing calendar and sent some delightfully friendly and threatening messages when I wasn't on track; Tashan Mehta, the voice of reason and my trusted partner in navigating life as an author; and Charley Miles, who – you know what, fine. People wanted this book. You are literally always right.

One day I was very down about writing being solitary, at which point my girlfriend told me to join a writing group, which I initially resisted very strongly. (I'm shy! I pretend not to be, but I am! Really!) So first, thanks to Megan Crawley, who is incredibly supportive and sometimes knows what's good for me before I do. And second, a huge thanks to all my friends in WWF, which in my (unbiased, honestly) opinion is the best writing group on earth. I hope you all know that you keep me sane. I couldn't waft around a castle, scream at a book club, drink tea, or hunch goblin-like over my laptop in a corner of a bookshop/cinema cafe with a better group of people. You are kind, talented, supportive, and funny as hell. Occasionally disturbing too. But never boring.

It's also true that no book gets near the shelves without an amazing team who knows far more about publishing than they do. So here's to my wonderful agent, Stevie Finegan, who immediately understood the vibe of the book and continues to champion it everywhere. I'm convinced she is the best agent on this mortal plane. There's also Eleanor Willis, editor extraordinaire, who somehow makes the long process of editing a chunky book enjoyable and satisfying and has made all the difference in the world to Fourspires. Thanks also to Ben Schlanker, assistant editor; US editor Kei Nakatsuka; and the whole Bloomsbury team in the US and UK, including Jessica Bellman, Charlotte Webb, Sarah Taylor-Fergusson, Danielle Rippengill, Mike Young, Tim Hardy and Isabelle Tucker, for everything they've done to get this book on the shelves.

I'm also ecstatically happy with all the artwork that features in and on *These Shattered Spires*, which is thanks to Danlin Zhang, Lolloco and Virginia Allyn. I can't believe I'm lucky enough to have everything under the Desecrae brought to life by them. If you've read this far, go find them on Instagram and support their work! R. Haven has also been the best sensitivity reader anyone can hope for; I appreciate those notes so much.

A bit of a strange but long overdue acknowledgement now. When I was a kid I was obsessed with Tanith Lee, whose children's (and later, adult) books are what spurred me to start writing. She kindly responded to all of my letters, sent me books that are among my most precious possessions today, offered to read chapters of my first-ever attempt at a novel, gave me my first real feedback, and told me that I would be mad to stop writing. I recently re-read all those letters, and now I'm grown up I realise just how wonderful that correspondence was and how important it was to getting where I am now. It was always my plan to send her my first published novel, but that wasn't possible. So here, instead, to the author who both got me started and influenced my heavy and enthusiastic use of em dashes: thank you for taking a young writer seriously.

Look out for the next book
in the **Wyrdos** trilogy

THESE HOLLOW RUINS

Coming March 2027

One

After the fall of the Desecrae

At the end of the world, with the tooth-filled sky cracked open and the dead lying in piles, Alix gave a bloody smile. Stripped of everything they knew and finally wielding their true name, Alix was newly born. They were the king of the universe.

Nobody knew who they had been. Nobody knew what they could do next.

They were the only victor of the slaughter that was meant to kill them. The apocalypse had been halted and the ghost of Sobweb banished. Now Alix, who used to be a familiar, was in charge.

And it felt phenomenal.

If only Nixie hadn't—

Don't think about that.

Alix's smile died, a knife-twist of anxiety reminding them that they were, in fact, totally screwed. They were standing in the wreckage of Fourspires Castle, at the crest of the Fifth Tower. The walls had fallen away and the twisting steps had collapsed. There was no way down. Even if there was, the decimated city below was filled with nothing but shattered spires and twisted bodies. Books flapped miserably in the remains of the gargantuan library

Alix had once called home. Rubble was piled around Alix's feet, along with the shard of mirror that Taro had vanished through when she'd strolled into the netherworld, chasing the soul of her ex-girlfriend.

Nixie's soul. Because Nixie was—

Don't think about it!

Alix picked up the mirror shard, squeezing it so tight it split their skin, and wishing they could hide it inside their flesh. They couldn't lose Nixie's path back from the dead.

The sky howled. Alix stumbled as the air ripped the pencil from behind their ear and flung it over the edge of the tower. They braced themself against the invisible pressure, panting, until it slackened.

Alix had read about the wind in books, but nobody had said it would batter them like they had cursed its mother. Or that the sky would be so boneless, so upwards and endlessly deep that it made Alix feel like they were falling out of their body, so bright that noxious splodges of colour exploded across their retinas every time they blinked.

Alix looked out again. The endless landscape reared up to swallow them, so impersonal in its vastness that they couldn't breathe. They had spent their whole life hemmed in by rock and teeth, bones and books; it had been a cage, but they had known everything about it. Now the cage was in ruins, with miles of scattered molars and puddles of spittle stretching out from the castle. The only home that Alix had ever known was irreversibly obliterated.

The bile rose in Alix's throat. They weren't a king. They were an irrelevant speck of dust, and they were going to die out here alone.

A moan tugged Alix out of their panic. Elliot, the blood disciple from hell, was drifting in and out of consciousness at their feet. Somehow – *I beg of the newly infinite universe to wipe that look off your face*, Alix thought – he was still smirking.

Unfortunately, they needed him.

Because Nixie had to come back. There was still so much for Alix to say to her, like: *You were a shitty friend, but I forgive you. I've been waiting my whole life to laugh with you again.* When Alix had imagined being free from Fourspires, they'd pictured Nixie standing next to them. That was why they'd agreed to her insane plan to flee the Desecrae in the first place.

Then, before the Desecrae fell, Nixie had apologised for being a bad friend. And Alix had said *nothing*.

I just wanted you to feel bad for a bit longer. And now—

Alix finally lowered their eyes to Nixie's body.

Nixie's warm-brown cheeks were still flushed with fury. Her head was tilted to the side as though she couldn't stand to look at Alix. There was no blood, nor bruises, nor visibly broken bones under her green robes. She lay where Taro had dropped her after screaming hysterically. She looked like the girl Alix had known years ago, before she'd transformed into a stranger: unguarded, uncynical and moments away from a grin.

Alix, choking up, squeezed the mirror shard again. They could fix this. Taro was unthinkably idiotic for strolling into the netherworld after Nixie, but she was also insane enough that it might actually work. *As long as Nixie is a ghost and hasn't vanished completely*, Alix thought nauseously. Alix just had to make Elliot use his blood arcania on Nixie's body, then find somewhere to hide before the ruins collapsed.

Alix crouched by the rocky lip of the tower. The broken steps began a few yards below, far away enough that a bad landing could be paralysing. Alix couldn't bridge the gap with their stone arcania because they had used all their strength, and even two more seconds of wresting would incinerate them. Maybe they could use Elliot as a cushion for a soft landing. He was still unconscious, so he wouldn't tense up when Alix dropped him, which theoretically meant fewer broken bones. Still – if Alix miscalculated his trajectory, he would smash like an overripe pumpkin.

Alix was still considering kicking Elliot over the edge when the ruins vomited people.

They burst over the lip of the tower in explosions of flowers, thrust up from the mangled castle by long tendrils of ivy. Incantations unfurled in unison from the strangers' tongues. *Botanic arcania.*

Alix barely had time to fling themself to the floor and feign unconsciousness.

The strangers' hands flew to the knives in their belts. Alix could tell how tightly they were coiled, waiting for death to jump out at them. Glistening columns of stone and blood and bone punched upwards into the sky, propelling another clutch of intruders into the Fifth Tower. When their feet hit the ground they stood back to back, fingers against hilts, eyes darting from ruin to ruin.

Alix hadn't truly believed in other people outside the Desecrae, but here they were: taller and less crooked, unfazed by the screaming wind, so unfathomably clean that Alix felt gross.

A pale woman with coppery hair shook her hands out, dislodging flecks of dried blood. Alix could tell she was trying to hide the shaking of her fingers. She nodded curtly; the others fanned out, slipping vials of blood and finger bones and crushed flowers from their pockets.

They had to be familiars, since they were carrying wresting materials. But they were dressed in achingly beautiful clothes, all gold leather and white silk and silver-scaled armour. And Alix had just seen them incant like arcanists.

What kind of twisted world is this?

The pale woman plucked the mirror shard from Alix's bloodied hand. It took everything for Alix to stay limp. It was so fragile, so *tiny,* this sliver of glass that Nixie needed in order to come back. The woman walked away and held it to the light, her mouth quivering with disbelief.

Alix slowly twisted their neck to look at Elliot. The warmth had drained from his face, leaving his olive complexion pallid. His shoulder was probably infected from the Unholy Mother that had sunk its teeth into him, before Alix had saved him. After *he* had saved Alix from being strangled. What a messed-up start to their burgeoning friendship.

I hope you appreciate what I'm about to do for us, vampire.

Alix pinched Elliot. His bloodshot eyes popped open. Alix, now miserably pencil-less, had to crack their mouth open and try to speak.

'Save Nixie,' Alix whispered, voice hoarse with disuse. Alix had only broken their years-long silence that morning, deep in the catacombs beneath Fourspires Castle. Their tongue already ached.

'What?' he mumbled.

Alix struggled to get the words in place. They knew what they wanted to say, but their mouth wouldn't cooperate. *Speak, Alix. You've done it before.*

The anxiety made them sick. They hooked their index finger under Elliot's chin and dug their nail in so hard he twitched.

'Listen,' Alix rasped. The strangers' eyes were fixed on the woman with the mirror, but if any of them tore their attention away for a second, they would see Alix was awake. Panic made Alix's heart thrash. 'Keep Nixie's body … alive. Don't let her …' A rock sat in their throat. They fought it. 'Don't let her go cold. Understand?'

'No.'

'*Elliot.* I swear to god.' They didn't have time for this. Alix had to get the mirror shard back. But first they had to secure Nixie's body. Alix grasped for Elliot's hand and pushed it into a sticky, bloody puddle on the floor. 'Do it. Or you'll never sleep again.'

Elliot's other hand flew to his pocket. Alix already knew it was empty.

'It's not there,' Elliot said. His face was wild and sickly as he fumbled for the necklace he had worked so violently to claim. 'Who took it? *Who do I kill?*'

Alix stared at Elliot's twitching face, trying to summon the pitilessness that had helped them survive the library. They tightened their fingers around his chin and forced him to look into their face.

'Taro … stole it.' Alix pressed their fingers in hard enough to bruise. 'She went to the netherworld. To save Nixie. Keep Nixie's body alive, or Taro won't come back with your necklace.' Elliot looked bewildered. Alix dug a nail in. '*Do it.*'

Elliot, as Alix had long suspected, responded particularly well to authority. He curled his fingers into the blood on the floor and dragged them over Nixie's neck – the only part of her he could reach – daubing her in red. Then he plunged his hand back into the puddle and wrested. The blood dried and cracked as it gave up its power, invisible but so painful that Elliot shuddered. His lips twisted as he drew the arcania into his mouth, shaping it with his teeth and tongue until Nixie's eyes twitched, responding to the sudden pulse in her neck.

She almost looked fine, and Alix could almost – *almost* – pretend that Nixie was sleeping.

'How long can you hold it?' Alix croaked.

Elliot's pupils slipped. He was almost unconscious again.

'Not long,' he said, then his eyes rolled to the back of his head.

Alix pinched him, but Elliot was unresponsive. What was *not long*? Did they have days? Minutes? *Shit.* Alix needed to get the shard of mirror. It was the only way Taro and Nixie could walk back out.

The copper-haired woman finished studying the mirror and tossed it to the floor. It landed a few inches away. Alix crept their fingers towards it, teeth gritted as they fought the urge to snatch it.

Just a few more inches.

The woman stamped on the shard and ground it to a fine powder.

Alix whimpered. They were powerless to stop the noise, which, in the silence, was as loud as a scream. Then someone *did* scream, and Alix knew from the circle of horrified faces that none of the strangers had expected to find anything but corpses.

'Take that one,' the woman barked, stepping back quickly from Alix. 'The one that's awake. Dispose of the other two.'

One of her men was already wresting, clutching a stone that sizzled under his grip, turning it into a force that he could shape with his mouth. Alix could taste the stone arcania in the air, gritty under their tongue; they heard the shape of his incantation. He would use his power to entomb Nixie and Elliot in the flagstones before carrying Alix off.

A bright flare of panic was followed by cold desperation.

Where Nixie and Elliot went, Alix would go too.

Alix grabbed Elliot's and Nixie's hands. The smoothness of Nixie's palm was a painful memory: it was the hand that had found Alix's in the dark of their shared bedroom in the Pit, comforting them, before Taro became the centre of Nixie's universe. Nixie was there at the beginning of Alix's remembered life, the only person who hadn't mocked Alix for being silent, the one who said: *We'll look after each other until we die.*

It gave Alix the strength to squeeze their eyes shut and steal the man's stone arcania.

It was disgustingly easy, physically speaking; and although it tasted all wrong, like licking the sweat off someone else's skin, it was as instinctively pliable as Alix's own power.

The man's entombing spell broke off. The arcania that gathered on his skin and trickled into the air around him was pulled into Alix's mouth by their incantation. He screamed as Alix took and took, but they couldn't stop, even though they had never done something so monstrous, so sickening. There was no other choice. Alix didn't have the strength to draw from their own resources; they barely had the strength to twist their mouth into the right shape.

The moment of theft was perverse. Achingly wonderful, too, in a cold and hellish way, because for the first time in Alix's short life arcania held no pain.

So it's this easy, they thought, and in the second it took to steal arcania from that man, Alix knew that in another life, had they been sent to Fourspires' University instead of given to the undead nuns at the Pit as a familiar, they would have done this without thinking, every day.

Alix shivered as cold rivulets of stone crawled from the floor and over their hands, forming marble chains, locking them and Elliot and Nixie together.

Their hands encased in stone, everything done, Alix finally let their shoulders slump into the floor. They were exhausted. They wanted to smoke.

Do they even have cigarettes out there?

'Monsters,' someone shrieked. The arcanist Alix had used threw up in a corner. 'They use other people's arcania.'

A woman loomed over Alix. She was holding a lump of something red and sticky, which meant she was a blood arcanist, otherwise known as *the worst kind*. Red liquid dripped on to Alix's forehead as she squeezed her fist and muttered.

I beg of the endless new world that things are better out there.

But I doubt it.

The blood ran into their eyes, and Alix slipped into the deep grey of forced sleep.

Alix woke up to someone sticking a needle through their foot. The needle dipped in and out of their skin, pulling together the edges of the ragged wound where Mr Fingers, the disembodied set of digits and Alix's once-friend, had stabbed them in the burning library. Alix bit the inside of their cheek to stop themself from screaming, trying to be as still as the cold stone slab they had been dumped on.

The needle stopped, the thread was snipped, and the fireworks behind Alix's eyes fizzled out. They could finally mentally scan their bones. *Unbroken.* But something ached deep in their marrow, and it wasn't natural.

Nails drummed against the stone by their head. Alix suppressed a flinch.

'… the girl in the green robes has a pulse, and it's forcing most of her organs to work. But it isn't a normal coma. Apparently it stinks of blood arcania.'

The nails tapped away.

'This is a bad omen, Dorian,' a second person said. 'First the trouble with Aerie, then the Null falls. And there were *people* under it. What are they capable of after surviving that?'

The Null? Did she mean the Desecrae?

'At least Sobweb wasn't in there,' Dorian said drily.

'That we know of.'

'Either way, this one doesn't look dangerous.' There was a pause in which Alix had the distinct impression that both people were staring at them. *I'll show you dangerous*, Alix thought, but they held still. 'We've put a bone bind on this one, and the other non-comatose one, so if they try to leave the castle grounds they'll automatically be pulverised. They'll become bags of bone slurry. I'll be surprised if either of them are allowed to live, anyway. It'll be a knife through the throat at Convocation.'

'Where's the one with the chewed-up shoulder?'

More rustling. A sigh. Alix cracked one eye open and saw Dorian smile grimly. She – Alix intuited from the crop of her curls and the deliberate cut of her armour that Dorian was a woman – lit up the tiled room in don't-touch-me armour, each scale bright silver against her deep umber skin. An articulated tentacle clasped a sheathed sword to her waist. The other woman, slim and ivory-pale, wore a plain smock; the air around her was metallic in a way that Alix could only describe as surgical. There were more stone slabs in the room, each covered in a cloth. Scalpels lay scattered on the floor, as if swept there by an earthquake.

Alix was in a hospital. It was also a mortuary.

'We locked the violent one in a room with a doctor,' Dorian said, as her companion nervously stroked the spine of a scalpel, 'and the doctor came out screaming.'

Alix lurched to their feet and ran.

Tried to run. The room tilted and smacked them in the head. They grappled with the floor, stood again, then ducked as the surgeon screamed and flung the scalpel, which barely missed.

Dorian swore as Alix took off again.

This time Alix made it through the door. It only took seconds for them to smash their fingers into the marble wall, wrest, and utter a crude spell that collapsed the frame. Then they were sprinting into the vertiginous unknown, their arm burning, their injured foot throbbing in time with their wild pulse.

This wasn't Fourspires – they understood that much – but everything came in panicked flashes. It seemed more like a palace, with blindingly bright walls and jewelled windows in the shape of fish, their crystalline eyes refracting the light from outside. The floor was so intricately patterned with swirling mosaics it made Alix dizzy, and their sense of direction, which relied on claustrophobic ceilings and shadows, was blown to pieces. There was too much colour, then light – sound – light – more colour –

Just! Keep! Running!

Alix swerved, knocked into an arched window, and slipped on a long slick of water.

They dragged themself out of the freezing puddle as the unfathomable world swung around them. Alix hadn't considered that everything outside the Desecrae would smell and feel and taste different, or that the air would be colder to breathe. Their body rebelled against the new world by narrowing their vision to a pinprick.

Now another guard was behind them, shouting as Alix took off again. The floor exploded in ankle-shredding shards as someone spat stone arcania at Alix's heels. Another corner – a blind turn into searing light – and Alix crashed into a crowd of people at a cracked window. It had been flung open to reveal the smoking ruins of Fourspires, visible over the rooftops of a nearby white city. Seeing Fourspires, which had once been Alix's whole world, reduced to a blur on the horizon was sickeningly weird. They tore their eyes away and elbowed through the crowd, their bloodied face and tattered Fourspires robes making several people scream.

'Sobweb!' one of them howled, and someone barked a bone incantation in panic, but judging from the agonised cry they had accidentally broken the guard's ankles instead of Alix's.

Another turn, and another, ornamental debris crunching underfoot as though the fall of the Desecrae had shaken the palace even this far away. No one followed now, but Alix kept running until they tripped over something blubbery. They slammed into the ground.

It was a tentacle, deep russet and pocked with white suckers. It trailed from a grimly ornate fountain embedded in the wall, where the rest of the creature pulsated furiously. *An octopus.* Alix had one on their arm, self-tattooed, copied from an ancient book in Fourspires' library, back when they had thought everything they read was a fantasy. It felt like a piece of their imagination had been yanked through their nostril and thrown at their feet.

Alix, exhausted, crawled away from the probing tentacle before it could tighten around their ankle. Their rotten cloak dragged over the broken stone strewn across the floor. A long, rubbery weed – something given mock-sentience by a botanic arcanist – oozed past Alix's feet, scooped up the debris, and flung it out a window as a shoal of skeletal fish animated by bone arcania cleaned the walls with their pin-sharp teeth.

Alix wormed into an alcove with a salt-crusted window and wrapped their arms around themself, damp and shivering.

Find Nixie – find Elliot – get out –

Cool air licked the back of their neck. Something was moving outside, deep and dark and ceaseless. Alix prayed for benevolence as they rose, shaking, to look through the glass.

The front of Newspires faced a white city and, beyond it, Fourspires. The *back* of the palace, here, revealed the whole thing to be teetering on a cliff. The ground at the bottom was huge and grey and *wrong*. It moved like a rug being shaken, with fraying lines that thrashed and broke and reformed. Alix tried to measure its breadth, contain it like it was contained on the page, but it was too big.

The ocean.

The books hadn't prepared them for this. The afternoon light made it burn like the end of a cigarette, while it moved so violently it spattered vertically up the rock face.

Alix was at the edge of the world, and the world laughed at how small Alix was.

They pressed their bitten nails into their leg until the clarifying pain brought them back to their senses.

Find Nixie. Find Elliot. Get out.

And do it before a knife was shoved through their throat, or they were turned to *bone slurry*, as the sword-wielding Dorian had said.

Alix slid out of the nook and wobbled on. Their pursuers, if they were anything like the Unholy Mothers, probably intended to carve Alix into pieces as punishment for using arcania and running away. *I beg of the cosmos that there are no undead nuns here.* Sweat prickled at Alix's temples at the thought of the Mothers' long yellow teeth. *I swear on my writing hand that I'll never curse again if you allow me this one mercy.*

Alix felt too exposed. They needed claustrophobia the way a spider needs a dark corner.

A library.

They were born for the suffocating weight of the written word. They could gather themself in a library. Find information about where these people might be hiding Nixie. Alix could deal with the enormity of this new world – its awful brightness and oceanic monsters – once they had their best friend back.

What would she do?

Nixie would force her breathing to slow and walk like she belonged. Like this.

Alix floated numbly through the palace. They stepped on to a marble landing, which was freshly cracked from some cataclysm – *the fall of the Desecrae*, they thought – and looked down into a sprawling hall. The people below were too preoccupied with their own horror to notice Alix. A woman kneeled at the foot of a statue, sobbing 'Hallow be merciful' and pressing fish bones into its cold hands. Others stood by the crooked doors, which hung from their hinges to show a sprawling garden, staring at the distant stump of Fourspires beyond the city. The tiles at their feet were rucked up like an old handkerchief.

Alix descended, praying nobody would see the blood and dirt coating their skin. One elderly man glanced up, but he was too busy pouring a toxic-looking concoction into the mouth of a barnacle-crusted set of pipes to see anything wrong. The pipes stretched from floor to ceiling, where they splayed out and burrowed into the walls, groaning as they drank.

Just. Keep. Walking.

There were three archways in the wall ahead, named *Attendant*, *Visitant* and *Scholar*. Alix stepped through the *Scholar* arch and found a dark and deathly throat that drove into the guts of the cliff like a corkscrew. As they walked doors slipped past on either side, tight-lipped and watchful.

Only one door was open. Five letters – *GRAMM* – were carved into the wood above it. Alix gratefully slipped inside the tiny room. The damp green curtains were drawn, and the only light came from a candle the deep yellow of animal fat, its stench not quite masking old leather and mildew. Hundreds of books lined the shelves. A bowing desk overflowing with papers had been wedged lengthways against the wall.

Alix wanted to huddle under the desk. Instead, they went to pull secrets out of the small library like a cat would pluck meat off a chicken bone.

They yanked books off the shelf, flung them open, and tossed them over their shoulder. It was all trash – encyclopedias and diatribes on arcanic theory. No map saying *You are here* or *Secret hiding place for almost-dead people*. Alix finished with the books and tore through the papers on the desk, stopping only to grab a pencil and stick it behind their ear.

They had almost destroyed the office when a man cleared his throat behind them.

Alix turned so fast, the stranger in the doorway twitched. He couldn't have been older than forty, but his fine, swept-back hair already had strands of white in it. Silver rings gleamed from his light fingers, which were frozen like fish hooks over the textbooks in his arms. His gaze travelled down Alix's robes, which were still covered in globs of apocalyptic viscera.

Alix was so bone-tired that planting their hand on the stone wall and wresting wasn't an option. They would just have to smash this man's head in with an encyclopedia.

'Are you lost?' the man said after an awkward pause.

Alix realised they still hadn't moved.

'I'm sorry about the mess,' he added, as though Alix hadn't broken into what was presumably his office. 'The books must have fallen when the Null collapsed. Awful business. They felt it a hundred miles away, and the other cities are already demanding to know what we're doing about it.'

He pushed his glasses up his nose with an index finger, and the movement was so pathetically nervous that all the tension left Alix's body. The man blinked at the pencil behind Alix's ear, then fumbled in his pocket for a small roll of paper. 'Perhaps ... ?'

Alix snatched the paper from him. Patronising asshole. But yes, Alix wanted it. They didn't take their eyes off him as they scribbled, leaning against their own thigh.

Where am I?

The man gazed at Alix's scrawl, tilting his head to read it upside down. His face did an alarming set of acrobatics. He looked at the robes again.

'Hallow be merciful,' he said. He took a step back. Now he held the books like a shield. 'You're one of *them*. From the ruins.'

Shit. Alix reached behind him and slammed the door before he could call for help. He flinched away.

'You're meant to be under guard,' he said, his fingers tightening on the books. 'You shouldn't just be wandering around –' Alix took his dusty jacket in their fist and pushed him, gently but firmly, into the middle of the room – 'but I'm happy to help,' he finished, sweat beading on his forehead.

Alix released him. He wriggled into the chair behind the wonky desk and, apparently too nervous to remain still, started fussing with the creased edges of a red notebook he'd placed in front of him. Alix pulled the opposite chair out and sat.

I'm Alix, they wrote on the desk. Not threatening enough. They gritted their teeth in frustration. *Your worst nightmare.*

Part of them expected him to say: *That's not your real name.*

'Alix,' he repeated, nodding vigorously. 'Neophold Gramm. Recently promoted to Head of Monstrous Defence. I work at a university just outside Newspires. Which is, uh, here.'

He looked at them hopefully, as though this would satisfy Alix enough to release him. They pressed the tip of the pencil into the wood and watched Gramm squirm.

Tell me where my friend is. And give me a mirror.

Gramm glanced at the red notebook on the desk, a small and unconscious movement that immediately made Alix want to grab it. Gramm saw Alix looking and defensively folded his hands over the cover. One of his rings, a blank silver signet, flashed in the candlelight.

'I can't,' he said, somehow terrified and apologetic at once. 'I don't know where they keep prisoners. And there's only one mirror in the palace, and it's protected. I'm sure you know they warp arcania and produce malefici. We already have enough of those.'

Alix locked eyes with Gramm. He gripped the edge of the desk so hard it could have splintered.

'Do you – *did* you have malefici under the Null?' he said, clearly desperate to fill the silence. Alix didn't blink. 'We thought everything under the dome of teeth and bones was dead. And are you all … silent? Something to do with lacking nutrients? I would love to ask some questions about the ecosystem. The light levels alone—'

Alix was considering jamming their pencil up Gramm's nose when he suddenly went very still, his gaze pinned behind Alix's shoulder.

Alix smelt it before they saw it: rotten meat and necrosis. They froze at the sound of wet suckers dragging across the ceiling, stopping right above their head.

A glob of clear jelly hit the desk. Alix looked up.

The maleficent was a pinwheel of mismatched elbows, each terminating in a splay of sucker-covered fingers. A cluster of eyes wobbled in the middle of its body, some double-irised, all pink and gummy with infection. It blinked and its pupils bobbed, each surrounded by a white foam of sclera, like a mass of raw eggs splattered into a hot pan.

Alix's stomach flipped when they saw what else was embedded in its lumpen skull. A twisted metal bar, poking out as though someone had already tried and failed to bash its brains in. Alix had seen the iron bar before: they knew that crooked bend, the flakes of rust.

The last place they had seen it was in Taro's hands right before she strolled into the netherworld.

The creature grinned sloppily and proffered a bouquet of spectacles with one hand, the lenses cracked and smeared with slime. When Alix didn't move, the maleficent released each of its fingers from the ceiling with a wet sucking sound until it was dangling by a single pinkish thumb.

'Do you have a sword?' Gramm whispered.

The maleficent drew in a great rattling breath. It was bigger than any of the starvelings in the Ulcer. Those malefici were always hungry, and they had worn their desire on their bodies, which were made of food scraps and turkey bones and pudding bowls. This one was new and unknowable.

Unless ...

Alix wrenched Gramm's spectacles from his face and flung them into the corner. The maleficent ran backwards down the wall to catch them, gobbling and dribbling. Gramm shot up and slammed his fist into a copper pipe on the wall. The pipe above his head groaned, the noise rising in pitch and cascading into the hallway, followed by a wet, full-throated scream that Alix just *knew* came from the haunted-looking pipes in the entrance hall.

The maleficent hit the floor and mashed its face into the spectacles. When it looked up, Gramm's glasses were stuck to its bubbling flesh.

Alix couldn't afford to give in to terror. They had exploded an amphitheatre and clawed at skeletons in the Fifth Tower. They had stood at the edge of the world as flesh pattered down around their ears, and they had smiled. This was nothing.

The maleficent vaulted over the desk, which Gramm was now hiding beneath. Its mouth split open, revealing blubbery tonsils that had their own eyeballs. Alix grabbed their chair and swung, smashing its legs into the maleficent mid-leap. The creature's momentum drove Alix into the far wall, and the chair legs into its head. This did not slow it down. It kept pushing against the wooden legs, which slowly slid through its skull as it strained to reach Alix's throat. Alix kicked it away. It crawled backwards stickily and Alix followed, brandishing the splintered furniture.

Gramm muttered feverishly under his breath as Alix flicked their eyes over the scattered papers, landing on the red notebook. Taking the weight of the chair in one hand, Alix grabbed the notebook and stuffed it into their pocket before Gramm could notice.

'Watch out,' Gramm quavered from his hiding place.

It had only taken a second for the maleficent to slink up the wall. It jumped at Alix's face. Alix jerked the chair. The monster impaled itself again, puncturing another part of its cranium but this time driving Alix into the floor. The maleficent writhed, then pulsed and revealed a long, multi-jointed arm that had been nestled beneath its body. It reached for Alix's eyes.

I beg of the universe that you go blind a million times and die in agony, you shitty, malformed lump of gristle!

Alix crawled their fingers over the cold stone floor.

As it turned out, no matter how close to death Alix felt, there were always more reserves of strength. They felt the life inside the stone and let it transform inside them, scorching their bones and burning their flesh. As the arcania bloomed on the surface of their skin they breathed it into their mouth, slipped their tongue around it, and incanted.

The ceiling cracked and a chunk of stone smashed through the top of the maleficent. Its thick skull whistled as it decompressed. Brain matter foamed through its cranium.

A long silence followed, then there was a single, sad *clang* as the maleficent toppled over and hit the floor, the metal bar and half the chair still embedded in its head.

There was a long, horrified pause.

'Quick thinking with the glasses,' Gramm said weakly. He pulled himself from under the desk and wiped his forehead with a damp handkerchief. 'A dead optometrist, I think. Or perhaps someone who passed away looking for their spectacles. That will teach me to leave my door open.'

Alix looked at him blankly.

'They each have their obsessions,' Gramm said. 'Apart from killing people. They all want to do that.' He peered at Alix curiously. 'You look surprised. Does that mean there were no malefici in Fourspires? We have thousands. More, even.'

Alix rearranged their face into what they hoped was a suitably bored expression, which was difficult with a corpse at their feet and slime all over their face. The red notebook bulged guiltily in their pocket.

Alix wrote in the goo covering the desk, using their finger.

We had some. Not many. Sounds like YOU have an infestation.

'Basically, yes,' Gramm said, looking pained. 'They terrorise whole towns and kill at least a dozen people a day, then they converge *here*, in the palace.' He slumped back into his chair. He seemed to have forgotten that he was terrified of Alix. 'I have no idea how to stop them proliferating, and it's my whole job. They'll drag me to Convocation with you and demand answers, especially now they're all wound up by Fourspires reappearing. If I don't do something clever …'

Alix tilted their head in question.

'You don't know about Convocation.' His gaze drifted to the ceiling, as though he was suddenly very interested in the cornices. 'It, uh, takes place here in three days. It's an emergency meeting. At Convocation, the governor of every city will gather for your … execution.'

That was what Dorian meant by a knife through the throat. Alix dug their pencil into the wood, cutting it like a flesh wound. Gramm couldn't pretend not to see it.

Execution?

'Yours, and the boy's,' he said. 'And the destruction of the body you dragged here, no doubt. We were perilously close to war already, and now …' His eyes flicked towards the window. To where Fourspires lay, broken and blood drenched. 'Do you know what you've started by coming out of the Null? By being *alive* in that evil place? You're fulfilling a terrible premonition. They will kill you, in public, to show everyone that they're still in control and keeping them safe.'

Alix dug their nails into the pencil. They hadn't started anything. They were just here to get Nixie back, because she was the only person Alix had ever cared about, and Alix had to tell her that. And these people wanted to *kill* them all? Fury burned in their throat.

And if I leave?

'You won't get far,' he said. 'I heard that they put the survivors of the Null under a bone binding. If you go beyond the beach at the rear of the palace, or the gardens at the front, your bones will disintegrate. I'm afraid it would be quite painful. Fatal, of course.'

Alix remembered the ache in their bone marrow when they woke in the mortuary. A curse. The *slurry.*

And the only bone arcanist who would lift it, because she wasn't terrified of the people from the Desecrae –Taro – had marched into the netherworld after Nixie.

Gramm held his breath, waiting for a response as Alix boiled with rage. They wanted to bring the room down on his head. But that wasn't what Nixie would do. In the Pit, after Alix had learned how arcanists used familiars until they were rotten corpses, Nixie – who was a full year above Alix – had reached for their hand in the darkness, stilling their furious sobs. *You can't be violent*, she'd said coolly. *They're animals, and we're their toothless prey. You want to survive? Use your brain, because it's all you have now.*

Alix pulled the goo-sodden roll of paper from their pocket.

You're desperate to get rid of the malefici infestation, Alix wrote finally. Gramm's silence spurred them on. *Fourspires was trapped under the Desecrae – the Null – for centuries. We had mirrors, and we had malefici. Search the ruins and you'll find both as proof.* The mirror that the woman had crushed under her foot, anyway, and the starvelings in the Ulcer. *But we kept them under control, even though we were trapped with them. I wouldn't be alive otherwise.*

Gramm looked hungry. Alix almost felt sorry for him.

You want to know how we did it?

'Yes,' he croaked.

The answer was violently simple. Everything under the Desecrae was controlled by undead nuns. They kept the starvelings contained within the Ulcer and ate any that attempted to crawl out of it. The one mirror that existed – hidden in Nixie's bedroom – didn't produce malefici because there was a despotic ghost blocking their way. Very occasionally, malefici oozed out of the Desecrae and terrorised the people at the bottom of Fourspires, but they were quickly caught by the Unholy Mothers.

It occurred to Alix, now, that the malefici that got through the Desecrae might have come from outside. From *here*.

Gramm didn't need to know any of that.

I'll tell you how to control the malefici if you take me to my friend's body and give me a mirror.

They had gone too far.

'Alix,' Gramm said, and the use of their name, still so new, sent a pang of recognition through their chest. 'I just can't.'

Footsteps pounded outside. The guards were coming for the source of the screaming pipes. Alix clenched their jaw.

There had to be something they could get from him. Something they could use to find Nixie *and* a mirror before they were executed at Convocation.

Fine, they scrawled. *Give me something else. Then I'll consider helping you.*

Doors burst open in the hallway. Alix's hand cramped as they scrawled, almost illegibly.

I know I can't leave the palace grounds. But I want to move around inside.

Gramm didn't even pretend to think about it. He was too desperate.

'I'll tell them you're helping me with my research,' he said quickly.

And give me a room next to Elliot.

'The boy who's giving everyone nosebleeds?'

Alix hesitated for just a second. But they couldn't turn back now.

AND I want new clothes.

'What?'

Alix jabbed their finger into the paper. *Right now.*

The door slammed open. Dorian strode in, her boots spattering the guts of the dead maleficent, her sword drawn.

Alix, the last stone disciple of Fourspires, snatched a pair of dark glasses from the maleficent and put them on. They smiled at Dorian, who flinched.

That's *what Nixie would do.*

But the botanic disciple had been wrong about one thing. Alix wasn't anyone's prey. In this world, where the survivors of the Desecrae were objects of abject terror – where their approaching execution meant there was nothing left to lose – Alix had teeth.

Cassidy Ellis Salter is a fantasy author who lives with a pile of bones and historical oddities they've rescued from the Thames. They hold a bachelor's degree and MA in Writing from the Warwick Writing Programme. They live and work in London, England.

cesalter.com
TikTok: @cesalter